The Accidental Agent

Andrew Rosenheim was born in Chicago and came to England as a Rhodes Scholar in 1977. He has lived near Oxford ever since. He is the author of eight novels, including *The Informant*, *Fear Itself*, *Without Prejudice*, *Keeping Secrets* and *Stillriver*, and a memoir, *The Secrets of Carriage H*.

Praise for *The Accidental Agent*

'There is much to praise in this complex and ambitious narrative, not least the adroitly handled ticking-clock scenario.'
Financial Times

'A truly intriguing, intelligent, engaging novel. Loved it.'
Jim Crace

'Outstanding ... combines a crackerjack plot and multiple nuanced characters with a convincing portrayal of WWII America ... The dramatic twists work to propel the plot to a powerful and moving conclusion.'
Publishers Weekly

'Taut with suspense ... a compelling novel.'
Historical Novel Society

Also available by Andrew Rosenheim

Stillriver
Keeping Secrets
Without Prejudice
Fear Itself
The Informant
The Secrets of Carriage H

The Accidental Agent

Andrew Rosenheim

arrow books

1 3 5 7 9 10 8 6 4 2

Arrow Books
20 Vauxhall Bridge Road
London SW1V 2SA

Arrow Books is part of the Penguin Random House group of companies
whose addresses can be found at global.penguinrandomhouse.com.

Penguin
Random House
UK

First published by Hutchinson in 2016
First published in paperback by Arrow Books in 2017

www.penguin.co.uk

A CIP catalogue record for this book is available from the British Library.

ISBN 9780099557890

Typeset in 11.38/13.44 pt Sabon LT Std, by Jouve (UK), Milton Keynes
Printed and bound in Great Britain by Clays Ltd, St Ives Plc

For Clare

Part One

1

IT WAS THE third week of Torts, and America was at war at last – though Nessheim knew his own war was over. He sat near the back of the large lecture room in Stuart Hall at the University of Chicago, trying not to yawn. The room was only sparsely filled, for enrolment in the college had declined dramatically since the Japanese attack on Pearl Harbor the year before.

The few law students remaining consisted of what Winograd, who sat beside Nessheim now, called 'cripples, COs, and girls'. A charmless description which Winograd told Nessheim he felt entitled to make since he was himself classed 4-F and exempted on medical grounds. A beefy Minnesotan, he looked like perfect cannon fodder until he took an awkward step or two, and you saw that his foot was encased in a thick boot that had a specially built four-inch heel. 'A run-in with a tractor,' he'd explained. 'They ought to call me 1-F since I've only got two feet and just one of them is fucked up.'

'Mr Nessheim.' The voice broke through Nessheim's thoughts, and he looked up to find Professor Fielding staring at him.

After war had been declared the previous year, half the faculty had decamped to bear arms or serve the burgeoning needs of the government in Washington. Fielding was one of those emeritus professors persuaded to come out of retirement to fill these vacancies, but unlike others who were keen to step into their old shoes, he clearly resented the lame ducks he was now teaching. He had served in the final months of the last war

3

with the American Expeditionary Force in France and had mentioned this in the very first class, as if to distance himself from his non-combatant audience. Not that he looked like any kind of soldier: he was a dapper figure, smartly dressed today in a three-piece suit of sage-coloured tweed that had been tailored in a more luxurious peacetime era. He had a thick greying moustache that he stroked tenderly on the rare occasions he listened to a student.

Now Fielding went on, his tone a mix of insincere optimism and authentic impatience. 'You looked a million miles away, Mr Nessheim. Where were you, I wonder? Guadalcanal perhaps, or North Africa?'

Pearl Harbor actually, thought Nessheim, though he wouldn't have dreamed of saying so – his presence there, on the day the Japanese attacked, wouldn't have been believed.

But Fielding was happy to continue on his own. 'I acknowledge that the conflicts we engage in here may seem pallid by comparison, but this is the theatre of operations we have all been assigned to. So would it help, Mr Nessheim, if I repeated the question?'

It wouldn't help at all, thought Nessheim, wondering how this was going to unravel. His written work so far had been well received, but in class he found his mind wandering. Fortunately Fielding was distracted by a new arrival. A young woman walked confidently down the far aisle of the lecture hall, heading for the seats at the front. Usually students who were late entered quietly, slinking into the back rows of the lecture room. But this woman made no effort to disguise her entrance, and her heels clicked like match strikes on the parquet floor.

She was a breath of fresh air in this stuffy balloon of a room, and somehow familiar too, although her face was shielded by the angle from which Nessheim viewed her, and by thick glossy hair that fell back upon her shoulders – it was the colour of burnt honey. She wore an elegant overcoat the same colour as Fielding's tweed suit, but of softer-looking, finer material. As she slowed down Nessheim caught a glimpse of her charcoal stockings and of well-shaped legs he was pretty sure he'd seen before. Winograd nudged him with an elbow, and said in a whisper that could have carried downtown to the Loop, 'Catch a gander of that.'

At the lectern, Fielding looked suspiciously at this new arrival, for he didn't like to be upstaged. 'And you are, miss?'

'Very late, Professor.' Her voice was smoky and low. 'Three weeks late, I know. But I couldn't get a train from the Coast for love or money – all the soldier boys have priority. Heavens knows why. There ought to be a law against it.'

Even Fielding smiled at this, though briefly. 'You're going to have a lot of catching up to do, Miss . . . ?'

She ignored the question. 'I know – I usually do, Professor.' She sat down, having spread her coat out on the chair behind her and taken off her neat black gloves, then used both hands to push her hair back. Suddenly Nessheim could see her profile, and understood with a sudden awful clarity why she seemed familiar. She said, 'Don't worry. I always seem to get there in the end.'

When class ended Nessheim left quickly, ignoring Winograd's entreaties to stick around. 'Don't you want to say hello to the new gal? You can't leave her with Hobson the CO – he'll bore her to death with tales of Quaker persecution.'

'Got to run,' said Nessheim tersely. From the rear

doors he turned and saw the late arrival talking to Professor Fielding. Remarkably, Fielding seemed to be chuckling. He looked beguiled.

Outside, Nessheim took a deep breath, walking out into a sky of surprising blue after days of lint-grey haze had seemed to portend an early winter. He was glad to get out of the stale air of the lecture room, where cigarette smoke drifted like low-level clouds beneath the high ceiling of the room. It had been unseasonably mild and the trees of the Quadrangle had been slow to turn, with only the faintest streaks of scarlet and yellow among their leaves despite it being the very end of October.

At the east end of the Quadrangle the street ran through pairs of tennis courts on either side. They were net-less now, requisitioned by the navy for drills. A small group of sailors stood at the street end of the high fence surrounding the courts, taking a break from preparations for the next day's navy parade along State Street – it was billed as the largest parade since the war began, with over 6,000 uniformed men and women expected. Fresh-faced, absurdly young, wearing their dress blues and white Dixie cup hats, they looked like the cast of a maritime musical.

As Nessheim passed them, a cigarette stub came sailing through the hooped wire of the fence and landed at his feet. He stopped walking and turned to face the court, where the sailor closest to the fence stared at him without affection.

'Thanks,' said Nessheim, kicking the cigarette butt into the street gutter with the toe of his shoe.

'What's your excuse?' the sailor said. He was short and pug-faced, with shoulders suggesting a former wrestler who worked with dumb-bells to keep his shoulders wide.

'Excuse me?'

'You 4-F or something?'

'You could call it "something",' said Nessheim.

One of the sailor's pals began to sing, clutching his heart mockingly: 'He's 1-A in the Army and He's A-1 in My Heart.'

Nessheim started to move on but the sailor said sharply, 'You're 4-F, I bet. Four is for 'fraidy cat and F is for fairy.'

Nessheim stopped and sighed. 'Now there we were, getting along so well, and you have to go and spoil it.'

One of the other sailors laughed. Nessheim gestured at the separating fence. 'Let me know if you're ever allowed out of your cage. Then we could continue the conversation in private.'

'You'd like that, I bet,' the sailor sneered. 'The private bit.'

This time Nessheim's sigh was heartfelt. I am thirty years old, he told himself, not a school kid reacting to a playground insult. He stared hard at Pug Nose nonetheless.

'Come on, Willy,' one of the other sailors said. 'The lieutenant's calling. Break's over.'

Pug-nosed Willy made a show of stepping back reluctantly from the fence. He said to Nessheim, 'I'll see you again.' And then he gave a chicken-like squawk before turning to join his colleagues.

Nessheim walked away, trying to clear his head of the sailor's taunts.

Being called a fairy didn't bother him as much as being called a coward. He wasn't avoiding military service; it was avoiding him. He had tried to enlist twice. The first time a phone call came in from Washington alerting the local Wisconsin draft board to his ropey medical history. His second attempt, made the previous spring before he left Los Angeles, had also foundered, though this time because halfway through his physical his old concussion-caused dizziness had struck out of the blue. When they'd taken his blood pressure the systolic number had been over two hundred.

He liked Chicago, a grey city which sat on the shore-line of Lake Michigan but otherwise had no natural physical advantages; it had to build its own beauty and had done so in only seventy years or so, after Mrs O'Leary's apocryphal cow had knocked over a lantern and burnt most of the city down. He thought now of going over to Jackson Park by the Lake, six blocks away. But along the Midway, mile-long lengths of lawn sand-wiched by boulevards that had been created during the 1893 World's Fair, he would see soldiers in drill forma-tion, and feel again the inadequacy of his own civilian status. He had always had the advantage in life of sticking out – in a good way. In his football days he had even briefly been semi-famous. But now he stood out for the wrong reason – he wasn't in uniform, when every other able-bodied man his age was.

He turned at Kimbark and walked up to 57th Street, passing the large houses that lined both leafy sides of the street. The only local material had been prairie sod, so these residences were built in a bewildering variety of brick, stone and white pine lumber. At 57th a row of stores extended to Kenwood Avenue. They were busy these days, after more than a decade of Depression-era struggle, and outside the grocery store there was a line of customers; sugar had been rationed at the beginning of May and many were waiting to buy it, their ration books in hand. People had cash to spend, now that anyone could get a job, especially if they were willing to move – to California, where the airplane manufac-turers were struggling to fill newly launched assembly lines with anything on two legs; or to Detroit, where, as part of Roosevelt's 'great arsenal of democracy', the motor-car companies had rejigged their factories to produce weapons of every conceivable description.

Nessheim wondered how long the new exuberance would last. Until the year before, America had fought the war solely through its imagination; now the battles were real and bodies would soon be coming back. And although people felt flush, there wasn't a lot to spend it on – it was as if they had been given a windfall on condition they spend it all in a dime store. You could buy a new suit, as long as it was a single-breasted number without a vest and had fly buttons instead of a zipper (the metal saved could make casings for ammunition shells). But new cars weren't being made, and it was virtually impossible to find tyres for the old ones. Rationing of gasoline would start on December 1 in the state of Illinois, with coupon books to be issued, allowing four gallons per week. Daily advertisements in newspapers reminded the public that cars and tyres were national assets, exhorting people to contribute to victory by conserving vital rubber and metal to provide for tanks and planes. There were neighbour-hood scrap campaigns and posters everywhere encour-aging citizens to buy US Victory bonds.

A car drove past which he noticed right away – a new Packard Eight deluxe convertible the colour of late-picked cherries. The driver had the top up, a curving mogul of cream-coloured canvas. It must have snuck in under the wire before all of Detroit's car-making capacity was turned to military purposes. When Nessheim cut diagonally across the street he saw the red Packard slow down and stop. It sat double-parked for a moment, ignoring the soft toot of a car waiting behind it. As Nessheim moved north on Kimbark he heard it suddenly accelerate away.

He passed Ray School where the kids were all in class, and the sports field was empty. There were the remains of a Victory garden laid out in one patch of ground, littered by flattened vegetable leaves and loose string which had demarcated the rows that had been picked clean. At the corner he came to the small complex of four-storey buildings where he had his apartment. He was crossing the street, looking right, when he saw the same convertible cross 56th Street a block away, heading north on Kenwood. This time the top was down, but his view was blocked by the row of elms bordering the sidewalk and he couldn't see the driver.

Probably nothing, he told himself, though he remembered his drive east from California the previous spring. He had left LA after uncovering a web of Russian intrigue, fronted by an alluring but ultimately poisonous woman named Elizaveta Mukasei; he had been forced in self-defence to kill one of her henchman. Mr Mukasei was the vice consul for the Russian mission in LA, and now that the Russians were allies, Nessheim couldn't lay a finger on either of them – despite ample evidence to convict the pair of espionage and murder in more normal times.

There had been a night he spent en route at a motel in Nebraska; the following morning, twenty miles east of there, he realised he'd left behind a pair of shoes and had doubled back to fetch them. The motel clerk had said, 'Your friend catch up to you?'

'What friend?'

'Skinny guy with a fedora. He sounded foreign to me.'

'He must have been looking for someone else.'

'He described you good enough.'

'Did he know my name?'

'He didn't mention it and I couldn't have helped him there anyway – the register wasn't much help.' He

10

laughed and passed the big bound book across the shelf of desk. Nessheim had scrawled his usual illegible autograph – his name might have been Nussbaum for all the ink blur said. The incident had been unsettling enough for Nessheim to detour off Route 40 for a day, then take an extra day driving to Chicago. Since then there had been no reason to worry. He might have stood out, but the only people who seemed to notice were – like Pug Nose – men in uniform.

His apartment sat at the base of a long U formed by two flanking wings of brick. He turned into this small recessed courtyard and saw two men waiting by the entrance to his own tier, a good fifty yards from the street. One of the men, powerfully built and looming in army uniform, was pacing back and forth; the other, dressed in a black raincoat that had seen better days, sat huddled with his hands in his pockets on one of two low piers that jutted out at knee height from either side of the entranceway.

Nessheim thought briefly of turning around. He could go through the alley that led to the rear entrance to his apartment, where in his bedroom closet he still had his Bureau-issue .38. But if these guys had come to get him would they be waiting out in the open? To hell with it, he decided, moving forwards. He was just a student now.

The sitting man spotted him, then stood up, leaving his hat on the brick pier. He was shorter than the army man, but heavyset, with a biggish soft-looking nose, dark strands of receding hair, and a wistful expression on his face. No one would mistake him for military – for one thing, his shoes could use a shine.

'Hello, Harry,' Nessheim called. 'Been waiting long?'

The man shook his head. 'About twenty minutes, but it's not that warm out.'

'Give it a month and you'll really feel the cold. We

11

had snow back in September. This is summer compared to what's to come.'

The man named Harry said to the other man, 'This is Special Agent Nessheim. Nessheim, this is General Groves.' Groves nodded curtly.

Nessheim said, 'Unless it's the Communist philosophy professor on the third floor, I reckon you're here to see me.'

'That's right,' said Groves. His steel-blue eyes gave nothing away.

'You'd better come upstairs then.'

Nessheim led the way into the building, unlocking the inner door of the atrium. He went past the front door of the janitor's basement apartment and up a carpeted staircase with a creaking mahogany banister. One flight up there was an apartment on either side of the landing. He opened the door to the left one, motioning Groves and Harry Guttman inside.

They all stood for a moment in the small hallway, then Nessheim took their coats and hats and hung them up in the hall closet. He pointed to the living room at the front. It was glowing softly from the light of the lowering sun.

'Have a seat,' he said. There was an easy chair he'd plucked from a yard sale down the block, a long grey sofa the landlady had thrown in, and a wooden kitchen chair.

Guttman took the sofa while Groves hesitated, then sat down as well, though he didn't settle, perching uneasily on the easy chair's front edge. Groves had a moustache that put Professor Fielding's in the shade, and an imposing frame – he was maybe an inch or two shorter than Nessheim, but much heavier. He would have played tackle on his high-school football team.

'Nice place,' Groves said curtly, looking around as Nessheim sat down on the kitchen chair. 'Tidy.'

'He grew up on a farm,' said Guttman.

'What's that got to do with it?' asked Nessheim. Guttman shrugged.

Groves was examining the bookshelves, which were half full, mainly with novels. He said, 'I don't see any football trophies. Guttman says you were all-American. Why not put the certificate on the wall?'

'There isn't one – it's just an invention of the sports writers. I was second team, anyway. That doesn't seem worth a shrine.' The only relics were a bunch of newspaper clippings he'd given his mother, which lay in an old shoebox under the stairs of her house in Wisconsin. His mother had never liked him playing.

Silence filled the room awkwardly, like a semi-visible gas. What did these two want? Nessheim finally broke the silence. 'I've got some cold beers in the icebox, and a warm bottle of Scotch.'

Groves started to shake his head but Guttman said quickly, 'I'll take a beer, thanks. General?'

Groves shrugged. 'I'll join you.'

Nessheim nodded and walked down the hall to the small kitchen.

He left the bottle of Scotch alone, figuring he'd need the drink after this conversation, not before. He grabbed two bottles of Blatz from the refrigerator and opened them with a church key he took from the drawer of the kitchen cabinet. It felt stuffy in the apartment, so he opened the outer back door, leaving the screen door on its hook. He heard a scraping sound from down the back staircase, then another; he stopped for a moment and listened, then realised it must be the janitor moving his garbage cans.

Returning to the living room he found the two men

13

sitting in silence again. He said, 'What's this about? My mother phoned me yesterday and my father's long gone. So who's swallowed a fork?'

Groves took the beer from Nessheim and held it for a moment, his lips tight. 'I'll let Guttman begin.'

Guttman was shaking his head. 'Nobody's dead, and nothing's happened – yet. But we need your help.'

'I thought I was just a student now, Harry. I resigned, remember?' He had made it clear he didn't want a desk job at the Bureau's Washington HQ.

Groves said brusquely, 'Guttman told me you never took a BA.'

'That's right. I lost my scholarship.'

'What happened – you forget to go to class?'

Nessheim said sharply, 'I got hurt playing ball. You can't keep your scholarship if you can't play.'

'So how'd you wangle your way into law school without a BA?'

Guttman spoke for him. 'Chicago lets you in if you've done three years of college.'

'Is that so?' asked Groves without any real interest. He turned back to Nessheim. 'You've got to admit it's a pretty irregular billet. How much is tuition?'

'Three hundred seventy-five bucks a year.'

'You got some dough socked away?'

'Enough,' said Nessheim truthfully. He'd been well paid as a Special Agent.

'Sounds an easy life to me, even if the place is stinking with pinkos.' Groves gave a snort, his nostrils dilating like rubber.

'If you say so. I tried to enlist, twice in fact, but the army wouldn't have me. Would they, Harry?' he asked pointedly.

Guttman didn't reply. Groves took a deep breath and exhaled noisily, like a moose clearing its nose. 'All right, let me explain. I've recently been appointed the head of a new military project. It's based in locations across the country – one of them is in Illinois. I can't go into details, it's top secret, but the project involves the finest scientific talent in the world.'

He paused – why? So Nessheim would nod, suitably impressed? When Nessheim failed to, Groves continued. 'It's all classified. Like this entire conversation. Is that understood?'

Nessheim looked at Guttman, who was nodding thoughtfully in non-interventionist mode. 'Sure,' Nessheim said slowly, damned if he was going to say 'sir'. 'I'm all ears and no mouth.'

'You know anything about physics?'

'I had a year of it in college.'

'How'd you do?'

'I'd never make a scientist, but I know more about it than he does.' He pointed at Guttman, who laughed: six months before, Guttman hadn't been sure what a physicist was. 'What is the project?'

'You don't need to know much about it. In fact, it's probably better that you don't. Leave it to the scientists.'

Nessheim wasn't a reader of comics, but you couldn't help but be aware of Flash Gordon and his fantastic gizmos and space rockets. 'Another secret weapon, huh?' Groves flushed slightly, so Nessheim knew he'd hit home. He looked at Guttman. 'Is it what that guy in California was talking about?'

'What guy?' Groves demanded.

Nessheim kept looking at Guttman. 'You know, Harry. The guy we saw last spring in Berkeley.'

Guttman said to Groves, 'Nessheim was with me when I saw Professor Oppenheimer on the Coast.'

'Why did you take him along?' Groves asked with obvious irritation.

Guttman said mildly, 'It's a good thing I did. We don't have to worry about his getting curious when he's already got a good idea of what's going on.'

'I guess so,' Groves said grudgingly. 'Do you know the Argonne Forest?'

'No.'

'It's about fifteen miles west of here. We have an installation there. The work is at a critical stage, but we've got some labour problems. Not everybody seems willing to help the war effort,' he added angrily. 'So we've moved it here to the university.' Groves took a swig of his beer. Despite his bull-like manners and appearance, he seemed uncertain what to say next. Nessheim saw no point prompting him. Either he had something to tell him or he didn't.

Guttman interjected, 'This project of ours is of interest to the enemy. We think they're running their own in parallel to ours.'

'The Japs or the Germans?'

'The Germans,' Groves declared. 'Your people.'

'My people?'

Groves ignored the sharpness in Nessheim's reply. 'Well, just how German are you?'

Nessheim shrugged. 'My parents were both born here. Their parents weren't. I thought by now I was American.'

'Guttman says you speak the language.'

'Not really. My parents spoke to each other in German, especially when they didn't want my sister or me to understand. Naturally I picked some up. But I understand it better than I speak it – my father discouraged that.' Nessheim's father had been eager to have his son assimilate in a way he never could.

'Were your parents Catholics?'

'No, Lutheran.'

'The scientists I mentioned – many of them come

16

from Europe, and almost all of those are Jews. Have you got any Jewish blood?' Groves sounded a little anxious.

'Not that I know of.' He glanced at Guttman, who looked as if he was trying not to laugh. 'I'll keep looking, though, and let you know.'

Guttman said, 'We believe the Nazis may have infiltrated the Argonne project, and that most likely it would be someone masquerading as a refugee. Probably pretending to be a Jew – there couldn't be better cover for a Nazi.'

Nessheim decided this was going nowhere fast. He said impatiently, 'I've got mid-terms coming soon and lots of studying to do, so are you going to tell me what all this has got to do with me?'

Groves said, 'We need to find this guy if he's there.'

'Don't look at me. I'm no physicist.'

'Yeah, but you were FBI, you're experienced, and we're moving the project about three blocks from here.' Groves went on, 'I gather you were undercover once.'

Nessheim tried not to look at Guttman. Hoover hated agents going undercover; Nessheim's time spent doing just that had been entirely unauthorised – he'd been an undercover "undercover agent".

'That's right,' Nessheim said quietly.

'Infiltrating the *Bund*.'

'Yep.'

'Did you use a different name?'

'You mean an alias?'

'Yes, that's exactly what I mean.'

'It was Rossbach.'

'Why aren't you using it now?'

'Why should I? I'm not undercover; I'm not even *over* cover. I'm in law school.'

Groves ignored this. It was clear that he had already

17

decided what Nessheim was going to do, even if Nessheim himself didn't appreciate that. 'Could you use it again?'

Nessheim considered this, then shook his head. 'Not in Chicago. I know people from before.'

'Ah. The famous football star.'

'That's not what I meant. There are people who will have heard of Rossbach. I wouldn't want to run into them using that name.'

'Former *Bund* members?'

'That's right.' The German-American *Bund* had disbanded when war was declared; that didn't mean the former members had abandoned their allegiance to the Führer.

Groves suddenly thumped the chair. He had come to a decision, which seemed to mean they had all come to one. 'Then Nessheim it's got to be. No big deal. Hopefully it's never going to matter either way. Not if you succeed.'

Nessheim looked at Guttman, but his old boss retreated to pursed-lips mode, his eyes fixed on the far wall. 'Succeed at what?' asked Nessheim.

'Deciding if there is a spy inside the project here and then finding him.'

'Who says I'm going to try? I've told you, I'm no longer with the Bureau.'

'Don't you want to help your country?'

'I tried enlisting – "my country" didn't want to know.'

'We can't all be heroes. Look at me – I thought I was getting a military posting, and instead . . .'

Instead I'm talking to a nincompoop like you – this seemed to be the implication. Nessheim said, 'I think you'll find if you ask Harry here that I've done my bit and then some. And I won't work for Hoover again.'

Groves stared angrily at Nessheim. His cheeks had

18

puffed out like muffins, and his mouth was as contorted as a corkscrew; he seemed half a second away from an explosion. But when he spoke his voice was measured. 'I report direct to the White House about this.' Groves pointed at Guttman and added, 'And so does he.'

So the Bureau wasn't telling Groves *or* Guttman what to do. The President was. Which meant forget Hoover; forget his sidekick Tolson for that matter. Neither was part of this. 'And I would report to . . . ?' asked Nessheim, telling himself it was only a theoretical interest.

Guttman cut in quickly. 'Me,' he said. 'But you're used to that.'

'And you don't talk to anyone else about this, got that?' said Groves, waving his forefinger like a baton. 'Except for the head of the project. We've just seen him. He's an Eye-talian, a physicist named Enrico Fermi – he won the Nobel Prize. But not another soul.'

'Not even –'

'Not even anybody, unless the President himself shows up here in his wheelchair. You can forget the normal chain of command.' He paused, then added, 'Harry can give you the dossier we've prepared.'

Nessheim shook his head. There was no point misleading the guy, even if he was annoying. 'You don't get it. I'm not an agent now, I'm a student.'

'For Christ's sakes,' said Groves, exasperated, though even now he didn't raise his voice. 'You can be a frigging law student any old time.' His voice softened just a touch. 'We're not asking for a lot. Just an hour or two each day to keep an eye on things. You can still go to class.'

'It doesn't work like that and you know it.'

Guttman added, 'It should be over by Christmas. We're talking two months maximum.'

19

'And what if it isn't?'

Groves threw up his hands in frustration. 'Where's the can?' he demanded, standing up quickly. Big as he was, there was a lithe, cat-like quality to the man.

'Down the hall on the left.'

Nessheim waited until he heard Groves stride down the hall and shut the bathroom door. 'Harry, I just want to say how sorry I was about Isabel.'

'I got your letter. Thanks for it.'

Nessheim had spent hours composing the simple sentences, ripping up draft after draft in case he sounded too formal or too mawkish or somehow insincere.

'Are you okay?' he asked.

Guttman nodded slowly. 'Yeah, I'm all right.' He added flatly, 'Life's just kind of different now.' He could have been talking to himself, thought Nessheim, feeling the man's loneliness. But he also sensed Guttman didn't want any more condolences about his wife. He nodded towards the bathroom and said, 'What's this all about?'

Guttman replied without inflection. 'What it sounds like.'

'You trust this guy?' asked Nessheim, his own scepticism undisguised.

Guttman smiled wanly. 'There isn't much choice. The President thinks he cuts the mustard – that's what matters.'

'He doesn't seem wild about me.'

Guttman shrugged. 'Probably because you're not his idea. I don't think he believes we've got a problem – he's got Military Intelligence crawling all over the place.'

'Do *you* think there's a problem?'

Guttman looked him in the eye, which Nessheim knew was a good but not infallible indicator that he was telling it to you straight. 'I just don't know. Odds are not, but it's a risk we can't afford to take.'

'And this project – you're telling me that Director Hoover doesn't even know it exists?'

'Yes, that's right,' Guttman said, looking slightly ill at ease. He added defensively, 'It's not as weird as it sounds. Everything's being run under the military's control. Military Intelligence has always been stand-offish – the Bureau never gets a look-in, no matter how hard Hoover tries. We got South America as a sop for that.'

Nessheim nodded reluctantly. 'All right. But are you going to tell me what I would be supposed to *do*? Stand around waiting for an egghead to say "*Heil Hitler*"? It's not like I can pretend to be a scientist – I'd stick out like a sore thumb.'

'Fermi's got some ideas for that. He'll tell you, and I'll leave it to you to use your judgement.' Guttman shifted uneasily on his seat. 'We're not asking a lot, you know. Just a couple of hours a day, like the General said. Chances are there's nothing to be found, but I'll feel a lot better if I know you've had a look. I'd want you to trust your instincts – *I* do.'

Nessheim said nothing, refusing to be flattered.

Guttman reached down and opened his briefcase, then took out a black box file. 'This will get you started. It's got the relevant background info, including the personnel files. Fermi's team isn't that big, maybe a dozen scientists who know enough to do it damage. The rest are minor players, though there're a lot of them.'

'And the Bureau isn't involved?' When Guttman gave a slight nod, Nessheim said, 'I'd be on my own?'

Guttman paused. 'I've got you local support at the Field Office here, but the SAC doesn't know about it.'

Nessheim asked, 'What's the support then?' He realised he was being drawn into the details of how he'd be operating, but decided he might as well humour his old boss.

21

'Tatie.'

'I thought she'd transferred to D.C.' Along with a million other single women, seizing the opportunities provided by the war.

'Nope. Maybe she heard you were here.'

Not Guttman, too, thought Nessheim, remembering his colleagues ragging him.

Guttman went on. 'She's expecting you to make contact. As for the Lab, Fermi will give you access to what you need. If he doesn't, or if he can't for some reason, then call me.'

'What about Big Boy here?' He gestured towards the bathroom.

'If the General wants info from you, give it to him. But if he doesn't ask, don't tell. Keep me posted, however – every week or so. But no written reports. Telegrams or phone are best – you've got my other number at home.'

'And at the office?'

'So long as I answer the phone when the switchboard puts you through. Or Marie in a pinch.' Guttman added, 'She's the only one who knows I'm here.'

Nessheim nodded. Guttman was never one for prescription; that was the good thing about working for him. On the other hand, it often meant prolonged periods of bewilderment, especially at the beginning of an assignment.

'So can I count on you, Nessheim?' Guttman averted his eyes from the younger agent, looking towards the hallway instead. Nessheim heard the biffy flush and the water run in the bathroom basin. When Nessheim hadn't answered, Guttman added, 'I'd offer you more money but technically you're on leave.'

'How's that? I quit, Harry. You had my letter of resignation.'

'Did you ever get a letter back accepting it?' he asked.

Before Nessheim could respond, Groves was standing in the wide doorway. He didn't sit down again. Looking at Nessheim he said, 'Are we all set?'

Nessheim said, 'I'll let you know. I need to think about this.'

Groves looked at Guttman as if the Bureau man had failed his assignment. He turned back to Nessheim. 'You got more questions?'

'No,' said Nessheim, who actually had about a hundred of them, but none that Groves would want to answer, or that Guttman would answer in front of Groves. 'Like I said, I'll let you know.'

When they'd gone Nessheim sat down on the hard kitchen chair, watching out the window as his odd pair of visitors marched away towards Kimbark Avenue, Groves striding as if on parade. Nessheim thought about what had just transpired.

Law school was hard. How could he keep up with the workload if he was engaged in a wild goose chase on the other side of the Quadrangle? For he figured that's what it was – a hiding to nothing, searching for an infiltrator who didn't exist. Nessheim had ample experience of Bureau suspicions that proved entirely unwarranted – arguably, Hoover owed his longevity in his post to an ability to generate false alarms. And the briefing (as usual when it came from Guttman) seemed as clear as mud. Nessheim was supposed to inveigle his way into a wartime project he couldn't understand – and, according to Groves, wasn't allowed to either.

Nessheim hadn't been a student for almost ten years; it hadn't been easy re-entering a world where you had to read so much (and so carefully), think clearly, and write so much. Especially since he was entered in a wartime course that would see him graduate with a JD in two years instead of three. The University of Chicago had been reluctant to accept him for the accelerated programme, but he had tested well in the exams they made external applicants take. And done well so far in his coursework; he'd had straight A's at the end of his summer quarter. No one could fault his commitment.

But he also knew his interest was stirred by what Guttman and Groves had said. The simple fact was that law was not only difficult but often remarkably uninteresting. For the first time in months he felt excited about something, and it certainly wasn't Fielding on Torts. Yet having rued for years the abbreviation of his education, and the removal of any prospect of a legal career, how could he admit that the realisation of this long-held ambition was actually proving so much dreary smoke?

Goddamned Guttman, he thought, half-angrily, half-admiring the older man's ability to work on Nessheim's susceptibility to adventure. He got up, thinking he could use a whisky now. Maybe he should play the 78 he'd bought the day before from the new record store on 53rd Street – Billie Holliday singing 'Until the Real Thing Comes Along'. That would calm him down.

But as he walked through the hall towards the dining room, he saw a car through the back window, parked in the alley that ran between 56th and 55th Streets. It was the red convertible again.

He had been taught by Guttman never to believe in coincidence – and it had stuck, even though he was a law student now, not an agent. He went back to the bedroom and drew the Smith & Wesson .38 from its holster hooked on a hanger in his clothes closet. Returning down the hall, he stopped in the dining room, standing

24

on the little round rug which, like a rolled-out pie crust, extended beyond the circular table. He slipped out of his shoes, then tiptoed into the kitchen, aiming the gun at the open back door. As he inched his way carefully into the kitchen, slipping the safety off, he felt foolish more than scared. But he had felt that way before and almost been killed as a result. Then he saw the figure sitting on the back stairs.

It was the woman from the law school. She was perched on the second step, with her skirt covering her knees and her hands in her lap. She looked incongruously elegant in the surroundings – like a princess visiting the palace kitchens. Looking up, she seemed unalarmed by the sight of Nessheim holding a .38 in both hands.

She said, 'I know things ended badly between us, Nessheim, but I didn't expect you to carry a grudge this long.'

He lowered the gun and exhaled, half in exasperation, half in relief. 'You shouldn't sneak around like that, Stacey. You could have got shot.'

'I wasn't sneaking around. I was waiting for your visitors to leave.' She stood up, smacking dust from the backside of her coat. 'Are you going to ask me in, or do you always entertain on the back porch?'

He sighed and lifted the hook off the screen door. As she came through the door he saw an envelope in her hand. 'I found this on the mat,' she said, handing it to him.

When he put it on the little pine kitchen table, she said with the bright curiosity he remembered so well, 'Aren't you going to open it?'

'It's the paper boy's bill.'

'Oh,' she said, disappointed. 'There I was thinking it would be in invisible ink. You being a G-Man and all.'

'My least favourite phrase. How did you know where I lived?'

'I have my methods, Nessheim.'

Then it came to him. 'You drove here?'

She nodded. 'You know me. I like the great outdoors best from behind a wheel.'

He laughed. 'You've got a pretty fancy car.'

It was Stacey's turn to look surprised. 'How do you know?'

'That was you in the Packard Eight. The first time, on Fifty-seventh, you had the top up. Then on Kimbark you had it down.'

'It seemed a clever disguise.'

He shook his head. 'Don't drive a car the colour of a fire engine if you're trying not to be noticed.'

She didn't reply, but walked through to the dining room, looking at the textbooks and notebooks stacked on the table there. When he came in to join her she walked quickly along the corridor to the front hall, where without so much as a by-your-leave she opened the door to his bedroom. Taking a step inside she stopped and surveyed the room, while he stood in the doorway behind her. Thank God I made the bed, he thought, looking over her shoulder at the spartan room. It held a night-time side table, a small closet, a maple dresser for clothes, a couple of planks he had set up on bricks for the books of his late-night reading – a mix of what his mother called 'proper books' and the paperbacks being produced for the military which Woodworth's sold illicitly on 57th Street – and the bed, an old iron one, with a white candlewick bedspread pulled tight across the blankets.

Stacey turned to leave the room. 'I can tell you haven't had a lot of company here, Nessheim.'

'Why's that?'

'No girl worth her salt would spend more than a night in a room this bare.'

'I must have been waiting for you to fix it up.'

'I thought you had a girlfriend in Washington.'

'Who told you that?'

'I don't know.' She walked past him into the hall, then turned into the living room and went and sat on the sofa vacated by Guttman. Nessheim stood in the open doorway and looked down at her. 'I suppose you want a beer.'

She shook her head, and her hair swayed easily on her shoulders. 'I'm off the sauce these days.' She waited a beat. 'Unless you've got some Scotch going?'

'You haven't changed.'

He went to the kitchen and poured them each a good stiff inch, then filled the glasses half-full from the sink faucet – the water was cold and hard here in Chicago, almost good enough to substitute for ice.

When he came back he found her lying with both legs up on the sofa. Her head was propped against a cushion she'd rearranged at one end. He gave her the drink, then sat in the soft chair and looked out the window. It was getting dark; in the courtyard the shadows were fading to black. 'Chin chin,' he said, raising his glass.

'Cheers,' she said, lifting the glass and taking a long pull. She nodded her approval and pointed vaguely at the walls. 'I was expecting a bachelor's slum, but this is kind of nice – bedroom excepted. Too bad. I was hoping you'd need me to clean the place up.'

'You mean, you'd send your maid to sort it out.'

'I've given up Drusilla for the duration of the war.'

'You let her go? After all these years?'

'Of course not. But she only comes once a week now.'

'A sacrifice, I'm sure. For her, I mean – she must miss the dough.'

'I pay her the same amount.'

'That's big of you.' He paused, then said, 'So what are you doing back in school?'

'A girl's got to eat.'

'I thought that's what they had men for.'

She looked at him with cool eyes. 'I tried that. It didn't take.'

He wasn't sure what she meant. There was always a man in Stacey's life; once it had been Nessheim. 'Don't tell me you're hard up now.'

'I'm not.'

'So why law school? To help the poor and defenceless?'

She looked at him with the studied calmness that meant she was getting annoyed. 'Nessheim, I know you think I'm a hypocrite, a rich girl toying with the poor for amusement's sake. But would it really be better if I thought I *deserved* to be rich?'

'That sounds familiar,' he said and took a long slug of his highball. It tasted soapy to him. 'So now that you've found me, is there a purpose to your visit?'

'Ouch,' she said very quietly, but he didn't look at her. She said more brightly, 'You haven't got a smoke, have you?'

'I don't smoke,' he said with annoyance. 'You must be thinking of another guy. Is it that hard to keep track?'

'I'll let you count,' she said with a shrug, though he could tell she was still cross by the way she was trying not to show it. They sat in awkward silence for a moment, then she gave a small sigh and said, 'You've changed, Nessheim, though I'm not sure it's for the good. What happened?'

'What didn't happen? I was in the FBI for eight years, Stacey.'

'Funny that, I never saw your name in the papers. You didn't shoot Ma Barker, now did you?' She gave a

28

playful laugh, trying to make things light again. 'I bet you never shot anyone.'

Stacey saw the look on his face. 'Oh, Jim, I'm sorry. I was being stupid, wasn't I? And you're still connected to the Bureau, aren't you?'

'Nope. I resigned before I came back to Chicago.'

'Then what were those two VIPs doing here?'

He shrugged and got up from his chair, and stood with his back to her, gazing out of the window. He didn't want to look at her. Her face wasn't flawless – she had a small curve to her nose, a dot of a mole on one cheek, one eye that was greener than the other, and little, slightly prominent teeth that she'd always complained were squirrel-like. Yet Nessheim thought she was the most beautiful girl he'd ever known. She'd also been the funniest, sexiest, most *alive* woman ever willing to take up with the likes of him. But then she'd done a bunk and left Chicago, returning three months later with a deep tan and a new boyfriend. Nessheim, whose spirits were usually high, had felt pancake flat for a year. More than a year, actually.

It was dark outside now. 'What do you want from me, Stacey?' He kept his voice down and was trying to sound detached.

'I'm three weeks behind, Nessheim. That's a lot of Torts. Somebody's got to help me catch up.'

He still wouldn't look at her; that would be fatal. 'Hire a tutor.'

'How much do tutors cost?' There was that familiar bounce to her voice.

'With you, more than any tutor can afford.'

She laughed at the jiggled logic. 'I had someone in mind, but he'd need to tell me the going rate.'

Nessheim snorted. She was playing him like a fish

29

too small to worry about if it didn't take the bait. 'What if he says no?'

'Be positive. You mean what if he says "Yes"? That means nobody at school finds out he's with the Feds.'

He didn't bother to deny it again, for he was suddenly overwhelmed by the return of old feelings. He had forgotten the extent of his desire for her. It was not only physical desire – simply being with Stacey had eclipsed any other happiness he'd known. He'd once made the fatal mistake of telling her that. 'Even more than football?' she'd replied, her sarcastic tone running like a piano scale across his feelings. His declaration of love reduced to schmaltz, he'd had sense enough not to go mooning on, and had merely bandied back, 'Well, maybe not football.'

Now he found himself moving to the sofa, and Stacey pulled up her legs to make room for him at the far end. Was she serious? He told himself that's why he needed to look at her face, though when he did he found her eyes laughing at him. But there was a hint of warmth, maybe even generosity, he hadn't ever seen before, and it almost took his breath away, since he thought he'd learned not to hope for anything from her.

'Okay?' she said in a whisper, and he nodded despite himself. She swung her legs off the sofa and leaned forward, and he waited for her to make the first move, trying to restrain the impulse to take her into his arms.

But she only kissed him on the forehead, once, lightly, while he closed his eyes. 'I'll see you soon,' she said, still in a whisper. 'I'm kind of glad I found you.'

By the time he opened his eyes she had gone. He heard the screen door slam in the kitchen, and when he roused himself and walked to the rear of the apartment, he only caught the quickest flash of her, heading towards the alley and her car.

He stood in the kitchen for a minute, resisting the temptation to go out on the landing and watch her. He noticed the envelope she'd picked up and tore it open, idly wondering how much the newspaper bill would be. Two bucks? Four? He couldn't remember when he'd last paid. He was surprised to find no calculations on the piece of paper which he unfolded, a piece of onion-skin typing paper. There was one typed line, and as he read it he suddenly felt a chill, warm as it was outside:

Welcome Home, Herr Rossbach.
We know where you are.

Part Two

2

As the *Liberty Limited* moved east through the dark flatlands of Indiana and Ohio, Harry Guttman sat in the dark in his grand compartment. With the lights off, he didn't have to stare at his own reflection in the Pullman window, and could see instead the occasional light of a distant farmhouse, or closer up the platforms of the stations they passed through at speed. South Bend, Valparaiso, and the improbably named Warsaw – which looked a small and sleepy town, unlike its counterpart, where Guttman knew for a fact people were being slaughtered on a daily basis.

Guttman was travelling on his own nickel. He had originally reserved the last upper berth in a section sleeper, anticipating a restive night from the snoring of other passengers in the bunks behind the dark green curtains and the rowdiness of the soldiers turning in after late-night games of pinochle in the bar lounge. He needed to be back at Bureau Headquarters in Washington the next morning (a Tuesday); he'd told his secretary Marie to say he was sick today, but Hoover didn't like illness among his staff, and had the irritating habit of calling you at home when you were out more than a day.

Revelling in his recent promotion from colonel to general, Groves had commandeered a 'drawing room'. But at the last minute he had decided to stay over in Chicago to compare construction notes with the executives at the new Merchandise Mart, the world's largest commercial building – though smaller than the new pentagon-shaped headquarters built for the War

Department, which Groves told Guttman proudly would eventually consist of 6.5 million square feet. Having changed his own plans, Groves had offered his compartment to Guttman – not without an almost royal whiff of condescension. The Pullman porter had looked so disappointed when the General proved a no-show that Guttman had handed over two bucks to keep him happy.

The compartment was embarrassingly plush and spacious: wood-panelled and carpeted, with two lower berths, one of which doubled as a couch while the other lay hidden in a recess of the wall. There was a pair of deep-cushioned lounge chairs by the windows, a small writing table, and best of all, a separate, private washroom. Quarters fit for a . . . general, Guttman supposed, since no regular soldiers travelled this way. Director Hoover did, of course; on his trips with Clyde Tolson he went nothing but first class. His subordinates, however, were expected to pursue a relentless frugality.

He thought about Groves and their meeting in Chicago with Fermi. The Italian scientist had been forthcoming, almost voluble in his descriptions of the set-up at the University of Chicago, where they had met in Fermi's office. They had been introduced to no one else, since Groves was at pains to keep Guttman's presence secret.

Guttman wished he could have got a better feel for what Fermi's scientists were doing. Groves had cut short Fermi's scientific explanations of atoms and energy, and focused on logistics – how many employees, where did they live, how many knew the true import of their work, and how many were immigrants (especially from Germany)? That was the way Groves's mind worked. Learn what the problem was, allocate resources, drive your staff hard, and see the job home. Simple as that. It made him simultaneously insufferable and impressive, and it was how the Pentagon had got built.

But unless it was a construction project you were running, life tended to be more complicated when people were involved. Fermi's reactions had been hard to read, but Guttman had watched Nessheim's aversion for Groves grow from the moment they met. Groves was too imperious and offhand; for all his easy-going manner, Nessheim had never been one to be pushed around.

He worried about which way Nessheim would jump, and deep down doubted the agent would agree to help. But was he really going to hide himself in Contracts and Jurisprudence while the world was at battle? In fairness, the guy had been through the wars before the rest of America had even heard a shot fired in anger. Guttman wished he'd seen Nessheim alone. Groves wouldn't have a clue how to find a spy.

If there were a spy. He thought of the meeting that had triggered his trip to Chicago. Marie had taken the call. 'It's Justice Frankfurter's office.' Guttman had been asked by the clerk to meet the Justice at his home, an elegant Georgian-style house on Dumbarton Avenue. Guttman's neighbour Annie Ryerson worked half-days as the Justice's secretary for non-judicial business, but fortunately she hadn't been there on the day of Guttman's visit – it was nice having her as a neighbour, but it would have been awkward to find her at work, steno pad in hand.

Guttman had climbed the stairs up to the main floor of the house, where the maid had answered the door and led him to the small study where Frankfurter worked at home. It was furnished by Frankfurter's favourite interior decorator – his wife – with oriental rugs on the buff-coloured carpet, a small French walnut writing desk, and hand-coloured lithographs of nineteenth-century Washington. Behind the desk hung a photograph of

Roosevelt shaking Frankfurter's hand two years before, after Congress had reluctantly approved his nomination to the Supreme Court.

Guttman wondered why the judge wanted to see him. It sounded important; on the phone his secretary at the Court had been insistent on an early date. Though Frankfurter was physically unprepossessing – almost tiny, with a friendly rather than handsome face – Guttman was always impressed by him, sometimes uneasily so. The Justice cut an elegant figure with his sleek white hair combed straight back. He wore beautifully tailored three-piece suits, bespoke shirts, an old-fashioned tie pin, and handmade shoes always buffed to a high shine. These vanities were nonetheless belied by an unaffected manner, which suggested that he would leave other people to take him seriously. Though he also seemed to assume they would.

Their relationship originated in a common concern for the plight of Jews in Europe. They had met through charity dinners, which provided a useful cover for their further dealings: as a Supreme Court Justice, Frankfurter had no business pursuing what critics would see as a partisan effort to bring yet more immigrants to America; similarly, Guttman was proscribed by his post at the Bureau from activities that could be construed as 'political'. But they did what they could – Frankfurter through his closeness with the President, who had a famous soft spot for the Jews; Guttman by gathering information from contacts in British intelligence and from Switzerland, about the only European country left where intelligence was not Gestapo-controlled or suborned. Not that the Swiss were naturally disposed to help; they were simply neutral businessmen, happy to reward the occasional 'donation' from a Jewish welfare organisation located safely in the country's cantons with information that no Jewish (or come to that, Allied) institution could amass on its own.

That morning Frankfurter greeted Guttman with a brisk handshake and ushered him to one of the pair of green-and-white damask armchairs positioned by the small fireplace. Above its mantelpiece hung a lovely pen-and-ink drawing of Mrs Frankfurter as a young woman. 'My family didn't have their portrait painted,' the Justice had once complained tartly. Like Guttman, he had married outside the faith, though there the resemblance ended: Frankfurter's wife was from an ancient Yankee family; Guttman's Isabel the daughter of Polish Catholic immigrants.

As they sat down Guttman saw a tiny wooden rocking horse in a corner of the room. Noticing him looking, Frankfurter laughed. 'One of the Gates girls'.' Guttman nodded, remembering that three English children had stayed with the Frankfurters for several months during the Blitz, until their mother had come over to reclaim them. Frankfurter's associations were so often with the great and the good that there was something touching about this personal philanthropy.

Frankfurter got down to business right away. 'Thank you for seeing the fellow in Berkeley. The President and Vannevar Bush are both very grateful.'

'He's a remarkable man.' Guttman had been impressed by Robert Oppenheimer.

'He is. From what Bush tells me, he's not at Einstein's level as a scientist, but that's like saying DiMaggio's not the equal of Babe Ruth. He's won the Nobel Prize after all, so any other scientist will have to respect him.'

Guttman said, 'You told me there had been doubts raised about his politics. I looked into that, and I have to tell you that he's had some iffy acquaintances. But there's no evidence he would ever be disloyal.'

'You sure of that?'

'As much as you can ever be.' Hoover saw Reds under almost every bed, but Guttman's inquiries suggested Oppenheimer's problems were in the bed itself. He had an exotic love life, and some of his paramours (not to mention his wife) had strong connections with Communist Party members. But the two hours he'd spent with Oppenheimer had convinced Guttman that the man's worst political sin was naivety.

Frankfurter said calmly, 'The military people don't agree with you.'

'I know that. And I'm giving you my own opinion, not the official one of the Bureau. The Director might not share my view.'

'He probably wouldn't, but it's not his opinion the White House wanted,' Frankfurter said with a touch of acerbity. 'You mentioned last time that you were worried security had been compromised at the Bureau.'

'I think it may still be a problem.'

'Another Nazi effort?'

'No, it's not the Nazis who are doing the infiltrating.'

'I don't think you mean the Japanese.' Frankfurter's eyes widened. 'If I understand what you *are* suggesting, I doubt that very much. Those people are our allies now. They wouldn't dare threaten the relationship.'

'Are you sure about that?' He found the man's innocence startling.

'My view isn't important,' said Frankfurter with deceptive mildness, since he added more sharply, 'but the President's is. He wants everyone focused on fighting the Nazis and the Japs, not investigating our allies. Why, just the other day he had somebody tell him that one of my former clerks – he's in the State Department now – was a Russian agent. The President sent him packing with a flea in his ear. Worth remembering that.'

40

Guttman accepted the rebuff in silence. He had hoped to take things further with Frankfurter, feeling that if he could enlist the Justice and perhaps even the President on this issue, he'd have a useful ally should Hoover ever discover his own suspicions. Now this prospect had evaporated. So what did Frankfurter want from him?

'Your opinion of Oppenheimer is important because he's being given a big job. Technically, you're not supposed to know anything about it. Hoover doesn't, and I don't want that to change.' It was said amiably enough, but there was a warning in his voice.

Guttman was intrigued now. 'I'll keep shtum,' he said.

Frankfurter chuckled. 'You can take the boy out of the Lower East Side, but not the Lower East Side out of the boy.'

Guttman smiled politely. Frankfurter had grown up near Delancey Street, a few blocks from Guttman's own childhood home, and both of them had attended the local grade school, P.S. 25. Each had left that world far behind, though Guttman's progress in life was unremarkable compared to Frankfurter's star-like ascension.

'Let's have some coffee,' said Frankfurter, 'and then I'll tell you why I asked you here.' He picked up a small silver bell with a bone handle and gave it a shake. 'I never used one of these on Hester Street,' he said.

The maid came in with a tray, and then while Guttman munched a dainty biscuit and juggled his cup and saucer on one knee, Frankfurter briefed him.

Three years earlier a letter had arrived at the White House, delivered by an acquaintance of the President's named Alexander Sachs. 'A *landsman*,' Frankfurter acknowledged, 'and a good enough fellow, if a bit of an operator.' Guttman almost choked on his biscuit; Frankfurter was the operator par excellence: countless numbers of Washington bureaucrats owed their jobs to him.

Frankfurter explained that the letter was written by Albert Einstein, who wanted to alert the President to a matter of national importance. Recent scientific advances had suggested that it could be possible to set up a controlled nuclear reaction, using large quantities of the element uranium, which would release vast amounts of energy. This in turn would allow the construction of a bomb larger than anything previously thought possible. It would have the destructive power of 20,000 tons of TNT and be capable of wiping out a major city.

Frankfurter said, 'I don't think we have to concern ourselves with the scientific details.' He paused and smiled. 'Mainly because I don't understand them.'

'Was Einstein saying we should build such a weapon?'

'Yes, but not because he thought it was a good thing to do. I think Einstein felt we had to follow this up, simply because if we didn't the Germans would get there first.'

'Have we done that?'

'Absolutely.' And Frankfurter explained that a project of unprecedented size was under way, at locations all over the United States. 'Though the advisers are starting to think we should centralise our efforts in one location. They are waiting for the results of a particular experiment going on in Chicago – it's being directed by an Italian physicist named Enrico Fermi. If it's successful, then we'll know this can be done. We'll be able to build a bomb. An atomic bomb.'

'Just how far along are the Germans?' Guttman asked.

Frankfurter explained that nobody knew for sure. The Nazis had lost a tremendous amount of expertise when Jewish scientists fled, but considerable talent remained, as well as a dedication to destruction which the West so far didn't share. Until recently, many scientists in the United States had been acting as if there wasn't a war going on – the scientific community was used to being an open book and had a long tradition of transparency. It was only now that they were managing to keep scientists from publishing papers about their work on the project. 'God knows what secrets their colleagues in Germany have gleaned just by reading the journals.' He shook his head wearily.

'Enough to catch up with us?'

'Let's hope not,' said Frankfurter. 'But that's where our problems begin.'

The scientists at work on this new project were a tremendously mixed bag. Many were refugees from Europe, and the impetus for the whole shebang, as Frankfurter called it with obvious relish, had come from America's most famous immigrant, Einstein, and another eminent scientist, a Hungarian Jew named Leo Szilard. If you counted the heads at the various labs already engaged with the project – in Berkeley, Chicago, Columbia, and soon Tennessee – there were hundreds of people involved. Security was tight, and everyone involved seemed to understand the need to keep the project secret. 'People aren't even telling their wives,' said Frankfurter in wonder.

'Have they all been checked out?'

'Yes – by the Military Intelligence Division.'

'That sounds okay.'

'Does it now?' Frankfurter asked. 'The MID concluded this man Fermi was a fascist.'

'Is he?'

Frankfurter snorted. 'He had to leave Italy because his wife is Jewish, so I doubt he thinks a lot of Mussolini. MID claimed Szilard was a fascist too. A somewhat extreme judgement, in my view, since Szilard got Einstein to write the letter in the first place. Why would a Nazi want to do that?' He added acidly, 'Especially a Jewish one.'

'Why wasn't the FBI involved?'

'It was. The MID findings were so patently absurd that we asked the Bureau to do its own checks. But Hoover merely confirmed what Military Intelligence had to say. I suppose he didn't want a ruckus with the MID.'

Guttman wasn't surprised; Hoover didn't like fighting battles he might lose. But then who did? The Justice continued. 'Anyway, this project has the code name Manhattan, but the problem's said to be in Chicago, where work is going on at the university. The worry is that there may be a Nazi agent who's been infiltrated into the team there.'

'How did we find this out?'

'I don't know precisely. This all comes from Harry Hopkins, so that's the horse's mouth as far as I'm concerned. Hopkins said the President was absolutely insistent that this be followed up. So I asked you to come and see me.'

Did the President really believe the Nazis had a spy in Chicago? It seemed improbable to Guttman. But he didn't press this – Frankfurter could be quick to take offence, as prickly if challenged as he was emollient when making the effort to charm. And the Justice's belief in Roosevelt was unshakeable, outdone only by his belief in himself.

Frankfurter scratched one cheek thoughtfully. 'The White House has appointed a man named Groves to run this entire project. He understands the seriousness of this information, and accepts that MID are the last people we want traipsing around the scientists. Yet we do need someone to look into the operation in Chicago.'

'So you want the Bureau to do it?'

44

'Not exactly.' He turned his hazel eyes on Guttman. 'When Director Hoover ran security checks on the scientists, he wasn't told what the scientists were working on.' When Guttman looked surprised, Frankfurter added, 'You said yourself security may have been compromised at the Bureau.'

Guttman wondered where this was leading. 'If you don't want military security and you don't want the Bureau, what's left?' The Chicago Police Department, he was tempted to say, but he knew the Justice liked to make the jokes.

'I was thinking of another alternative. The President knows you've played an important role in ... certain matters in the past, and he knows you're someone he can trust.'

Flattery will get you everywhere, thought Guttman, determined to resist it nonetheless. 'I can't exactly up stakes and move to Chicago,' he said.

Frankfurter gave an understanding smile. 'No one's expecting you to. But the last time we met, you mentioned that young agent who was involved before.'

'Nessheim?'

'That's the one. Miss Ryerson knew him, I believe.' Frankfurter's face showed the hint of a smile. 'I have the feeling she was sweet on him – or maybe he was sweet on her.'

Guttman merely nodded.

'You said he was in Chicago, didn't you?'

'That's right,' said Guttman.

'Annie said he'd left the Bureau to go to law school.'

'That's what he thinks,' said Guttman.

There was a sudden sound of a chime scale coming from the corridor, and Guttman's reverie was broken. 'Second sitting for dinner,' the dining-car waiter called out.

Guttman got up and went into the compartment's tiny bathroom, where he washed his hands and face, then looked in the mirror. He hadn't shaved very well that morning, but then his five o'clock shadow started to show by lunchtime whatever he did. He straightened his tie as best he could, brushed dandruff off his shoulder that turned out to be chalk. As he went out into the corridor, he heard the Pullman porter say clearly from one end, 'He's in Room D.'

Guttman was in D. But when he walked down the corridor whoever had been asking was gone. Maybe they had meant the next car.

The dining car was filling up but the steward found him a seat at a table for four that was occupied only by an elderly lady, sitting rigidly upright by the window. She was dressed for dinner, in a simple black wool dress and a solitary cameo pin for jewellery. When Guttman sat down across from her she gave a curt nod.

Guttman said, 'Evening. I hope you don't mind my joining you.'

'I can't expect a table all to myself,' she said, with the clipped tones of the New Englander. Guttman could see it: Vermont bred and born, a Congregationalist church-goer with a life of few fripperies and fewer words, sustained by $1 million in government bonds held in an old shoebox, tucked away under the back stairs of her large Federalist house.

The waiter, in a spotless white jacket and black bow tie, came and handed him the menu, then asked if he'd like a cocktail. 'Only got rye if you'd like a highball, sir,' the waiter said. 'There's gin as well.'

'Give me a beer,' said Guttman, ignoring his table companion's small frown. When the waiter went away he examined the menu. Dinner cost $2.00, though service personnel got 10 per cent off and parents could share their portions with children. He was told to Eat Fast and to Buy Victory Bonds and Stamps. For the entrée, there was a choice of Spring Lamb Steak Sautéed, Fried Spring Chicken Maryland, Boston Pot Roast, or Creamed Fresh Shrimp. Guttman had hoped for Prime Rib, but beef rationing was making choice cuts scarce.

He decided on Hot Clam Bouillon to start, followed by Pot Roast. He picked up the pad and pencil by his plate and wrote down his order. It was an old-fashioned system to keep waiters from stealing – otherwise a customer would ask for the T-bone steak, the waiter would write down the order as a salad bowl, charge the customer for the steak, pay the railroad for the salad bowl, and pocket the difference.

He looked at his dinner companion but she wouldn't meet his eye. So they sat in silence, as she ate her main course and Guttman spooned up his soup. He was remembering the end of his conversation with Frankfurter. It seemed clear that Frankfurter had apprised Roosevelt of Guttman's fears that the Bureau had been compromised. Equally clear, Roosevelt must have taken this to mean it was compromised by Nazi sympathisers. Since Roosevelt's source of information (and what exactly was it?) claimed a Nazi had infiltrated the project in Chicago, then naturally the President wouldn't want to engage the Bureau in smoking him out.

Which made sense – sort of. For if the President distrusted the Bureau, why had he continued to add to the power Hoover wielded? The President had in recent years expanded the FBI's powers enormously, undermining his own Attorney General's efforts to keep Hoover under control. Why had FDR done that? It seemed a direct contradiction of what Guttman had learned from Frankfurter.

47

Unless ... Guttman chewed thoughtfully on a piece of stewed beef and then reached the only conclusion. The President was scared of Hoover.

When he'd finished his pot roast Guttman broke down and ordered dessert, writing 'One peach pie' on the pad just as a woman came into the car from the far end, passing the galley and almost colliding with a waiter coming out with a hot plate. She was wearing an eye-catching, peacock-blue cocktail dress. Her thick black hair was brushed back in a wave, with a long ivory clip to hold it in place, and her eyes had enough mascara applied to make her lashes shine like dark stars against the pale skin of her face.

Two of the soldiers, at a table for four, looked up at her with interest, and one of them opened his palm wide to show there was a free seat. The dining-car steward was about to lead her there when she said something and he nodded, then led her past the soldiers' table and pulled out the aisle chair next to the old lady.

'Hope you don't mind,' she said, impersonally addressing the table. The old lady didn't respond, and Guttman felt obliged to say he didn't mind at all.

The waiter was back with Guttman's pie and the menu card, and the new arrival looked at it intently for a moment. Her features were strong: a long nose, flattened very slightly at the end, a mouth lipsticked cherry red, and a strong chin that was saved by a small dimple that broke the blunt monotony of its cleft. No one would ever have called her beautiful, but she certainly served to brighten up the dining car, which was filled with soldiers, sailors and bureaucrats.

She put down the menu with a neat slap on the white linen tablecloth and unfolded a starched napkin across her knees. 'Well, at least there's a choice,' she said chirpily, with a voice more youthful than the rest of her – Guttman figured her for forty and a bit. 'Going west we had sandwiches until Utah.'

The old lady looked disapproving, as if an unpatriotic complaint had been voiced. The woman in peacock blue winked at Guttman, and he half-smiled and looked down at his plate.

'You start out in Chicago?' she asked him, and he nodded. She nodded back, then turned to the old lady. 'Where are you travelling to?'

'Washington, then New York,' the lady said. 'And then home – thank goodness.'

'You don't like New York?'

'Not much. Not my kind of people.'

Guttman said nothing. The younger woman extended her hand to him. 'I'm Lois,' she said.

He stuck a mouthful of pie behind one cheek and put down his fork to shake her hand. 'Harry,' he said.

The old lady ignored the exchange, but the woman named Lois seemed determined to include her, asking, 'Have you come far?'

'Just Chicago.' The voice was like flint. 'My grandson's stationed at Great Lakes.'

'Nice of you to visit him,' said Guttman. Maybe she would warm up now that he was not her sole dinner companion.

She shook her head. 'Not when I had to tell him that his brother's dead.'

'I'm so sorry,' said Guttman, slightly stunned.

The old lady glared at him. 'He was a marine, killed by the Japs in the Solomon Islands.'

Guttman didn't know what to say. Lois turned to him and broke the silence. 'So where are you getting off, Harry?'

He said, 'Washington.'

'What are you doing there?'

'I work for the government.'

'That sounds exciting.' She said this without sarcasm – or conviction – then looked at her menu. 'What's it gonna be?' she mused out loud. 'Shrimp for me, I think. Don't see that on the trains much.' She looked at Guttman. 'Any chance I could borrow your pencil?'

'Sure,' he said, blushing slightly, and handed it over. Lois scribbled her order on the little pad, and handed it back to him. When he took the pencil she seemed to make sure their fingers touched.

Seeing that he'd finished his peach pie, the waiter came and asked if he wanted coffee. Guttman hesitated, feeling the woman Lois's eyes on him. Part of him wanted to stay and talk to her; suddenly he felt his loneliness like a running sore. But part of him – irrational but large – felt it would be a betrayal. And he had papers in his compartment to look at, and God knows he could use some sleep, something he couldn't get at home these days.

So he shook his head and stood up, leaving a quarter on the linen tablecloth, while the white-jacketed waiter moved aside to let him out, clutching the hot silver coffee jug with a linen napkin.

'Excuse me,' Guttman muttered as he edged out into the aisle.

The old lady didn't reply, but Lois looked surprised, even disappointed. 'Going so soon?'

He nodded. 'I had a long day.' He got a curt smile in return as he said goodnight.

The Pullman porter had been in his compartment to make down the bed with freshly laundered linen, fluffed-up pillows and a brownish-pink blanket. Guttman took off his clothes, reaching absent-mindedly for his holster and gun only to remember that he hadn't brought them with him. His business had been too unofficial for that. He put on his pyjamas, a blue flannel pair his wife had bought from Hecht's. He turned off all but the night light above his bed and got in, deciding the stuff he'd brought from work could wait until the morning, when he would be back behind his desk. He took Steinbeck's *The Moon is Down* to bed with him, but found it hard to concentrate on the book. He was tired.

He wondered if he had been right to make the trip. *You and your missions,* Isabel had said once, fondness and concern vying in her voice. It made a change, anyway, for in the last months his regular duties had become emotionally meaningless to him – war or no war. It had reached the stage where recently he had thought seriously about leaving the Bureau. Not that he knew what he'd do then. He couldn't hang out a lawyer's shingle; it was twenty years since he'd taken his night-school law degree, and he doubted he would even be able to pass the Washington Bar. A job as security chief for a department store had been his mental fallback each time he thought Hoover was about to get rid of him. And with so many ex-cops now in military uniform, it was true that he could walk into that kind of post for the asking. But the prospect appalled him – of days spent in an office tucked behind women's lingerie or the shoe department; eight hours interrogating shoplifters and contemplating the place his life had come to.

He was dozing off now, starting to dream about his childhood down on Manhattan's Lower East Side. His friend Max was there, and they were playing stickball. The same Max who got polio ten years later and now lived in calipers. But the dream had the Max of old, whipping the ball in while Guttman stood over the sewer top they used for home plate. He swung and missed with the broomstick, then swung and missed again. Guttman was growing frustrated, desperate to hit the ball ... suddenly there was a knock on the compartment door.

He came to with a start, to find the night light still on and his book sitting like a flattened gable on his chest. Had he imagined the noise? He waited tensely. Then there was another knock.

He got up, feeling in his oversized pyjamas like the ten-year-old boy in his dream. He shuffled to the door, still groggy. 'Who is it?' he asked.

'Open up, please.' It was a woman's voice.

Guttman opened the door a crack and looked out cautiously. It was the black-haired woman from the dining car. He opened the door wider. The corridor lights had been dimmed, but he could see that she was alone.

She was smiling at Harry, pyjamas and all, and seemed to be swaying slightly. He wondered if she were drunk, though she hadn't had anything but coffee at dinner. She said, 'I thought you might like some company, Mr Guttman.'

The lines seemed out of a bad movie. He felt embarrassed. 'I was going to bed. Sorry.'

'Won't you stay up a while for me?'

He didn't answer. He didn't want a scene but he also didn't want this woman inside his compartment. She said, more sharply now, 'What's the matter? We could have some fun.'

'Nothing's the matter. I'm married, that's all.' The lie seemed necessary.

'I guess I got it wrong then. You sure you're still married?'

He bristled slightly. 'I'm sure. Goodnight.'

He closed the door and locked it, hoping she wouldn't

knock again. When he got back into bed, he realised he was shivering. Had the woman mistaken him for Groves?

Then suddenly he sat up. When the woman had sat down at dinner, she'd introduced herself. *I'm Lois.*

Harry, he'd said.

So how did she know his last name?

3

IN THE MORNING the dining car was nearly empty – the soldiers were taking the rare opportunity to sleep in and there was no sign of the woman named Lois. Guttman returned to his compartment just as the train went through the Ivy City locomotive coach yard, full of dark Tuscan-red Pennsylvania Railroad coaches and, above them, a cat's cradle of overhead wires for the new electric line between D.C. and New York. Ten minutes later they arrived at Union Station. On the platform he couldn't see Lois either. Maybe she had got off in the early hours; he dimly remembered they had stopped at Harrisburg while it was still dark.

He went through the crowded hall, a blur of bustling khaki-clad soldiers, past the sign for the Servicemen's Lounge and the long line at the ticket window, and got into one of the taxis waiting outside. He'd left his car at the Bureau, hoping no one would notice that it had been there since Sunday. The cab moved slowly towards the Capitol, the driver complaining that the war had brought too many people to town. When Guttman suggested that must help business, the driver said he'd gladly sacrifice the extra fares for lighter traffic.

Guttman got out discreetly at 12th Street and walked the long block to the Bureau. The temperature was in the mid-sixties, and chances were the coming winter would not be harsh – it very rarely was in what was essentially a southern city. A good thing, thought Guttman, since he hated snow – its association with a childhood spent struggling with hand-me-down galoshes and buckled rubber boots.

At the Bureau he found Marie behind her desk in the anteroom outside his office. There was a young agent standing by her desk. Probably a new recruit from one of the field offices, making the rounds. Guttman didn't recognise him, though the way this guy was hanging around Marie was familiar enough. The field guys would hover in the little anteroom like bees around a honeypot, drawn to the mixed kind of attraction Marie exuded, part lustworthy, part maternal – most of the agents were younger than Marie, who Guttman figured was in her early forties (he could never bring himself to ask). She was a well-built redhead with a pleasant, lived-in face; attractive in a way that made even the ugliest rube feel it was not inconceivable he had a chance with her. She was welcoming, *gemütlichkeit;* to a raw-boned kid in from the Butte office for the first time she must have seemed soothing and redolent of home – like a re-assuring malted milk at a soda fountain.

As Guttman came in, the young agent stopped talking.

'Morning, Marie,' Guttman said.

'Morning, Mr Guttman.' This was unusual – Marie only called him *Mr* in Tolson's presence.

Guttman turned to the agent, who wore a dark blue suit, white shirt and a tie without discernible pattern. The young man stood there confidently, a good four inches taller than Guttman, and handsome in a Clark Kent kind of way.

'You waiting to see me?'

'No, sir. I was just dropping off a memo with Miss Boudreau from Mr Tolson. It's to all the assistant directors.'

'I see. Have you managed to do that now?'

'Sir?'

Guttman nodded at the memo on Marie's desk. 'Message received, Mr ... ?

'Adams, sir. Thomas Adams.' He extended his hand and Guttman shook it grudgingly.

'Was there anything else requiring your presence here, Mr Adams?' Guttman said laboriously.

The young man blushed. 'No, sir. I'm all through. Thanks, Marie,' he said and scooted out of the room.

Marie looked knowingly at Guttman. 'You're in a good mood. Was your trip that bad?'

'Don't know yet. Who was that kid?'

'T.A.?'

'Is that what he's called? They're taking them young these days.'

'You're just feeling your age. You see the resemblance?'

'To what? Of whom?' Miss Lewalski from the sixth grade, strict with a ruler and a stickler for grammar, came flooding back.

'Doesn't he remind you of someone?'

'My nephew Seymour?'

'Go on, be serious. Can't you see it?'

'No, Marie, I can't. Who does the young T.A. remind me of?' He felt grumpy, and was getting grumpier.

'Frank Sinatra.'

'I think I've heard of him. Scrawny guy, yeah?' But it was hard to put a face to the name; he thought of Sinatra as a syrupy voice on the radio.

Marie shook her head. 'Sometimes, Harry ... Even you know who Sinatra is. All the girls in the pool think so. Down to the Adam's apple.'

'Has our "Sinatra" finished high school yet?'

'You sound jealous.'

This was true. Guttman had never looked as young as this guy. Even in his early twenties, Guttman's hair had been deserting him. What remained were long strands, splayed across his pale-coloured pate like black threads on an ivory pillow. 'I've seen the guy before, I think.'

'Of course you have. He worked for Mr Tolson a few years back, then went to the Chicago Field Office.'

'Did he now?' Tolson specialised in young male assistants. Clean-cut individuals, usually former athletes, as Tolson liked to pretend he was as well.

'Yeah,' said Marie, 'I think he was out on the Coast for a while too. But I guess Mr Tolson thought he was wasted out there, and brought him back to work for him again.' Marie played it straight, but her eyes were mischievous.

'Other than the arrival of young Sinatra in your life, did I miss anything yesterday?'

Marie shook her head. 'Don't think so. The mail is on your desk. You've got the Executives Conference at ten-thirty. Otherwise your day is clear.' He started to move through the doorway to his office when she added, 'Oh,' and he noticed her voice had lowered. 'There was a call for you. I didn't want to leave the message on your desk.'

'Who was that?'

'Your Canadian friend.'

It had taken J. Edgar Hoover over fifteen years to recognise the importance of counter-espionage and to accept that operating within America's borders were foreign agents who the FBI needed to do something about. Through the Depression of the thirties, Hoover would not countenance the idea. His objectives were combating conventional crime (especially bank robberies) and accruing power for the organisation he ran.

When war broke out in Europe in 1939, however, Hoover had created a new division, separate from the all-encompassing General Intelligence Division. It was named Division Five and was run by Edward Tamm, a trusted Hoover lieutenant. Div 5 comprised four sections, and Guttman ran the one devoted to counter-espionage. Yet he still reported to Tolson, not Tamm – which Tamm resented.

Guttman's anomalous status had come after intense negotiations in the spring of 1942 with Hoover himself, when Guttman's priority had been to arrange his own transfer from running the Strategic Intelligence Service, or SIS, another new division created after America's entry into the war to track German activities in Latin America. With an invalid wife back then, the last thing Guttman had wanted was to traipse around Caracas or Santiago looking for Nazis. He was in any case more comfortable fighting the enemy at home. In his own way, he supposed, he was an Isolationist himself.

At 10.30 he went upstairs for the weekly Executives Conference. It was chaired by Clyde Tolson and was held in a meeting room down the corridor from the Director's quarters, a suite of rooms that included Tolson's own office. The meeting was attended by all the assistant directors and a few other senior Bureau officials. The only junior person usually present was Miss Caccioppo, a legendary stenographer said to hold the unofficial world record for shorthand speed, so Guttman was surprised to see Tolson's new assistant there, the kid T.A.

The rest were all familiar faces, and most of them had been at the meeting every week for the last ten years. Only Pop Nathan was missing from the old days; he was in San Diego, where he'd gone to be Special Agent in Charge. An early Hoover appointment, he had been the only other senior Jew at the Bureau, but Guttman didn't miss him much, since Nathan had always displayed a loyalty to Director Hoover which was both blind and impermeable.

Tolson began with a summary of the field office reports, focusing on crime trends. The most recent ones were a surge in war-related fraud, including a rash of scams in which phoney life-insurance policies were sold to newly drafted soldiers.

Then each of the assistant directors reported on their own bailiwicks. Normally Guttman's attention would have wandered by now, but he found himself studying the faces round the table, as old hands like Glavin from personnel and Louis B. Nichols, the Bureau's head PR man, gave their reports. Did Guttman really know these old familiars as well as he thought? Could not one of them have some terrible secret? Not the usual kind of secret – the hidden liking for a morning whisky; a fondness for other men's wives, or for teenage basketball players; even an undeclared conviction for petty theft – but something on an incalculably larger scale.

Why not? The Bureau itself had changed incalculably, with a wider remit, a bigger role not just in the country but the world as well. Despite Glavin's moaning, the Bureau had expanded fourfold in less than four years, and there were now over 3,000 Special Agents. Even so, the old guard still held sway, and it seemed incredible that one of these staid, white-shirted, white-skinned, old-school agents would so fundamentally betray the country they were paid to protect. He couldn't believe it of any of them.

It was Tamm's turn next. Guttman could never really figure him out. Tamm made it no secret that he couldn't stand Tolson, which might have made him an ally. But Guttman knew that in a pinch Tamm would always do Hoover's bidding, hoping to be restored as the heir presumptive – and he knew too that Tamm had checked up on him more than once in the past at Hoover's behest. Recently it was rumoured that Tamm nursed secret ambitions of becoming a judge; he was said to be building relationships at the Justice Department upstairs, and had been spotted coming out of Attorney General Biddle's eyrie, high in one corner of the building.

Tamm started by reporting on the growing evidence of Communist influence in industrial disputes, long a Hoover preoccupation, and he cited continuing trouble with the miners' union, whose leader John L. Lewis was a particular Bureau bête noire. Guttman, who was claustrophobic in his own basement, let alone hundreds of feet underground, found himself secretly sympathising with the miners. Tolson asked Tamm about RACON, the programme launched by Hoover himself earlier that summer to investigate agitation among Negroes, especially those involved in the March on Washington Movement. Although President Roosevelt himself had met in a spirit of conciliation with the movement's head, A. Philip Randolph, this had cut no ice with Hoover – who claimed Randolph was a mere figurehead, and that the real levers of Negro power were controlled by James W. Ford, a member of the American Communist Party, who'd had the temerity to run for Vice President on the CP ticket. Tamm reported that wiretaps had been installed in Ford's office and home; at this, Tolson nodded meaningfully at Miss Caccioppo, who stopped writing until Tamm was finished. Not for the first time, Guttman was glad he wasn't running Div 5.

At last it was Guttman's turn. He had hastily cobbled together notes from his own field reports in the hour he'd had at his desk since returning from Chicago. He began with the Nazis. He'd personally turned another Nazi agent named Sebold two months before, and persuaded him to send misleading transmissions for well over a year to the German High Command. Sebold had led the Bureau to the other members of his network, which had just been rolled up – unbeknownst to their German masters. Tolson was nodding approvingly as Guttman turned to the Hawaii Territory, where the SAC, a straight shooter named Shivers, had forcefully argued against extending the internment of Japanese-Americans. Hoover, in an atypical display of liberalism, had agreed, and persuaded the President to exempt Hawaii from his Executive Order. There had been howls from xenophobic elements of the West Coast press, so it was gratifying to hear from Shivers now that there had been no evidence of espionage activity in the Islands. Finally, Guttman mentioned a case in Milwaukee, where a former *Bund* member had been found in possession of an arsenal – though Guttman omitted the fact that this 'arsenal' had only consisted of five shotguns.

Tolson asked, 'Nothing further on Dasch?'

'No. I'm confident we got them all.' Dasch was a spy who'd landed on Long Island in June, courtesy of a U-boat, but within a week of his arrival he and seven co-conspirators had been arrested. The case had been a sensation in the press and a major public-relations triumph for the FBI. The trial of the saboteurs had ended two months before in early August.

'Dasch is lucky to be alive,' interjected Tamm. 'If you hadn't written to the judge he wouldn't be.'

That was true, and Dasch's reprieve had caused outrage. What the public didn't know was that Dasch had not only given himself up, but had also led the Bureau to his co-conspirators, including four Germans who had landed in Florida. Without Dasch's help it might have taken months to catch them all, giving the others time to wreak havoc along the eastern seaboard. Considering the value of Dasch's crucial assistance, Guttman had been perfectly happy to write to the judge asking for clemency on his behalf. Looking now at

Tamm he felt a sudden surge of anger. 'They executed six of the eight. That's a pretty good batting average, even for a hanging judge.'

Tamm's cheeks flushed. He looked about to reply when Tolson cut in: 'Okay, let's move on.'

'That's all from me,' said Guttman.

Reports done, Tolson took over; he liked to finish the meeting with a short sermon of his own. Guttman never understood the point of it. Half-homily, half-directive, the little talks were unpredictable in their choice of topics. One week Tolson might inveigh against the perfidy of the American Federation of Labor or, as he did the week before, speak scornfully about Charlie Chaplin's Communist associations and predilection for underage girls (to Tolson's annoyance, Tamm had asked if the girls were also Communists).

This week Tolson's target was conscientious objectors. There weren't very many of them (the last figure for those registered by the Selective Service was 12,000), and to Guttman they seemed by definition not to pose a threat to peace. Tolson saw things differently, and now ordered that instructions be relayed to field offices to increase surveillance of COs. Guttman wanted to sigh out loud. Most COs were either in prison or doing alternative service, so this seemed a more than usually pointless exercise. Guttman might have said as much if he'd felt Tamm would support him, but their spat had put paid to that.

The meeting ended and Guttman was getting up to leave when Tolson called out – 'Harry.'

'Harry' was as rare as Marie calling him 'Mr Guttman'. Guttman waited warily as the others left. The kid T.A. was collecting the press clippings from the table and Guttman expected Tolson to wait for him to leave too, but he didn't.

Tolson said, 'How are you doing?'

'Okay,' Guttman said cautiously. Tolson was not one for personal concern.

'Must be tough being on your own,' said Tolson. Guttman shrugged. He was embarrassed to have this exchange in front of T.A.

Tolson went on, 'The boss is pleased about your handling of this Dasch business.'

'Is he? I haven't had a blue page.' Hoover communicated congratulations to senior members of the Bureau on blue-tinted paper.

'He wouldn't want it to go to your head,' Tolson said edgily. 'And he doesn't want you to take your eye off the ball.'

'I'm not.' It was important to sound emphatic. You didn't just toe the line; you had to hug the goddamned thing.

'Good to hear. I had a feeling something else was bothering you.'

'Who, me?' All innocence.

'Yeah, in the meeting.'

'No. Not at all. I've just got my hands full at the minute.' Then, in case it sounded as if he were complaining, he added, 'Like everybody else.'

Tolson said, 'Well, like I say, the boss is pleased. And it seems you've also got a fan at the Court.'

'Oh?' Guttman wondered what Tolson meant. Hoover's court? Not likely.

'The boss was leaving the White House the other day and ran into Justice Frankfurter.' Tolson chuckled. 'I guess the separation of powers doesn't extend to FDR's cocktail hour. Frankfurter was full of praise for you. He told the Boss you were a "stellar G-Man". Ha!'

'Nice of him,' Guttman said dutifully.

'Sure it was,' said Tolson. His speech was speeding

up – never a good sign. 'Thing is, when the Boss mentioned this to me, I couldn't help thinking, how does Frankfurter know whether you're good at your job?'

It had been cool in the room during the Executives Conference, but Guttman felt he was breaking into a sweat. He threw his hands out, like an Italian. 'He doesn't, Clyde. We know each other from other stuff. You know, Jewish fundraisers.'

Tolson nodded neutrally; it was impossible to tell if he bought this. 'You people do stick together. Still, it doesn't hurt to have an ally at the Court.'

Downstairs, he walked towards his end of the corridor and the small bunch of offices which Tolson, in a moment of dubious comic inspiration, had nicknamed Guttman's Ghetto. Coming through the open door to Marie's anteroom, he found her on the phone. 'Have a good trip,' she quickly said into the mouthpiece, then put it down, looking flustered. He wondered if she'd found a fellow. She deserved to.

'Marie, wasn't Powderman supposed to come see me?' The new New York SAC.

'He came by yesterday. I explained you were sick,' she said, raising an eyebrow. 'He went back to New York last night.'

He nodded but looked at her sharply. 'Are you okay, Marie?' It wasn't like her to forget things.

'Of course I am. But what about you? You've lost weight, Harry.'

'Have I?' No one had ever said this to him since . . . He thought hard. Actually, no one had ever said this to him before. He flexed his shoulders. It was true; his suit jacket felt looser than normal.

'It's not good,' Marie said.

'Why not?' He'd always wanted to lose weight.

'It doesn't suit you. You're a big man – you don't want to shrink all of a sudden.'

'Okay,' he said, a little flustered now himself.

'You need feeding up. I bet you're living on leftovers.'

'Well,' he said hesitantly. On his way home he would have so many work things on his mind that he never remembered to shop. On the days Annie Ryerson came in to help out she usually left supper, so twice a week he had a proper evening meal. Other nights he usually ended up eating a bowl of cereal.

'Come to dinner one night, Harry. I'll cook you a proper meal.'

'You don't have to do that, Marie.'

'I'd like to. And little Jack is dying to meet you.'

Big Jack had departed some time before Marie had come to work at the Bureau. Guttman had no doubt her abandoned son could use a father figure, but Guttman already had his hands full with Jeff, Annie's little boy, who had taken to coming over at weekends to play.

'I'll give you a date,' said Marie.

He nodded unenthusiastically. 'Hold my calls, will you?' he said and went into his office, closing the door behind him. Lifting the phone on his desk he gave the switchboard a number in New York.

After a minute a female voice answered the phone. 'British Passport Control Office.' This was the cover name for the British Security Coordination Office, where a Canadian, William Stephenson, was in charge. A former pilot in the Great War, Stephenson was a self-made businessman who had volunteered to help the British lobby for support during the two years when Britain was at war and America was on the sidelines.

'Hi, Katie, it's Harry Guttman. Is your uncle in?'

'Oh, Mr Guttman, you've missed him. He may be back this afternoon.'

'I thought you'd transferred to Bermuda.'

'No such luck. Uncle Bill won't let me go. Do you want me to leave him a message?'

'Just tell him I returned his call.'

4

HE LEFT EARLY, suddenly tired. The travel back and
forth had caught up with him, and he swept a stack of
memos into his briefcase, explaining to Marie that he
was heading home. His car, an ageing Buick sedan, was
parked around the corner and thankfully started up at
once. It was dark by the time he passed the White
House, and he could see the lights on in the living
quarters upstairs where Roosevelt would be sitting now,
before the cocktail hour he enjoyed with cronies and
anyone interesting who was passing through town.

He drove through Georgetown, not far from the house
where Nessheim had boarded for several months in
1940. Frankfurter had helped the young agent find
accommodation there, and Guttman felt a sense of déjà
vu about the re-emergence of the connection between
the three of them. Crossing the bridge, traffic was light,
and ten minutes later he was home, at the new house
he'd bought over ten years before on the outskirts
of Arlington. It was part of a suburban development
that had stalled during the Depression, but now the
once-empty lots all held houses.

He parked his car in the driveway, outside the garage
he'd had built next to the side of the house. In a sudden
inexplicable fit of busy-ness he had started to clear the
contents of the garage before leaving for Chicago, and
now boxes full of old clothes filled the space where the
car usually went. He stopped outside at the twin mail-
boxes, propped at chest height by the sidewalk. Both
were empty and he wondered what had happened to
his newspaper. Inside, there was a light on in the living

room and one in the front hall. It soothed him momentarily, but then he realised there would be no one there;
nowadays the lights were just a beacon to mislead
burglars into thinking someone was home.

When he walked through to the kitchen he saw mail
on the table in a neat stack, a folded copy of the evening
newspaper waiting for him, and a telegram envelope.
Annie had been in, even though he'd told her not to
bother. A plate sat covered by a dish towel; when he
lifted it he saw a big sandwich of ham and cheese, some
carrot sticks and a handful of potato chips. Bless her;
the last thing he felt like doing was cooking.

He went outside through the kitchen door and stood
on the little deck, peering into the dark of his backyard.
A nice suburban plot, decent neighbours, a still night;
it seemed difficult to believe that seventy feet away by
the back of his garage someone had fired a bullet at his
head. The unreality of it had grown since he'd been
alone.

Most nights now he paced the yard, almost willing
his assassin to return and finish the job – such was his
misery since his wife's death. But something had
changed: as he surveyed the yard, its shapes gradually
emerging as his eyes grew accustomed to the dark, he
gave a slight shiver when he looked over to the dull
dark patch of grass by the garage. An odd feeling filled
him, one which he dimly recognised as fear. He hadn't
thought he would ever feel that again.

He went back inside and took the plate with his dinner
to the living room, where he poured himself two inches
of Johnny Walker, turned on the radio, and ate while
a reedy voice told him American soldiers fighting on
Guadalcanal were making advances against fierce oppos-
ition from Japanese troops. When he started to nod
off, he got up and turned off the radio and lights and

went into the bedroom. He took his clothes off, put on fresh pyjamas, brushed his teeth and got into bed in the dark, not even pretending to read. He waited for a moment on what had always been his side of the bed; he was trying not to give in.

He yielded at last, rolling over to lie face down on what had been Isabel's side. People would think it was nutty if they knew, but it was the only way he had to try and reach his wife. On his belly he kept still for a moment, inhaling as deeply as he could, his nose pressed against the bottom sheet, hunting for the faintest perfume.

It was no good; the traces of Isabel weren't there. Lately they hadn't been. Either the sheets had been washed too often since her death or enough time had passed to make her scent disappear. He sighed and turned on to his back, moving over to his side of the bed, even though he could have the whole of it now if he wanted.

Someone had told him it would be two years before he felt any better at all. Somebody else told him he had to take life a day at a time. Heeding that advice, he lay still on the bed, wondering what the next day – number 117 since the death of his beloved wife Isabel – would bring. He wasn't optimistic.

In the morning the phone woke him. He sat up, shaking the sleep fog out of his head, then looked at his watch: 6.15. It must be Nessheim or Marie, he thought, but why were they calling him this early? He reached for the phone and grabbed it on the third ring.

'Harry?' The voice was mild, mid-Atlantic, familiar. Neither Nessheim nor Marie.

'Who's that?' he demanded. It was still dark outside.

'It's Bill Stephenson. We've been playing tag with the telephone. I thought I'd try again before I left town.'

'Hi, Bill,' said Guttman, slowly regaining his composure. 'How are you?'

Stephenson chuckled down the line. 'More awake than you from the sound of it.'

'Sorry. I've been away.'

'Anywhere nice?'

'Not really. Business. Kind of unofficial business.'

'Ah – I'll ask no more questions. So how can I help?'

'I need to check up on some people,' he said hesitantly. He had asked Stephenson for assistance before, but still felt uncomfortable that it was so obvious he couldn't use the Bureau's own resources. It felt peculiar to be trusting a foreigner more than his own colleagues, but it was not the first time.

'Here?'

'In Europe. You know we haven't got people over there. I was hoping you could help.'

'Is there a list?'

'I'll send it to you tomorrow.'

'What are we looking for?'

'Confirmation mainly. That people are who they say they are. But it could also be that they've left people behind who could be used against them.'

There was a moment's silence. 'We're talking about recent émigrés to America then?'

Guttman just grunted.

'Jews?'

It was a factual enquiry; Guttman knew Stephenson well enough to recognise that. 'Yes, pretty much all of them. It's a question of whether the Nazis could put pressure on someone over here by threatening people who got left behind.'

'In normal circumstances they probably could. The thing is, from what we've learned, they're going to kill all the Jews they can anyway.'

70

'I think you'll find they've started.'

'These people I'm checking for you – are they all working on the same thing?'

'Yeah.'

Stephenson sighed. 'Is this still a safe line, Harry?'

'Absolutely.' He'd had it put in under his wife's maiden name several years before. 'All right,' said Stephenson. 'We're talking scientists, aren't we?'

How on earth did he know that? Taking Guttman's silence for assent, Stephenson went on. 'You know we're cooperating with you on this project.'

'Yeah?'

'You don't have to say anything, Harry. We're on the same side. Though it would help if General Groves saw things that way.'

Guttman was flabbergasted. 'I don't know what to say, Bill.'

'I know you don't. It will all be a lot clearer when we can talk face-to-face. Unfortunately, I'm leaving today. I'll be back in ten days. But send the list tomorrow to Katie, and we'll get started.'

'Where are you going?'

'Bermuda. We've made some interceptions you can hear all about when I'm back. I may have some other news for you then as well. From Norway.'

'Norway?'

'Yes, news from Norway. I think you'll be surprised. By the way, what's happened with the problem you told me about?'

They each knew what he was talking about. Guttman said, 'Nothing. I've been wondering if I've got it all wrong.'

'Really? It didn't sound that way to me.'

Guttman felt something niggling at the back of his mind. For no reason he knew of he said, 'There is one

71

other guy I'd be grateful if you could check out for me – here on home soil, I mean.'

Stephenson waited a moment to reply. It was a big thing to ask, and begged as many questions as it hoped to answer. 'Okay. Send me that name too. I'll be in touch when I'm back next week.'

Guttman said goodbye and hung up the phone. He remained sitting on the edge of his bed, thinking about 'the problem'.

It had begun with a telex sent from Washington under Clyde Tolson's name to the Office of Naval Intelligence in Hawaii, requesting that surveillance of a suspected German agent be called off. The agent was thought to be meeting with Japanese intelligence officers, and the failure to continue surveillance meant both that Agent James Nessheim had nearly lost his life and that information had been received too late to prevent the attacks on Pearl Harbor.

The problem was that Tolson had been in New York when the telex was sent from D.C. He denied all knowledge of it, and of ordering it to be sent by proxy. At Bureau HQ, moreover, no record could be found of the telex in the logbook kept of all official communications with other government agencies – including the Office of Naval Intelligence. When Guttman had asked the recipients in Hawaii to send him a copy of the original text, they had explained that, along with 80,000 other documents, the telex had been destroyed in the Pearl Harbor attack. Someone had been both careful and lucky.

That, it seemed earlier that spring, was that, but Guttman had hoped that if he worked away at it something would emerge. He could be bloodhound-like once he found a hint of a trail. But then he'd been sidetracked, for almost four months; not by the lack of leads but by

Isabel's death. One week she was sitting peacefully in her wheelchair, reading the society column out loud while he made stew; the next week she was in Walter Reed in a hospital bed with a tube in her mouth; the week after that it was all over. Guttman had barely had time to say goodbye to his wife.

She would want me to follow this up, he decided, feeling uplifted by the thought – even though he'd always told her he had no causes when it came to work. Except, of course, to find and punish the bad guys. 'Like a Western,' she'd said with a smile; his favourite kind of picture show. 'That will do just fine as a reason. You go and round 'em up.' And for the first time since he'd lost his wife Guttman felt he was back in the saddle again.

He got dressed and went out into the kitchen, where he saw the telegram Annie had left on the table. It would be from Nessheim, he figured, telling him no. He wondered what had happened between Nessheim and Annie. For a while he had thought they would end up together – Nessheim had been eager to, Guttman was sure of that. But then he'd gone away and probably tomcatted around – and Annie's mentions of him had grown infrequent. Guttman thought Nessheim was a fool not to have seized his chance.

Still, Nessheim had unique abilities as an agent – at least in Guttman's view. He earned people's trust, and he could read the fine print of somebody's character like Helen Keller touching Braille. He took the initiative and required little direction; he was adaptable, even ingenious; and he could look after himself. It was the perfect mix for an undercover man, yet now it looked as though he meant it when he said he didn't want to stay with the Bureau.

What a waste. He would be a perfectly competent

lawyer, but the kind who was a dime a dozen in the city practices Guttman knew. Though it was more likely (he had declared the ambition often enough) that Nessheim would become a big fish in a little Podunk pond up in Wisconsin. There was something special about the guy; it was just a shame Nessheim didn't know that himself.

Guttman opened the telegram at last. He read its terse message with surprise.

Count me in. JN

Part Three

5

THE DOSSIER GUTTMAN had given him was thin, unhelp-fully so. A series of short biographical sketches with a litany of institutional names – labs and universities from Heidelberg to Vienna, Prague to Basle, from Harvard to Berkeley, and even the University of Minnesota. Nessheim had to assume the affiliations had all been verified or were being checked by Guttman; he was in no position to do so himself. But it didn't seem likely that any infiltrator would make up a résumé, since it would be the easiest thing to check about him. If the paper trail was not going to help, he would have to hope something emerged when he got to know the Lab and its mysterious crew. If there was anything to emerge. He remained a doubter, sensing Guttman was doubtful as well.

He rang the Bureau's Chicago Field Office and spoke to Tatie. She had been expecting his call, she told him, even though Guttman hadn't been confident that Nessheim would be coming aboard again. 'I know you better than that,' she added. Nessheim arranged to have a drink with her in the Loop the following week, begging off dinner by claiming an appointment back on the South Side. After he'd hung up, he went off to find Fermi.

It proved unexpectedly difficult. The main home of the Metallurgical Laboratory, or 'Met Lab' as it was commonly known, was on Ellis and the corner of 57th Street, kitty-corner from the north-west perimeter of the Quadrangle. Before leaving his apartment, Nessheim dressed carefully in a dark grey worsted suit, a white shirt and a blue- and yellow-striped tie. He needed the jacket to cover the bulk of the shoulder holster and gun he had been wearing since finding the '*Rossbach*' note on his kitchen table. It was still just warm enough to leave his Chesterfield at home, though as he headed down 57th he saw someone up the street in an identical coat. It was an expensive coat for a student, and the guy wearing it also had on a black homburg, something a student wouldn't do. Curious, Nessheim was trying to get a better look but the man was walking fast. Once he turned sideways and Nessheim saw a youthful face with a long straight nose. He looked vaguely familiar.

Then he heard *thump thumpa*, *thump thumpa* behind him.

'Winograd,' he said before he'd even turned around.

'None other,' said the man, half-breathless from trying to catch up. He wore a thick woollen sweater, corduroy trousers, and his specialised boot. He had a burly farmer's build, with the beginning of a pot belly and forearms like Indian clubs from swinging hay bales.

'Why aren't you in Torts?' asked Winograd.

'I could ask the same of you.' They kept walking, and Nessheim slowed his pace to accommodate Winograd's syncopated walk.

'Doctor's appointment. I'm off to class now.'

'Mine's the dentist,' Nessheim said. 'Dicky tooth.'

Winograd nodded. 'Hey, I talked to that new girl – her name's Stacey. Quite a gal. She was here as an undergrad. Don't know how I missed her.'

Winograd had taken a BA in the college and then spent a couple of years 'bumming around' as he liked to say, though as far as Nessheim could tell he had never gone further west than Kansas. 'How old is she?' Nessheim asked.

'Dunno. She said she'd lived in LA for a while. I bet she was trying to break into the pictures. What do you know about that?'

'Less than you,' said Nessheim truthfully. He and Stacey must have overlapped in LA, but he hadn't had any idea she was there. Typical, he thought; she reappears when it suits her, not a minute before.

They reached the corner of University Avenue and Nessheim stopped. 'I'll see you,' he said.

'Where's this dentist?' asked Winograd, baffled.

Nessheim pointed towards Washington Park. 'Over on Cottage Grove.'

'She was asking about you, you know.'

'My dentist?' asked Nessheim with deliberate obtuseness.

'No, the girl. Stacey Madison.'

'Great,' said Nessheim without enthusiasm. 'I gotta go – my tooth's killing me. See you Monday.'

The Lab office was housed in a new limestone building that resembled the original buildings of the university, though lacking the Gothic ornamentation – the exterior had no grotesques, finials or fleurs-de-lis – and the walls inside were bare. On the second floor Nessheim found a series of small cell-like offices running along one side of a corridor; on the other side there was a large open room for typists and junior technicians. No one asked him what he was doing there. At first, in fact, no one paid him any attention at all.

Finally, a voice called out. 'Are you looking for someone, young man?'

Nessheim stopped. A man was striding down the corridor towards him, moving quickly, almost fussily. He wore an ancient three-piece suit of mocha-brown wool and heavy brogues, and looked just old enough to call Nessheim 'young man'. He was tall but slightly stooped, as if his hunched shoulders were being gently pulled towards his abdomen. He had a bulb-shaped chin, and a downturned mouth that gave him the lugubrious look of a basset hound. A few remaining tufts of hair curled behind his ears, but the top of his head was bald, and sat like a dome above his elongated face. Dark-skinned, he might have been Greek or Italian, and he surveyed Nessheim carefully with dark brown eyes.

'I was looking for Professor Fermi.'

'He is not here.' The English was precise, and sounded school-learned.

'So I was beginning to discover.'

'Perhaps I can be of assistance. I am Professor Kalvin.'

So not a southern European – the dossier said that Kalvin was a Pole who had escaped from Europe by the skin of his teeth. Nessheim said, 'No, thanks. It's Fermi I need to see.'

The man raised an inquisitive brow.

'Very well. His office is over in Eckhart Hall. Do you know it?'

'I'll find it,' said Nessheim, who passed it every day. 'Thanks.'

He left the building and walked down 57th Street. At the corner with University Avenue, he turned and passed the Reynolds Club, which had a barber shop where Nessheim had his hair cut and listened to Floyd the barber bemoan the new price controls – which extended even to haircuts. Next to it sat Mandel Hall, the biggest auditorium on campus, with a seating capacity no one who'd had high-school history could forget – it held 1,066 seats.

He walked through into the main Quadrangle, next to the college tennis courts where the sailor had taunted him; they were empty now. Eckhart Hall was intended to blend with the other light grey, Gothic university buildings that were spread around the Quadrangle. It was four storeys high, with gables, hipped roofs, tall narrow windows and archway entrances, ornamented with symbols depicting the subjects housed within, including Euclid's proof of Pythagoras' theorem in honour of the mathematicians whose building it was – though they had now decamped to one of the towers of Harper Library. Above the entrance two gargoyles with sombre faces sat above the lintel of the arched doorway. The directory on the ground floor said nothing about the Met Lab, but at the bottom little wooden letters on a board read, *'Professor E. Fermi Top Floor'.*

This time he had to show his ID and was directed upstairs. Here he found nicer quarters than in the other building, with fresh paint in the wide sunny corridor. Nessheim moved along, peering at the small typed cards held in brass holders on each door. He found Fermi at last and knocked on the door. No response.

'Ah, we meet again.' He turned to find Kalvin once more, behind him in the hallway. 'Is the Professor not there?'

'No.'

'You are not having much luck.'

No thanks to you, thought Nessheim. 'Do you know where else he might be?'

Kalvin said, 'That's classified.' He saw the sceptical look on Nessheim's face and added, 'He could be in Commons having lunch.' He walked past Nessheim and disappeared into another office.

Nessheim moseyed around the floor until he found an open door. Inside, two women sat typing. Seeing Nessheim they both stopped work. The older woman said amiably, 'You look lost.'

He explained he was searching for Fermi. The younger

81

woman's eyes widened and she stood up suddenly. She was wearing a homely black dress speckled with tiny pink roses. 'Are you Mr Nessheim?'

'That's right.'

'The Professor's been expecting you – he wasn't sure when you would show up. You'll find him a block from here. Do you know Stagg Field? It's the football stadium.'

'The *old* football stadium,' the older woman reminded her.

'I do,' said Nessheim. 'What's he doing there?'

The younger woman shrugged. 'I'd better let him explain. You'll find him under the West Stands, right along Ellis – that's one street over.'

He knew Stagg Field all right, the vast football stadium that had been sitting unused since President Hutchins's abolition of intercollegiate football at the U of C. One summer almost a decade before, Nessheim had played in a scrimmage there before the official season began. He had intercepted three passes thrown by an inept predecessor to the legendary Jay Berwanger, and Northwestern had won easily in a lopsided contest. The U of C players hadn't seemed to mind; it was as if they knew they were for the high jump. It had bemused Nessheim, who had always played with intensity, to compete against a team that didn't seem to care.

He walked along the stadium's west side, which could have been transplanted from the Scottish Highlands – a long exterior stone wall, crenellated and ready for archers, and octagonal corners, each the size of a castle's keep. Halfway along, Nessheim came to an opening two storeys high, where once thousands had poured in for football games.

He went through and found himself standing in a bare, cavernous space underneath the stands, where at last he encountered security of a sort. A soldier sat at a table just inside the entrance, wearing a sidearm – it looked like a Colt .45 from the length of the holster. Down the hall, Nessheim saw half a dozen men standing in a circle, smoking cigarettes. They were in civilian clothes, and one of them wore a long apron.

'Pass,' the soldier demanded.

'I haven't got one.'

'State your business.'

'I'm looking for Professor Fermi. He's expecting me.'

'And you are?' asked the soldier, reaching for a logbook on the table.

'James Nessheim.'

'Nature of your visit.'

'Classified.'

The soldier shook his head wearily as he scribbled. 'Yours and everybody else's. ID?'

Nessheim showed him the little wallet with his Bureau identification; the paper ID had expired, but the soldier seemed satisfied by the shiny metal badge. 'On you go, pal.'

Nessheim passed by the table and walked towards the circle of men. He caught the eye of the man in the apron, who was smoking a cigarette.

'Where would I find Professor Fermi?'

The man gestured with a dirty hand at a door on the inner wall of the vaulted hallway. 'In there.'

Walking over and opening the door, Nessheim stepped into a high-ceilinged room, lined in dark grey slate and brightly lit. A spectator's gallery perched above the court on its northern side. In front of him on the floor, there were stacks of dark brick-sized blocks set neatly against a side wall. An outline had been drawn on the floor in thin black paint, marking off about a quarter of the court in a circle – it looked like the floor plan of a house. Two men, one quite tall, the other quite short, both in lab coats, stood peering down at the black line. From the photographs in Guttman's dossier, Nessheim recognised the smaller man.

'Professor Fermi,' he called out.

The man looked up vaguely, then his eyes seemed to focus and he snapped to. Saying something to his colleague, Fermi came forward, peeling off his lab coat as he did, and shook hands. He was neatly dressed, in a grey houndstooth suit, white dress shirt and maroon silk tie. Trim and compactly built, he exuded an athletic energy that suggested a man who knew what he was doing. 'Ah, my head of works is here,' he said with a smile. The voice was deep, friendly but firm.

'Wrong guy. I'm Nessheim. I think General Groves told you I'd be coming.'

'As I say, my head of works. Just as the General promised. I need one, so let's hope you can play the part, no?' Fermi pointed at the other man, a tall blond young man in grey overalls who was still inspecting the outline on the floor. 'My colleague Walter Zinn is tired of doing all the work himself. He wants to get back to physics – especially after this morning. We have had a small disaster.' He motioned Nessheim to follow him out of the court. As they reached the door, he stopped suddenly. 'People say this is a squash court, but I am told by one of my colleagues who went to Yale that it is actually a racquets court. Do you know which it is, Mr Nessheim?'

'No.'

'Me neither,' he said, sailing out the door, looking pleased that his ignorance was shared.

In the outer hallway the smokers had dispersed. Fermi led Nessheim to the north-west corner of the block, where two massive wooden doors had been swung back, revealing another entrance into the hall, as wide and high as the one Nessheim had come through. Above the lintel framing the high doorway, several bricks were missing, and Nessheim could see the grey sky outside through the gaps they'd left.

'That is this morning's work,' Fermi said gloomily.

'What happened?'

'The truck arrives and picks this entryway to deliver. It comes into the hall and we unload the graphite bricks. Filthy stuff to handle and extremely heavy. That is why the truck comes inside. But when the driver left he took something with him.' He pointed up at the gaps. 'The university authorities don't know yet. But they will be – how do you say it? – tied to be fit.'

'I think it's fit to be tied,' Nessheim said gently.

Fermi flashed a smile, as if they both knew English was a ridiculous language. 'Can you explain why the truck can come in without problem and then leave with such destruction?'

'I think so,' said Nessheim, wondering if Fermi was testing him. 'The truck came in fully loaded, right? So it would have been sitting low.' He motioned down with his hand, palm extended. 'Then when it had been unloaded it would have sat a lot higher.' And he brought his palm up.

Fermi nodded approvingly. 'See, you are a natural for the role. You don't even have to act.'

'But –'

'I know, I know,' said Fermi, 'that is not what you are here for. Though it would be more useful for me if you could prevent this disaster happening again than spend all your time on this wild chicken chase.'

'Goose chase. It's called a wild goose chase.' He laughed. 'And let's hope that's exactly what it is.'

Fermi was no longer smiling. 'Believe me, Mr Nessheim, I am completely confident of that. I know my colleagues and none of them would do anything to help the Nazis. Not one. In fact, all of them are desperate to beat the Nazis to it.'

Nessheim didn't reply to this. 'What deliveries do you have in the next few days, Professor?'

'More graphite and wood from the Sterling Lumber Company.'

Nessheim suddenly remembered the short tutorial given to him and Guttman by Oppenheimer, explaining how a chain reaction had to be controlled or the neutrons would escape harmlessly. Heavy water – that had been one solution. Graphite was another, though back in Berkeley, Oppenheimer had worried that it would be impossible to find graphite pure enough and in sufficient quantity. They must have succeeded.

Nessheim said now, 'Okay, I'll try and sort it out so there isn't another disaster.'

Fermi looked at his watch. 'You've had lunch?'

'No.'

'Neither have I. Come and we will go to eat.'

Moving towards the west entrance they passed another door, identical to that of the racquets courts. 'What's in there?'

'Sandbags in case of fire. And some stored materials,' Fermi said elliptically.

Nessheim remembered what the scientist had said in Berkeley. 'Uranium?'

Fermi looked at him sharply. 'I thought you weren't a scientist.'

'I'm not. It doesn't take Einstein to guess what's in there.'

Fermi grinned. 'That is a new expression for me – "It doesn't take Einstein." I like it. I will tell Einstein when I see him next.'

They walked to 57th Street and turned east. Nessheim

assumed they would eat at Hutchinson Commons, but as they approached the doors a group of people came around the corner. 'Enrico,' one of them called cheerfully, and Fermi stopped.

'Hello,' said Fermi. 'I am just showing my new acquaintance the place.' He pointed to Nessheim – 'Gentlemen, may I introduce Mr Nessheim. He has come to assist us in our labours. Not,' he said quite clearly, 'a physicist, but an expert in running things. Is that fair, Mr Nessheim?'

'More than fair,' said Nessheim, and the men laughed. They seemed a friendly bunch, and now Fermi introduced them in turn. Nessheim listened intently for their names, and they were all familiar from Guttman's dossier: Szilard, the eminent Hungarian physicist, a short podgy man who shook hands formally, like a dignitary; Anderson, tall with a crew cut, acting like a regular Joe; Nadelhoffer, a bearded giant of a man whose birthplace Nessheim had noted, since it was less than forty miles from his own in Wisconsin; Leona Woods, the only woman, who was shy and serious-looking; and Kalvin, the man Nessheim had met an hour before.

'You coming to lunch, Enrico?' the youthful Anderson asked.

Fermi shook his head. 'No, you go ahead. I will see you later on.'

Fermi kept walking, crossing University Avenue. He stopped at the first building they came to, a Georgian-style mansion of rust-coloured brick. Holding the front door open for Nessheim, Fermi said, 'We'll eat here – it is a club for faculty and more private.' He added with a touch of pride, 'They made me a member when I joined the Met Lab.'

Inside, Fermi nodded at the receptionist, standing behind a counter that held candy and cigarettes, then turned right sharply. Ahead of them there was a long mahogany bar set in a slightly sunken room. It was empty, except for two old men who sat across from each other at a card table, studying their hands, and closer to the window, a man in a dark jacket and patterned bow tie who was playing billiards by himself.

They climbed the slate-tiled staircase, then at the next floor went down a few steps into the dining room, a large room with chandeliers hanging from its high ceiling, though now ample daylight poured in through the tall windows on the building's southern side. A maître d' led them to a discreet corner, away from all the other tables, overlooking the rear gardens where men in tennis sweaters were playing doubles on the clay tennis courts.

A waiter in a white coat poured iced water into their glasses while they scrutinised the printed menu and ordered. When the waiter left, Nessheim tried to make small talk. Did the Professor like Chicago? How about his wife? Were his kids enjoying America? He sensed Fermi knew it was etiquette rather than genuine interest at work, though the Italian answered patiently enough. At one point he looked out of the window at the tennis players.

Nessheim said, 'Do you like tennis?'

Fermi nodded. 'Yes. I am a good player. Do you play?'

'No.'

'The General said you were a football hero. The American football.'

'I used to play.'

'You are modest, I see. Forgive me, but I am somewhat surprised now that I see you in the flesh. You are tall but do not seem . . . brutal enough for football. I thought the players were all enormous and like to crush each other.'

'Lots of them are. I could run fast and stay out of their way.'

Fermi smiled. 'As for me, I am not a team sportsman. I exercise a good deal – bicycle, and walking, and swimming. All summer, I swam at The Point, almost every afternoon.' Fermi laughed before sighing. 'I suppose we cannot spend all lunch discussing sports. Shall we talk now about the goose chase?'

Nessheim nodded. 'I need to make a start somehow. Security needs to be tighter in the offices used by the Met Lab, but I will talk to the General about that. For Stagg Field, I will need to know who has keys to the courts, what the work shifts are, and so on.'

'Of course,' said Fermi without conviction.

'Tell me, are new people still arriving at the Met Lab?'

'People are joining all the time. We have a meeting every two weeks to introduce them. There is one next week in Ida Noyes Hall. And – this will please you – we talk about security.' Fermi dropped his voice. 'How they mustn't talk about anything in public, not even mention any scientific words. That there is a secret at all is a secret, is what they are told. You should come; we even show a film.'

'What's that?'

'It's called *Next of Kin*. Someone is careless with a briefcase full of top-secret military plans, and it is stolen by foreign spies. The result is catastrophic,' Fermi said with delight.

'I'll come to the next meeting,' Nessheim said. 'But in the meantime, I'll need a list of newcomers. Are you still recruiting senior people?'

Fermi shook his head. 'No. The new ones are technicians and junior scientists, working on very specific problems. We do not tell them about the larger objectives,

89

so none of them will have the big picture. Even if I believed in this spy of yours, I would not worry about the new people arriving.'

'All right,' said Nessheim, hoping Fermi was right. 'But what about your senior colleagues – how did you find them?'

'I did not need an advertisement. We physicists are not a very big community. Some I approached myself. Some Szilard did. He got the programme started and he knows everybody.' Fermi's voice was admiring.

'They would have been vetted by Groves's people?'

'Always. And they come with formal references. In writing,' he added a touch astringently.

'I saw from the file that many of them are foreign.'

'Of course. Like me. Some are even registered aliens. Like me.'

He said this so dispassionately that it took a moment for Nessheim to register the resentment behind it.

Nessheim said mildly, 'I didn't know that. It seems ridiculous.'

'Does it?' Fermi's voice still gave nothing away. He drank his iced water. 'That is not for me to say.'

'It's a free country, Professor. Say what you like.'

'Even to the FBI?' he said, amused.

'Even to me,' Nessheim said firmly.

'When I used to visit here before I moved from New York, each time I needed a special permit. Finally, they gave me the extended permit. But not for my wife,' he said, openly angry now. 'If, for instance, I take her to Milwaukee to celebrate our *anniversario matrimonio*, and do not get her a permit for the trip, I could be thrown into . . .' He stopped, searching for the word.

'The pokey.'

Fermi smiled. '*Si*. "The pokey." '

Nessheim said, 'To be honest, Professor, if your idea

of a romantic getaway is a weekend in Milwaukee, then you probably deserve a few days in the clink.'

For a moment Fermi stared at him, baffled. Then the sense of it sank in, and he laughed out loud.

Their food came. Fermi looked at his tuna sandwich and potato chips as if Oysters Rockefeller sat on his plate and declared, 'In Italy right now people are eating dried beans and green potatoes. It was the same in the other war when I was a boy.' Fermi picked up half his sandwich and examined it almost lovingly. 'People here have more food than they can eat, heating in their houses, and hot water and toilets. I am not sure why they feel they must complain about the cost of gasoline.'

'Americans drive everywhere, especially in the country. If you live on a farm it can be a long trip to town if you haven't got wheels.'

'Wheels? Ah, a car. I get it. You have lived on a farm then?' Fermi's curiosity seemed authentic.

'I grew up on one.'

'Your family owns a farm?' Before Nessheim could explain, Fermi went on excitedly. 'That is my dream.'

'It is?' Nessheim decided not to say his father had lost the farm ten years before.

'I told my wife that when I was forty years of age I would become a farmer. That was before the war, of course. It has delayed my plans. I –' He paused awkwardly, as if realising it sounded as though he viewed the war chiefly as an obstacle to his personal ambitions. 'You see, physicists are no good after forty. I will only be remembered for the work of my years before that.'

Again this startling self-confidence. But presumably that was how you won the Nobel Prize. And it had the benefit of being said without vanity or arrogance, as well as letting Nessheim steer Fermi back to the project.

'Professor, here's my phone number – you can call me any time there's a problem.' He handed over a slip of paper. 'But there's actually only so much I can do. You're the one who understands the project, and who knows the staff. You're the one who has to tell me if anyone is behaving suspiciously, or badly, or out of character. You know them; I don't. I have to rely on you.'

Fermi smiled with what Nessheim was beginning to see was his perfunctory smile – quick, tight-lipped. The genuine article broke out like sunshine all over his face.

'These are scientists, Mr Nessheim. We are not like other people. Scientists do not believe in secrets. How can they, when they spend their lives searching for the truth?' He picked up a potato chip and looked at it appraisingly. 'You will understand that my colleagues are sometimes tense. They understand the importance of their work here.'

I wish I did, thought Nessheim. Then he heard a woman's throaty laugh from a nearby table, which was blocked from view by a pillar. An older man's voice declared, 'Now that, my dear, was *war*.'

Fermi said, 'The General was insistent that I not discuss the project with you – or anyone else, of course.'

'I understand.'

Fermi stared at Nessheim, his eyebrows raised. 'Do you? I sense you know more than Groves would like. I did not mind the General, though I liked more the other man – Guttman. Groves is nonetheless . . . impressive.' He looked at Nessheim intently. Nessheim made sure his face gave nothing away. Fermi said, 'He is a general, after all . . .'

'Hitler only made corporal.'

Fermi laughed appreciatively, then wiped his mouth

with his napkin. He leaned forwards, serious now. 'If this experiment succeeds, then we will have truly opened the box of Pandora. And the lid of the box will never be put back.' He whistled through his teeth, imitating a sudden gust of wind, then waved a hand dismissively. 'Some of the staff are frightened by this.'

'Do you feel the same?'

'I did,' Fermi acknowledged. 'But if we don't do it the Nazis may get there first. That would be catastrophe. They want to take over the world. And they are trying to.'

'Okay.' There was nothing to contest.

Fermi said more calmly, 'The Russians are another matter. Many people sympathise with them, and now of course they are allies.'

'Yep,' said Nessheim drily.

Fermi said, 'I share your enthusiasm.'

'How dangerous is your experiment?'

'In my view not at all. Others may disagree, because any time you travel into the . . .' He hesitated.

'Unknown?'

Fermi nodded. 'People get scared.'

'Is there *any* chance that you could blow up Chicago?'

'No,' said Fermi, and carefully ate the last corner of his sandwich. 'Unless I am wrong, of course.' He was smiling as he wiped his mouth with his napkin.

'But if someone did want to sabotage the project what would they do?'

Fermi pondered this for a moment. 'They would take advantage of the fear.'

'What fear?'

'That I might blow up Chicago. Or the world.'

'How would they do that?'

'They would cause an explosion, perhaps. Or make

93

a fire. Anything to demonstrate this is a process that cannot be trusted.'

'But they can't blow up Chicago, can they?'

'No. They can only suggest it might be blown up if people tried this experiment again. They would be trying to scare off the authorities, you see, to do enough to stop the work on the experiment. And that would be disastrous.'

'Really?'

'If General Groves decided he had to slow things down to be sure it was safe, or perhaps even stop for some time, we could waste a year, maybe more until "the coast is clear", yes?'

'I can understand why he'd do that.'

'Can you?' Fermi shook his head. 'I can't. It would be worse than sabotage because it would be unnecessary. And let the Germans catch us. So the sabotage would have its desired effect.'

Some of the tennis players came in, now showered and dressed in coats and ties and looking hungry for lunch. The waitress arrived with a coffee pot in her hand, and when Nessheim shook his head no, Fermi motioned for the check. 'I need to get back to my work,' he said to Nessheim as the waitress totted it up.

'When is the next delivery?'

'Monday, in the late morning. Zinn will be there. I will explain to him you are coming.'

I'll miss Jurisprudence, thought Nessheim, but there didn't seem an option. The waitress put the bill down between them and he reached for it. 'I'll get this.'

'But no,' Fermi said, sounding horrified. 'You are my guest here.'

'The FBI can afford a lunch,' Nessheim said, wondering if in fact he could claim expenses. Since the SAC in Chicago didn't know he was on the payroll, it wouldn't be easy. 'It can be on your tab next time.'

On their way downstairs, Nessheim looked to see who was at the table behind the pillar. No wonder the laugh had sounded familiar. Stacey was sitting by the window, looking half-flirtatious and entirely attentive, while Professor Fielding sat with the expression Nessheim knew so well from other men Stacey had flattered – puffed up with pride, but apprehensive that the rapt interest of the beautiful woman with him required a more entertaining performance than even the Arthur McNeil Professor of Jurisprudence (Emeritus) could deliver.

They left the club. At the corner as Fermi started to say goodbye, Nessheim asked, 'Will I see you Monday?'

'Absolutely. Come to Eckhart Hall first. The graphite truck will not arrive until eleven or so. Thank you for lunch. Or should I thank Mr J. Edgar Hoover?'

'I'll be glad to convey your gratitude.' Though Hoover was the last person Nessheim would tell about this conversation.

Fermi didn't laugh. He looked at Nessheim. 'When the General told me a security person would be arriving, I expected a dumb policeman. You sometimes try to play that role, Mr Nessheim, but it is not convincing. I think you are more than you let on.'

They shook hands and Nessheim started to head back to his apartment. He had liked Fermi, but could not help feeling that the man was often acting. The flash of resentment, the excitability – these stuck in Nessheim's mind as much as the automatic smile. He sensed an unease in the scientist about something, but couldn't even begin to guess its cause.

He was being careful now. Crossing 57th Street, he turned around, trying to look like a man who'd suddenly discovered he'd left something behind. He stared ostentatiously back at the entrance to the Quadrangle Club, but let his eyes float, as if adjusting to the dark. He was very long-sighted; his father had always called him 'my binoculars' when as a boy Nessheim would accompany him hunting for deer. So he spotted the dark Chesterfield coat he'd seen on his way to Eckhart Hall that morning; its owner was moving east along 57th Street, only now he had removed his homburg.

The kids from Ray School were outside now, throwing a football, and Nessheim walked halfway down Kimbark Avenue, then stopped and stood by the school fence. Again he looked back in the vaguest way, and then he saw the Chesterfield, waiting on the corner at 57th. Nessheim walked quickly now to try and draw the guy out. When he reached 56th he stopped by the first of the big oak trees lining the block; when he looked back he could still just make out the Chesterfield, standing there. The guy was good: too smart to come out in the open, but still making sure Nessheim was heading home. Damn, thought Nessheim, spy or no spy, something was going on.

6

HE STAYED IN for most of the weekend, only venturing out as far as the little grocery store on 55th. There was hard frost outside on the front courtyard, and the wind was picking up, so he turned the heat up and started revising for mid-terms. Nothing interrupted him, except for a phone call on Saturday afternoon from Winograd, inviting him to a party in International House, a vast tower on the edge of the Midway where foreign students lived. He begged off, and putting down the phone realised he had half-hoped, half-dreaded that it was Stacey calling. She could have done so easily enough – his number was in the phone book, part of the openness he could enjoy as a student.

On Monday morning he left early for Torts at nine o'clock – on Wednesday and Friday it was held at eleven, but all the schedules were erratic now, thanks to the influx of so many military students and there being too few teachers. Conscious of having been followed once, he took a circuitous route, walking along 56th to Ellis, then cutting down and coming through the Quadrangle from the north-west. He was slightly late for class as a result and, coming in quietly through the back doors of the lecture hall, saw Winograd in their usual place, and next to him Stacey. He sat down in the back row, so as not to draw Fielding's attention and a reprimand for tardiness. When class ended he tried to get out quickly, but somehow Stacey was quicker and caught up to him before he got out of the building.

'What's the rush, sailor?' she asked. She wore a boxy, knee-length coat today that could have passed for a hand-me-down except for its grey fox collar. He could smell French perfume as she leaned towards him.

'Places to go and things to see,' he said lightly, and made to move off.

'I thought maybe we could start my tuition this evening.'

'Sorry, but I'll be downtown. I've got to meet somebody.'

'What's her name?'

'It's not like that.'

'Sure. Where are you meeting . . . *it*?'

'The Palmer House.'

'What time?'

'Six.' He wanted to tell her to mind her own business. This pushiness was unlike the Stacey of old.

'So meet me at seven. I'll be on the steps of the Art Institute.'

'It'll be closed then.'

'That's why I'll be on the steps, stupid.'

Before he could protest, she walked away, heading for a place where he couldn't follow her – the ladies' powder room. He didn't understand what she was doing. She'd never been the jealous type, far from it; Stacey had always acted as if the other women in Nessheim's past were negligible – preliminary trials for her, the real thing.

By now Winograd had emerged from the lecture hall. 'So you met Lady Godiva, I see. All we need is the horse.'

'And fewer clothes.'

'I'd be happy to take care of that part of things.'

Nessheim looked at him sharply, but Winograd was unabashed. 'Well, wouldn't you?'

'See you later.'

'Another dentist appointment?'

'Never seems to end.'

He found Fermi in his office in Eckhart Hall, working a slide rule and jotting down the results on a piece of paper. It was a remarkably tiny room, simply furnished with a small desk and a typewriter. On one wall, a blackboard was covered with a spider's web of mathematical equations. Fermi could see what Nessheim was thinking: 'You think I should have a palace then?'

'No, just a room big enough for a visitor to breathe.'

'I advise you then to hold your breath.' Fermi smiled.

They left the building and walked to Stagg Field, where Zinn was waiting in grey overalls. Fermi made introductions, and Zinn explained that the delivery was waiting around the corner on 58th Street. Fermi asked Nessheim to drop by Eckhart Hall when he was through, and left them to it – Nessheim went with Zinn to find the graphite.

Outside there were about a dozen teenage boys waiting around, and Zinn instructed them to follow him. He explained to Nessheim that they'd been recruited to unload the heavy lengths of graphite (some were fifty inches long) from the trucks that would now be coming regularly, and then to shift them again once they'd been machined and smoothed into uniform-sized bricks. The boys were mainly Irish kids from the stockyards neighbourhood who were waiting to be drafted. Zinn said they were happy to work for peanuts in the meantime, since they had nothing else to do. They wore jeans and sweaters and sneakers, and some of them looked young enough to still be at school. With a jolt, Nessheim realised that in twelve months some of them would be dead.

On 56th Street they found the dump truck, with a canvas cover tied firmly over the load, and a bewildered driver who was talking to the soldier meant to be guarding the second entrance. When Nessheim and Zinn joined them, the driver made it clear he had heard all about the disaster of the earlier delivery. At first he refused even to try to get his truck inside Stagg Field, but when Nessheim patiently explained what he had in mind he eventually relented.

It took ten minutes to coax the truck through the archway, but it cleared by a good three inches, and no further bricks were dislodged. The driver parked close to the door of the racquets court, and the unloading began. Soon the Irish kids started to look like members of a minstrel troupe, their faces coated by graphite dust. When they were done, Nessheim asked Zinn to open the second racquets court, where sandbags lay stacked near the door. He had the boys take these out, each bag between two of them, and dump them on the back of the truck. After fifty or so, he reckoned the truck was as weighed down as when it came in. The driver seemed to have developed faith in Nessheim, however misplaced, for he shot out of the archway, clearing it by a heart-stopping inch or two. Having seen the effect of the sandbags, the stockyard boys didn't object when told to unload them again and take them back to the second racquets court.

With Zinn as tour guide, Nessheim saw the other rooms being put to use under the stands. In the visitors' locker room, Zinn introduced him to Knuth, who turned out to be a master carpenter. Work would start going full blast that week, and Zinn added that they would be working two shifts – one under his supervision, the other under the physicist named Anderson.

Nessheim said goodbye to Zinn and returned to Eckhart Hall. He found Fermi still working intently on a paper covered in figures and notations, and explained what he'd been doing. Fermi nodded, then asked mischievously, 'No spies yet?'

Nessheim laughed. 'Not yet. But tell me something – if

100

the Nazis did have an informant inside this project, what exactly would they learn?'

'Just that a controlled chain reaction is possible. Though we don't know that yet.'

'When will you know?'

Fermi got up and walked over to a calendar on the wall. He pondered it for a moment, then lifted up the page for November, showing December. With his free hand, he spun a spiral in the air, then suddenly stuck out his finger and jabbed a date on the calendar page: *December 10*. 'I'd say then,' he declared. Coming back to sit in his chair, he said, 'Maybe sooner.'

'That's quick.'

'Yes and no. You see, we have been making prototypes for almost a year. The only thing that is changing is the scale of the experiment.'

'I understand. To go back to the Nazis, if all goes well and they know about it, could they duplicate the result?'

'Not easily. They would have trouble finding enough pure graphite – it has taken us many months to find a reliable source. And enough uranium. Besides, they have gone the path of heavy water.' He peered at Nessheim. 'You understand what I am saying?' He sounded sceptical.

'I do. It's another moderator.'

Fermi looked simultaneously pleased and alarmed that Nessheim knew this. 'It is not, in my view, the right path.'

'So what would be the value of having a spy here?'

'I honestly cannot tell you. That is why I don't believe there is one.'

There was a formal knock on the door, and when it opened Kalvin stuck his head in. He nodded perfunctorily at Nessheim, then addressed Fermi. 'Enrico, I will miss the tea dance, I'm afraid. I have an appointment for my dental work.'

'Of course.'

Nessheim spoke up. 'Is your dentist okay?

Kalvin looked as if he'd been asked if his wife was any good in bed. Nessheim added, 'I'm having some gyp with a molar.' He figured he'd better have a real dentist lined up in case Winograd kept asking questions.

'Mine is rather specialised, and expensive. He works downtown in the Pittsfield building.' Kalvin could have been describing a pedigree racehorse. 'You'd do better with someone more local.'

'Okay,' said Nessheim, never having been snubbed about a dentist before.

'See you in the morning,' said Fermi, then as Kalvin retracted his head he turned back to Nessheim.

'Tea dance?' asked Nessheim.

Fermi laughed. 'We meet each week to review progress. Kalvin, Anderson, Zinn, Szilard when he's in Chicago, Nadelhoffer and me. At first we were all so polite with each other that Szilard said it was like a *thé dansant*. But tell me, is everything all right at Stagg Field?'

'Seems to be. I'm going to phone General Groves tomorrow. You may find security a bit tighter – the soldiers were kind of lax checking IDs.'

Fermi opened and closed a hand to indicate that he took this on board, but wasn't especially interested. 'We will begin constructing the materials now into something we're calling a "Pile". This "Pile" will be enormous – it will take up half the court and rise almost to the ceiling. Once we start I will be very occupied, so please tell me now if there's anything you want me to do.'

'That's easy. I just need to know who has keys to the courts, and the storeroom next door. And anything that happens which strikes you as unusual.'

'I have the keys; so do Anderson, Kalvin, Nadelhoffer and Zinn.'

'Fine.'

'Anything else?' Fermi was looking longingly at the calculations on his piece of paper, and Nessheim realised he was being politely dismissed.

'No. I'd better be going.' He made a show of looking at his watch.

Outside Eckhart Hall he looked again at his watch, this time for real. He had plenty of time to kill before meeting Tatie, but decided he might as well spend it downtown. He could go and stare at the window displays in Marshall Fields or look at the French paintings in the Art Institute or even walk over to the marina at the Lake. Whichever, it would make a break from Hyde Park and the university, which was suddenly seeming claustrophobic.

On University Avenue he turned right and walked across the opening to the main Quadrangle, heading for the Midway. He passed the President's house, a big brick mansion that sat without pretension right on the street. The wind had picked up from the north-east and turning on 59th he buttoned his coat, and jammed his fedora firmly down on his head. It was then that he saw Kalvin, maybe half a block ahead of him, walking in the same direction. Heading for the Illinois Central train to take him downtown to see his dentist.

He thought briefly of catching up to the man, then decided against it. He hadn't taken to Kalvin any more than Kalvin had to him; it would be a strain if they travelled on the train downtown together. He crossed 59th Street and angled across the grass field, moving east along Midway Plaisance, the middle road of the three that ran in parallel, virtually from the Lake to Washington Park over a mile west. Two long rows of now-leafless elm trees lined this middle row, mature almost fifty years on from their original planting at the time of the World's Fair.

He kept an eye on Kalvin, slowing down so that the man was a block ahead of him. When Kalvin reached Dorchester, Nessheim moved over to 59th Street again at the Laboratory School, another grey limestone Gothic monster, this time a junior model housing the school for the faculty's offspring. Thomas Dewey himself had helped found it, and Nessheim had heard it was a hotbed of precociousness – the kids were tested within an inch of their lives from first grade onwards.

The railway tracks were elevated and just east of Harper Avenue, a hidden street tucked against the railway embankment and darkened by overhanging trees in the otherwise obvious grid of Hyde Park. The tracks themselves went over 59th Street, and beneath them the street ran through a dark tunnel with raised sidewalks for pedestrians on either side. The station entrance was on the near side of this tunnel, and Nessheim took his time, thinking that with luck Kalvin might catch a train before he got there himself – the service was frequent, with one downtown train every ten minutes.

So he was surprised when he looked ahead to see a figure emerging into the light at the far end of the tunnel – tall, taking quick but itsy-bitsy steps. It could be no one but Kalvin. It seemed the man wasn't going downtown to his highfalutin dentist, so why had he told Fermi he was? Intrigued, Nessheim walked through the tunnel, ignoring the station's entrance. He hung back a little at the far end, waiting until Kalvin reached Stony Island before stepping out into the light.

He assumed Kalvin was heading for Jackson Park, though it seemed odd, since it would be dark soon. Kalvin would be hard to follow, even though Nessheim knew the park well. He liked to walk there, especially on the Wooded Island, a hangover from the World's Fair of 1893. It had a restored Japanese pavilion and a rose garden that sat nestled between two adjacent lagoons. At the southern end of the island there was never anyone around, except for an old Negro man fishing for carp, who would exchange a few remarks.

When he got up to Stony Island, he saw that Kalvin had crossed the avenue and moved north on a diagonal. He was heading for the one building that remained from the World's Fair, the Museum of Science and Industry. It was a massive Beaux-Arts building that stretched over fifteen acres on the edge of Jackson Park, tucked between the Lake and the rest of Hyde Park. Nessheim had been there several times, and had never seen a museum like it. It had a coal mine sunk deep in its foundations, where schoolchildren and adults alike could see how the fuel was extracted. There was a vast room-sized train set, and a mechanical game of noughts and crosses that no human had ever won. On the ground floor unhatched chick eggs sat behind glass in an enormous flat cabinet filled with straw. It had glass sides and a glass top, so the chicks could be seen from all angles. Every so often you would see a shell tremble, a crack appear, then another crack, until suddenly a tiny chick struggled and flapped its way ferociously out of its albumen cover into the great world outside.

He couldn't see Kalvin anywhere in the main rotunda, which was filled with children on school outings. He wondered which way to go, and finally chose the first gallery to his right. Walking in, he found a room dedicated to the history of the American Indian, with large murals tracing the different tribes and little pictorial cameos of their daily life and *mores*. At one end of the room loomed a large wooden model of an Apache warrior, with warpaint on both cheeks and a headdress of feathers spread out like a hand of playing cards.

He still couldn't see Kalvin. Nessheim moved through the throng into the next gallery, which was so dark that it took several seconds for his eyes to adjust. The room was shaped like a stretched football, oval and elongated, and from his position he could see at either end a large disc of darkened glass. Each was placed on a low platform and faced its counterpart at the other end of the room.

Two small schoolboys stood on one of the platforms, giggling and speaking in exaggerated whispers. Next to them, waiting impatiently, was Kalvin.

Nessheim stepped back through the entrance, taking cover behind a standing placard that said 'The Whispering Gallery'. He watched as the boys left their place in front of the large glass disc, and Kalvin quickly stepped up. He stood there, his back to Nessheim.

What was he doing? Nessheim moved a little closer, until the angle of view improved and he could glimpse the side of Kalvin's chin. It was moving up and down, almost as if the scientist were chewing gum; then Nessheim realised the man was talking to himself. Why? Kalvin's jaw stopped, then resumed moving – it was as if he were talking to himself, since there was no one within earshot.

This went on for another minute or two, to Nessheim's increasing bafflement. Then Kalvin seemed to be done with whatever ritual he had been absorbed by, and he stepped down from the platform, his place taken immediately by another gang of kids. Nessheim retreated again behind the placard, but Kalvin went out of the far exit, heading into the depths of the museum and its famous coal mine. Nessheim remained mystified, until he glanced at the placard shielding him and understood what had transpired. It read:

The Whispering Gallery has a magical effect that also demonstrates a scientific principle. The room is designed in the form of an ellipsoid and has two arch-shaped dishes at either end that serve as points of focus. This means that if you whisper directly into one dish, your voice will travel across the room to the other focal point, and will be heard – and heard only – by the listener standing in front of the other dish.

He gave himself a mental kick. Kalvin had been talking all right, but not to himself.

But where was the other participant in the dialogue? He moved to the gallery's entrance and stared at the other disc of glass, at the far end to his right. Whoever had been there to receive Kalvin's words was gone. A little girl and her mother were standing on that platform; at what had been Kalvin's end her father stood, whispering. No adult had come out of the entrance where Nessheim had been standing; he (or she) wouldn't have gone to Kalvin's end, in case they were seen together – disguising their conversation must be the whole point of this weird exercise. Which left one entrance at the far end.

Going through it quickly Nessheim found himself in a small hallway, with a staircase leading to the museum's upper floor. A corridor led back to the main Exhibition Hall. He walked along it, and stood in a doorway a few steps up from the Hall. He wasn't sure what he was looking for. For all the schoolchildren, there were plenty of adults. But since Kalvin had turned into the museum's interior recesses, wouldn't his listener have moved as far as possible from him?

Nessheim half-ran to the entrance, nearly bowling over two women with shopping bags, just avoiding treading on a toddler who came up to his knees. Exhaling apologies, he slipped outside and stared out through the evening's darkening gloom at the vast parking lot. It was lit dimly by ancient standing lamps, relics from the Fair rewired to use electricity and spaced at regular intervals between the parking spaces. They provided the only source of brightness in the grey: a woman walking to her car was suddenly revealed to be wearing a yellow coat. And there was a man, in a midnight-blue Chesterfield ... Nessheim stared hard. Could it be?

He ran down the front steps of the museum, desperate not to lose sight of the retreating figure. Nessheim prayed that he didn't have a car here; there would be no way he could follow him. But the man was still walking, and each time he passed a lamp Nessheim drew closer, until he was confident that it was the same Chesterfield he had first spotted that morning, topped again by a homburg hat.

Coincidence? Never, thought Nessheim, increasing his pace. As Guttman had told him many times, it was better to be 'paranoid', in the newfangled language of these new doctors of the mind, than to be complacent about unexpected connections.

The Chesterfield was moving fast, crossing Stony Island Avenue and heading for the tunnel that took 57th Street underneath the tracks. Nessheim struggled to keep up, but there were no lights on this block of the Inner Drive.

Underneath the tracks a solitary bulb lit the entrance to the station. He saw the Chesterfield turn and enter through the iron turnstiles. Nessheim stopped at the edge of the tunnel, and gave it twenty seconds. Then he moved forward quickly, buying his ticket from a visor-capped man behind a grilled window. He asked for a round trip to Randolph Street and paid his fifteen cents, then rushed up the stairs just in time, for a train was coming in.

A couple of doors opened and a few people got out, while the conductor hooked an arm on an opening door from inside the coach and swung out over the platform, scanning it in both directions. There was no sign of the Chesterfield, and Nessheim scooted back to the last car, just before the door slid shut and the conductor blew his whistle.

He tried to scan the occupants of the compartment casually; it was less than half-full and he could see all the passengers. Still no sign of Chesterfield. Nessheim sat down by the door on one of the cane-covered reversible seats as the train started up again. It was cold in the car, helped by the IC's famous 60:40 air conditioning: sixty miles an hour and forty open windows meant the train made its own cooling system, which worked even in the dripping heat of a Chicago summer.

A copy of the *Chicago Herald American* sat next to him on the seat, and he picked it up and pretended to read, barely taking in the headline, which seemed a classic even for that paper: *'Mother of 14 Kids Kills Father of 9 in Police Station'*.

He was trying to figure out what was going on. Who was this guy? He'd been following Nessheim, of that he was pretty sure, but why then meet with Kalvin? Kalvin was a Jew – why would he be helping the Nazis?

The train stopped at 53rd and Nessheim didn't get up, figuring Chesterfield wouldn't take the IC for one short stop. At 47th he did stand up and went to the door and peered out of its window just in case, but only an old Negro lady got off. The next stop was 23rd

Street, so he flicked through the paper, unwilling to look into the next car. The mid-term elections had been two days before, and Roosevelt's Democrats had lost forty-five seats in the House, yet just managed to hang on to a majority. In the South-Western Pacific fierce fighting continued on Guadalcanal, but Carlson's raiders, a unit of marines, had wiped out a Japanese garrison on Little Makin Island. Rommel was in retreat in the sands of Western Egypt, and had lost 600 planes and 160 tanks to the British Army. It was day seventy-three of the siege of Stalingrad. And here I am, thought Nessheim wearily, playing spies and taking the IC downtown.

At 23rd Street no one disembarked. Heading downtown again, the train curved on to an inside track and he could see the tall buildings of the Loop looming toy-like against the northern sky.

Then Roosevelt Road, and 14th Street, where buildings became commercial – warehouses, small factories, stores. Chesterfield must be going all the way downtown, thought Nessheim, since everybody else was. So it was fortunate that Nessheim stuck his head out of the window at Van Buren, since he would never otherwise have seen the man emerge from the front car. Without a backward glance, thank God, since Nessheim had to leave the train and move conspicuously fast to keep up.

At the subterranean shelter of the waiting room, Nessheim stopped for a moment, anxious not to climb the stairs to Michigan Avenue and find himself standing next to the man. He counted slowly to ten, then went up, in time to see his target heading across the avenue and proceeding along Van Buren Street. The man crossed under the busy L tracks that ran north and south over Wabash. At State he turned north and walked up to Jackson before turning left again. He seemed oblivious

110

to the possibility of being followed – almost too much so, and Nessheim slowed his own pace.

He was right, since when Nessheim turned the corner, he saw him less than a hundred feet ahead, ostentatiously staring at a store window. Nessheim turned on a dime and waited around the corner of the building for over a minute; when he came round into Dearborn again he saw Chesterfield far ahead, striding towards Adams Street, passing the massive brick Monadnock Building, then turning left on Adams. Nessheim followed, starting to feel nervous, since this was highly familiar territory to him, and the last thing he needed was to run into someone he knew.

Wherever this guy was going, he was doing it in a roundabout way. It suggested either that he'd been well trained or that he was new to the city. Nessheim was wondering which when he turned the corner on to Adams and found the likely answer. It was one he would never have expected; he watched with disbelief as Chesterfield entered the revolving doors of 105 West Adams Street. Among its many occupants were the headquarters of the Chicago Field Office of the FBI.

He ignored the questions multiplying in his mind and this time sprinted towards the building, daring this new connection to be untrue. He hit the brass-lined revolving door at speed, accelerating the outward journey of a businessman who had been calmly leaving on his way home. 'Hey,' the man shouted as he was sent flying on to the sidewalk by the swinging door. Nessheim ignored him and raced towards the bank of elevators on the left side of the mezzanine.

There were no elevators waiting and he went from one to the other, checking the floor number that clicked floor by floor in little windows to the side of each shaft. Most of the cars were high up in the building, which was over forty storeys. But one was on twelve and still ascending. It must be Chesterfield's. Nessheim had no way of knowing who else was in the elevator car, but it wouldn't be full at this time of day – people would be going down, leaving work, rather than going up. The car stopped at sixteen, long enough to mean someone was getting off. Then it ascended again until it reached the nineteenth floor.

Bingo, thought Nessheim; the nineteenth was where he had started out with the Bureau, little more than an errand boy until given a chance by the SAC Melvin Purvis to become an agent.

He wanted to go up himself to the nineteenth floor, and find out who the guy was. But he couldn't – Guttman had been explicit that this operation was off the books. If he went upstairs, chances were good that he would run into the current SAC – Nelson, a hard nut who had cleared the Chicago Field Office of agents hired by his predecessor. Nessheim would have been one of them, sent like the others 'to Butte' in the parlance of the Bureau, had not Guttman arrived to recruit him.

'Jimmy,' a hoarse voice cried. No one called him that any more; when he turned round he saw Lenny, the one-armed owner of the kiosk in the building's lobby. Lenny was gregarious and knew everybody – he could tell you the condition of the sick cat owned by Mrs Fergus who worked on the third floor.

'Still here, huh?' Nessheim answered. 'What happened to Florida?'

Lenny laughed. 'I keep losing the big hands. What about you? I haven't seen you for ages.'

'Oh, I've been around.'

'Not here you ain't. You still with the Feds?'

He shook his head. 'Nah, just visiting.'

'Well, visit some more.

'Say, Lenny, did you just see a guy come through? Young-looking, wearing a blue Chesterfield.'

'Yeah, I saw him. Nice coat.'

'Who's he work for?'

'Beats me. Never seen him before.'

7

Nessheim went outside, where the sidewalks were crowded with people leaving work. He killed time walking along LaSalle Street towards the Corn Exchange, which sat hunkered down at one end like a squat bulky guardian of America's agricultural future. He turned, moseying around on State, absent-mindedly checking out the window displays at Carson Pirie Scott and Marshall Field's while he tried to figure out what he had uncovered.

The Chesterfield guy was with the Bureau, but what did that mean? That Kalvin was an informant? If so, why hadn't Guttman told him? Lenny hadn't recognised Chesterfield, which could only mean the guy hadn't been in the building before – Lenny didn't miss a trick. So was he brand new here? Sent to Chicago to run Kalvin? Or was he in town for the one weird meeting in the Museum of Science and Industry? In which case, what did Kalvin know that was important enough to summon a Special Agent?

He got himself so immersed in questions and possibilities that he ended up being late for his meeting with Tatie, just two blocks away at the Palmer House. Only five minutes late, but that would be enough to prickle Tatie.

Eloise Tate, middle name unknown, was probably in her late forties now, nearly twenty years older than Nessheim, and with a long-standing ability to make him feel all of fifteen years old. Like everybody else, he'd always been a little scared of her, though she'd always been nice to him. In his first year at the Bureau, when he'd been little more than a glorified gopher for

Purvis, and the agents ignored him and he had no friends at work, he'd come down with flu so bad he couldn't even make it to a phone to call in sick. Tatie had come to his boarding house, bringing him soup. None of the older guys had ever let him forget it, though what they didn't know is that she'd come back every evening after work. Young as he was, it hadn't even occurred to Nessheim that Tatie could be sweet on him.

He went through the Wabash entrance to the hotel, then through reception to the Grand Lounge. He stood at the top of the short staircase and stared at the hotel's famous showpiece. The two-storey gilded room was furnished like Louis XVI's salon, with rich patterned carpet on the floor, Tiffany 24-carat gold chandeliers, and an array of walnut and maple tables, plush sofas, and armchairs padded with thick velvet. The ceiling was especially famous, a series of frescoes created by a Frenchman brought in at unprecedented expense in the 1920s. He had depicted the most famous figures of Greek mythology in lustrous blues, reds, and gold, with the nude figure of Venus ascending as a centrepiece. It was trumpeted as an American rival to the Sistine Chapel; there had never been anything modest about Chicago.

Nessheim spotted Tatie at a corner table, sitting stiffly on a ruby-red velvet chair. She was wearing a neat wool jacket and a pleated skirt, both charcoal grey, and though fashionable they had the unintended effect of making her look much older. He felt as though he was having drinks with a country relative, come to the big city to keep an eye on the family's prodigal son.

He shook her hand awkwardly since she stayed seated. Apologising for being late, he pulled up another chair and sat across the little pie-shaped table. 'Would you like a drink?' he asked.

'Just some tea, please.' So he ordered that and little sandwiches that came on a three-plated affair, the contraption held together by a centring rod with a handle that the waiter swung with practised ease. Nessheim hated to think what this was going to cost him.

He said, 'It's nice to see you again. I thought you'd gone to Washington.'

She shook her head. 'They offered me a post there, restructuring the Records department. I'd have been reporting directly to Louis B. Nichols.'

'That's a big job,' said Nessheim politely. 'But I guess I've always thought of you as part and parcel of this place.'

'You and everybody else. Sometimes I feel I'm just part of the furniture. And almost as dusty.' She sighed wistfully, and suddenly Nessheim saw that she was becoming a lonely old maid. He was startled by this thought. She said with an artificial brightness, 'Still, my friends are all here. I'd like to think you were one of them.'

'Of course, Tatie.' But he felt embarrassed. Friendship was not how he would have described their relationship. She'd been like that older sister to him – scolding, tough, but giving out an underlying sense of affection. That wasn't the same as friends.

'I'm sorry you couldn't have dinner with me,' she said. There was something pathetic about her voice.

'So am I,' said Nessheim, trying to sound as though he meant it. He ploughed on, thinking how forced he sounded as he explained that he had to see someone in Hyde Park that evening.

Tatie picked up her pack of cigarettes from the table and shook it until one stuck its neck out, then offered it to Nessheim. He shook his head, and she said, 'Still clean then, Jim?'

He shrugged. He had smoked one cigarette when he turned sixteen and promptly puked behind the bakery where his girlfriend worked in Bremen, Wisconsin.

'My clean-living Mr Nessheim,' said Tatie, but there was no affection in her voice.

'I wanted your help on something,' he said, since their small talk was going nowhere.

'Shoot,' she said.

'It's about the German-American *Bund*. It's supposed to be disbanded, but I wonder if there's been any activity still here in Chicago. Could you check the file for me?'

'Of course, but I think you're right – it's defunct.'

'And could you check two names for me? Just in case they're still around?' He passed her a piece of paper. Schultz the *Bund* leader in New York was dead – of natural causes while he served his time in Sing Sing. Beringer, on the other hand, had been alive and well when last seen by Nessheim, and there was Alex Burmeister to consider, husband of Nessheim's high-school girlfriend and once a prominent figure in the Wisconsin *Bund*.

'And there's something else – if I wanted to know if somebody was working in the Field Office, how would I best go about it?'

'You know their name?'

'That's the thing – I don't.'

'How about age?'

'Young, younger than me, I'd say. Mid-twenties. Nice-looking fella, kind of tall, thin build, bordering on skinny.'

'There would be a large number of candidates, Jim. Everybody looks young to me these days, and there are a lot of new recruits. Would you recognise him if you saw him again?'

'I'm pretty sure I would. But I wouldn't want him to see me, if you get my drift.'

'I got that, thanks, Jim,' she said sharply. She was prickly about even the remotest hint of condescension. 'Your best bet would be the mug book.'

'The what?'

'We call it the mug book. It's got mugshots of every employee in the office, along with their personal details. They're all in one big book – it's like a photo album. That way you don't have to go look at each individual file. The SAC has one, and so does Miss Clory.'

'She's still there?'

'Agnes soldiers on,' Tatie said drily. Miss Clory was an ancient spinster who looked after payroll and small personnel matters – if you lost your wallet Miss Clory helped you get fixed up with a new licence and social security card (though if you lost your badge there wasn't much she could do – usually you got fired). Tatie seemed to recognise that one day not too far off, people like Nessheim would be asking the same question about her.

'This mug book, do you have one?'

She shook her head. 'But I can get access to it easily enough.' There wasn't much Tatie didn't know or couldn't find out in the Field Office. Tatie added, 'This sounds pretty mysterious. Is it to do with Harry Guttman's business?'

'Could be. I don't want to say more than that right now – I could be dead wrong.'

Tatie stubbed out her cigarette in the china ashtray. The last half-inch broke off and Nessheim watched as she chased the still-smoking end with the longer stub, stabbing it until it gave a last tiny exhalation and died. She said, 'Okay, I'll keep it on the QT. Give me a call when you're ready and we can meet up again – here's as good as any place. I'll bring the book with me.'

They kept talking, but it was hard-going, oddly

formal. Nessheim said, 'Tell me, have you heard from Mr Purvis?'

'I had a card from him a few months ago. He's left Hollywood. They're making a movie of his experiences, though I don't think the Bureau has done much to help.'

'I bet not.' Hoover's animus towards Purvis was legendary within the FBI. The Director had never liked anyone else grabbing the limelight, and after Dillinger's death in a shootout, Purvis had threatened to become equally famous – he'd even been put on Wheaties boxes for a time. But not for long, thanks to Hoover.

Then Tatie asked him about law school and what he'd been up to; asked him about what car he was driving these days and where he was living; and, Nessheim felt sure, was about to ask after his mother when another voice said, 'Hi, stranger.'

He felt a hand on his shoulder, and looked up to find Stacey standing beside him. His heart went thump – because she looked so good, because he hadn't expected her, and because he couldn't believe she had shown up while he was talking to Tatie.

'Hi,' she said again, in the low breathless voice that made his back tingle. She didn't even acknowledge Tatie, but then, she had never been a girls kind of girl. 'I'll be in the bar.'

He was blushing when he turned back to Tatie. Her face was thunderous. She lifted her china teacup and finished her tea in one long draw. Putting the cup down sharply, she declared, 'I've got to be going.'

'Tatie, wait. Can't you stay a while?'

She stood up to leave. 'I wouldn't want to keep you from your meeting back in Hyde Park. Let me know when you need the mug book.'

When she'd left he paid for the tea and went to the

bar, feeling terrible. He should never have told Stacey he was meeting Tatie here; Stacey was too unpredictable. How like her to horn in, without so much as a by-your-leave to Tatie.

He found her sitting on a bar stool, with her right leg crossed over her left knee. A Cuban-looking man at the far end of the bar was giving her the eye, while Stacey, fully aware of that, was chatting with the bartender. A pack of Pall Malls and a gold lighter sat on the bar top in front of her, next to a frothy drink in a frosted glass.

He sidled on to the stool next to her, and Stacey said to the bartender, 'Ask this good-looking guy what he's drinking.'

'Sir?' the bartender asked uncertainly. Nessheim realised he couldn't decide if Stacey and Nessheim knew each either.

'I'm *not* having whatever she's drinking,' Nessheim declared. 'Give me a bourbon on some cubes.'

While the bartender fetched a bottle of Four Roses, Stacey said, 'Who was that grim old bird?'

'Someone I used to work with,' he said neutrally.

'I hope you're not spending much time under *her* wing.'

He didn't reply; there was never any point remonstrating with Stacey.

'It's good to see you,' she said as the bartender set his drink down. Nessheim took a long sip, and felt Stacey's hand on his arm. 'So how's Agent Nessheim tonight?' she asked.

The bartender was studiously drying glasses with a cotton dish towel, but Nessheim could tell he was listening. 'Hurry up and guzzle that down,' Stacey said.

'What's the rush?' he asked. 'The damage has been done.'

'I'm starving. Should we eat at the doghouse I'm in?'

He couldn't help laughing. 'How about the Berghof? I haven't been there since I came back to Chicago.' They had gone there often in the old days.

'Once a Kraut, always a Kraut. If you can stick the *Thüringer*, so can I.'

The usual line outside the Berghof moved fast on Adams Street, and soon they were sitting at a little table half-sheltered by the screen in front of the serving station, which Stacey commandeered over the captain's objections. She took her coat off and stood for a moment, as if on display. There was a lot to look at: in her raspberry-red rib-hugging dress, Stacey and her honey-blonde hair caught the eye of every man and woman in the room.

The waiter came up, pad and pencil in hand. He wore a long white apron, like the bartenders next door. 'Can I get you folks a cocktail?'

'A double Manhattan with an orange slice,' said Stacey, and Nessheim ordered a large stein of the dark bock beer. Stacey reached across the table and put her hand on his. 'Could you stand sharing the porterhouse for two? You can have your *Kartelhosen* another time.'

'*Kartoffeln*, I think you mean. They're potatoes and come with it.'

'Whatever you say. That way we can both be happy.'

When their drinks came the waiter also brought a basket of dark rye bread, and Nessheim took a piece, then gave their order. Stacey shook her head. 'You do like the heavy German stuff, don't you?'

He nodded as he took a swallow of his beer. 'Mother's milk for me.'

'My mother wouldn't cook. Said she'd had enough of that in Dakota.'

'Your mother's from Dakota?' He had never met the

woman. From Stacey's earlier accounts he would have expected New York or even Paris to be more likely candidates.

'Yep, though she doesn't like to admit it.' She gestured towards the bar next door. 'Do you go there sometimes?'

'I used to when I worked downtown.' It had a long slab of dark mahogany, with barmen who wore white aprons and kept their sleeves rolled up. The right mix of bustle and relaxation for a drink after work. At lunch a beer got you the makings of a free lunch laid out in little wooden bowls on the countertop – raw onions, pork crackling, tiny hot dogs with toothpicks and hot brown mustard on the side, and pickled pigs' feet for the strong of heart.

'*I'd* drink there,' Stacey declared, 'but they won't let us girls in.'

'I know.'

'It's not fair.'

'My heart bleeds for you. What are you complaining about? You've got the vote.'

Her nostrils flared momentarily, then she realised he was kidding. But she was not entirely appeased, and said seriously, 'It's not right. One day it's got to change.'

'Why not worry about bigger injustices? Like your coloured brethren and how they're treated. Now that's not fair.'

'I know. Did you realise Hyde Park has restrictive covenants through the whole neighbourhood? You could be a doctor but if you're also Negro you can't even buy a railroad flat. The university has a lot to answer for.'

This jarred with his view of the neighbourhood's endemic progressivism. 'I'm sure you'll find plenty of law students ready to protest.'

'Maybe,' she said doubtfully. 'Your friend Winograd seems to think they're all Reds.'

'He's not my friend.' He had gone to a dreary party at Winograd's place, a railroad flat above a radio repair place on 53rd Street, and in return had invited him over once to his own apartment, where Winograd had drunk all of the beers in the icebox.

'He thinks he is. What do you know about him?'

'Not a lot. He graduated a few years ago, but it's never clear to me what he's been doing. He's 4-F obviously. He likes Billie Holiday, and that's good enough for me.'

'So you think his heart is in the right place?'

'You mean the left place, don't you?'

'No, I don't, and certainly not for Winograd. But forget about him. Let's not talk politics.'

Really? It was as if Lindbergh had asked a dinner companion not to mention aviation.

'Anyway,' said Stacey, 'did you have a good meeting?'

'It was going swell until you interrupted.'

Stacey looked completely uncontrite. 'That lady gives new meaning to the phrase "old flame".' She added loudly, 'You must have been in short pants when she lost her cherry.'

He saw a woman at a nearby table flinch. 'Stacey,' he said reprovingly.

Stacey turned to the woman at the table. 'Sorry,' she said, looking no more apologetic than before, though Nessheim was impressed, since he'd never heard her apologise before. She turned back to him, and said more quietly, 'But honestly, Nessheim, you can do better than that.'

'I told you before – it was business.'

'I thought you'd left the FBI, remember?'

'I have. It was family stuff.' He scrambled about

mentally, trying to find a safe foothold. 'To do with my father's estate.'

'Estate?' She looked at him with disbelief. 'I'm sorry about your father, but what's a Wisconsin farm boy doing, seeing somebody in Chicago about his father's will?'

He shrugged but didn't answer. She went on, 'Something's up. You can't fool me.'

The waiter came with their steak, still sizzling from the broiler. It was the size of a flattened catcher's mitt. Balancing the plate carefully on a little stand he carried with his free hand, the waiter deftly carved the meat in two. He gave them each a plate of sliced pink beef, then set down dishes of hash browns, green beans and creamed spinach on the table.

Stacey ate hungrily, snaring the lion's share of the creamed spinach as well as most of the potatoes. 'Very fine *Kartelhosen*,' she said, chewing appreciatively. 'But tell me, if Winograd's not your friend, who is these days?'

He thought for a moment. There had been Devereux in San Francisco, another Special Agent at the Bureau. His old pals at the Bureau here in Chicago had been dispersed in the mass cull initiated by Nelson, the SAC. His college friendships had withered after he'd left Northwestern early. He shrugged. 'I keep myself to myself these days.'

'Oh.' She looked surprised.

He asked her about herself, but she wouldn't play. 'I haven't done much of interest,' she said bluntly. 'Not like you.'

She continued to deflect his questions about where she'd been with a laugh or by helping herself to more of the side dishes. 'The food hasn't changed,' she said appreciatively. He learned only that her mother was still alive, and that law school seemed the best of a lot of bad options, but she was spare with other specifics of her recent past. Yes, she'd been in LA, she admitted, but not for long, and no, she hadn't tried to get into the movies. Each of his questions seemed to lead to her asking her own, but he found it easy being with her, easy again to talk to her. He thought of Fielding, and that apprehensive look as the man tried to entertain her, but he didn't feel similar pressure himself – this was her date, he figured; he hadn't sought her out. He left out anything serious about his escapades, and she smiled at his account of the ludicrous antics at the Hollywood studio where he had been based for a year, then laughed out loud when he demonstrated how he'd shown a B-movie actor how to hold a gun.

Finally, to change the subject he said, 'I saw you the other day, you know.' She was eating *Apfelstrudel* by now, while he sipped a mug of steaming black coffee.

'Where was that?' she asked between bites.

'In the Quadrangle Club. You were lunching with Mr Torts himself.'

For a split second Stacey's eyes widened in surprise, like an innocent girl in a Mack Sennett movie. 'How . . . ?'

'I was behind a pillar at the next table. *Now that, my dear, was war,*' he said, imitating Fielding's stentorian tones.

Stacey grimaced. 'I didn't see you there. It was strictly a duty lunch.'

'Sure it was.'

'You sound jealous, Nessheim.'

'Never,' he said, then burnt his tongue with the coffee.

She shook her head. 'When I decided to go to law school, it turned out there was a professor who'd known my dad once. And the professor –'

'Was Arthur Fielding?' It seemed implausible that a manufacturing paper magnate had been pals with the Arthur McNeil Professor of Jurisprudence.

'If it's any consolation, Professor Fielding spoke very highly of you. He said you were one of the few able to distinguish between the illegal and the immoral. He wanted to know all about you.'

'And you obliged?'

'I said you were a closed book, an enigma to your fellow students.' She laughed when she saw the incredulous look on his face. 'Don't worry – I don't think he even knows what you look like. But he does think the world of your coursework.' She laughed again before he could feel flattered. 'Actually, I think he just wanted to know whether you and I were seeing each other.'

'The old goat. How did your dad know him?'

'It was during the last war. They were both in France in 1917.'

'I bet Fielding gives a pretty good account of himself.'

'Dad said Fielding never saw combat. He was a quartermaster, stuck in a tent behind the lines, counting cans of beans – or having someone else count them. My father was an officer. I learned later he'd done some serious fighting. But the only stories he ever told were funny ones – how his buddy got kicked by a horse, and what happened when his men got served snails in a bistro.' She examined her nails, keeping her eyes on her hand. 'I think you're doing the same thing with me, Nessheim. You tell a good story – when you describe your time as a G-Man it's one big laugh after another.' She pointed her index finger at him, then cocked her thumb like a gun, and let her hand shake and flop all over the place.

Nessheim laughed heartily.

126

'See what I mean?' she said, and she was serious again.

When they finished dinner, Nessheim paid and they went out on to Adams Street.

'Where are you parked?' Stacey asked.

'I'm not. I took the IC.'

'Oh, good, you can be chauffeur then,' she said happily, and handed him her keys. An L train clattered overhead behind them as they walked towards Michigan Avenue, and Stacey took Nessheim's arm. Ahead to the east the neo-classical Art Institute stood like a bulwark between them and the Lake. 'You still in Lincoln Park?' he asked as he unlocked the passenger-side door and held it open for her. He wondered how he was going to get home.

'No. I've moved south for the duration. Hyde Park.'

'Must be a big sacrifice.' He remembered the glamour of her previous place. Two bedrooms and a living room fronted by glass with a magnificent view along the beach all the way to the Palmolive Building where the Lake bent out in a large bow.

'Not really. It's three minutes to class instead of thirty-five. Worth slumming for.' In the car Stacey was quiet as Nessheim joined the Drive at the south end of the Loop. It was too cold to put the top down, but the Packard purred contentedly, cat-like, as Nessheim worked through its gears and moved over to the fast lane. Ahead of them, the Field Museum and Planetarium loomed like colossal monuments in the dark, unlit in token obeisance to the blackouts diligently obeyed on the country's coasts.

They were moving fast past the 23rd Street exit when Stacey spoke up. 'Nessheim, why aren't you in uniform?'

'I couldn't find one that fit.'

'Seriously, it's not what I'd expect. Don't you want to be at war?!'

Once there was nothing he wanted more. He exhaled slowly. 'Believe me, I tried.' He didn't want to explain any further. Fortunately she reached for the radio, then leaned back in her seat as 'Smoke Gets in Your Eyes' filled the car.

He left the Drive at 51st and drove, at her direction, south on South Shore Drive towards her apartment building. It was a handsome tower of cream-coloured brick, just down from the Shoreland Hotel.

'There you go ma'am,' he said. 'Door-to-door service.'

'I haven't got the fare. You'd better come up while I find my purse.'

He shook his head. 'Pay me next time. Where should I park this baby?' He could walk home in ten minutes.

'I need my first tutorial, Nessheim. We've got Torts in two days and I'm floundering. Mid-terms are only ten days away.'

'You can wait a day or two.'

'Says who?'

'Says your tutor.'

She gave a perfunctory nod. 'I understand that, and I recognise that Torts and Malfeasance may not be enough to lure you upstairs. What if I said I just wanted to talk to you?'

'I'd say it's so much phooey.'

She nodded again, sympathetic but unconvinced, like a psychiatrist listening to a patient. Nessheim leaned forward and turned his head sideways towards her, until his cheek rested on the steering wheel. He felt quite helpless.

'Okay,' Stacey declared, 'let's cut to the chase. Would it help if I said I want you to come upstairs so you can take all my clothes off?' She suddenly looked away, as

128

if the brashness of the words came as a surprise even to herself.

No, Nessheim told himself. No, he thought again; don't give in. Then he lifted his head from the steering wheel, reached for the handle and opened the door. 'Now you're talking,' he said.

Her apartment was on the sixth floor, and they took the elevator up. She said it had an operator during the day but at night it was automatic, and as soon as its gold-framed doors slid shut, she put her arms around Nessheim, a hand behind his neck, and brought his lips down hard on to hers. It was a slow ride up and she used every moment of it to arouse him; another two floors and he would have had his clothes off.

Stumbling out, they disengaged long enough for Stacey to find her keys and open the door. Once inside, he barely noticed the Lake-front view from the living room, as they clung to each other like a pair of marathon dancers, holding on for dear life as they moved along the parquet floor to the bedroom. They fell on each other like little kids on Christmas morning, ripping the wrapping off their presents.

Later, he woke in the middle of the night, drowsy but happy as he made out the sleeping form of Stacey next to him. She wore a silk slip that was pushed halfway up her hips, and her hair, golden in the faint light from the bathroom, lay splayed either side of her face on the pillow.

He got up quietly and went out to the living room. Leaning against the waist-high bookshelf that ran against the wall beneath the large picture windows, he could see a few passing cars six storeys below, mainly Checker cabs, cream bodies with green checks. The window opened easily, sliding to the side, and he listened to the noise of breakers hitting the rocks at The Point on 55th Street. He knew he should be focused on the man in the Chesterfield and his odd rendezvous with Kalvin, and knew too that he should be calling Guttman right now, to hell with the hour, and trying to find out what was going on.

But any urgency had been bushwhacked by the woman sleeping next door. What am I doing? he asked himself. It will end in tears, just like last time. My tears, thought Nessheim. It was so obvious that Stacey couldn't stay still for more than a second or two – in her love life as well as in her choice of places to live. Nessheim had moved around himself, but for him it was enough to last a lifetime. He wanted to settle. This is not the way to go about it, he thought, closing the window with his palm, leaving a sweaty map of his fingers on the glass.

8

THEY GOT TO law school in time for Torts the next morning. This time Stacey drove. As they got in the car she said, 'You look like the cat who's got the cream.'

'Don't be so sure of yourself,' he said, but this only made her laugh.

'What are you doing tonight then?' she asked.

'Not what you think, that's for sure. I've got to study, Stacey.' He was already trying to think how he'd pass his mid-terms if he was going to spend time at Stagg Field and Eckhart Hall, much less a luxury apartment off South Shore Drive.

'Let me come over.' She saw his face. 'Don't worry, I have to study too. I'll cook supper – I can get groceries on 57th Street.'

'You don't have to do that.' He liked the idea, but he sensed he was supposed to like it. He wondered what was going on. Stacey didn't pursue men; they pursued her. 'I can get them on my way home.'

'No, let me do it. I've got something special in mind.'

'Well –' he said.

'I'll be there about six.'

'I may be out.'

She was undeterred. 'Then leave the kitchen door open. Or have you got a spare key?'

'Maybe.' He realised this was to argue the details; on the main point of her coming over he had given way without noticing.

'Under the mat?'

'Not any more.'

'Why, you thought I'd find it?' She was smiling but there was an edge to her voice.

'Something like that.' Since receiving the *'Rossbach'* note he had moved the spare key from such an obvious hiding place and tucked it instead deep into a cranny on the underside of the wooden stairs at the rear of his apartment. No one could find it there without half an hour's search. He told Stacey now exactly where it was.

They walked together into Stuart Hall and Stacey came with him down the centre aisle, then sat down in the seat on his left. A moment later, Winograd arrived. He stood for a moment, looking stunned to find Stacey sitting there. He sat down as Fielding came in at the front and went to the podium. As Fielding gave a preliminary cough and started to speak, Winograd whispered, 'That was fast work. How the hell did you manage that?'

Nessheim opened his notebook, and shielding the page so Stacey couldn't see, wrote rapidly, *'She's just using me to get to you.'*

Back at the apartment he phoned Guttman first. It rang twice and a woman answered. He realised it was Marie.

'Hello there,' she said when he asked for her boss. 'He's upstairs, duking it out with Tolson.'

There was always something refreshing about Marie's irreverence, which was not limited to commentary on Guttman's idiosyncrasies. 'When can I reach him, Marie?'

'You an hour behind us?' she asked, and he realised that was her discreet way of asking if he were in Chicago.

'Yeah, and I'll be here all day.'

'He may want to call you from home, Jim.'

That would be evening, with Stacey in attendance. No, thanks. Were things so fraught at HQ that Guttman thought his calls were being listened to? 'I'll be out tonight, Marie, but I need to talk to him.'

'Sure thing. I'll tell him it's important.'

Next up was Groves. Less urgent, perhaps, but it would at least show Nessheim was on the ball. A switchboard operator answered, and while he waited for the call to go through he tried to visualise where the large moustachioed figure of Groves was based – was it somewhere in the labyrinthine corridors of his new creation, the pentagonal behemoth on the Virginia side of the Potomac, or was he in the old quarters of the War Department on Massachusetts Avenue, not far from the White House? He wished they'd invent a phone that told you the location of the person you called.

He was put through to one secretary, then another, and the second time he heard someone in the background say gruffly, 'Put him through,' and seconds later a voice said, 'Groves.'

'General, it's Nessheim, checking in.'

'Yes.' He sounded impatient.

'You may need to tighten up security some more at Stagg Field.'

'Why? What's the problem?'

Groves listened in silence as Nessheim described the laxness he had found from the sentries. He felt a little sorry for the soldiers in question, who were about to get a dressing-down they'd always remember. But he didn't feel he had a choice. When he'd finished Groves stayed silent for a moment, then said tersely, 'I'll see to it. Let me know right away if the situation doesn't improve. We can't have that.'

'I will.'

'Anything else?'

'No. I –' but Groves had already hung up.

When the phone rang an hour later he was expecting Guttman at the other end of the line. 'Is that you, Jim?'

said a curt female voice, and it took him a second to recognise Tatie's clipped tones.

'Yes, it's me, Tatie.'

'I've got some stuff for you. You staying home for the next hour?'

'I can do. Listen, about the other evening –'

She cut him off. 'Don't go anywhere, okay? I can't do this twice.'

For forty-five minutes he sat in the living room trying to study but with half an eye on the clock. He was slightly nervous about seeing Tatie again, wondering how best to apologise for their aborted last encounter. He didn't want to hurt her feelings and he could use her help, but he was no longer a young pup happy to take instruction.

But when the buzzer went and he asked who it was, a young male voice replied. 'It's Pete. From the Field Office.'

Nessheim buzzed him through, then opened the front door, watching as a fresh-faced young kid in a suit a size too big came up the stairs, carrying a Gladstone bag in one hand.

Once in the living room, the kid named Pete sat down on the sofa, and declining anything to drink while calling Nessheim 'sir', opened the bag. Nessheim stood as Pete handed over an envelope, then lifted an oversized book out with both hands and put it on the coffee table. The mug book.

Nessheim opened the envelope and read the note inside. It was from Tatie – he recognised the typewriter face – but wasn't signed. It said:

```
Local Bund membership once reached 500 in
the Chicago area, but declined to 136 by
1941. Then, right after Germany's declar-
ation of war on the U.S., the organisation
```

disbanded. We have no reports of any
further activity in the Chicago area.

  No Beringer appears on the Chicago
membership roster at any point, but
inquiries with Bureau HQ indicate a Max
Beringer was released from Ossining State
Prison in October 1941 and deported to
Mexico. The Milwaukee Field Office reports
that Alex Burmeister was a member of the
Wisconsin Bund (joined 1937), and President
of the mid-Wisconsin chapter, but publicly
disavowed the organisation in 1940. He
is currently serving in the US Army in
North Africa.

He reached for the vast volume on the coffee table;
it was the dimensions of a wedding album. Sitting down
across from Pete, he went through its stiff pages one by
one. Each photograph was pasted on to thin board,
then pasted down again on to the album's pages. The
photos were standard Bureau employee ID shots.
Nessheim remembered his own being taken, in a brightly
lit corner of the basement in the Justice Department
building in D.C. There the lab photographer snapped
all the new agents, one at a time, standing against a
background cloth of brown.

  There were almost a hundred agents in the mug book,
and Nessheim looked at them all. Several faces were
familiar from his own time at the Field Office, which
had ended only five years before, when Guttman had
plucked him out for special duties elsewhere. Of the
others, perhaps a dozen qualified as possibles – males
under the age of thirty, dark-haired, sharp-featured – but
none triggered even the remotest link to his visual
memory of the Chesterfield man.

Finished, Nessheim sighed and put the book back on the table. 'You want to leave that with me?' he asked, thinking maybe he would go through it again that evening just in case.

Pete shook his head. 'No can do, sir. More than my life's worth. Miss Tate would flay me alive.'

'*Miss* Tate?' Nessheim asked drily.

Pete blushed. 'You know Tatie, sir?'

'Sure. She's a tough cookie. But with a big heart,' he added.

The kid blushed again. 'Anyway,' said Nessheim, 'thank her for the info and for sending the book. Tell her I'll be in touch.'

'Wilco,' said Pete, and they both stood up. Pete must be a Tatie favourite, or she wouldn't have trusted him with such an unorthodox errand. Why had the kid blushed when Nessheim had praised Tatie? Unless . . . For the first time in his life Nessheim saw exactly how age was going to start to creep up on him. In Tatie's eyes, he realised, Pete was the Nessheim of ten years before, another kid she'd taken under her wing and possibly then some.

When Pete had left, Nessheim contemplated what he'd just learned – or not learned. He wasn't surprised Beringer was in Mexico; that had been the deal when the man had grudgingly supplied information about his fellow Germans operating in America before the war. Fair enough, thought Nessheim, but Alex Burmeister was something else. He'd married Nessheim's old high-school sweetheart Trudy after he'd knocked her up, which had seemed unfortunate but forgivable. But he'd also given information to the *Bund* in New York that had got Nessheim in terrible trouble, and that was a score Nessheim hoped to settle one day. It pained him that a man of former Nazi sympathies got to serve, while Nessheim poked around the detritus of the Nazi-lover's former organisation. But one thing was clear: neither Beringer nor Burmeister could have left the '*Rossbach*' note by Nessheim's back door.

At three the phone rang again and this time it was Guttman. He sounded snappish.

'Marie said you called me here. What's the problem?'

By now Nessheim had had time enough for his puzzlement about Kalvin to turn to anger. 'You didn't tell me that the Bureau had a source in Fermi's unit, and you didn't tell me this same source would be meeting up with a Special Agent right under my nose. How am I supposed to operate with some goon crawling all over my patch, talking with one of the lead scientists in the project?'

There was a silence over the phone. Then Guttman said firmly, 'Let's start over. A – I don't have the faintest idea what you're talking about. B – which scientist met which agent? C – are you sure about this?'

'You think I've gotten rusty? Hell, I followed the agent back to the Bankers Building. I don't think he's working for an ad agency.'

'Well, kid, what can I say?'

Kid. When was Guttman going to leave off with that? Nessheim was thirty years old, for God's sake.

Guttman went on. 'Who was the scientist he was meeting?'

'Kalvin.'

'He's one of the senior guys, isn't he? A Polish Jew. I don't understand.'

'Neither do I. That's why I called you. He's an odd fish, Kalvin, and I was going to ask you to double-check his credentials. But if he's being run by the Bureau, I'll keep my distance. I just wish I'd been warned.'

137

'He can't be working for us. This is my patch – I'd know if this guy was ours. Let me check it out, and I'll get back to you. So what else have you found out?'

As if this weren't enough. 'Nothing,' said Nessheim tetchily.

'Have you heard from Groves?'

'Yes. Though I called him. Security here is quite lax. A couple of dozy soldiers my grandmother could have hoodwinked. He's on the case, thank God.'

'This note you got – do you still think that it's the *Bund*?'

'I don't know what to think. Beringer has gone to Mexico, and the other candidate is in the army. The US Army. Some of the *Bund* members here might have heard about Rossbach, but I can't see how they would link him to me, much less know I was here. It's a mystery.'

'Another one. Listen, I'll do the rounds and make sure somebody hasn't got some connection with Kalvin. But like I say, I doubt it. Let's speak next week.'

This time Nessheim hung up first, still annoyed. It was all very well for Guttman to pooh-pooh the idea that Kalvin was a Bureau informant, but what other explanation was there for the meeting Nessheim had witnessed? And come to think of it, how could Guttman be so confident about the goings-on in his 'patch'? If Nessheim's own work for Guttman was being kept secret from Tolson and Hoover, who was to say that two couldn't play that game? Maybe this Chesterfield guy was working for Hoover.

9

'IT SAYS HERE, "Intention is not a criterion for determining a Tort." Why not?'

Stacey lay on the living-room sofa, a glass of soda on the floor within arm's reach. Nessheim was in the soft chair, going through his class notes in preparation for the mid-term exam.

Nessheim said, 'Intention isn't always relevant – only the actual action is. You didn't *mean* to forget to pay the rent, but that's not going to wash with the landlord, or with the judge.'

'But it's relevant in other parts of the law. If I kill you accidentally, I get charged with manslaughter. If I meant to do it, I'm for the chair.'

'Think of Torts as a magnificent exception.'

Stacey snorted. 'Some exception. It's got to be the most boring part of the law.'

'What are you finding interesting?' he asked, genuinely curious. She wasn't in any of his other classes, which were required ones, and she hadn't talked about her other courses either.

She shrugged.

'Just what else are you taking, Stacey?'

'Military law. Wages and prices regulation.'

New courses had been rushed in after the war broke out, and were not respected; most of the faculty resented their presence on the curriculum and saw them as a cynical pandering to the government. Nessheim looked at her and shook his head. 'That's it? No Jurisprudence. No Constitutional Law? Not even Corporate Organisational?'

'The teachers said I'm doing really well,' she protested.

'I've caught up all the weeks I missed already. I'll do okay.'

'I bet you will. Mickey Mouse could pass most of them magna cum laude.' He regretted this as soon as he'd said it, and watched as her mouth closed, almost protectively, taking the hit of his words. 'I'm sorry, Stacey. It was a rotten thing to say. I guess mid-terms are getting to me.'

She nodded, but he sensed he'd hit home. Why was she taking this cockamamie brew of stuff? He wanted to apologise again, but sensed this would only compound the offence.

She said quietly, 'Check the chilli, will you?'

He went back to the kitchen and looked at the stove top. Stacey had commandeered his biggest pot, and after a quick half-hour's preparation its contents were bubbling nicely: chuck steak, cut in thin strips and first browned in a skillet, tomatoes slowly melting in the heat of their simmering juice, and maroon pinto beans. As well as enough chilli powder to rip the lining off a man's throat.

Fortunately, Stacey had lugged eight bottles of beer back with her, and he took two out of the fridge now, opened them both and went back into the living room. He put on Ella Fitzgerald and Stacey put her textbook down and they both listened to the record. Then they ate the chilli in the dining room, Nessheim drinking two more beers to dampen the fire raging in his mouth after every forkful. Noticing this, Stacey said lightly, 'You get used to it, Nessheim. I promise. But next time I'll tone it down a bit.'

After dinner he was surprised to find Stacey intent on studying some more. She was deep in the Military Law manual, or so he thought, for without lifting her eyes from the page she said, 'Nessheim, why is there a gun in your clothes closet?'

'It's a souvenir from the Bureau.'

She digested this for a minute. 'You're still doing stuff for them, aren't you?'

He shrugged. 'I'm a law student, remember? We don't have enough time to moonlight.'

She said, 'Let me know when you want to tell me the truth.' And she started reading again.

At eleven they looked at each other, and by silent agreement decided to go to bed. When she joined him there in the dark she was naked, and soon made sure he was too. They made love less frantically than the night before, which reassured him somehow, making him feel that this time was as much about emotion as simple lust. She fell asleep in his arms, and when he tried to disengage she stirred. 'What?' she asked sleepily.

'I didn't mean to wake you up.'

'That's okay,' she said, putting her hand on his chest. He had his own hand under the bedclothes and lay it on her thigh. Her skin was at once so soft yet taut. He knew that she sailed and played tennis and rode bikes and swam.

'Are you always like this these days?' she asked, but without any hint of complaint. She sounded wide awake now. 'You're a parched man who's found a well. How long has it been?'

'Don't ask.' He sighed.

'I'm surprised – women like you, Nessheim. You must know that. They see a tall, blue-eyed, good-looking guy, who's confident enough to treat them well. And yet you manage to suggest vulnerability on your own part – which any woman loves. "A secret wound that only she can heal ..."' she added facetiously, then seemed to think about this for a moment. 'Though I have to say, you've changed. You're not the happy-go-lucky guy I used to know.'

141

'It's the same me,' he said, thinking of his feelings for her.

'I don't think so.' She sat up and turned on the bedside light, then reached for the pack of cigarettes on the night table. Fishing one out, she lit it, inhaled sharply, then blew out a grey plume of smoke in the room's warm air. 'You're still pretty vulnerable, but I'm not sure you're still so nice. So, do you want to tell me about her?'

'What?'

'The girl in D.C.'

'Nothing to tell. I thought it might work out but it didn't.'

'When did you last see her?'

'At the beginning of the summer. I went back to Washington for a while – I was going to work for Guttman, my boss there.'

'What happened?'

'It turned out to be a desk job. Dull and pointless. He was being sidelined – that made me sidelined too.'

'I meant with the girl there. Is that the last time you've been to bed with anybody?'

Nessheim was reluctant to say. 'It wasn't like that. We were never . . . together.'

'You mean you never . . . ?'

His embarrassment was fully fledged now. 'Yeah,' he said huskily.

She took a deep drag and then crushed out her cigarette on the plate she'd brought over as an ashtray. 'That's the problem. It's bad enough getting rejected, but because you never got to the nitty-gritty, there's nothing to work on in your mind except fantasies.'

'You talk about rejection like an expert.'

'See, that's not very nice.'

He turned towards her under the sheets and slowly drew his hand up along her thigh. 'I'll show you nice,' he said.

10

HE WORKED HARD for mid-terms during the next few days, and was glad to find that Stacey did too. Soon they were in a routine – except for Torts they didn't see each other during the day, but convened in Nessheim's apartment around six o'clock. One of them would have bought groceries, and Stacey usually cooked since Nessheim's expertise, she claimed, was limited to 'greasy food': hamburgers and pork chops, steaks and bacon and chunks of liver – anything that would fit into a skillet with some lard. Meat like this was hard to find, which accelerated Stacey's appropriation of the kitchen.

That was not all she took over. Reading on his bed one afternoon, Nessheim was moved to complain when Stacey came in at the end of a day. 'Honest, Stacey, how many drawers do you need? At the rate you're going I'll have my own clothes in the dining room. Maybe I should get Drusilla in to sort the place out.'

Stacey blushed.

'Don't tell me,' he said. 'You already have. When was she here?'

'She liked the apartment,' Stacey said defensively.

'Oh, yeah, I bet. It's so glamorous compared to your view on South Shore Drive.'

'I've never heard class resentment from you before, Nessheim.'

'You still haven't,' he said. 'It's Drusilla I'm speaking on behalf of. I said a drawer, Stacey. You've taken two.'

She jumped on the end of the bed on all fours and crawled up to him, tickling his stomach as he went. 'I'm a girl, Nessheim. Come on, girls have clothes, lots of clothes. Girls need space. You have a sister; you should know this.'

'She had her own room,' he said, trying not to laugh as Stacey tickled him with both hands. 'You've got a luxury apartment. What do you want to move in here for?'

She stopped tickling him, and swung her leg over until she was straddling him. She leaned over, her hair falling almost to the pillow, and looked down at him, her lips faintly creased in the beginnings of a smile. 'It's homey here. I like it, dust and all.'

'I can't believe it. You've got a view people would kill for.'

'View, *schmew*,' she said, in what sounded to Nessheim like a terrible approximation of Guttman. 'It's like the story my mother told me.'

'What's that?' he asked, trying not to sound intrigued. He was having to readjust his picture of her mother with each mention; all he'd known before was that the two had never got on – Stacey was a daddy's girl through and through, and had in the past talked exclusively about him.

'She told me once that if she could pick one place in the world where she could live, it would be the farmhouse in North Dakota where she spent six months as a girl. Not the North Shore mansion, or the palatial apartment on the Gold Coast – nope, it was the rickety house three miles outside Fargo where she lived for just a little while. But her daddy died and they had to move into town. And then another town, and another town.'

'Like an army kid?'

'Yeah, but without the army. My grandmother had five mouths to feed on her own.'

'How did she get by?'

'She took in sewing. Alterations, repairs – anything

she could find.' Stacey stared at Nessheim, a little defiantly. 'When there wasn't enough sewing work she took in men. That's when they'd have to move to another town.' She laughed and, clambering off Nessheim and the bed, stood up. 'I'd better warn you that I used some hangers too.'

'That's okay.'

'You sure?' She was looking away from him, her breezy confidence all gone.

'I'm sure. This can be your Dakota,' he said. For a while anyway, he thought, trying to protect himself.

On Sunday afternoon they went for a walk, an unpredictable meander through the neighbourhood, with Stacey at the helm, suddenly deciding to turn this way or that. The unpredictability jibed nicely with Nessheim's new caution, though he didn't mention it.

Almost all the trees had shed their leaves now. A bright refractory sun lit the interstices of pavement between them, casting a low bleached flare of irregular light. It would be dark in an hour, and Nessheim wanted to get home, quickening his pace a little until Stacey took his arm and subtly slowed him. Ahead, another couple was approaching, also arm in arm. The man wore a formal overcoat and a brown fedora; there seemed something European in his aspect, and Nessheim realised it was Fermi. The woman next to the Italian was almost his height, with a striking, pretty face and black wavy hair tamed by a short-brimmed red felt hat.

'Professor,' said Nessheim hesitantly when they were within a few steps of each other.

Recognising Nessheim, Fermi stopped and smiled; it was the genuine version. 'Mr Nessheim,' he said. Then he added formally, 'My wife, Laura.' She was wearing smart black gloves and did not offer to shake hands, so Nessheim merely nodded hello and she smiled back shyly.

'This is my friend, Miss Madison,' Nessheim replied. There was something Continental in the scene: they could all have been on a Sunday promenade in some small Italian town, where you could count on running into people you knew.

'I am honoured,' said Fermi. He seemed about to introduce his wife to Stacey when suddenly Signora Fermi gave a little cry and stepped forward, opening her arms wide. To Nessheim's astonishment, the two women embraced while Fermi looked at them, nonplussed.

Laughing, the women broke off. Laura Fermi turned to her husband. 'This is the lady I spoke to you about, Enrico.'

'Of course,' Fermi said weakly.

'Yes,' his wife insisted. 'Who helped me in the *negozio di alimentari*.'

'How nice,' said Fermi, clearly thinking it was time to move on. But his wife spoke to him in a burst of Italian. He started to reply, but she talked right through him until he nodded obediently. He said to Nessheim, 'On two Saturdays from now we are having a few people from the Met Lab to our house. We would be very privileged if you could come.' He then added, as if an inducement were required, 'It would be a good opportunity to meet all my senior colleagues.'

'It would be my pleasure,' said Nessheim, though it was the last thing he wanted to do. On a Saturday night, he'd much rather take Stacey to the Rhumboogie Club.

Laura Fermi interjected again in Italian, gesturing towards Stacey with one hand while her other did a conductor's dance, in time with the rapid-fire tempo of her words. Fermi's face grew slightly flushed. 'My wife says to make it clear that you would be most welcome too,' he said to Stacey.

'Yes,' said Laura Fermi unequivocally.

'Wonderful,' said Stacey before Nessheim could speak. 'Can we bring anything?'

'No,' said Laura Fermi. 'Not even olive oil.'

Relieved to have discharged his wife's orders, Fermi tipped his hat and moved on, as Laura gave Stacey another hug.

As they walked on, Nessheim said to Stacey, 'What was that about? How do you know Fermi's wife?'

'We met on 57th Street when I was buying us dinner,' she said crisply. 'She was trying to buy olive oil.'

'What for?'

'To cook with, you big dope. Italians use it instead of lard. I had to explain she wouldn't find it in Schumacher's – she'd have to go to a drugstore. I drove her down to Blackstone and we got some at Sarnat's. When I dropped her home she asked me in for coffee. She's very nice.'

'Sure, but I don't think you want to go to the party.'

'Why not? She's my friend.'

'She said you only met her a few days ago,' he protested.

'So what? Are you trying to tell me that you and Enrico go back to grade school in Wisconsin? I don't think so.'

'I can't take you with me. Anyway, Winograd said he's having a party that night.'

'I hope you enjoy it then. I'll go to the Fermis on my own. You heard the Professor – I'm invited too.'

'But . . .' He started to protest, then couldn't think of an argument that didn't involve telling Stacey much more than he wanted her to know.

'Are you embarrassed to take me?' she demanded.

'Yes,' he said, and savoured the look of shock on her face. It mutated into what he thought was just a sulk, but then he realised it was sadness, a resignation that he was accustomed to seeing on less attractive faces. He took her arm, recognising that he could only get his way through bullying, and he wasn't that kind of man. 'You win,' he said, and saw her spirits lift tentatively. 'God knows what it will be like. And it's your job to tell Winograd we got a better invitation.'

Mid-terms came and mid-terms went, and Nessheim was fairly confident he had done well. He was not an ascetic, and didn't like studying more than the next man, but he figured that even if he bailed out of law school halfway through he would like to feel he had done himself justice. And if it turned out he liked the law after all, then doing well would be the best way to set him up for work he enjoyed.

With Stacey it was hard to tell, for though she worked pretty diligently there was a lot to make up – whatever the easiness of her courses. He just hoped she would get through; he realised, as barely an evening went by that they were not together, that he couldn't bear it if she flunked out – and went away again.

At the Met Lab work was under way in earnest, with two twelve-hour shifts that left Zinn and Anderson respectively in charge, looking exhausted. Fermi, by contrast, seemed even more energetic than usual, and tried to encourage his colleagues, saying, 'It won't be long now,' again and again.

There were three more loads of graphite, and each time Nessheim had gone over to guide the trucks through. Timber also arrived in quantity, and soon Zinn transferred the planing and cutting of the boards to the second racquets court, since the graphite had made the locker room start to resemble a car mechanic's workshop, clogging Knuth's saws and making the floor oily and dangerously slick.

Security had been radically tightened within forty-eight hours of Nessheim's call to Groves. Now, in addition to the sleepy military policeman sitting at a table, there were also two standing soldiers at each entrance, carrying M-1 rifles. Stricter identification protocols were now in force as well, and Nessheim himself had to be photographed in Eckhart Hall and given an ID card. He persuaded Fermi to change the locks on both the racquets courts and the locker room, and though the same people received keys, it reassured him that no others could be floating around.

The 'Pile' itself was growing with each day, though it was still low enough to be added to without ladders or scaffolding. Fermi was present every afternoon to supervise the insertion of cadmium rods into cored-out graphite blocks, and to decide their placement – usually in consultation with Zinn and Anderson. They worked their long hours uncomplainingly, and Zinn was an excellent taskmaster with the Irish stockyard kids when they were needed to move the graphite.

Nessheim gave Kalvin a wide berth, waiting for Guttman to come back with news of the agent the Pole had met with in the Museum of Science and Industry. Kalvin was rarely at Stagg Field in any case, and they only encountered each other occasionally in the hallways of Eckhart Hall. The scientist seemed to reciprocate Nessheim's mild aversion, which made it easier for Nessheim to avoid him.

All in all, the work proceeded with a quiet but professional urgency. There were no setbacks Nessheim was aware of, only the tension of knowing that the work was of critical importance, needed to succeed, and needed to succeed as quickly as possible. If anyone found it possible to be calm in such circumstances, it was Nessheim, who thought the likelihood of a German spy at the Met Lab to be increasingly improbable. His thoughts, unprofessional as he knew this to be, lay mainly elsewhere: he found himself looking forward to the end of each working day, and his return to Kimbark Avenue and Stacey.

11

ON THE NIGHT of the Fermis' party, Stacey took over the bedroom, with her clothes spread out on the bed, three pairs of shoes in the middle of the room and the top of the dresser covered with vials and tins and jars of creams and lotions and powders. Nessheim sat in the living room, reading the *Tribune* while she moved around in the bedroom, alternately cursing and singing. She came out at one point, barefoot in a sheer pearl slip, holding a hairbrush in her hand. Standing in the doorway she asked, 'Do you know most of the people who will be there tonight?'

'Not really. But could you do me a favour – and a second one by not asking me why I'm asking?'

'Maybe.'

'Don't say I'm at the law school with you.'

'Why?'

'That's my second favour – remember?'

'What is this Met Lab anyway?'

'Metallurgical Laboratory. Fermi runs it, and the others work there.' He said this as if it should have been obvious.

'But Laura Fermi told me her husband was a physicist. He won the Nobel Prize.'

'He did,' said Nessheim, trying to shut down the conversation.

'That's not metallurgy.'

'Metallurgy mixes chemistry and physics.' He was pretty sure this wasn't true.

'So is it to do with the war effort?'

'Isn't everything?'

This seemed to work, until Stacey suddenly said, 'Okay, but what's it got to do with *you*?'

'If I answer your question will you leave it alone?'

'Of course.' Her eyes lit up.

'Promise?'

This only made her more eager. 'Cross my heart and hope to die.'

'It's got nothing to do with me.'

And he returned to his book, ignoring the look of frustration spreading across her face. She stomped off to the bedroom, while Nessheim struggled not to laugh.

Eventually he went into the bedroom to change. Stacey was standing, still in her slip and stockings, staring down at the bed where two outfits lay spread out.

'Are you sure you want to go to this?' he said.

'What, you think I'd rather go to Winograd's instead? Now be a good boy and tell me which one to wear.'

He stared at the bed. The choice was between a green moiré dress tied with a bow at the waist, or a simple grey wool number that would show off her figure. 'Go grey,' he said.

'You sure?'

'I'm sure. It will be a lot more fun to take off later on.'

'Don't count your chickens, buddy.'

She pulled on the grey dress, which lived up to expectations. While she went to the bathroom to fix her make-up and hair, Nessheim started to change. He was in boxer shorts and a T-shirt when Stacey came back.

She said, 'Nessheim, I've been meaning to ask you, what are you going to do? I mean, after law school.'

'I do not know.' And he didn't.

'It's not like you to withdraw.'

'I told you – I tried enlisting but it didn't take.

What should I do instead – sit in Washington helping buff J. Edgar Hoover's reputation? How's that going to help the war effort?'

'I know you've seen some bad things,' she said, pursuing her own thoughts – she was relentless that way. 'Is that what's got you in the time-out box?'

He shrugged.

'You got hurt, didn't you? That's not an appendix scar on your side.'

He fingered the long scar reflexively. It had hardened gradually, and no longer gave under his touch. 'I'm fine now.'

'What about the other guy? Did he get hurt?'

He nodded.

'Permanently?'

'Yep,' he said, then threw his hand out dismissively. 'Can we stop the interrogation now?'

She went out again and he put on a blue Brooks Brothers shirt and picked out a grey suit which, like all his suits, was one size too big in the jacket to leave room for his gun. He reached into the closet behind his other suits and brought out the holstered .38, hooked it carefully over his left shoulder, then put on his jacket and buttoned it just as Stacey came back into the room. 'Even tonight?' she said.

'How's that?'

'Well, either that's a gun in your armpit or you're getting overexcited.'

He laughed despite himself. Stacey said, 'I didn't know metallurgists were dangerous.'

'It's a regulation. I have no choice.'

'A regulation for *life*? You keep saying you resigned.'

He sighed; she was penetratingly persistent. 'I don't suppose if I asked you to leave it alone, you would?'

'That's about the third "leave it alone" in a half an

hour, Nessheim. Comes a point when a girl wants in on *something*.'

'I would if I could,' he said, and kissed her hard enough that she couldn't reply.

The Fermis were living on Woodlawn Avenue between 55th and 56th. Two doors down, a fraternity occupied a double-sized mansion, and a banner above the front door proclaimed Open House for new pledges. Despite the November cold, a bunch of guys stood out on the large porch, warmed by big mugs of beer they carried in their hands. They hooted amiably as Nessheim and Stacey went past, and Nessheim waved like a fellow player of frat games.

'What do they want?' asked Stacey, taking his arm.

'Beats me. Even with your coat on you seem to attract masculine attention.'

'I hope so,' she said freely. 'I suppose you were in a fraternity at Northwestern.'

'Not on your life.' He could have been; half the football team had been Dekes, but he hadn't wanted to join. He figured that you could be a football player, affable, a regular guy, yet still want to preserve something of yourself that fraternities were designed to crush. He was no maverick, but he was not a natural joiner either.

The Fermi place was a tall three-storey red-brick house squeezed into the row, which Stacey said the Fermis were renting from a businessman who'd gone to Washington for war work. Nessheim wasn't sure what to expect – a decorous affair, most likely, stiff and European, with little booze or none, high-flown conversations and a sense of relief when he and Stacey could leave.

Laura Fermi opened the front door, in a black party dress and with flour on her hands. She smiled shyly at

Nessheim, then beamed when she saw Stacey. They hugged so hard that flour fell like fairy dust from Laura's fingers. She introduced them to her two children, who were already dressed in their pyjamas and shook hands with a grave European formality. 'Off to bed now,' said Laura with false sternness. She showed Nessheim where to put their coats in the front closet, and Stacey went with her towards the kitchen, over Laura's protestations.

The living room was large and square with a high ceiling, and the furniture had been pushed back to the perimeter to let people stand freely in the middle of the room. At the far end Fermi was presiding over a long table that held empty glasses, bottles of ginger ale, some cartons of apple juice and a couple of soda siphons. He was talking to the other guests – Nessheim recognised Szilard, and next to him Kalvin and Knuth, the work-shop man.

As he joined them Fermi said, 'Maybe you can help.'

Kalvin said, 'Does your expertise extend to the making of punch?'

'I'd say I had experience more than expertise. What have you got there?'

In the punch bowl there was a large block of ice but no liquid. Fermi reached under the table and brought up two bottles of gin. 'Is this enough?' he asked doubtfully.

'Should be to start,' said Nessheim. 'Unless you want people carried out of here on stretchers.'

Fermi laughed. 'But what shall I mix it with?'

Nessheim surveyed the table. 'Not ginger ale,' he said. 'I'd put soda water in to make it fizzy. But you want some flavour too.' He picked up a small bottle of grena-dine. 'This will do – it will sweeten it and make it look pretty.'

'Could I beg you to do the mixing for me?'

'Why not?' He began making the punch while Fermi looked on as if this were a novel experiment. Szilard and Kalvin drew closer. They looked like a comedy duo: Kalvin tall and balding; Szilard short and stocky, with a face like a frog, and hair brushed back above a high forehead.

Szilard said amiably, 'May I ask where you acquired this set of skills, Mr Nessheim?'

Kalvin said, 'I believe he means, where were you educated?'

'Northwestern. It's the other university in town.'

'Is it good?' asked Szilard.

'I think most would say it's the Second City's second college. Academically, at least. But a powerhouse when it comes to parties.'

Fermi laughed. 'His degree is not in parties, I assure you.'

'I assume you are an engineer,' Kalvin said. 'Civil or structural?'

'Civil,' said Nessheim. 'My particular interest is in bridges.'

'Any particular kind of bridge?' asked Kalvin.

'Cable-span bridges.' This seemed to satisfy Kalvin, and Nessheim thanked God for his old room-mate Reissmuller, an engineering student who talked bridges non-stop, sometimes even in his sleep.

More people had come by now, and Laura Fermi came out of the kitchen with her apron still on, followed by Stacey. They were carrying trays of sandwiches, and moved around the room, offering them to the guests. Reaching Nessheim, Stacey declared, 'Eat up, pal.'

Szilard inspected the offerings. 'Egg?' he asked.

'*Si*,' said Stacey with a smile.

Szilard took one. Kalvin was staring at Stacey, then realised she was waiting for him so he took a sandwich as well. When Laura moved on, Kalvin said, 'Is that the Fermis' maid?'

Szilard shrugged to show he didn't know.

'I don't think so,' said Nessheim.

'If I were Mrs Fermi I don't think I should like to have her in the house,' said Kalvin. Szilard laughed, and Nessheim tried to laugh as well.

The room was filling up, and Nessheim found himself separated from Kalvin and Szilard, and next to the drinks table where Fermi was conferring with his wife and Stacey. He turned to Nessheim. 'We think we should have some music. I know Americans like to dance.'

'That would be nice,' said Nessheim.

Laura Fermi said, 'There is a problem. Enrico has bought a new record player. Excellent in every way.'

'But . . . ?'

'We have no records. They are in boxes back in New York.'

Fermi gave a sad smile. 'I blame my wife, she blames me. Either way, we have no music to play.'

'That's all right,' said Stacey. 'We can listen to the radio. There's lots of music on a Saturday night.'

Laura Fermi looked downcast. 'We have no radio now. They took it away – just yesterday.'

'What do you mean? Who took it away?'

'The authorities.' She didn't look at Nessheim. 'It was a Capehart and had shortwave, and they said we couldn't be trusted not to listen to broadcasts from overseas.'

'Like where?' Stacey was incredulous.

'Italy. Germany. I suppose almost anywhere in Europe.'

'But that's moronic. I can listen to the same things.'

'Ah, but you are not a registered alien.' She sounded almost apologetic; there was none of her husband's asperity in her voice, just the resigned sound of someone being bullied who knew there was nothing they could do about it.

Stacey looked at Nessheim and he could see she was furious. He wanted to say it had nothing to do with him, but then he had a thought. 'Hang on two secs. I don't live far away – only a block and a half. I've got lots of records. Let me go get them.'

Laura Fermi said, 'No, it is too much trouble –'

'Hurry up,' Stacey said, cutting in. 'It's the least you can do.'

So he went outside, passing half a dozen new guests to the party, including the Canadian physicist Zinn, who had cleaned up any graphite traces from his hands and wore a spiffy blue double-breasted suit. His wife had also come, as well as several younger women with bright lipsticked mouths, excited to see the home of their husbands' fabled boss.

Outside it was starting to spit with rain, and the frat-house boys had all gone inside. Nessheim hurried up to 56th Street and went east a block. As he entered the courtyard of his apartment block on Kimbark he looked ahead to his living-room window at the far end, where he always left the table lamp on by the sofa – just enough to suggest someone was home without celebrating the fact. Lately he had been vigilant about this.

His apartment windows were completely dark.

Maybe the light bulb blew, he thought, but it sounded weak even to the hopeful side of his nature.

He stopped halfway down the courtyard by a side entrance to the wing that formed one side of the court-yard's U, watching his windows. They remained black, lifeless. He tried to think what he should do – move forward naturally, and maybe get a bullet in the head? Go back to the alley and come in through the kitchen?

158

Thank God he'd paid no attention to Stacey – at least he had his gun.

In the event he concocted a compromise. He took his felt fedora off, thinking that if he'd been watched earlier, this might now disguise him. He moved silently across the back half of the courtyard to his entrance, and gently opened the ground-floor door. Once inside the tiny atrium he pressed the little black button, no bigger than a courtesan's mole, for his apartment. This would tell anyone inside his place that it was a stranger calling, looking for Nessheim. Then he pushed the buzzer of the apartment two floors above, that of the Communist philosophy professor who had previously rented Nessheim's apartment before moving upstairs. As he'd hoped, the door clicked and gave way against his pressing hand.

He moved through the ground-floor hallway, past the janitor's door, and went quickly but quietly up the stairs two at a time. On the landing he stopped. In the thin glow of the hallway light his door looked undisturbed. Above him he heard the Professor's door open, and a thin voice called out, 'Who's there?'

He went up another half-landing and said, in a low quiet voice, 'Sorry, I pressed the wrong buzzer. I'm seeing my friend down here.'

The Professor did not reply, but Nessheim heard him go back into his apartment. He came back down again and stood close to his own door, listening. He couldn't hear a thing from inside, just the muddled sounds of movement in the other apartments, the clank of a radiator taking a break, the high pitch of water being run through the pipes.

He took his keys out of his pocket and put them in his left hand, while his right extracted his pistol from the holster inside his jacket. He got the key into the lock with his left hand and slowly turned it, simultaneously pushing the door with his right foot. The door swung open, creaking like the effects in a hokey ghost story. He stayed back for a moment, trying to adjust his eyes to the dark interior of his apartment, knowing that if he stepped forward he would be framed by the light of the hallway.

He finally stepped forward, keeping the swung-open door between himself and the hallway leading to the back of the apartment. He pointed his weapon towards the living room in front, then in one quick movement hit the light switch, ready to fire.

In the light he saw there was no one in the living room, and the door to his bedroom was closed. Had he left it that way? He started to step forward, just beyond the edge of the open door, then hesitated. As he did, he heard a *phhttt* and something thudded ahead of him. He saw a splinter fly from the bedroom door.

He stepped back quickly into the hallway, breathing hard. Someone was in the dining room to his left. Could there be a second guy in his place? Not likely; the fellow in the dining room wouldn't have pulled the trigger if his associate was in the bedroom and right in his line of fire. Nessheim reached in again and switched off the hall light, then got down on his hands and knees and crawled into the hallway of his apartment, turning with his gun pointed at what he approximated was his dining-room table.

What now? He didn't want to crawl down the corridor, waiting until he was spotted and shot like a sitting duck. But it was too late to retreat, go downstairs and outside, and run round the whole apartment complex to the alley at the back.

Then he heard noise from the kitchen, the swing of the screen door, and the loud bang of the outer door as it swung shut. He stood up and ran down the hall, banging a dining-room chair that had been pulled out from the table, and swerving into his small kitchen. He flicked the light on and ducked in case anyone still stood on the outside landing. Getting his bearings, he turned the light off and opened both the screen and the outer back door, then moved out on to the porch, his gun level in one hand, the other ready to swing like a club at close quarters.

There was no one on the porch; instead he heard running down the alleyway towards the street at the back. Nessheim half-ran, half-jumped down the stairs and ran at full speed along the alley. He had once been timed in eleven seconds for the hundred-yard dash, and he was running as hard as he could now; not even eight years in the Bureau had slowed him down much. He was confident he would catch the intruder – if he didn't get shot in the process. He heard the gate swing at the back entrance to the alley that ran parallel to Kimbark Avenue, but he didn't hear it close – instead there were running steps on the bricks of the alleyway and another rumbling sound. A car.

He hit the gate with his hand, stiff-arming it open as if hitting a safety while running for a football field's end zone. He saw a running figure to his left, maybe fifty feet away, and a waiting car, the passenger door open. The figure jumped in and the car shot off, its door staying open for a second or two until the new passenger managed to swing it shut. Nessheim raised his gun as the car accelerated down the alley, swerving to avoid the unrepaired potholes. In the light of the one street lamp, fifty yards away, he could just make out the model. It was a dark Plymouth with no licence plate on the back – though even had there been one he would not have been able to make out the numbers.

He lowered the gun. He had had no adequate reason to shoot – what if he killed the driver? Or the passenger who had fled his apartment? You could kill an intruder you caught in your home with impunity, but you weren't entitled to shoot him after you'd chased him for a hundred yards outside. Even if you were a sort of FBI agent.

He stood watching as the car reached 55th Street and went right. Towards the Lake and the Drive, Nessheim noted, which suggested both that they knew the quickest way out of Hyde Park and that they weren't from the neighbourhood. It wasn't much to go on, he thought grimly. And when a woman in a long coat turned into the alley at the far end, walking a small dog, he headed back towards his apartment.

He wondered how they had got in. The windows were all closed – he'd made sure of that when he and Stacey had left for the party. The front door lock had been untouched and was in good order. When he walked up the back stairs now, he examined the kitchen door; it was okay, too, though since the burglar had left it wide open as he escaped there was no way of knowing if he'd come in that way. Contrary to popular perception, picking a lock usually damaged it noticeably but the back lock was okay; it could have been picked but no one had smashed it out and pushed their way in.

He reached up and checked the hidden crevice on the back of the stairs; the key was still there. That surprised him; when he'd told Stacey where to find it, he had assumed she would keep it with her.

Inside he went through the apartment room by room, having first locked the kitchen door. Nothing seemed to be missing, and his three-drawer filing cabinet in a corner of the dining room was locked and untampered with. He heaved the cabinet out away from the wall and found that its tiny key was still taped behind the middle drawer.

He checked himself in the mirror on the back of the bathroom door and saw that he'd somehow ripped his suit trousers at the right knee. There was no disguising it; sighing, he went and changed into a dark blue suit. He knew he should be getting back; any longer and Stacey would want to know what had happened to him. And the others would want their records. He went to the record player and opened the little door to the standing cupboard it sat on. He'd been only an occasional and pretty indiscriminate buyer of records, happy for the most part to listen to music on the radio. There were maybe thirty 78s standing upright and he picked through them quickly. He took some big-band albums in case people wanted to dance, and a few singers: Billie Holiday, Louis Armstrong, a new one by the Tommy Dorsey Orchestra with Frank Sinatra. He put them in a paper grocery bag and tucked it under one arm. This time he left a light on in the kitchen as well as the living room, but he didn't believe the intruders would be back. He'd surprised the guy, he was sure; he'd been looking for something and it hadn't been Nessheim.

At Fermi's he found the party in full swing, if music-less. There was no sign of Stacey, but then she emerged from the kitchen, where she must still have been helping Laura Fermi, and came over right away.

'You've been gone a long time.'

'Sorry,' he offered. 'I thought I'd dropped my key. Have you still got yours?' he asked casually.

'No. I put it back under the stairs. I thought that's what you wanted. But why have you changed clothes?'

'I was kind of hot in the other suit,' he said.

She stared at him. He could see she'd had some punch: her eyes looked especially alive, the pupils sharp and reflective as mirrors. 'Are you okay?'

'I'm fine. Have you met some of the people here?'

'Every single one. Laura's a dutiful hostess. You going to dance with me?'

'Maybe later,' he said, just as Laura Fermi approached, lifting her hands with delight when she saw his bag of records.

A minute later Tommy Dorsey's Orchestra was playing and almost everyone was dancing, with people spilling out into the front hall and the kitchen. Fermi brought out two more bottles of gin which Nessheim mixed with the dwindling soda supply, adding more grenadine to temper the harshness of the raw spirit.

He was standing by himself in a corner, when he was joined by the enormous bearded man called Nadelhoffer. He wore a tweed jacket with patches at the elbows, and had a thin wool sweater underneath and an open-necked shirt. He didn't look much older than Nessheim, but he had three inches on him and must have weighed 250 pounds. In his hand, the cup of punch looked like a shot glass. He eyed Nessheim grimly. 'You like parties?' he said gruffly.

'Sure. This is a good one.' He was struck by how little it resembled his preconceptions.

'They're not for me. You know, I recognise your name.'

'Really?'

'I grew up in Wisconsin, just outside Waupaca.'

'Is that so?' said Nessheim, though he knew this from the dossier. 'I'm from just outside Bremen myself.'

164

'I thought so. If you're the same James Nessheim, you used to make the papers.'

'I am, if it was about football. You played ball yourself, I take it.'

Nadelhoffer shrugged. 'It was unavoidable when I was growing up. The excitements of a small town.'

A dry sense of humour, but with a melancholic undertone. Nessheim said cheerfully, 'I know what you mean. Eating the big dinner is the main event.' Nadelhoffer didn't seem to get the allusion, and Nessheim realised most physicists probably didn't read Hemingway.

Fortunately, Kalvin and Fermi joined them now. Fermi pointed to the middle of the room. 'Miss Madison is an excellent dancer.'

Nessheim turned and saw Stacey jitterbugging with one of the young physicists; the other dancers had moved to give them space.

'That is a remarkable young woman,' said Kalvin. 'I was talking to her and it turns out she speaks very good Spanish. Do all maids in America speak Spanish?'

It was hard to tell if Kalvin was joking; Fermi looked baffled by the reference to a maid. Nessheim said, 'She's been to Mexico.'

Kalvin stiffened almost imperceptibly, then relaxed. 'That would explain the accent, I suppose.'

Zinn came up and put a friendly arm around Nessheim's shoulder. 'Thank God you showed up at the Met Lab, buddy.'

Fermi laughed and looked at Nessheim. 'I told you Mr Zinn did not enjoy the transporting of graphite.'

Zinn raised his glass. 'Here's to Nessheim. My replacement in the Labours of Hercules.'

Kalvin said sardonically, 'Don't worry, Walter. You are irreplaceable.'

165

'Everyone can be replaced,' said Fermi firmly. 'Everyone. Though I am reluctant to say this, that includes me!' They all laughed.

Zinn said, 'You've done a terrific job getting the people you want, Professor. What's your secret? No one ever turns you down.'

'That is true, but it is not to do with me. Once they understand the importance of the work they all want to come. They realise that they will be present at the birth of a new kind of creation.'

'God help them,' Nadelhoffer intoned and Nessheim saw that he was serious. His beard, dark and Lincolnesque, gave an Old Testament gravity to the pronouncement.

Fermi looked embarrassed by the intervention, and Zinn tried to lighten things: 'Go on, Professor. Has anybody turned you down?'

Fermi thought for a moment. 'In fact, no. We did have one person who did not come after all. But that was different. He had an accident.'

'A bad one?' asked Nessheim.

'The worst,' Nadelhoffer interjected. 'A fatality.'

Dourness again hovered over their talk. Fermi looked keen to go and see to his other guests, while Zinn's wife was gesturing for him to join her. Nessheim spoke up quickly. 'Who had the accident, Professor?'

Fermi frowned and shook his head unhappily. His eyes had turned into dark pools of sadness. 'You would not have heard of him, but he helped to bring me to America. I owe him a lot. And I am told he did remarkable work when he was much younger. His name was Perkins. Professor Arthur Perkins.'

12

WHEN THEY FINALLY left the party, just short of midnight, Stacey clutched Nessheim's arm as much for support as from affection. He had stuck to apple juice, for he had wanted to stay alert even if the horse had already fled the barn, but Stacey had made up for his shortfall. The wind had died, and as they walked the block over to Nessheim's apartment, Stacey yapped away as he guided her home.

'What's the pencil factory?' she asked. 'I met some man tonight who said he was its foreman.'

It must have been Zinn, making a joke about graphite; he liked to say they could go into the pencil business with the graphite offcuts from their work. 'I'm not sure who you mean,' said Nessheim.

'And who was that morose giant of a man?'

'You mean Nadelhoffer? He works with Professor Fermi.'

'What's eating him? You'd have thought the war was over – and we'd lost twice.'

'He gets weighed down by things, I guess.'

'I would too.'

'What do you mean?'

'Don't play me for a mug, Nessheim. Anyone could tell these guys are doing hush-hush work.' Stacey exhaled with exasperation. 'I bet those guys tell their wives what they're up to,' she said. He knew she was trying to taunt him into indiscretion. 'Especially Nadelhoffer.'

'He's not married, Stacey. And I doubt Professor Fermi tells his wife a thing.'

'I wouldn't count on that. And I bet the others do.'

'Maybe,' he said neutrally, hoping she would leave it alone.

'I mean, if you and I were married, you'd tell me.'

It was an odd thing to say. He looked at her strangely; she seemed unperturbed. At last he said, 'We're not married.'

Stacey squared her shoulders and said 'Humph' in a curiously old-fashioned way. Then she recovered, saying, 'Don't look so scared, Agent Nessheim.'

When they reached the courtyard on Kimbark Avenue, he was relieved to see the light still on in his living room. Inside the atrium he opened the outer door, and they went up into the apartment. He entered first, but though there was a faint whiff of cordite inside, and the splintering on the bedroom door, Stacey had hit the punch hard enough not to notice, and everything else was as he'd left it. When he came out of the bathroom dressed only in his boxer shorts, he found her under the covers, naked, alluring, and out for the count.

He didn't feel sleepy, so he went to the kitchen and poured himself a small Scotch, then sat in the dining room so as not to disturb Stacey. He realised he hadn't been back to her apartment again since their first night together.

What did this mean? Was there a chance of a life with her? he wondered. It would certainly be eventful: there would always be the equivalent of a Spanish-looking guy at the end of the bar, eyeing her up. That wasn't the problem: Trudy, his first girlfriend back in Wisconsin, had been a pretty girl who drew more than her share of admiring stares. But unlike Trudy, Stacey would stare back, or smile, or flirt. Sometimes all three.

He supposed he could deal with that, or at least try to get used to it. Maybe if she got married and had kids she would lose some of that 'look at me' business.

Wasn't that true of most women? They had kids, and suddenly instead of worrying about themselves, they found a new world to worry about. But it was hard to see Stacey Madison ever settling down. She was the kind of woman who drank life dry, moving from waterhole to waterhole (man to man, bar to bar, party to party), never sated, never full, never happy with the same source of the energising fuel she lived on.

When he went into the bedroom, the bedside lamp was on. Stacey stirred and then sat up drowsily. She said, 'Hand me a smoke, will you? I've lost my lighter. There're matches in the wooden box.'

He found the box and opened the lid. Inside he didn't find matches, but instead a bracelet, a small necklace, and a ring. His eyes fixed on the ring, and he slowly brought it out of the box. It was gold, simple, unadorned; it could only be for one thing. He sighed involuntarily.

'What's the matter?' Her voice came from the bed, alert now.

'Nothing,' he said. But he had to know. 'What's this?'

He could see her sit up to peer at him – she was short-sighted but too vain to wear glasses.

He brought the ring over to the bed. Without a word he held it about a foot from her eyes.

'Ah, I brought the wrong box. Damn.' She sounded unruffled. She added, 'That's my wedding ring. Pretty, isn't it?'

'When did that happen?' he asked, trying to keep the anger he felt out of his voice.

'Are you going all puritan on me, Nessheim? Don't tell me you haven't slept with a married woman before.'

'I'm not telling you anything,' he said.

'Mr Pious, is that it?' Her scorn seemed affected.

'No. Mr Careful if the husband has a gun.' He was

trying to show he didn't care, but he couldn't carry it off.

Stacey must have wanted the same thing, for she tried to laugh. She reached her hand out for his, but he ignored it. She said, 'Cat got your tongue? You've done it before. Why's this so different?'

'Because –' he said, then stopped, too shook up inside to speak. He wanted to tell her it was different because he loved her and didn't want her married to another man. But it was not a confession he could bring himself to make. He'd done that once with her and been burnt. Never again. So he said only, 'You might have told me.'

'Why? Does it matter?'

'Of course it matters. It makes me feel . . . feel like . . .'

'A gigolo?' Stacey laughed out loud to his fury. 'You're many things, Nessheim, most of them good, but you're not a gigolo.'

He didn't join her laughter. 'So what about this husband of yours?'

'Do you really want to know?'

'Not really.'

'I'll tell you anyway. He's in Reno as we speak. In two weeks – actually fifteen days and yes, I'm counting – we'll be divorced. Satisfied?'

'Sure.' He wanted desperately to believe her.

'I'll tell you all about him. His name is George Tweedy. Not a name to be reckoned with if you ask me. He's –'

'I don't want to know,' he said angrily.

'Okay,' she said mildly. 'Everybody's got a past, Nessheim. Even you. Now get me that smoke, will you?'

He did and soon Stacey was snoring gently, while he lay there, willing himself to sleep as well. But he was too much on edge, after the break-in earlier and after this new revelation. Did he believe Stacey about her impending divorce? He didn't really know. Did it matter? He didn't know that either.

He thought back to the evening. How had the intruder got in? Stacey had borrowed the only other key, but for some reason she had put it back. It was conceivable that the intruder had found it, though very unlikely. But say he had found it – why had he put it back before he was done inside?

The only conclusion was no conclusion. If there were others, Nessheim couldn't see them. Or didn't want to.

Part Four

Part Four

13

'This is a buffer. They've saved a lot of lives.'

But not the one Guttman was interested in. He tried to look appreciative as the man named Mullen from Otis Elevators pointed to an oil barrel at the bottom of the elevator shaft.

Next to Mullen stood the building superintendent, Schuster, who was anxious and ingratiating. The police would have been here after the accident, maybe half a dozen times, and it was a wonder Schuster had kept his job. He had greeted the phoned news of Guttman's visit as if it were a call from the dead.

They were standing in the basement of 185 Riverside, on the outer edge of Manhattan's West Side at 91st Street. After taking the train very early that morning from D.C., Guttman had come up on the Seventh Avenue Line from Penn Station.

Now Mullen said, 'Go on,' as though he was teaching a reluctant kid to drive. 'Step in and have a look for yourself.'

Guttman did so gingerly, ducking under the little door's lintel, emerging at the bottom of the shaft where he craned his neck and stared up nervously. At the very top of the shaft there was a skylight, and tinsel trails of light drifted down on either side of the elevator car, which he could just make out many floors above. Though the professional part of Guttman overcame the apprehensive, he was still scared that at any minute the elevator might come plummeting down.

He cursed Nessheim for getting him into this. They had got nowhere looking for the mysterious man Kalvin

175

had met at the museum, and in the absence of any other leads, Guttman had felt obliged to do something when a new name surfaced. Once Guttman learned more about Arthur Perkins, RIP, it had seemed worth a trip just to make sure his death had been the freak accident the local New York police said it was.

Guttman pointed to a bunch of thick looped wires that were dangling from the shaft above. 'What are those?' he asked.

'The compensating cables,' Mullen said confidently, stepping through the door to join him in the bottom of the shaft. 'There are a dozen of them above the car – each one's strong enough to support the elevator on its own in case the others break.'

'What happens if *all* of them break?'

'Slats come out from the side, hook on to the guide rails and stop the car from descending further. If for some reason that doesn't work, we've got the buffer down here to cushion the impact.' Mullen added with a touch of pride, 'The only time that's happened, the occupant of the elevator survived.'

Guttman stepped back through the opening, relieved to be out from beneath the elevator. The basement corridor seemed a safe if unattractive haven; the walls had been painted a dingy vanilla. What a contrast to the opulent lobby upstairs, with its marble-tiled floor, gold rococo sconces, and a pair of six-foot deco mirrors that gave a magnified sense of space. Even the elevator, which Guttman had travelled in briefly and apprehensively because of its history, was luxuriously panelled in cherry wood; the plum-sized buttons for each floor were padded in gold plush. Riverside Drive wasn't Fifth Avenue, and the tenants here were affluent rather than rich, but these buildings had been created to attract the *crème* of Manhattan's West Side, and in that they had succeeded.

'But not this time,' said Guttman. He pointed to the shaft.

'How's that?' asked Mullen.

'The cables didn't work, did they?' Guttman asked impatiently. He could visualise the elevator car falling, splintering on impact when it landed. What did people say? If you timed it right, and jumped into the air just as the elevator landed, you could survive.

He was contemplating this when Mullen said abruptly, 'That's not what happened here. There was nothing wrong with the elevator car.'

'What do you mean?' Guttman was alert now.

'The elevator car didn't fall. The victim did.' And when Guttman looked puzzled, Mullen explained. Professor Arthur Perkins had left his apartment on the eleventh floor just before nine o'clock in the morning – like he always did. He pushed the elevator button on his floor. And when the doors to the elevator opened, Perkins stepped forward to get in. Only the actual elevator compartment was on the twelfth floor, which meant that he stepped into space.

'I didn't know that,' said Guttman. He felt sickened. Forget timing your jump; this would be a descent filled with desperation and panic. What a horrible way to die. Guttman tried to imagine what Arthur Perkins had been thinking as he fell, imagining the feelings of terror as the man realized nothing was going to break his fall. Perkins would have fallen eleven storeys to ... right where Guttman had just been standing.

Surprised to learn how Arthur Perkins had died, Guttman grew angry, partly because he was struggling with his own fear. He said, 'How did it happen? I don't want to hear how the Otis Elevator Company takes precautions against everything from power cuts to acts of God. Something went wrong.' Then he turned to the super. 'And

177

don't tell me you were too busy moving the Festerwalds'
refrigerator or squashing cockroaches in Mrs Du Vivier's
bathroom. I want to know why the elevator stopped on
twelve, but the doors opened on eleven.'

'I don't know,' the two men said, almost in unison.

Guttman turned to the super. 'Is there an elevator
man for the building?'

Schuster shook his head. 'The doorman doubles as
the elevator man.'

'And that morning?'

'The doorman was off sick.'

How convenient, thought Guttman. 'I'll want to talk
to him.'

Schuster said, 'He's called Stokes. I fired him ten days
after the accident.'

'You got his address?'

'I have his old one. Right now he's of "no known
abode". Your best bet would be the Bowery.'

'A boozer?'

'And then some. You might as well know, he's my
wife's cousin and yes, that's why I hired him. Do I regret
it. He was off sick more than he was on.'

'So that day, who ran the elevator for the residents?'

'Nobody. It's automatic anyway – the doorman runs
it as a kind of courtesy. I was doorman, but still
super too.'

'And you were too busy fixing the Festerwald's icebox
to work the elevator.'

'Actually, I was finding a cab for Mrs Monroe.'

Guttman thought for a minute, then said abruptly,
'Okay, you can go now.'

Schuster seemed surprised. 'Really? That's it?'

'Yeah. Unless you've got something else to say?'

'No, no. It's just that the cops talked to me for hours
last year.'

'I'm sure they did. So no sense duplicating the process.'

The super left and the Otis man, Mullen, started to follow him. 'Not so fast,' said Guttman.

'Yeah?' said the man warily.

Guttman softened his voice. 'Can you give me any idea how this happened? I'm not holding you to it – I just want your best bet.'

Mullen seemed to take this as a challenge. 'Well,' he said, and Guttman could see he was in his element now. What followed probably lasted only a couple of minutes, but Guttman felt as though he was trapped with the club bore on a long trip in a small car. *Flyweights, ratchets, sheaves,* a mysterious *governor, hoistway doors* and *car doors* and of course the *hoistway door interlock* followed by the *hoistway door keyhole.* The terms were spat out without explanation until finally Mullen paused for breath.

Guttman said quietly, 'Can you tell me what all that means?'

Mullen looked deflated. 'It means I can't figure out how this could have happened. It's a mystery to me.'

'You absolutely sure of that? I'm not asking you as the representative of your company. I'm asking you as a man who understands, talking to a man who doesn't.'

The Otis man nodded. 'I'm positive. The last service was only two days before the accident. The check list was complete. All A-Okay.'

'Then I have another question for you.'

Mullen looked intrigued. 'Yeah?'

'If you wanted this to happen, how would you go about it?'

Mullen looked alarmed. 'You mean *cause* the accident?'

'Yeah.'

'You're suggesting –?'

'I'm not suggesting anything – it's strictly hypothetical. But try and tell me how you'd do it.'

And this time, though the vocabulary remained alien and technical, Guttman could make out the gist of what was being said. It would have required two men, and would have needed two different days. The first day was almost certainly that of the service; it was then that the controller had been rejigged so that it could interpret floor numbers differently from how it should. It wouldn't have been before then, since according to Mullen that would have been detected during the service check. On the day of the accident itself, timing would have been critical. Someone had to gain access to the elevator controller and recalibrate it to read eleven as twelve, then nip downstairs to the eleventh floor and unlock the hoistway door – or else, regardless of the controller, it wouldn't have opened. Though couldn't the man doing the service have done this already? Guttman put it to Mullen.

The Otis man looked horrified. 'Why would he do that?'

Guttman shrugged. 'We're talking hypothetically, remember? Who was the service guy?'

'Bergen. Nice fellow.'

'Still with the firm?'

'Funny you should ask. He was too old to be drafted but he signed up anyway. Wife and kid too. Guess he can't be wild about the wife.'

'You know where he is?'

'Last I heard he was at Fort Sheridan. He sent a postcard to the guys in the repair shop.'

'Okay. But what I wonder is, if you primed the controller at the time of the service, wouldn't that do the trick?'

'No, otherwise you'd have elevators stopping on

wrong floors or not opening at all. You'd have to do it right before you wanted the wrong door to open. Then you'd have to be sure someone pushed the button at eleven. That way, the elevator car would go to twelve but the hoist door would open on the floor below.' He paused, seeming suddenly to appreciate the implications of this. 'What are you driving at? Is Bergen in trouble?'

'Of course not. I'm just working out the possibles. That's what I get paid for.'

'Should I be worried about this?'

'Nah. I get paid to do the worrying too.'

It was raining as Guttman waited for the crosstown bus on 86th Street. He had on the old black raincoat Isabel had made him buy years before, and underneath a brown double-breasted suit and a striped Brooks Brothers tie. Without his wife to supervise him sartorially, he knew he was in danger of becoming entirely slovenly, but he was doing his best – and he'd shaved with special care early that morning, nicking himself only once and tending to that with a styptic pencil instead of sticking toilet paper on the cut.

From the bus stand he could see out to the Hudson, where a navy biplane flew low over the river, then turned hard left towards New Jersey. Two Negro ladies waited with him, done with their morning jobs and heading to the East Side now to work for other masters. They were complaining about the service – how late the buses were and how crowded. 86th Street was in bad shape, full of potholes from the previous winter that had still not been filled. The war was imposing new priorities, and anything without a military benefit was being put on hold.

As if to confirm this, a black Ford came barrelling

by and hit a pothole full of water, soaking a passing man's coat with a black spray of filthy gutter water. As the car kept going, Guttman saw that the pothole had left it with a warped hubcap, turning like a wobbly plate with every revolution of the wheel.

Finally the bus came. Once across Central Park, he got off at Third Avenue, and caught the L train downtown. It was virtually deserted, and half of the cars were the old sort, pressed back into service. As on the bus he found himself about the only passenger under the age of seventy, and one of the few men. New York seemed to have regressed in the war; and the city seemed dull and deadened. What was missing? Young men, away in uniform? Maybe, but that was true in Washington too, where the influx of white-collar workers was two to one women.

As the ageing cars rattled and shook, he thought about the strange death of Arthur Perkins. Guttman didn't share Nessheim's intuitive sense of connections: he was best at *dis*connections, and at sensing when something was wrong. That certainly seemed the case with Arthur Perkins; Guttman had no doubt it hadn't been an accident. But how could you possibly prove it was a homicide after a year had passed? Even if Guttman could, who was he going to tell – and to what end? What link could there be between Perkins's death and Nessheim's search for a German agent in the Met Lab?

He got off at Grand Street, steeling himself for the transition as he moved back into the Lower East Side, the rough world of his childhood, where the superficial civility of uptown gave way like melting ice.

14

GUTTMAN'S MOTHER HAD dozed off within ten minutes
of his arrival, so he told Mrs Warshaw he'd come back,
though they both knew he wouldn't. He gave the woman
a sawbuck, guilt money paid in advance which she took
with insincere thanks. He knew she thought he was a
lousy son, but on the last visit his mother hadn't even
known who he was. That had spared him telling her
that Isabel had died. Not that his mother would have
cared. Isabel had never met her or Guttman's father,
and had been *persona non grata* without even being
seen by either of them. They had punished their son
ostensibly for marrying 'out', but really it was for finding
the kind of love they had never shown him, or each
other.

He went down the two floors from the small apartment which he paid for, and out on to Orchard Street.
On the alley wall someone had painted in harsh letters:
'*HITLER IS A PRICK*', the word '*prick*' resurfacing
in a milky pentimento behind the paint used to scrub
it out. Beneath it someone else had written: '*STALIN
IS OUR HERO*' – though now '*our hero*' had been
effaced, and substituted with '*A PRICK TOO*'.

Guttman laughed. The ins and outs of the political
Left down here were notorious – Trotsky himself had
lived in New York for a time, in the Bronx, and had
used the large neighbourhood library on East Broadway.
Guttman had initially been hired by the Bureau because
it was thought he understood them. He never had;
Isabel had once said he possessed the ideological sophis-
tication of a prune. His mentor hadn't been Marx (or

later on Lenin), but the lowly local cop, an Irishman named Keane, who wouldn't have known the theory of surplus value from a hole in the ground, but had been a towering one-man dispenser of justice, fearless and incorruptible.

At the intersection of Delancey, Guttman looked across the street and noticed a black Ford passing slowly by. It was heading towards the Williamsburg Bridge and its left rear hubcap was wobbling. He stopped, pretending to check his watch, keeping the corner of an eye on the Ford, hoping it was going to Brooklyn. When it turned right instead his heart began to race. He looked at his watch for real; he had ten minutes to shake them – if he was right that it was the same car.

It's your home turf, he told himself; use that advantage. He looked for anyone on foot following him, but saw only old Jewish women, wearing thick coats, heavy woollen stockings and stout dark shoes, out shopping for groceries. And a few stooped old men, taking their midday constitutionals.

Then a pack of small boys approached along the cracked Delancey Street sidewalk. Their leader approached him, bold as brass. He had his hair slicked back like a crooner popular with the ladies, though he barely came up to Guttman's belly. 'Any spare change, mister?'

'Not for you,' Guttman said. 'Why aren't you in school, kid?'

The boy looked affronted. 'We're collecting scrap for the war effort.'

'I bet.'

'What are you anyway, *der Inspector*?'

The school board official from the *Katzenjammer Kids*. Guttman tried not to smile. 'Maybe I am,' he said.

'Never,' the kid said emphatically and hitched up his

pants. He puffed his chest out before declaring, 'Anyway, I graduated.'

The boy couldn't have been more than twelve years old. 'What's your name, Mr Graduate?'

'They call me Doby.'

'All right, Doby, you want to earn two bits for three minutes' work?'

'Maybe,' the kid said. No flies on him.

'I'm going in there,' said Guttman, pointing to the drugstore on the corner. 'While I'm inside I want you to keep watch for a black Ford. Nice car – shiny, but with a funny back wheel. It will have a man in it, maybe two. If you spot it, I want to know. If you don't see it, I want to know that too. Don't make anything up, and don't let them catch you watching. Got it?'

'Yeah.' Doby considered the deal. 'Two bits, huh? How about one of them up front?'

Guttman considered this, then dug into his trouser pocket and came up with a dime. 'This is forty per cent down – consider yourself lucky. And if you run off on me you might discover you haven't graduated after all.'

Guttman went into the drugstore and walked the aisles, pretending to be interested in different brands of tooth powder and packets of safety razor blades and *Mr Comfort's Pills for Piles*, all the while listening as two adolescent-looking sailors on shore leave gathered their collective courage to buy condoms from the pharmacist. Before their transaction was concluded, Guttman went out and found Doby standing on the corner, his little mob waiting eagerly behind him like a passel of Fagan's followers.

'Did you see the car?' Guttman asked.

'Sure did. It's right over there, mister.'

Doby started to turn around and point, but Guttman

185

leaned forward and held his arm. 'Good going,' he said. 'How many people in the car?'

'Two guys.'

'Okay. Don't look at the automobile, and walk the other way. This is for your help.' He fished a crumpled dollar out of his pocket and stuffed it into Doby's little hand, then started walking quickly across Delancey Street. When Doby cried out, 'Gee, thanks, mister,' Guttman didn't look back, but turned his head sideways until he spied the Ford parked further along Delancey, facing against the traffic. A heavyset man in a dark overcoat was standing on the sidewalk next to it. As Guttman continued to cross he saw the man tap once on the window of the car.

So they had a guy on foot as well.

He set off the other way on Delancey Street, pondering his next move. Local knowledge, he told himself again; it had to be worth something. On instinct he turned on to Orchard Street. As a boy he had worked for many of the stores there, making deliveries. He could barely remember a time when he hadn't worked after school, or a time when his father hadn't complained that he hadn't worked enough.

He saw that Loesser had closed down, no surprise since Fine half a block up had always sold a better grade of vegetable. Guttman stopped by the vacant storefront and casually looked back up the street. The heavyset man on foot had stopped to inspect the storefront at Lilenthal's, an act which would have been more plausible had it not been a ladies' underwear store. In the distance beyond, closer to Delancey, the black Ford had moved and then pulled over. There were two guys sitting in the front.

Turning round, he saw Schneiderman's across the street, unchanged from his days there, nestled in the basement behind a plate-glass window with embossed letters: 'Dry Cleaning & Alterations'. Suddenly inspired, Guttman jaywalked and went down the steps to the store. Opening the door, he heard the bell tinkle as it always had, and found a small gaggle of women standing by the counter, jabbering among themselves while Schneiderman and his daughter Esther moved along the racks behind the counter, tickets in hand as they searched for the dry-cleaned garments. Guttman stood by the door for a moment, looking out through the embossed letters on the window.

The heavyset man ambled past on the other side of the street. He didn't even glance Guttman's way. A pro, thought Guttman, as the Ford moved forwards and slid into an empty space about a hundred feet down the street.

Schneiderman came from the rear of the store, holding a man's suit on a hanger. When he saw Guttman his face broke into a big grin. 'Harry!' he exclaimed. The women at the counter turned as one to inspect the newcomer.

He worked his way round them, taking care not to meet anyone's gaze, since at least one would have been a friend of his mother. Lifting the heavy wooden lid at one end of the counter, he stepped into the owner's side of the store.

Shaking hands, Schneiderman slapped Guttman on the shoulder. He was a little man, addicted to bad puns and loud bow ties. He had been the nicest of Guttman's various childhood bosses, always telling him to take his time, defending him once when Mrs Meltzer had complained he'd dropped her overcoat in the mud (he had). For a while he had tried to pair the younger Guttman up with his daughter Esther, but seemed to bear him no malice for declining the offer – Esther had even then been a sour girl, who took after her mother.

Now he called out, 'Esther, look who's here.'

From the far end of the counter, Esther contented herself with a quick wave. She didn't look as though she'd grown any nicer. Schneiderman shrugged, then said jokingly, 'You back to do some deliveries?'

Guttman smiled. 'Actually, Eli, I'm on my way to visit my mother.'

'How is she?'

'Not getting any younger. You know how it is.' Realising the women were listening to the exchange, he leaned forward, wincing as if in pain. 'Can you do me a favour, Eli?'

'What's that?' asked Eli, with a small note of concern.

'Can I use the biffy, please? I got caught short.'

Eli stood back and laughed. 'You know where it is. Not even a world war changes Schneiderman's prime ass-et.'

Guttman smiled weakly in gratitude, then headed towards the back of the building, while Eli went to serve the next customer. Passing the creaking door to the toilet, Guttman opened the store's back door instead. He estimated he had five minutes before the occupants of the Ford and the heavyset guy came looking for him.

Little had changed from the days when he used to sneak a cigarette here in the tiny backyard and hope Esther wouldn't tell on him. The same empty drums of the chemicals used for the dry cleaning, stacked by the back door; the same sodden grass that even in spring didn't seem to grow. And blessedly, the same low fence, separating Schneiderman's from the back of the building behind. That was a tenement in Guttman's time, three small apartments stacked like checkers on top of each other, filled with transient tenants. Unlike Schneiderman's, the building had a thin outside alleyway running from the yard to the street.

Guttman found the weak point of the fence, which years before he had hopped easily enough, as a shortcut for deliveries. Now he found he could step over the fence when he pressed down on its ancient wire, and ten seconds later he was out in front, on Eldridge Street. He turned right and hurried. He wasn't going to run – a telltale in this neighbourhood of a person in trouble – but he didn't hang around.

Five minutes later he was through the door of Katz's, just off Houston, certain that neither the Ford nor the man on foot were on his tail. At the counter he ordered a knish and a cream soda, then took them and went and sat in a booth by himself. A coat rack obscured the view in from the street.

'Sorry I'm late,' said a man sidling into the booth to sit across from him. 'The Second Avenue subway's closed but nobody told me.'

It was Stephenson, whose offices at the British Security Coordination group were in midtown, at 30 Rockefeller Plaza. Guttman hadn't wanted to meet with him there, now that the FBI had opened a liaison office next door. They had been spotted together there once before.

'I just got here myself. I had to take a detour – I'm pretty sure I had some company.'

Stephenson looked over Guttman's shoulder towards the deli's front window. He was about Guttman's age and had a square face and a fine bony nose. 'Do you know who it was?'

'No. I can't even prove they were following me. There's a black Ford and a heavy on foot. I lost them twenty minutes ago, and I doubt they'd wander in here just by chance.'

The waitress came up, pencil and pad at the ready. 'What'll it be?' she said impatiently.

Stephenson's eyes widened slightly as he looked at the

189

remains of Guttmann's knish. He hesitated, so Guttman decided to help out. 'Give him turkey breast on white bread, slightly toasted. A little bit of mayo.' He looked at Stephenson. 'Sound okay?'

Stephenson nodded. He looked relieved not to be eating the native fare.

'And to drink?' demanded the waitress.

'A cup of mud,' said Guttman firmly. He saw Stephenson's face and explained, 'That's coffee.'

'And for you, sir?' The 'sir' was sarcastic.

'Give me a half-order of chopped liver and an onion bagel. Plus another cream soda.'

'Half an order?' The waitress sounded annoyed. 'Since when have we got all hoity-toity, Harry Guttman?'

Guttman looked sharply at the woman, and realised he recognised her from grade school, almost forty years ago. Though back then Lilian Rabinowitz had worn her hair in long greasy braids, which she liked to chew on lovingly during math class.

'Haven't you heard of rationing? And if I was being hoity-toity, Lilian, why would I come here?'

She laughed. 'That's more like it. I'll be back with your food in a jiff.'

Stephenson was looking over Guttman's shoulder again. 'Okay so far,' he said. Then he shifted his gaze to Guttman. 'We've got a problem starting this conversation, Harry.'

'How's that?'

'Both of us know more than we're allowed to tell. But if we can't level with each other, then we can't help each other.'

'Yeah,' said Guttman uneasily, rubbing his chin with his fist. Guttman wanted to keep his distance from Stephenson's easy unaffected charm. 'I have a feeling you've got more to tell me than I have for you.'

Stephenson shrugged. 'I'm not so sure about that. Unless you understand the science – and I sure don't – then we're not in any danger of violating security.' He leaned forward, so there was no chance of being overheard. 'The thing is, we have all been cooperating on what for lack of a better phrase I'll call the Big Weapon. We know about the project and you can relax – we were *allowed* to know.

'Now, we checked out the names you gave me as well as we could. Nothing popped up for you to worry about, though there was one name we couldn't learn much about.'

'Which one?' asked Guttman, hoping the growing knot in his stomach was wrong.

It wasn't.

'Kalvin,' said Stephenson. 'He's a Polish Jew, but Poland's not a place where our sources can discover much these days. It's chaos, as you can imagine, and it's likely to get worse as the Russians advance. Jews there have either been slaughtered or are about to be. Obviously some are in hiding. Kalvin was there until 1933 – we know that much. He worked in a research laboratory in Warsaw. Then he came over here in 1940.'

'That sounds par for the course.' Most of the refugee physicists' careers followed this kind of peripatetic progress, especially the Jewish ones. 'But how did he get out of Warsaw in 1940?'

'He didn't. He popped up in Paris in 1938, working in the Curie Radium Lab.'

'So what's the problem?'

'We've got five missing years before then.' He looked briefly again over Guttman's shoulder, then said, 'Look, there's probably an innocent explanation. All our info is coming through Switzerland, and sometimes it's second, even third hand. I can't vouch for it as I could have done before the war.' He added with an unexpected sharpness, 'All I can say is I have people risking their lives to get it.'

Guttman bit his lip. 'I do know that, Bill. I'm very grateful.'

'Sorry, Harry. I didn't mean to get touchy.' He looked embarrassed. 'Relations on high are a little strained right now.'

Guttman looked at him questioningly, and Stephenson explained: 'This project's been turned over to the military. Our friend Groves.'

Guttman decided not to nod.

Stephenson said, 'He's worried – rightly – about security. I figured that's where your queries were coming from. But he also distrusts us Brits. He doesn't think we can keep secrets from other interested parties.'

'Is he right?'

'Possibly,' said Stephenson shortly. 'Let's come back to that, but first, can you tell me why you wanted this information?'

Guttman had been dreading the question, since he wasn't sure of the answer himself. Fortunately their food came, on vast oval-shaped plates. Stephenson looked at the mound of chopped liver on Guttman's plate. 'That's a half-order?'

'Welcome to *my* club. The decor's not up to the Century Club, but the food's okay.'

'They certainly give you a lot of it.'

They ate for a while in silence. 'This is good,' Stephenson at last acknowledged, between mouthfuls of turkey, while Guttman moved the bagel around the vast grey mound of chopped liver. He didn't feel hungry after his knish. At last he said, 'Do you remember Nessheim?'

192

'How could I forget him? He deserves a medal. I hope he got one.'

'He's in Chicago, actually.'

Stephenson stared at Guttman. 'For the Bureau?'

'Technically, he's a student at the University of Chicago Law School.' He figured if Stephenson didn't know where the 'project' was, this wouldn't mean much to him.

Stephenson's eyes widened. He said, 'And the rest of the time, he's at Stagg Field?'

So he did know. Good, thought Guttman; he was happiest coming clean with Stephenson. 'I'll tell you about it,' he said, leaving the chopped liver alone.

So as Stephenson continued to eat his turkey breast sandwich, Guttman explained how he had first been drawn in, leaving Frankfurter's name out of it, but making it clear that he had been privately consulted – and that the rest of the Bureau (he meant Hoover) was unaware of the project. He described how he had cajoled Nessheim to help out. And finally, sensing its thinness, he related what Nessheim had unearthed so far, though Guttman didn't mention Arthur Perkins. 'The thing is, if Kalvin's a Jew, I can't believe he'd be helping the Nazis.'

'Stranger things have happened. He may have family back in Poland who the Nazis have threatened – we had a Jewish refugee interned who was being blackmailed by the Gestapo. But it doesn't seem very likely. Is there any evidence the Nazis have infiltrated the project?'

Guttman sat back in the booth and sighed. 'That's the thing. There isn't any at all that I can see.' He thought of Kalvin's mysterious meeting with the man who'd then gone downtown in Chicago to the building that housed the FBI Field Office. It was impossible to see a Nazi connection there. He said resignedly, 'My orders came from on high.' He looked meaningfully at Stephenson. 'The highest high we have, lacking a monarch.'

Stephenson laughed; there was something refreshing about the delight which could spontaneously appear on his face, since otherwise he cut such a prim professional figure. 'The President himself, huh? But I tell you, I think he's got the wrong end of the stick. We're confident that the Nazis aren't working on building . . . on a project like this. They've decided it's not practical. There's a physicist named Heisenberg – he's been in charge of German efforts to build a Super Weapon. He confided in one of ours.' Stephenson paused briefly. 'Have you heard the name Bohr? B-o-h-r.'

He'd been on one of the lists – Guttman was sure of that. He couldn't pronounce names, he didn't recognise them when they were spoken, but he remembered what they looked like on a printed page. His memory was not photographic, but it was close. 'I've seen it. Where is he now?'

'In England. But before that, in Denmark. Heisenberg went to a conference there and saw Bohr. He could not have been clearer that the Germans don't believe a bomb is possible within the probable time limits of this war.'

What were they? Three years? Five years? Some days Guttman thought it might be ten. He said, 'Denmark? You said you'd have news from Norway.'

Stephenson smiled. 'Norway's our guarantee. Just in case Heisenberg wasn't telling the truth (though we're sure he was). The Germans have a factory – it makes something called heavy water.'

From his visit to Oppenheimer six months before, Guttman knew what it was. 'What about it?' he asked.

'We're going to blow it up. It may take more than one go. But we'll get there. And that won't leave the Nazis with any alternatives, even if they suddenly change their mind. They can't get the graphite for one thing.' He looked at Guttman to see if he was following.

He was. Pure graphite lay at the heart of the project in Chicago at Stagg Field; Groves had said so, in a throwaway line when he thought Guttman wasn't paying attention. 'So there's nothing the Nazis would gain by having an agent in Chicago?'

'Nothing. It's almost inconceivable. You know better than the rest of us how inept the Nazi espionage attempts have been in this country. But you also know their *targets* have always made sense – blow up a naval yard, disrupt communications, wreak havoc among civilians. It's the people they've chosen who've been their downfall.'

This was true. The few fifth column sympathisers had been easy enough to find, and the actual Germans who'd landed had almost rounded themselves up, so incompetent had they proved.

Guttman said, 'Maybe so, but there's something that troubles me. Nessheim had an anonymous note, saying, "We know where you are." It wouldn't mean much of anything – Nessheim used to run informants in the Chicago area, and he's got any agent's normal quota of enemies. But the note was addressed to "Rossbach". And that was Nessheim's undercover name when he infiltrated the *Bund*.'

'I remember. Who else would know that?'

'Nazi sympathisers, maybe the Nazis themselves.'

'Yes, of course, but who else?'

'What do you mean? Outside the Bureau, nobody else would know it.'

'Outside the Bureau?' Stephenson gave him a look that said *come on*.

Then he glanced over Guttman's shoulder again, and this time his eyes stayed there. 'Harry, there's a guy who's passed by the front window twice. Heavyset, tall, with the collar of his overcoat turned up. No hat. I'm just wondering.'

'If he comes by a third time you'll know. Twice is questionable – three times is bad news.'

'That's what I was thinking. Before we go, I need to tell you about that one other name you asked me to check. The one that wasn't foreign.'

'Okay,' said Guttman slowly, still digesting the import of their exchange about Stagg Field.

'We can't figure out where the man lives.'

'What do you mean?'

'We've followed him, Harry. Not every day – I just don't have the manpower now. But enough to know that he doesn't go home, or at least not "home" as you and I know it. He keeps going to motels. They're all in D.C., but not in what I'd call the most salubrious neighbourhoods.'

'Weird. I mean, I can see maybe he'd stay in a motel for a while, but even then you'd want to make a long-term deal. You know, get a room cheap if you stay a month. That would still be odd – he's not a new employee any more.'

'I know. And we're checking him out on the West Coast. But until then we've focused on his life in D.C. – and the motels. My chaps have the strong impression that he's not always alone.'

'Shacked up with someone?

'It's more like visitation rights. And from more than one visitor. We couldn't get a photograph – it was too dark. But we'll keep trying.' Stephenson started to reach into his coat for his wallet.

'It's on me,' said Guttman, reaching a hand out to keep Stephenson from proffering money.

'Let me contribute. It was delicious,' he said with a smile which suddenly froze.

'What's the matter?'

'Our friend just walked by a third time. Are you armed, Harry?'

Guttman shook his head. Strictly speaking, he wasn't on official business. 'I didn't think I'd need a gun today.'

'You never know. Anyway, I am. For two cents I'd take care of this guy but this is your turf and I'd hate to end my war in Sing Sing. Especially if he's not working for the enemy. Did that occur to you?'

'It did, Bill. It did.'

'I'd better leave first, Harry. I don't think he's spotted you yet.' He stood up, buttoning his overcoat. 'I'll be in D.C. the day after tomorrow. I'll call you if I've got any news about your young roving friend. Same number?'

'Yeah, or at the office if you get through to Marie.'

'Good.' Stephenson pointed to the bill. 'I think I will let you get the tab after all, Harry. I'm just sorry you've got two problems. It could be they both stem from the same place.'

Guttman waited ten minutes, then paid the bill and left Lilian Rabinowitz four bits. Outside, he stood and looked around. It didn't take long; within a couple of minutes the heavyset guy was coming up Houston and when he spotted Guttman standing there, he turned and signalled to a car way down the block. It was the Ford again. Guttman walked slowly and the car passed him, then went right down Essex Street. Turning round,

Guttman blessed his luck, for a cab stopped almost as soon as he raised his arm.

'Foley Square, and step on it,' he barked, showing the driver his badge. By the time the Ford had circled around the block he would be long gone. Looking back through the rear window he saw the heavyset guy standing alone on the far corner, waiting forlornly for his colleagues in the dark car.

In Foley Square, a Red Cross station had set up shop for blood donations, though the persistent drizzle was keeping volunteer numbers down. Guttman walked up the steps of the Courthouse, a monumental, classical Greek temple with Corinthian columns and granite-faced exterior walls. Adjoining it at the rear was a tall tower, thirty storeys high, which held government offices, including the Field Office headquarters of the FBI.

Going through the Courthouse halls, he passed lawyers, clients and cops mingling outside the courtrooms, waiting for the afternoon sessions to begin. There had been a time when Guttman had hoped to spend his career in just such a setting: defending the innocent (this was when he was still an innocent); prosecuting the guilty (as he grew more worldly wise); or testifying as an honest cop, tough but just – like Keane, the Irish policeman. Those aspirations seemed in the distant past, and he would not have wanted to say which role he was playing now.

The receptionist was startled when Guttman showed his Assistant Director's credentials. It was encouraging that she hadn't been expecting him, though he knew it didn't mean much. She phoned through to Powderman's secretary, and Guttman could envisage the resulting panic – especially since it turned out that Powderman was not in his office, but roaming the floor. After a few minutes a flustered woman in a pink blouse came and collected Guttman, apologising for the delay as she took him to see the new Special Agent in Charge.

Powderman had moved into the SAC's comfortable office overlooking Foley Square, though his desk faced the door so that he sat with his back to the window. Little American flags sat on each of his desk's front corners, and a poster on the wall showed two factory workers gabbing, while a sinister foreign-looking man with a moustache eavesdropped in the background. The caption read, 'Keep it to yourself!'

Powderman seemed genuinely surprised to see him. 'You should have said you were coming.'

'So you could lay out the red carpet?'

Powderman laughed, a little nervously. 'At least I'd have made sure I was in my office.' Guttman relaxed a bit, more confident now that Powderman hadn't known he was in town. It seemed the Ford hadn't been a Bureau car after all.

Powderman asked, 'What brings you to the city?'

'My mom's not well.'

'Sorry to hear that.' Powderman looked too young to have a dying mother; Guttman figured he was just shy of forty, and fresh-faced. A Nebraska native, who now that he'd been promoted to SAC wore a spiffier kind of suit, though he still spoke with the mild twang of the Midwest. The SAC's job here usually came with the title of Assistant Director, but either because it was wartime or because Powderman was unproven in the role, he was still just called the Special Agent in Charge. This gave Guttman a slight but perceptible advantage.

'I thought while I was here I'd stop by. Nothing new on the Dasch front, I take it?'

Powderman considered this, careful now that the small talk was over. 'No. We followed up the leads you guys provided. Nothing more's come up.'

Guttman nodded as if he expected this. 'I had three more names. Since I'm here maybe you could run them through the local files.' It was not an unusual request, for not everything held in the field offices would be duplicated in the files at HQ on Connecticut Avenue. Field offices would commonly hold unsubmitted lists of subversives, or more accurately, *suspected* subversives. Everyone knew the lists could be both grotesquely inclusive and wildly inaccurate – as if someone throwing darts counted even those that missed the board. These stabs in the dark could be the results of a neighbour's vindictive whisper, a suspect's meeting with a known 'agitator', an undivulged grudge on a Special Agent's part, or simply from the field office's need to show results.

'Sure,' said Powderman, reaching for the internal phone on his desk. He spoke into the receiver. 'Bonnie, check a few names in the internal subs files, will you?' Guttman could hear a high-pitched voice respond. Powderman said, 'Yes, right away. I've got someone from D.C. here and he's waiting.'

Powderman looked at him questioningly and Guttman said, 'The first name's Kalvin – with a "K". A refugee currently living in Chicago, but it was suggested he used to live in New York.' It hadn't been, but Guttman wanted to give three names to lessen the attention paid to the one he was actually interested in.

Powderman spelled out 'Kalvin', then raised his eyebrows at Guttman.

'Schneider. Ernst Schneider. Lives in Yorkville.' Guttman was making it up on the fly.

Reciting Schneider's name into the phone, Powderman then looked at Guttman again. 'The last one is Perkins – Arthur Perkins of Riverside Drive.' He didn't say that Arthur Perkins was dead.

Powderman relayed this last name, then put the phone down. 'It won't be long – Bonnie's quick.'

While they waited, they shot the breeze for a bit, talking sports mainly – Powderman bemoaning the decimation of Major League rosters by the wartime call-up. 'Ted Williams,' Powderman announced. 'He's going to lose a couple of years of home runs.'

A couple of years? Again, Guttman wondered. He was confident of the Allies' eventual victory, yet equally certain of the Germans' ability to resist a premature invasion of Europe.

When they had exhausted the last season's batting averages and Guttman was wondering when Bonnie would show up, Powderman said suddenly, 'You know, I think maybe I owe you an apology.'

'Why's that?'

'Do you remember when we last ran into each other?' Powderman continued: 'It was outside Rockefeller Center. You were with Bill Stephenson.'

Guttman looked at him as if to say, *and so*? But he felt his pulse pick up.

Powderman swivelled on his chair, avoiding Guttman's eyes. He seemed uneasy. 'I mentioned to Percy that I'd run into you.'

Percy Foxworth. Former SAC in New York and now Guttman's successor as the head of SIS. Guttman said, 'Of course you did.'

Powderman glanced at him, checking the tone of this; Guttman did his best to look benign. Powderman said, 'I thought I'd better say I'd seen you – it's not every day you run across an Assistant Director outside the shop.' He exhaled. 'I didn't expect Percy to think anything of it.' He added ruefully, 'I was wrong.'

'What happened?'

'Percy went bananas. He claimed you should have

201

told him you were seeing the Brits. He said he was going to make a formal complaint to Tolson.'

'Did he?'

Powderman nodded. 'He kept me there – or here, actually,' he said, gesturing to the room, 'while he dictated the memorandum. I saw him sign it.'

It must have gone out then, thought Guttman. But why hadn't Tolson ever said anything to him?

Powderman looked sheepish. 'I'm sorry if I landed you in the shit.'

'Don't worry about it. You did the right thing.'

Powderman seemed relieved – enjoying the double reward of purging himself without being punished for the confession. Guttman changed the subject. 'Tell me something. Have you sent anybody out to the Chicago Field Office in the last few months?'

Powderman stared at him curiously. 'Nope. And I'd know – it would need my okay. Why?'

Before Guttman could answer, there was a brisk knock on the door and an older woman walked in, carrying a file in one hand. She reminded Guttman of Tatie, the head of the typing pool in Chicago. Women didn't usually last long at the Bureau, but the ones that did – like Tatie, or Helen Gantry, Director Hoover's assistant – were tough as nails, and knew it too.

'What have we got, Bonnie?' asked Powderman. He added, 'This is Assistant Director Guttman from the Bureau.'

She gave Guttman a quick appraising stare, and he saw some of her assurance replaced by caution. Her boss was no longer the only man in the room she needed to please. 'Not a lot there,' she said, handing the file over to Powderman. 'There's nothing on a Kalvin or a Schneider.'

'In the *Bund* files?' asked Guttman.

'Anywhere,' she said firmly. 'I checked all the internal subs records.'

'Good girl,' said Powderman, and Guttman saw Bonnie wince almost imperceptibly. She had to be in her fifties. She said, 'Arthur Perkins didn't come up either.'

'Can't say I'm surprised,' said Powderman. 'Not exactly a Nazi name.' He opened the file she'd handed him and peered at the single piece of paper inside. 'So what's this?'

Bonnie explained, '*Missus* Arthur Perkins did make the files.'

'She did?' Guttman couldn't help himself.

Bonnie said nothing while Powderman scanned the paper. 'Well,' he said at last, 'I don't think we should get too excited.' Looking at the sheet, he went on, 'Mrs Perkins is a Forbes from Boston – apparently that counts for something up there. She attended Miss Porter's School for Girls and the Radcliffe College for young women, which she left prematurely, presumably to marry Mr Perkins, who was a graduate of Milton Academy and then of Harvard College.' He sighed and shook his head. 'This should be in the Social Register, not our files. Hang on, here's the kicker – in 1931 it seems Mrs P. hosted a lunch for Eleanor Roosevelt in 1931, at the Cosmopolitan Club here in New York.'

There was silence in the room. Eventually Guttman broke it. 'And . . . ?'

Powderman put the paper back in the file and chucked it on to the desk. 'And nothing,' he said crossly. 'It doesn't even tell us what they served for lunch.' He shook his head. 'Why that was worthy of a place in Records is beyond me.'

He and Guttman exchanged the knowing looks of Bureau veterans.

*　　*　　*

Guttman went out into Foley Square, where the rain was harder now and the line to give blood even shorter. He had forgotten that it was Powderman whom he and Stephenson had run into, well before Pearl Harbor, and was taken aback by Powderman's confession that he had told on Guttman. He couldn't understand why Tolson hadn't called him in and chewed him out. Everyone from agents to assistant directors was required to inform the local SACs if they ventured into their territories. Not doing so wasn't a major offence, incurring a reprimand but not much else, so maybe Tolson had decided to let it pass.

No. Tolson would never let go of an opportunity to give Guttman a hard time – he did that even when Guttman had done nothing wrong. Given a real reason, Tolson would have been down on the fourth floor in D.C. like a shot. In the whole kerfuffle about Guttman's actions pre-Pearl Harbor, Tolson had tried to throw the book at him – so why leave this page out?

But right now Guttman needed to concentrate on the more immediate problem at hand. From the Bureau files, and from his conversations with the New York police and Perkins's successor at Columbia, he was sure that Arthur Perkins was clean as a whistle. Yet if he were so innocent, why had he been killed? He hadn't been involved in high-security research. As far as Guttman could tell, Perkins's involvement with the scientists working in the Columbia lab he oversaw was confined to setting their salaries.

Guttman pondered this as he walked towards the Bowery again, trying to decide whether to go back to D.C. There was a train he could catch from Penn Station in forty-five minutes; if he got it, he'd be home for a full night's sleep before going to work in the morning.

His thoughts returned to Perkins. Could his murder then have been a terrible mistake? Had someone thought the Chairman of the Columbia University Physics Department was involved in the creation of a super-weapon? Maybe. And maybe they had mistaken him for Fermi, or Szilard, or any of the physicists now working so frantically on the South Side of Chicago.

But that didn't make sense. If enemies knew enough about the project to kill somebody in order to impede it, then surely they knew enough to pick the right individual. Unless . . .

Guttman stopped in the middle of the Bowery sidewalk, absent-mindedly fingering the change in his pocket, oblivious to the other pedestrians who were forced to move round this short, stocky man, standing like a squat deer caught in somebody's headlights.

Maybe they had killed Perkins because they wanted him out of the way. Guttman stood still and grappled with this unformed idea, inchoate as a jellyfish, until a further thought came out of nowhere. They hadn't killed Perkins because he was X or did Y, but because somebody else was Z.

15

HE WAS ASKING to see the widow without warning, so he wasn't surprised to be told to wait outside in the hall while the Negro maid consulted her employer. He'd given his card and hoped that would do the trick, since not many people would turn away an Assistant Director of the FBI, especially in wartime. Yet it seemed the widow of the late Arthur Perkins was in no hurry to have him admitted.

At last, the door opened again. The maid looked at him impassively. 'Mizz Perkins will see you now.'

He followed her into a short hallway with parquet floors, a mahogany coat stand and framed prints of English landscapes on the wall. The hall opened up into the living room. It had a dramatic view of the Hudson, though the foggy mist that had come in after the midday rain obscured the Jersey side. A chintz-covered sofa was positioned with its back to the window, and an armchair sat at an angle to it. A decorative fireplace hollowed out of the room's central internal wall was full of dried flowers, which gave out a faint whiff of cinnamon-like scent. On the mantelpiece an array of invitations stood, arranged like so many calling cards in a Jane Austen novel. The far end of the room led into a small dining room, and it was from here that a tall woman came towards him.

'Nancy Perkins,' she declared, coming across a large Persian rug to shake his hand. She didn't smile. 'And you are Mr Gootman from the FBI,' she said.

'Guttman,' he said, but she didn't seem to hear, for she was busy ushering him to a seat on the sofa while she sat down, straight-backed and legs uncrossed, in the armchair. She wore a simple, pale blue dress that Guttman's mother would have said was 'nothing fancy', but he could see it was beautifully made – as if its maker had understood that falls from fashion never last, and that quality survives until the wheel of taste comes round again.

'Thank you for seeing me, Mrs Perkins. I apologise for not phoning ahead.'

She didn't look impressed by this. 'What did you want, Mr Gootman?'

He didn't bother correcting her again. She was a Boston Yankee, after all. Not many Germans up there, and not many Jews with German names. 'It's about your husband, Mrs Perkins, and events just before he died.'

'My husband's accident was over a year ago, Mr Gootman. Why are you asking me about it now?' She sounded more curious than cross.

'I'm not, Mrs Perkins. I'm here about a project started on your husband's watch. I won't be very long – most of it is pro forma stuff.'

'You should know that I'm not a scientist,' she said with an intonation – dry, cynical and clipped – which Guttman had last heard on a visit to Yale.

'I realise that. Still, I wanted to ask if anything unusual happened in your husband's professional life in the months before the accident.'

'And if it had?' There was a daunting quality to the blue eyes.

'There was work of national importance going on in your husband's labs. There still is. I'm trying to establish how much he was involved with the work going on around him, or whether he stood back, as it were.'

'As it were,' she muttered, and when she looked at

207

Guttman it was with a superior knowingness. She said, 'My husband was the Chairman of the Department. It didn't leave him a lot of time for participating in research. It was something he felt most keenly. That's why he was so excited.'

'What about, ma'am?'

'He had decided to do science again. He planned to give up the chairmanship and join the team of Professor Fermi.'

She pronounced it Fir-me, and Guttman needed to be sure. 'Enrico Fermi? The Italian physicist?'

'That's the one. Very gifted, apparently, if a little intense for my taste.'

It was what people often said about the Jews – *a nice enough fellow, if a little intense*. Guttman tried not to bristle.

Mrs Perkins was saying, 'My husband was like a little boy at Christmas, even after I told him he might find it difficult to take orders from someone who had been his junior. He said to think of it as an officer with a desk job, who re-enlists as a private in order to join the fighting. It was rather touching when I look back at it, but at the time I'm afraid I wasn't very sympathetic.'

'Oh?'

She shrugged and gave a sigh. 'Arthur said we might have to move because of the new job. It was not a prospect that cheered me. After New York, the delights of Chicago were not apparent to me. Boston would have been acceptable, even if they say you can't go home again.'

'You said your husband was going to give up his chairmanship of the department. Was he concerned about who would take his place?'

She shook her head. 'He said a simpleton could do

the job. The only hard part was managing the physicists. Some of them could be impossible, especially the Hungarians.'

'Szilard?'

'Particularly Szilard.' She was emphatic. 'He should have been named "Lizard"; it's almost a perfect anagram as it is. There's something slippery about that man – he's been in so many countries by now you feel his only nationality is himself. Oh, I know he's meant to be brilliant, but he could have shown a bit of gratitude. It was Arthur, after all, who got him his position.'

'Was Fermi like that too?'

'Not at all. He *did* show gratitude, even though he has more reason to have a swelled head – he's won the Nobel Prize and Szilard hasn't.' She sat back decisively in her chair. 'But no, none of the administrative issues worried Arthur. I'd never seen him so determined. What bothered him was something else.'

Guttman wanted to ask what this was, but decided there was no point pushing; this was a lady who said what she wanted to say, no more and no less. After a pause, Mrs Perkins continued. 'What troubled him was the scientist whose place he would be taking. Unfortunately, Arthur had told the young man he could join the Fermi team. Then Arthur had to tell him he couldn't.'

'Tricky,' said Guttman mildly.

'If anyone could smooth things over it would have been my husband,' she said with a touch of pride. 'But not this time. Arthur said the young man had taken great exception to being left out, especially when Arthur – unwisely in my view – explained he was joining the team instead. Arthur said the man was not only upset, he was positively insulting.'

'Oh, dear,' said Guttman, hoping this was the right

thing to say. It was not a phrase he was accustomed to using.

Mrs Perkins nodded vaguely, and Guttman pressed on. 'Do you know the name of the scientist your husband was going to replace?'

She shook her head, but didn't seem interested.

'Was he foreign?' Guttman prompted.

'I wouldn't be surprised.' She smiled, as if both admiring his tenacity and recognising its futility. 'So many of them are.'

'Would anyone at the department know?'

'I shouldn't think so. Fermi was away when my husband made his mind up – he was going to tell him on the day he . . . on the day of the accident. He wanted Fermi to be the first to know. And of course, technically Fermi had to approve the move. Though I don't think there could have been any question – my husband had a very distinguished record in research, even if it was some time ago. No, what bothered Arthur was this other man's unpleasantness.'

'But you can't remember his name?'

'I can't, I'm afraid.' She seemed untroubled by this.

He had reached a dead end, doubly dismaying since his expectations had briefly risen so sharply.

'You're looking very disappointed, Mr Gootman.'

'Guttman,' he said dully.

'Of course. I've never been very good with names.'

He couldn't bring himself to reply. He decided to make his excuses and head for the train. Then Mrs Perkins said, 'I'd tell you to phone the university and ask Miss Debenne but I'm not sure she'd be willing to help.'

'Who's Miss Debenne?'

'She was Arthur's secretary. Forgive me for my bluntness, but she isn't awfully fond of Germans. Her family's suffered terribly since France fell.'

'But I'm not German,' Guttman protested. 'I'm a Jew.' He sensed he sounded ridiculous.

'Oh,' she said, undisturbed. 'That wouldn't help, I'm afraid. Miss Debenne isn't keen on the Jews either – you know the French. I suppose I could call her. You see, she kept Arthur's appointments diary –' Suddenly she stopped. 'I've just remembered. She sent all the diaries to me when spring semester ended. I didn't pay much attention.'

'You have your husband's diaries?' asked Guttman, surprised.

'Yes,' she said, looking as if she didn't know why Guttman was getting so worked up. 'They're not diaries as we know them, Mr Guttman. Just appointments and names.'

In the silence that followed you could have heard a pin drop. Gradually, like an awakening flower, Mrs Perkins understood the import of what she'd said. To her credit she seemed embarrassed. 'My goodness, I've been a complete booby, haven't I? Names are exactly what you want.'

'One name will do,' said Guttman.

Five minutes later, Mrs Perkins had deciphered Arthur Perkins's inscrutable handwriting in the relevant page of the moleskin book he'd used as a diary – the entries had stopped five days later when he'd had his all-too-final appointment. Guttman memorised the entry for January 18, 1942 like a catechism. *Ian Grant (Princeton) – 3.30 Fac Club.*

16

WHEN HE GOT back to Arlington it was almost midnight. It must have rained here as well, for the streets were shiny in the harsh beam of his headlights, and on the bridge over the Potomac his tyres hissed, rolling through the surface water.

He parked in the little driveway outside the garage, too tired to face the palaver of opening and shutting its door. When Isabel had been alive, this home had been a kind of paradise to them both, two city kids who'd dreamed of one day having a backyard. Now on his own, it seemed increasingly a burden.

As he walked up to the front door he noticed a light showing in the living room; Annie would have left it on since she'd been in today. He put his briefcase down and fumbled for his keys, then finally worked the right one into the lock.

He knew at once that something was wrong. The key turned too easily, as if the locking mechanism had been removed. He'd already moved forward, anticipating the slow swing open, but the door gave way as if snapped from a rubber band. He stumbled into his front hall, then the door hit something and Guttman nearly fell down. From the dim light cast by the living-room lamp he could just make out one of the kitchen chairs, upended by the opening door; it had been placed two feet back from the entrance, a makeshift burglar alarm.

A woman's voice came from the living room. 'Who's there?' it called out.

He recognised the voice. 'Annie? It's me.' What was she doing here?

He picked up the chair and set it down on its legs, then walked into the living room. Annie was standing by the sofa, dressed but slightly dishevelled, and he saw from the wool throw and the contours of the sofa cushions that she had been lying down. 'What's going on?' he asked, puzzled now more than alarmed.

'Oh, Harry, you gave me such a fright.'

'Likewise,' he said, bemused. 'What's that?' On the little table next to the sofa, on top of the stacked magazines, there was a little pistol, a .25 Beretta. It was meant to be a lady's gun, but only a fool would think it couldn't do what it was supposed to do.

Annie stared down at the gun. She stammered out, 'I-I-I thought . . .'

'Listen, you sit down while I close the front door – if it'll close any more – and put my case away.'

She nodded wordlessly and he went out into the hall. Inspecting the door, he saw that the lock had been tampered with – someone had rolled its barrel so hard that the lock wouldn't close.

He picked up his briefcase, stomped down the hall and put it in the bedroom, then went into the kitchen, where he turned the light on and fixed two set-ups in tumblers with ice and water before taking them through to the living room. He found Annie sitting in a corner of the sofa and as he turned on another lamp he looked at her. 'I'm having a large inch of the Director's special – how about the same for you?'

'It sounds a pretty exotic concoction.'

'Not really. Johnny Walker Scotch – I get a fifth every year for Christmas from Mr Hoover.'

'Even now?'

He nodded; she was aware of his rifts with the FBI's head man. 'However mad he gets at me, I'm still on the Christmas list. The day I don't get the bottle I'll know

I'm for the high jump.' Though, conversely, getting the whisky was no guarantee that he wasn't anyway.

He went over to the tray in the corner and lifted the bottle of Scotch, which was only half-empty. He wasn't much of a drinker, and when he had the occasional cocktail before dinner he drank cheaper stuff than this. Now he poured hefty shots into both of the glasses he'd prepared.

As he handed Annie her drink she smiled a little wistfully. 'You must think I'm crazy. To come home and find the door like that, and the chair, and then me brandishing a gun.'

'I didn't see the brandishing,' he said. 'But I admit the rest was unexpected.'

'I can explain.'

'I know. But try your drink first.' He could see she was in a state, and hoped the whisky would calm her down. They sipped in silence for a minute.

'Well,' Annie said, taking a deep breath. 'I was up early this morning while it was still dark. When I looked out the window I saw a light on over here. You said you'd be leaving before dawn, and I was worried that you'd overslept. But then I saw that the light was outside the house. I figured you were waving a flashlight, but I wanted to make sure it *was* you. So I put my shoes on and opened the door.'

'I left real early – at about five.'

She nodded. 'This was at six. When I went outside the light wasn't there. So I started across the street.'

'Why didn't you go back inside and call the cops?'

'And say what?' She sounded slightly indignant. ' "Officer, I saw a flashlight outside of Harry Guttman's house – please send a patrol car right away"?'

He laughed. 'What happened then?'

'When I got over here I heard a car drive away.

'I found the front door the way it is now – I think somebody's picked the lock. I tried to close it as best I could, then went back to get Jeff ready for school.'

'Okay. And then tonight?' he asked.

'Hold your horses, Harry. I sent Jeff to school, then I got Mrs Jupiter her breakfast and called the Justice to say I couldn't make it to work. After that I phoned a locksmith – he couldn't come today, darned man, but he's due first thing in the morning. If you're going to work I'll be glad to wait for him.'

'That's okay. I hope I didn't get you in Dutch with the Justice.'

'He understood I couldn't leave this place with the door open like that. Anyway, the Justice likes you, Harry. He told me once you were his "brother in arms".'

Like hell, thought Guttman. He looked again at the gun on the table. 'Speaking of arms, I didn't know you had a handgun.'

When Annie shrugged he added, 'You could hurt somebody with that, you know.'

Her face hardened momentarily. 'I am aware of that. But don't worry, I don't carry it around. I keep it on the upper shelf of my closet – safe from Jeff.'

Guttman nodded. Her son was a nice kid, but curious and energetic, with a boy's desire to search out everything.

'Well, thank you for guarding the place,' he said, thinking it would be nice to go to bed.

'I wasn't sure if you'd be back tonight. I figured whoever it was, they could walk straight in.'

Was there a faint note of reproof in her voice? He realised he wasn't sounding very grateful. He was; it was just that he was astonished by her initiative. She had been very brave, if also foolhardy. This woman had plenty of guts. Sleeping on his couch with a .25 by her side, ready to defend his house from intruders.

He took a long draw on his drink, feeling it warm his insides. 'You've done swell, Annie. I can't thank you enough.'

'Did you have a good trip?' she asked, and he realised she didn't want to go yet.

He tried not to yawn. 'Okay. I saw my mother, which is never a bundle of laughs. I don't think she'll be with us much longer.'

'I'm sorry,' she said.

I'm not, he thought. 'She's not really herself any more. It'll be a blessing in a way if she moves on sooner rather than later.'

'Was the train okay on your way back? They say there's snow coming up north.'

'It hasn't got there yet. Though the power went out in the dining car.' And the bar car had run out of peanuts. His supper had been two beers.

'So you didn't have dinner? Harry, you must be starving. Let me make you something.'

'Don't worry. I can fry an egg.' Actually, he was too tired to cook anything.

'Don't be silly. Sit still.' She ignored his feeble protests and went out to the kitchen, and within five minutes had given him a plate of scrambled eggs and two slices of toast. He realised he was ravenous, and perked up as he ate. He asked about Jeff, and heard about his school grades, and how Mrs Jupiter was starting to go slightly doolally. It was easy, familiar talk, and worked like balm – Guttman realised how agitated his day had been. He felt relaxed now, and suddenly gave a long sleepy yawn before he had time to suppress it.

Annie smiled. 'Bedtime for Mr Guttman,' she said, getting up and taking his plate and fork to the sink.

She started to wash them, and before he could say anything asked quietly, with her back to him, 'Have you heard anything from Jim lately?'

'Not for a week or so.' She had turned sideways to him, holding a dishcloth in her hand which she used to dry the plate. 'Have you?' he asked.

Her eyebrows arched involuntarily, but she inspected the plate calmly, and put it down on the counter. 'No, not since he was here last summer.'

'Oh.' He wondered if Nessheim had another girl now. He hoped not. Poor Annie. 'He's got his studies, and he's also doing some work for me.'

There was a small, private smile on Annie's face, and Guttman sensed that his efforts to explain Nessheim's silence were what was amusing her. He felt confused.

She said, the smile now gone, 'I hope it's nothing dangerous he's doing for you.'

He tried to look surprised. 'No, not at all. Routine stuff. But it keeps him busy – I'm sure that's why you haven't heard from him.' He stopped awkwardly, no longer sure what he thought.

'He's a sweet guy,' Annie declared. 'I hope he's happy. Someday he'll find himself a gal who's right for him.' She put down the dish towel. 'You'd better get some sleep, Harry – I'm going to. I'll be over on Thursday as usual.'

Harry followed her to the front door and said goodnight, then flicked the switch to turn off the outside light. He watched Annie cross the street and go into Mrs Jupiter's, then he stood for a minute with the front door open, breathing the cold air and listening as the leaves tumbled in the gutters of the street like whispers.

17

IN THE MORNING he woke early, but stayed at home until the locksmith came. It took him almost an hour to change the lock. Guttman retreated to his study to use the phone, wanting to catch Nessheim before he went to class.

He was surprised when a woman answered, and wondered if he'd got the wrong number. He wanted to hang up, but he had made the call station-to-station, so the operator put him through. 'Is Nessheim there, please?' he asked.

'You've missed him,' the woman said. She had a low breathy voice, and didn't sound like a college girl to Guttman. No wonder Annie hadn't heard from Nessheim. 'Can I take a message?' she asked.

'Tell him Harry called, will you? And get him to call me.'

'Sure I will. Has he got your number? And your last name?' The woman gave a throaty laugh, which tingled Guttman's spine like a spa masseur's roller.

'Yes on both counts. Will you be seeing him, miss?' He wanted to keep the conversation going.

'Not 'til supper time, Harry. You don't mind if I call you Harry, do you, Harry?'

He laughed. 'Be my guest. Since we're so familiar now, what would your name be?'

'You can call me MW if you like.'

'Okay. What's that stand for?'

'Mystery Woman. Don't worry – I'll give Nessheim your message. I'll say bye now, Harry. Nice speaking to you.'

Guttman put down the phone. It was nine-thirty his time, an hour earlier out there. He couldn't believe 'Mystery Woman' had gone to Nessheim's place just for breakfast. Was she shacking up with the guy? It sounded that way. Guttman thought of that voice again, and felt a mixture of envy and alarm.

He got to the office just after eleven, stopped a floor below his office and went down the hall to Records and Files. A young man in round-framed spectacles and wearing a bow tie came out from the stacks to the counter.

'Where's Ant?' asked Guttman impatiently.

'Mr Antrim has transferred to the Armory.'

'Since when?'

'I believe on reflection that it was in May.' Spoken like a small-town librarian, intent to show he was more cultured than the provincial baboons he was employed to serve.

'What's your name?'

'Luther Toobis.'

Guttman nodded, as if he'd been expecting this remarkable moniker. 'Well, Luther, I want to check a Germ-Am file.'

'Pardon?'

'The German-American Index. It's the sympathisers directory.'

'Ah, of course,' the man said, as if the misunderstanding were Guttman's fault. 'What was the name?'

Guttman told him, trying to suppress his irritation. Luther said, 'I'll just go and see.'

The Toobis guy was quick; you had to hand him that. He couldn't have been more than two minutes. 'Nothing in the index, I'm afraid. And of course no file.'

'Of course.' Guttman paused. 'While we're at it, could you have a look at the ACP register?'

The man tilted his head until he was looking at Guttman over the tops of his glasses. 'The ACP register? Same name?' He sounded incredulous.

Guttman's patience snapped. He had been pulling files while this kid was in short pants. 'Son, just do what I ask.'

Luther didn't dignify this with a reply. This time he was a little longer in the file rooms – sulking, Guttman figured. But when he returned he looked puzzled. 'He's listed in the register all right, but there's no file.'

'You mean there never was a file?'

'I don't know. My understanding is that for a name to be listed in the register it has to have a file. I guess I was wrong.'

I don't think so, thought Guttman. 'What was the register code?' he asked. There was a hierarchy for American Communists: M for member, S for sympathiser, A for associations with.

'A,' said Luther.

'Right. Now tell me, are the case files still here?' There was something else he needed to check, he realised, now that he'd learned that Grant's file had gone missing, but he was still reeling from discovering which directory Grant's name could be found in.

'It depends on the years,' said Luther.

'I'm talking before the war – 1935 to 1940.'

'Those would be at the Armory. Only wartime and current are here now.' Then, mistaking Guttman's newly relaxed air for friendliness, he said, 'How come you asked me to search both ways for this guy Grant?'

'How's that?'

'Well, I can understand if someone's a Nazi, and I can understand if they're a Communist. But you had me look at both registers.'

220

'Got to cover the bases,' said Guttman, trying to hide how startled he felt.

He left and took the stairs rather than the elevator. Perkins had been murdered all right, and Grant had been sent in his place. But not because the Germans had sent him there.

As he came into his suite, Marie looked up and smiled. She always seemed happy to see him. 'How's your mom, Harry?' she asked.

'Not so hot,' he said, and this was true.

'You see anybody else up there?'

'How's that?' he asked suspiciously.

'I don't mean business, Harry. I mean, did you have any fun?'

Fun? He had almost forgotten the word. Marie was watching him sympathetically. Or was it pity? He said gruffly, 'I've got a call to make.'

'Okay. Don't forget your supper date.'

'What supper?'

Marie exhaled with frustration. '*Our* supper. You're coming over day after tomorrow.'

There had been a lot of invitations in recent months from Marie. Had he actually accepted one? It looked that way. The prospect exhausted him but he nodded knowingly. Marie said, 'Six-thirty, Harry. I'll write the address down. If you forget, so help me I'll brain you.'

It took twenty minutes to track down the Chairman of the Physics Department, and only thirty seconds for Guttman to be surprised again.

'Are you absolutely sure?' he asked incredulously.

'Yes, Mr Guttman. I am absolutely sure. I saw him forty minutes ago and he was late for a seminar.' The Chairman sounded impatient.

'He hasn't ever worked at Columbia?'

'Not during my time here. And that's been ten years.'

'Or been working in Chicago in the last twelve months?'

The man sighed. 'Nor working in Chicago. Since it's eight hundred miles away, I think I'd be aware of that. Now I think of it, Professor Grant did spend one term at the Institute for Advanced Studies a few years back.'

'Where was that?' asked Guttman, his hopes rising.

'Here in Princeton, Mr Guttman. Sorry to disappoint you.'

When he put the phone down, Marie came in. 'Mr Tolson called. He dropped by yesterday. He wants to talk to you.'

'I'll call him now.'

Marie shook her head. 'He wants to see you in his office.'

'When?' He was puzzled by the formality of Tolson's request. Usually when he wanted to talk to Guttman, the Associate Director would come down and stick his head in through the door. Not that such informality meant anything – as he stood hanging by an arm from the doorway, Tolson was equally happy to shoot the breeze or berate him.

'You've got ten minutes,' said Marie, who though watch-less always seemed able to tell the time within a minute or two. Guttman, with the chunky Swiss watch his wife had bought him for a birthday, usually found he'd forgotten to wind the goddamned thing.

He slapped one cheek, trying to stir himself. A Tolson summons meant trouble, and Guttman would need all his wits about him. Out of self-preservation he had to duck Hoover's sidekick for now. 'I've got to go out. I'll see Tolson later.'

'What do I tell him?' Marie asked with alarm.

Guttman was already grabbing his coat. 'Tell him I had to see the doctor. Tell him it was urgent. Tell him I have a bad case of . . . I don't know. Corns.'

'*Corns?* Harry, that will never wash.'

Harry hunched both shoulders helplessly. 'Tell him it's serious. Think up something, okay? If he's free later, I'll see him after lunch.'

He was out the door before Marie could protest any more.

He checked his watch in the elevator and decided it was safe to leave the building now. Tolson wouldn't be leaving for another half-hour – with Hoover to have lunch, as they did daily at the nearby Mayflower Hotel.

They also drove to work together each morning, and drove home together at the end of the day. They were like a married couple whose mutual fascination had never flagged. Isabel, who knew some French, had told Guttman it was a *marriage blanche*, and contrary to the furtive commentary that was rife, Guttman was also convinced the relationship was entirely asexual. To Guttman, Hoover was as sexless as the Sphinx. If Tolson was not so neutral, his outlet must have been among the succession of handsome young agents working directly for him. Like his young assistant T.A. whom Marie liked so much.

What struck Guttman was that the emotional life of the Hoover–Tolson relationship also seemed inordinately sublimated, even in the privacy of their chauffeured car. Their driver Smitty had in an unguarded moment told Guttman that their demeanour was as unrelaxed there as in the office. They sat stiffly in the back of the chauffeured car, while Tolson deferred like an obedient junior to Hoover's opinions on everything, from the vulgarity of a billboard they drove by to the shortcomings of the Dallas Field Office. Tellingly, even alone with the man, Tolson addressed Hoover as 'Boss'.

Guttman now had lunch in a diner off DuPont Circle. It was far enough from the Justice Department building that he could be confident of not seeing anyone from work. He sat on a low stool at the counter, eating a grilled cheese sandwich and drinking a soda, letting the events of the last two days sink in.

He'd learned that sometimes a kind of half-conscious filtering process worked best for him. He could spend hours with a yellow legal pad and pencil, writing down the facts he knew, making links between them, trying to describe the motivations and intentions of the players he encountered – players being the apt word, since he always thought of complicated cases as taking place upon a playing field, or even a double-sized stage. But there were times when this detailed rational process only furthered his confusion, and this was one of them.

He walked back slowly to the Justice Department, his overcoat collar tipped up under his ears. The harsh westerlies blowing now weren't bringing rain, just a bitter gusting cold that made him wish he'd been sensible enough to wear his old wool overcoat. Isabel wouldn't have let him leave the house without it. Not for the first time, he missed her mothering of him, something she'd insisted on and he'd accepted, if only to balance the protective role he had assumed during the years of her illness. You're on your own, he told himself, and though he felt readier for Tolson now, the words ran through his head like a dirge.

Tolson had recently moved office, and was now separated from the Director only by Mrs Gandy and the duo of girls she kept employed typing reports under her demanding spinster's eye. Tolson's new office was modest, the size of a travelling rep's hotel room, and sparsely furnished with only a desk and chairs – for meetings Tolson used the conference room across the hall where the weekly Executives Conference was held. Unlike Hoover, Tolson had the drapes pulled back; a fresh-air fetishist, he kept the window open a good six inches even in November, which provided a chill counterpoint to the overheating radiators.

'You been travelling?' Tolson asked curtly. Guttman tried not to show his surprise; he had expected the usual enquiries after his health.

'Just to New York. Family stuff.'

'Anything new up there with Sebold?'

'No. He's still broadcasting, and the Nazis seem to be buying it.'

'You ever think of sending him back in?'

'How's that?'

'Like he was still operating as a spy. He could try and make contact with sympathisers. That sort of thing.'

'How would that work?' Tolson had spent about three weeks total in the field – in Buffalo, New York, a decade before. At times like this, his inexperience showed.

Tolson shrugged. 'Undercover.'

'We both know the Director's view.'

'That didn't stop you before.' He looked at Guttman with apparent sympathy.

'Once bitten, twice shy. It worked that time – as you know. But I don't think I'd want to try it again.'

'Nessheim used a Kraut name, didn't he? Ross-something.'

'Rossbach,' Guttman said flatly. He didn't understand what Tolson was getting at, but he didn't like it.

'That's right. How is our ballplayer these days?'

'Beats me. Not playing ball, that's for sure.'

Tolson pushed a paperweight along the desk with one

225

hand, then back with the other. Guttman watched it dully; it was a winter scene, with a little church in the middle. As it moved along the desktop the snowflakes whirled, obscuring the steeple.

'The reason I ask,' said Tolson, his eyes on the paperweight, 'is that if you don't know what Nessheim's up to, somebody else does. Otherwise, why is he back on the payroll?'

Guttman kicked himself. How stupid to fall into a classic Tolson trap. The benevolent pleasantry, the meandering comment, and then *bam!* – the trap closed tight, teeth sharp and lethal. That's why people underestimated Tolson at their peril. Where Hoover sat remotely atop the organisation, protecting it from without, Tolson guarded the regime with assiduous viciousness from within. He possessed a hound's fine nose for detecting any deviation from the company line, and with Tolson in place, there was never any credible chance of a coup.

Guttman sat silently for a minute, looking at the photographs Tolson kept on the top of a glass cabinet set against the side wall. When Tolson did this the trick was to stay calm; not to stutter or protest or too obviously prevaricate. So he stared at a picture of the young Tolson in football uniform – who looked singularly stupid with his leather helmet on, his uniform pristine.

'That is down to me,' Guttman said at last, turning his eyes to meet Tolson's unbenevolent gaze. 'Payroll messed up when Nessheim left – they owed him four weeks' salary. I tried to sort it out, but half the bookkeepers seem to be signing up. Finally, I just threw up my hands, and put him back on payroll for a month. He'll be off by Christmas.'

'Is he doing anything for the money?'

Guttman shook his head. 'No, it's due him, like I said. He's in law school now. It's what he always wanted.'

'So you've seen the guy? He's happy?'

'He was here in the summer. That's when he resigned.' Guttman told himself this was the truth. Just not all of it. He needed a diversion fast; fortunately, Grant in Princeton could provide just that. 'Listen, I've found something out that could be important.'

'Yeah?' Tolson's interest was piqued.

Guttman decided to keep the late Arthur Perkins out of his account, since that would only lead back to Nessheim. He was thinking on his feet, wanting to divert Tolson with a spiel that would lead the man anywhere except Chicago and Nessheim. He took a deep breath and started talking fast. 'You remember the State Department guy who was murdered in Rock Creek Park?' Thornton Palmer, an improbable Communist – born to wealth, a graduate of Yale – who had come to Guttman out of a mix of guilt for betraying his country, and hope that Guttman could clear his name and protect him. Guttman had not been able to do either.

'That was when you went hunting for spies all on your little lonesome,' Tolson said sourly.

Guttman ignored this. 'And Palmer led me to Sedgwick, that banker in New York who was channelling funds for the Russian Embassy.'

'Sedgwick bumped himself off, if I remember.'

'That's right. The Boss thought I'd hounded him to death.'

'You probably did. So what about it?'

'Both Palmer and Sedgwick said there was a third guy they knew who had also been recruited. A scientist at Princeton.'

'Yeah,' said Tolson, pointedly non-committal.

'Well, I may have found him.'

'Oh?' Tolson did not sound enthusiastic.

'His name is Grant. He's still at Princeton.'

'And still a Red, I suppose?'

'Who knows? But I intend to find out. It means we've identified the whole spy ring now. All three of them.'

Tolson shrugged. 'Two of them are dead.'

'Grant's not.'

'But you're not sure he's active any more. That means he's never going to see the inside of a slammer.'

'He should.'

'What harm can he do now?'

This was truer than Tolson could know. On the other hand, if Grant had made it to Chicago ... Guttman said spiritedly, 'What harm does any spy do? He can pass any secret information he lays his hands on to the Russians, that's what he can do.'

'Our allies, you mean. What secrets would they like? It's not as if we have a secret weapon at our disposal. I think everybody would be happy to give them "secrets" if it helped them push the Nazis back ...' Tolson scratched his forehead for a moment. 'I don't get you, Guttman. The Nazis are all over Europe, they're slaughtering the Jews, and you're hunting down some Red who's teaching in the Ivy League. I don't get it at all.'

Out of the blue, unbidden, and spoken before he knew what he was saying, Guttman said, 'Ask T.A. – maybe he would understand.'

Tolson stared at him. When he spoke, his voice was cold, unrattled. 'You want to explain yourself?'

'T.A.'s a bright guy, that's all.' This sounded lame even to Guttman. 'He majored in Political Science, I thought.'

'Fine Arts, actually,' Tolson said flatly. He stared at

Guttman with bloodless eyes. 'Anything else you got in that weird head of yours?' When Guttman didn't reply, Tolson said, 'I didn't think so. Meeting's over.'

Back in his office there was no sign of Marie. Most of his own files were kept in her anteroom; the most confidential he kept in a two-drawer steel box behind his desk. He went to that now and took his key chain from his pocket, where the key he wanted now sat anonymously among those for his car, front door, back door, garage, and Maryland beach house which, since Isabel's death, he no longer rented. He opened the top drawer, found a file, then wrote down the case number, which sat like damning evidence on the memo he had sent the Director two years before.

He had just grabbed his coat again when Marie came back. 'I'll be out for a bit,' he told her. 'Not sure when I'll get back, so don't stay on for me, okay?'

She looked at him questioningly. 'Everything okay, Harry? I mean, was it all right with Tolson?'

'Same old stuff,' he said dismissively. 'Listen, my cousin's in town. I need to see her before she goes back to New York. I don't think she realises how sick my mother is.'

Marie nodded, and Guttman went out, satisfied she had bought his lie. He didn't want Marie involved. If it all blew up, he didn't know if he could save her from Tolson's vengeance, but he'd do his best, including not compromising her now.

He went out of the building into a watery wintry light he usually associated with the dread months immediately following Christmas. Christmas: soon the lights would be up on the stores, and each night's drive through Georgetown's M Street would remind him of the holiday's approach. Annie would be going to Vermont, she had said, a further stage in her reconciliation with her parents there. He doubted he would be bothered to cook a Christmas dinner for one.

On his way east, he passed the Capitol, without noting it. Usually he felt a persisting thrill to be working among the major monuments of his country, but today his sense of threat was starting to overwhelm him. To take on a case he wasn't convinced was real was bad enough; to find it then leading to unexpected targets was worse. But he was making progress. Or doing a brilliant job of fooling himself.

18

ANTRIM WAS AN irreverent man in an organisation built upon reverence, a lover of crosswords who had a phenomenal memory, and was known to everyone as Ant. Out of curiosity Guttman had once consulted the Personnel file where he learned that Antrim's first name was Reginald – but he wouldn't have dreamed of using it. Antrim had clashed with Louis B. Nichols repeatedly over the years, and when Nichols had solidified his grip over the entire Records division once war broke out, he must have consigned Antrim to this semi-exile in the Armory.

'Well, well,' Ant said now, not unfriendly, 'if it isn't a big cheese. What can I do for you, Harry?' He stood behind a counter that looked virtually identical to the one back at Justice, and he pushed the sign-in book towards Guttman.

Guttman ignored it and held up a slip of paper. 'I got a couple of case numbers here – I wanted to have a look at the files.'

'Do you mind giving me a few minutes? I'm on a job for the Director himself, and I'm short of staff today – Mary Ann has got flu.'

'I'm a little pushed, Ant. What do you say I come through and get the boxes myself?'

'You think you can find them?' Antrim liked to think of himself as the sole master of the FBI's Byzantine filing system.

'I'll manage. I've had lessons from the best, remember?' said Guttman. Antrim made a show of scoffing, but Guttman could tell he was flattered.

'Are they recent files?'

'Within the last five years.'

'Okay, be my guest then. Give a yell if you can't find anything. The files from '35 on start at about the forty-yard line.'

'What?'

'You'll see.' Antrim pointed to a door. 'Through there.'

Guttman went through a pair of swing doors and found himself in one corner of the Armory's enormous interior hall, the space of a football field with room for bleachers to boot. The ceiling was a good eighty feet above the ground, and lamps dangled down on cords from the exposed steel rafters, though natural light was also supplied through cathedral-style windows at the Armory's far end.

This would have been the parade ground for the National Guard and any permanent military units stationed in the city. Now it had been given over to the Bureau. Roughly half the space was taken by row after row of drawer-filled wooden cabinets, the height of a grown man. The other half of the floor, closest to him, held rows of tables, with a desk lamp and metal office chair at every available space. Most were occupied, and here FBI technicians and clerks processed, filed and searched through the world's largest collection of fingerprints.

He remembered Antrim's directions, and figured if the fifty-yard line was halfway down, the forty-yard line would be two or three rows of carrels further along. Sure enough, he found the case files for the late 1930s beginning at Row C, and walked slowly along.

The files were held in Manila cardboard boxes, stored vertically with labels on their spines which showed the case number, case name (known as a Ghost) and the serial numbers of the documents held within. Complicated cases had more than one file box; Guttman remembered one investigation that claimed an entire shelf in the Justice Department building. Inside the boxes, stuck to the inner side of each cover, was a lined page held down by thick brown glue which had usually seeped out from the corners before drying. Anyone consulting the file was meant to sign this page, with their department and the date they looked at the file.

For the Dreilander case, there were three boxes, although Guttman was confident that there were others, placed by Helen Gandy in Hoover's personal archive. One of the trio he found now was subtitled '*Rossbach*', and two people had signed the lined page inside. The first was Tolson – it read '*C. A. TOLSON*' in block capitals, followed by the signature Guttman knew well: '*Clyde Anderson Tolson*', written in a sweeping flourish. Tolson was proud of his middle name, and for a while Bureau smart alecs had called him 'Andy' behind his back.

Tolson had examined the file during the previous year; in fact, almost exactly eleven months before: '*December 17, 1941*'. Guttman remembered the chaos in the days after the surprise attack on Pearl Harbor. Both Tolson and Hoover had ignored warnings that the Japanese would strike. Was this why Tolson had looked up the Rossbach file then – ten days after Pearl Harbor, when Nessheim was back in LA after actually witnessing the Hawaiian debacle from the cell of a navy stockade? Had Tolson been scrambling for any ammunition to excuse his and Hoover's negligence? It seemed the likeliest explanation.

Guttman opened the box, dimly remembering its contents and expecting to find the summary he had written when the case was officially closed. That should be here, along with reports from Nessheim, and transcribed accounts of conversations with principals in the case – including Palmer, the dead diplomat, and Sedgwick, the dead banker. Guttman wondered what else he would find.

The answer was nothing. The box was empty; someone had scooped the contents clean. The second signatory? But the handwriting there was an indecipherable scrawl, as were the date and department.

He recrossed the floor and went through the little doorway into the atrium where Ant was still standing.

'Thanks, Ant,' Guttman called out with a wave.

'You didn't sign the book.' Antrim looked at Guttman, with drawn eyes, and Guttman looked back at him neutrally.

'I get it,' Antrim declared at last. 'Good to see you, Harry. Come see us in Butte any time.'

19

LUNCH HAD BEEN over for an hour, but the smell of deep-fried oysters and fried potatoes wafted through the bar. The proprietor was a beefy man with a wart on one cheek; it seemed to have grown since Guttman's last visit. With a cloth rag in one hand and a flat tin in the other, he was working on the bar top, which was weathered to a deep glow by the rag-rubbed wax applied each day. Near the swing doors leading into the kitchen, a plump woman with curls the colour of a thin and artificial sun was drying glasses with a dish towel while the radio played 'I've Got a Gal in Kalamazoo'. Guttman ordered coffee, added cream in a sloppy slurp when the mug arrived, then took it to wait at a table at the back with a view of the front door.

He didn't have long to wait. There was a payphone, a two-piece candlestick set positioned on the wall near Guttman. When it rang the owner gave a final rub with his cloth, then ambled down to the end of the bar and answered it. After a moment he looked around, saw Guttman, and put the receiver on the bar. 'Call for you,' he said and went back to his waxing.

Guttman stood, then went and picked up the phone. He said a tentative hello into the mouthpiece set into the wall.

'It sounds pretty quiet, Harry.' It was Stephenson. 'The guy who answered the phone knew you right away. Is membership down over there? Maybe the dues are too high.'

'Wait until the shift's through next door. You wouldn't find room to draw breath then.'

Stephenson said, 'How are you fixed for time, Harry?'

Guttman looked at his watch. It wasn't yet four o'clock and he wasn't due for supper at Marie's until six-thirty. 'I'm okay.'

'Why don't you take a little drive? It's only ten minutes away.'

'Why am I doing that?'

'You'd better come see for yourself. Let me give you directions.'

Sundown was still an hour away, but a low sky of charcoal cloud gave the sky the grey tint of dusk. Guttman put the Buick's lights on and drove along the river, past warehouses and small factories, then turned north into a working-class neighbourhood of cheap apartments. The land here wasn't reclaimed but looked it – flat and unattractive, with scrubby trees, and in summer the area was as hot as a malarial swamp. Though now it was cold enough for Guttman to put the heating on in his car.

At the edge of the neighbourhood, where it was about to join the better parts of Georgetown, he came to a commercial stretch, the block filled with grocery stores, a hardware store, a diner that was empty inside, two corner bars, and finally, set back slightly from the street, a low row of units, built like a series of bungalows, which had a stand-alone neon sign that announced 'The Winking Eye Motel'. The sign, almost inevitably, winked slowly on and off.

Across the street a stretch of barren ground served as an informal parking lot for half a dozen cars – residents of the apartments above the stores and shoppers who hadn't found a space on the street. Guttman turned in and then pulled around on the bumpy gravel to park facing the motel across the street. He doused his lights after he saw Stephenson get out of his own car and gesture like a traffic cop for Guttman to stay put. The Canadian disappeared in the jumble of cars parked further along the lot, then reappeared suddenly by the passenger-side door and got in.

He was dressed impeccably, as always, unbuttoning a fine wool overcoat to reveal a dark suit with matching vest and a steel-blue tie. It was hard to say where the man looked more out of place – in Katz's, the Jewish deli, on the Lower East Side, or here, across from a sleazy motel near the Potomac.

'We found out why your friend is using bedbug joints. He's got a regular visitor – or two. Ladies. No boarding house landlady's going to put up with that.' Stephenson, for all his worldliness, sounded as though he wouldn't have put up with it either. 'He's in his room now, and not alone. It's the one with the Oldsmobile right outside. If he stays true to form he'll be out shortly – it seems he times these rendezvous to a T.'

A line of cars parked outside the rooms stretched along the walkway of the motel, but he saw the one Stephenson had referred to.

'It could just be a meeting,' said Guttman.

'I don't think so. Young Fletcher – he's sitting in a car at the other end of the lot – is an enterprising fellow. He bribed a maid to let him into the room. He said the evidence was incontrovertible.'

Guttman said, 'You said he had more than one visitor.'

'That's correct. Fletcher didn't go quite so far with the other lady, but he didn't need to. He walked by the room on the way to the soda machine. Fletcher said there was enough noise coming from inside the room to make it clear what was going on.'

'Golly,' said Guttman. 'The boy's got energy.'

237

'You sound surprised.' Stephenson laughed.

'I am,' Guttman admitted, wondering what Tolson would make of his protégé's way of ending the day. But he was also wondering what the point of spying on this was. It smacked of voyeurism, and seemed faintly prurient. T.A. liked to shack up of an afternoon with some dollies – what of it?

Guttman glanced at Stephenson, who was looking around in every direction, but slowly, barely noticeably. For an amateur he was very careful. Guttman said, 'When we met in New York you said there was a reason we were cutting off your information supply.'

'Did I?' Stephenson's eyes grew watery, a habit they had when he didn't like a question.

'Yes,' said Guttman firmly.

Stephenson said reluctantly, 'We had a problem that your guys in the military found out about.'

'Oh? What sort of problem?'

'Some secrets travelled east from England. Scientific information – about the project we were all cooperating so nicely on.'

'How far east?'

Stephenson said, 'Well, it went past Berlin without stopping, if you get my drift.'

'What's wrong with that? They're our allies now,' he said, trying to parrot Tolson's party line.

'But not privy to the project. As you must know.'

'So what's the upshot?'

'Groves learned about the leak. He managed to get an interdict on any further exchanges of technical information – there's been a transatlantic working group. It seems a bit unfair, since we helped get your guys started in the first place.'

Guttman wouldn't have been able to tell either way. Stephenson went on, 'We raised it eventually

238

with Churchill himself. He took it up with the White House.'

'I thought he and Roosevelt get on like a house on fire.'

'They do, but your President knows he's holding all the valuable cards. We figured he wouldn't directly override his Military Intelligence people's recommendations – or Groves's – unless he had other advisers telling him to.'

'Which ones?' Guttman asked. During the New Deal, FDR's kitchen cabinet had been famous – or notorious, depending on one's view. Tommy the Cork, Ben Cohen, and such a slew of Frankfurter acolytes that they were known as the 'hot-dog' boys, in vernacular recognition of their patron's surname. But by now many had either left government or taken senior positions in the administration outside the White House. According to Annie, Frankfurter had recently been lamenting his loss of a coterie around the President.

Stephenson said, 'Harry Hopkins visited London last winter.'

'I remember.' He had praised the pluck of the English loudly at the time. 'He loves you Brits.'

'Maybe,' said Stephenson cryptically. Guttman couldn't read his expression. Stephenson said, 'In any case, he's helped try to overturn the edict. We're hoping normal practice will resume early in the New Year. By that time, the project should be based in one place.'

'Really?'

Stephenson said flatly, 'They can't exactly keep it on the South Side of Chicago.'

Guttman was dismayed that Stephenson knew so much more about it than he did. He consoled himself that Hoover knew even less. 'I've come to the conclusion that you're right – the Germans don't have anyone in Chicago. Or anywhere else for that matter. Though I still worry about that note Nessheim received.'

'It could be a stray thing – some hangover from his work undercover in the *Bund*. You said so yourself.'

'I still think something's not right in Chicago.' He took a deep breath and then told Stephenson about his two visits to the Upper West Side building where Arthur Perkins had died. 'If Perkins was murdered, I decided it was to let someone take his place. I thought I'd found the substitute – his name is Grant, and he's a Professor of Physics at Princeton. There's just one problem – he's still in Princeton.'

'Who would have been trying to get him into the Chicago lab?'

This sounded oddly naive of Stephenson, and Guttman looked at him disbelievingly. 'The same people who received your classified info. As I think you know already. In fact, I think you've known all along.'

The ensuing silence was so suffocating that Guttman wanted to get out of the car. But he needed to hear Stephenson first.

The Canadian exhaled a long spiral of air, his breath misting on the windscreen. 'I tried to tell you – when we talked on the phone here and then in New York. If you look back I think you'd have to admit that. If I was a bit elusive, understand that I was – I *am* – in a difficult position. Here were your guys in Military Intelligence ordering the head of the project to cut off all ties with us – because they think we're a leaky sieve. So if we said you were leaky too, they'd just think we were trying to get our own back. And since the Bureau doesn't even know about the project, I couldn't express my concerns to you. You can see that.'

Guttman grunted sceptically. 'But you talked to me before.' After the debacle of Pearl Harbor, Stephenson had done more than talk – he had helped spirit Nessheim away from the military authorities when they'd decided the younger agent was a spy.

'Sure I did. But you're out in left field, Harry – sometimes I think you live there. It's not a question of trust – I trust you plenty. But from what I know of the man, Hoover will be gunning for you. You know too much. I hate to be so blunt, but I have to figure that one of these days you'll be out on your ear.'

Guttman felt a crushing sense of disappointment, though he wasn't sure why – nothing Stephenson had said was unreasonable. In the past Guttman wouldn't have minded Stephenson's candour, yet here he was dismayed that Stephenson felt forced to hedge his bets. Was Guttman going soft? He had never needed allies at work, except for tactical reasons. Isabel had been his ally through everything: work, money, their joint childlessness, all the problems of life. He must have got needy, he decided, living on his own. How pathetic.

'There's another thing,' said Stephenson, perhaps sensing Guttman's introspective gloom. 'It's the other problem we talked about. In the Bureau. I can't move on that – only you can, Harry. And for a while I wasn't sure you could be bothered.' He added gently, 'After Isabel died.'

Guttman didn't respond. There was nothing to contest. He knew he had been out of touch; he knew he had stopped following the trail.

'Hang on!' Stephenson said, and he pointed through the windshield towards the motel. A man had come out of a room, but instead of closing the door he stood holding it open. After a moment a woman also came out, hastily buttoning up her overcoat. They moved off along the walkway, the man striding fast, until he stopped to wait for his companion, gesturing for her to get a move on. They were hard to see as dusk began to darken the scene, but then they passed through a disc of light cast by an overhead bulb.

'What's the matter?' Stephenson demanded, and Guttman realised he had gasped involuntarily. 'Don't tell me we've got the wrong guy.'

'No, it's him all right.' T.A. from the Bureau, as he had guessed long before. The only surprise was that T.A. liked humping girls, when Guttman had taken him for Tolson's protégé in more than strictly professional ways.

That wasn't what had made him start, though he wanted another look to be sure. By now the couple had reached the motel office at the walkway's end. T.A. went inside – to lodge his key or ask for change or maybe even check out – and the woman remained standing outside, motionless in the yellow light of the outside lamp.

She moved her head to throw her hair back, and Guttman remembered when he'd seen her last. There was no longer any doubt in his mind. And as T.A. came out of the motel office and took the woman's arm, Guttman wondered how the Tolson protégé had come to know the black-haired temptress from the train.

20

MARIE LIVED ON the northern fringes of the city, near Rock Creek Park, in one of a series of three-storey apartment buildings erected just before the Depression hit. She had a long bus ride to work, but she'd explained that the neighbourhood was safe and the school for her little boy Jack was good. Guttman had never been there before, and when he parked outside on the street he found it nicer than he had imagined.

He brought a box of chocolates since it seemed an anodyne gift – booze would have suggested he was presuming an intimacy that didn't exist. When he pressed the buzzer he heard Marie shout for her son to answer it. The boy answered the door and stood staring at Guttman. He couldn't have been more than seven years old.

'Hi,' said Guttman.

'Are you Mr G?'

Is that what Marie called him at home? 'I guess so,' he said.

'Where's your gun then?'

'If I tell you, will you let me in?'

Marie came down the corridor from the back of the apartment. She had changed for dinner, and wore heels and a navy blue crepe dress half-covered by an apron – she was drying her hands on it as she walked towards him.

'Jack,' she exclaimed, 'invite Mr Guttman in! He's our guest.'

While Marie took his coat and hung it in the hall closet, Guttman walked into the living room. It was modestly furnished but comfortable, with a three-seater sofa with soft cushions and a couple of decent second-hand chairs. On the mantelpiece there was a line of small china figures, including a little painted Madonna which reminded him that Marie was Catholic. A card table with a mended leg was set for dinner.

'I bet you could use a drink,' Marie said, as Jack stared up at Guttman. She went to the kitchen and brought out an ice tray and a pitcher of water, and he poured himself a stiff drink and made Marie a weaker one at her request. They sat down on the sofa, while Jack buzzed around them. She was going to Quebec for Christmas, to see her parents and siblings. Instead of asking him what he was doing then, she asked about Thanksgiving, the following week.

'Gosh,' he said, then suddenly thought she might be thinking of asking him over again. 'I'll probably be down seeing Mom in New York.'

For dinner, Marie had gone to a lot of effort, giving him three courses, starting with pea soup. Then she brought out a big casserole dish, holding it away from her with oven mitts, while Guttman steadied the table. When she took the lid off, steam rose like a genie's breath. Jack laughed. Marie served, putting a big chop on each plate, with sauerkraut and potatoes that came from the casserole. She was handing Guttman his plate when suddenly she froze.

'What's the matter?' he asked.

'Oh, Harry, I'm so sorry. It's pork chops. Is that a problem?'

What? He was merely flattered that she'd used her ration cards on him. But then he got it. 'No, that's fine, Marie. Isabel made pork all the time.'

'She did?' Marie said, looking as though she thought he was just being polite.

'Sure. She wasn't Jewish, after all.'

'I didn't know that.'

She didn't? Guttman was surprised. How many times had Marie helped him buy his wife a Christmas present? How many times had he joked about what the nuns who'd brought up Isabel would make of her 'unsuitable' marriage? None of which had made a dent on Marie, it seemed.

He said forcefully, 'I eat anything, believe me. And it smells delicious.'

For dessert Marie had pushed the boat out – to the far shore, thought Guttman. She served *grands-pères*, sweet dumplings in maple syrup with vanilla ice cream. Marie explained that they reminded her of Canada, where her father had been a logger. With them she passed around a plate of whippet cookies, sweet biscuits topped by marshmallow that had been coated in a hard shell of chocolate. They were impossible to find in Washington, Marie explained, because the pure chocolate didn't survive the shipping, and she'd brought them down from her last visit home. Guttman nodded, struggling to clean his plate, feeling that if he ate one more spoonful of the sugar-filled dessert he would crystallise.

After dinner Marie put Jack to bed, then made coffee, which she brought out on a tray that held little china cups, two snifters and a pint bottle of brandy. 'Have a nightcap, Harry,' she said.

She sat down on the sofa next to him. Not too close, but not very far away. Guttman was starting to feel uncomfortable.

He turned down the offer of brandy, and to shift the mood he asked, 'How's your young friend, T.A.?'

She looked bemused. 'Okay, I guess. Very busy – Mr Tolson sends him all over the place.'

'I bet he does.'

'Why do you ask?'

'Just wondered. You made it sound like half the gals in typing were sweet on him.'

She shrugged and gave a half-smile. 'I guess they are. He's a nice boy.'

'How about you?'

'How about me what?' He saw she didn't like the question.

'Are you sweet on him too, Marie? He's a good-looking kid.'

'I'm almost old enough to be his mother, Harry,' she protested.

'Nah. Big sister maybe.'

'Flatterer,' she said and moved almost imperceptibly closer on the couch.

'I'm sure he'd be interested, Marie. It's obvious he likes you.'

'Well, *I'm* not interested,' she said firmly. 'Whatever you say, it would be robbing the cradle. Besides, I don't think you're right about him.'

'What, about being interested in you? Of course he is. No one in typing holds a candle to you.'

'For goodness' sake, he lives with his mother.'

'You can't tell a lot from that.' Guttman shrugged benignly. 'It's not something I'd have wanted to do at his age. But each to his own, eh?'

'He's not really interested. A woman can tell, Harry. I don't just mean me – the other girls would say the same thing.' She added slyly, 'Maybe that's why he works for Mr Tolson.' She put a hand to her mouth. 'Sorry.'

Guttman laughed. 'That's okay, Marie. You're probably right about that.' He was trying to make sense of this. Just a few hours before, he'd seen evidence to the contrary. The kid was obviously a bit of a ladies' man, yet that wasn't the impression he was making at work.

If Marie was casting doubts, then Adams must be giving that impression on purpose. Why?

He wasn't going to find out talking to Marie. Then she said, 'Did I mention, Harry, that my husband is finally divorcing me?'

'No, you didn't. I'm sorry.'

'I'm not. I haven't seen the bum in five years, so it's not like it's going to make a difference. He didn't even send Jack a birthday card this year.'

'So maybe it's for the best.'

'It is. Especially since I'm not initiating it.' She gave a laugh that was unlike her usual robust one. 'I'm a good Catholic girl, after all. I couldn't do it myself. But I'm glad he is.'

She leaned back now, though her scent lingered like potpourri in a drawer. 'He was a Wobbly. Worked the lumber mills, which is where he met my dad – and then me. He's still out there, only now he's an organiser, travelling all around.'

'Listen, Marie,' he said, glad he hadn't had another beer, 'why don't I help you do the dishes before I leave?'

He could see this startled her. She said, 'I'll do them in the morning. Don't go yet, Harry.' He could smell the scent on her neck. Lemon and sugar; it reminded him of lemonade. It was tempting for all of two seconds. During all the years with Isabel he had never found it hard to stay in line; even had he been tempted to stray, one no-go would have been anyone working for him.

Guttman said now, 'We've both got work in the morning. I'd better get some sleep in case Tolson calls me back again.' He gave a faint-hearted laugh, and noticed that her movement his way on the couch had stopped.

She said, 'Are you sure?'

They both knew what she meant. He said quietly,

'I'm sure, Marie.' He paused for a moment. 'Sorry,' he said. That was as close as he wanted to come to addressing this awkward situation.

'It's okay, Harry.'

'Maybe another time,' he said gently.

She nodded. 'Sure, that would be great. I'll cook something other than pork chops.' But her smile was doleful; Harry could see she was trying to mask her disappointment. She got up, brushing a crumb off her skirt. 'I'll get your coat.'

21

ONCE HOME HE suddenly realised how tired he was. When the phone rang he was half-asleep on the sofa, with the radio playing from Radio City Music Hall in New York. It was Nessheim, finally calling back.

'About time,' said Guttman crossly. 'Didn't you get my message from your room-mate?'

'I don't have a room-mate.'

'She sure sounded like one.'

'I thought my personal life was my own, Harry.'

'It is,' he said grudgingly.

'That's big of you. Thanks.'

Guttman suppressed a sigh. The last thing he needed was a quarrel with Nessheim right now. 'So, anything to report?' he asked.

But Nessheim had little news, other than to say that the project at Stagg Field was progressing quickly, and that Fermi was now hoping for a result well before his previous deadline of New Year's.

When he'd finished telling this, Guttman said, 'There are a couple things I want you to check.' He explained them, while Nessheim listened in silence. Finally Guttman said, 'You still there?'

'Just writing it all down. Bergen at Fort Sheridan and Fermi about Grant. Anything else?'

'That's it. But ASAP.'

'I'm on the case.'

Guttman hung up, annoyed and wondering why he felt that way. Was he cross with Nessheim for not being with Annie? No. So what was it? And then he realised:

Nessheim was *happy*. Like a child who wasn't, Guttman didn't think this was fair.

At the office in the morning, Marie was cheerful, polite, demurely dressed and slightly aloof. His heart sank as her conversation touched on every topic under the sun except that of the night before. Oh, Marie, Guttman thought, why couldn't you have left things as they were – my work confidante, my doorkeeper?

He had to say something. When she came into his office again he was about to speak, but something in the set of her lips stopped him. He decided he would wait a minute and then try, but Marie was already talking. She handed over an envelope, saying, 'This is from the Chicago Field Office, but by registered mail. *Highly confidential.*' She sounded simultaneously sceptical and cross. 'Not by telex,' she added significantly. Normally anything urgent from the office there would come that way. She looked at Guttman. 'You want to tell me what's going on?'

'Nothing's going on.'

'Then why do you keep sneaking in and out of the office? Why are you making mysterious calls and receiving confidential letters? And why did Tolson want you up in his office?'

'Honest, nothing's going on,' he said plaintively.

'Okay, don't tell me if you don't want to,' she said with a sigh, and retreated to the anteroom, closing the door behind her.

What the hell, he thought. He picked up the envelope, noticing the embossed Chicago Field Office address on its back flap, and wondering why they were communicating this way. He occasionally received the odd loony missive, easily dismissed, not even filed, but had never had one forwarded from a field office.

He extracted a single page and saw that it was typed on letterhead. Looking down, he found the signature of Eloise Tate, aka Tatie, and when he read what she had to say he thought his blood would turn cold.

Oh, Nessheim, he thought bitterly, how could you do this to me? The questions that had been plaguing him were starting to have answers, but there was little consolation in that. Nessheim had fallen for the oldest trick in the book, and he had taken Guttman with him.

Part Five

22

NESSHEIM KNOCKED FIRMLY, just made out a muttered *come in*, and opened the door. Professor Fielding had been Dean of the School before his retirement, and since his successor occupied his old quarters, Fielding had been given this large office on the third floor of Stuart Hall, overlooking the Quadrangle. Oak panelling, a mahogany cabinet bookcase, walls plastered with a slight handmade warp, and mullioned windows with black iron handles – like the outside campus, the interiors of its perimeter buildings were designed to mimic medieval Oxford rather than the Midwest prairie on which they were set.

Fielding was working at his rolltop desk at the far end of the room. 'Yes,' he said wearily from his books, without looking up.

Nessheim explained that he'd missed the class when exams had been returned. Still writing, Fielding reached blindly with his other hand for the small stack of blue books on a corner of the desk. 'Name?' he asked curtly.

'Nessheim.'

Fielding put down his pen and went through the blue books. 'Burgess, Merrick, Symonds, and here we are – Nessheim.' He studied the exam book, which had the grade on the cover, then looked up. He seemed surprised. '*You're* Mr Nessheim? Or are you collecting it on his behalf?'

'No, I'm Nessheim all right.'

'I see.' Fielding didn't sound convinced. 'Tell me, have you been in law school somewhere else?'

'No. This is my first year.'

'Hmm. Where did you take your BA?'

'I didn't. I left Northwestern before graduating.'

'What have you been doing since then?'

'I was with the Federal Bureau of Investigation.'

'Is that what they're calling it now?'

'Yes.'

'I take it you're exempt from military service?' It was clear both that the question was rhetorical and what he already thought of the answer. 'So now?'

'I'm in law school,' said Nessheim mildly. He did not want to be drawn into the subject of his deferment.

Picking up the blue book, Fielding waved it as if in reprimand. 'Well, I have to say this is outstanding work.'

'Thank you.' He felt almost childishly pleased by Fielding's praise.

'It's the best exam I've had this year. If it hadn't been taken under supervision, I'd be suspicious you'd had assistance.' He gave a thin malicious laugh as he handed back the exam.

Nessheim said, 'I'm as surprised as you. I don't find Torts easy.' This seemed to allay Fielding's scepticism. Had Fielding really thought he was a cheat, and too stupid to do well legitimately? Nessheim was about to leave, but Fielding wasn't through. 'I've seen you in class, Mr Nessheim.'

'I hope so, Professor. This was my first absence,' he said drily.

'You sit with Miss Madison. Is she a friend of yours?'

Nessheim was too old to be coy. 'Yes. A good friend.'

'Ah.' Was this a check to the old boy's hopes? Fielding said, 'I don't know if she's mentioned it, but I was an acquaintance of her late father's.'

'I see,' said Nessheim neutrally.

Fielding brought a hand to his mouth and coughed. He cleared his throat and said, 'That girl is trouble.'

256

'Trouble?' asked Nessheim, surprised.

'I said *troubled*.'

'She makes a lot of people happy.'

'I'm sure she does,' Fielding said, staring at Nessheim. 'I hope they make her happy too.' He sighed, then said, 'People think money solves everything. But she's not had an easy life. Her father was a very busy man. Businessmen tend to be. Successful ones, anyway.'

'I never met him.'

'He's been dead some years. He was devoted to Stacey. If he'd lived I doubt she'd have gone off the rails.'

'Did she?' said Nessheim coolly.

Fielding nodded, undeterred. 'Too much money, too little direction. If something could be counted on to shock the staid ladies of Lake Forest, then you name it – Miss Madison did it. She was just plain wild all around. She drank – though she came by that honestly from her mother. She smoked – I wouldn't be surprised if there weren't some dope-taking too. She travelled the world like an heiress in a novel by Edith Wharton – Paris one year, Rome the next, then even Mexico. She was rarely alone – she always had men in her sway – and she's a beautiful girl. You can't deny that.'

Nessheim wasn't about to try, but Fielding was in any case now in full flow. 'For a while she was pink in her politics. More than pink, in fact – she was positively vermilion. Fortunately she seems to have had most of that political nonsense knocked out of her by her time in Mexico. As I say, her father was devoted to her. Her mother . . .' and he sighed to show both that it was sad and that he was being fair, 'is not a happy woman, but she has always tried her best. She came to see me when her daughter wanted to enrol. I was happy to help, even though it was a late application – very late. I have to say that I don't think her new-found interest in the law runs very deep.' He looked at Nessheim, as if he could count on his understanding. 'Fortunately, she's a smart girl, even if her previous record here was not what anyone would call outstanding. Still, it seems better for her to be occupied and out of harm's way than hanging around with a bunch of Jewish Communists in Hollywood. Nice to see you, Mr Nessheim.'

Nessheim collected his blue book, thanking Fielding. The buoyancy of doing so well in the exam had been punctured by Fielding's account of Stacey. Leaving the office, Nessheim felt he was the troubled one now.

23

Snow came, just a sprinkling at first, but accompanied by a blasting icy cold. The temperature sank. There was a thermometer bolted to the outside of the Kimbark living-room window and when it hit minus 5 degrees Fahrenheit outside, its strip of mercury stopped moving and wouldn't budge. That night four inches of snow fell, then another three on the following day. Winter had begun.

With the training of a Wisconsin childhood to fall back on, Nessheim put on thick woollen socks, long johns and an extra T-shirt for warmth. His boots were ridged and didn't slip on the snow. Stacey laughed at the get-up, but she wore heavy boots as well, though characteristically they were fur-lined with the same soft beaver pelt stitched inside her leather gloves.

At the Lab the foreigners suffered the most, especially the Southern Europeans. Szilard waddled around with a homburg on his head and an oversized black coat that made him look like a snowman crossed with a penguin. He wore two woollen scarves wrapped around his throat, one clockwise and the other counterclockwise; once safely inside, it took him almost a minute to free himself from their snake-like embrace, and for the first time Nessheim saw the lugubrious Nadelhoffer laugh. Their leader, Fermi, had purchased a pair of oversized gloves, a cotton face mask, and black rubber boots with buckles he struggled to undo, since their web-like clips filled with snow during his short walk to work.

At Stagg Field braziers had been brought in for the guards at the entrance, who got up every few minutes to stand by the coals and rub sensation back into their hands. They were cold even in the racoon-fur coats they had purloined from the abandoned lockers. In the racquets courts, heating was primitive and draughty, the wind whistling through the old concrete stands above, but the pace of the physical work going on meant nobody was truly cold. Knuth, working his saws and lathes, was actually sweating on the morning Nessheim came by.

He was looking for Fermi, and found him alone with the battery of neutron counters on the balcony ten feet above the court where the Pile was being erected. He was reading a book. When Nessheim looked closer at it, he saw to his surprise that it was *Winnie-the-Pooh*. Fermi turned his head and met his quizzical look. 'It helps me improve my English,' he said with a smile. 'I call some of the instruments here by names of characters from the stories. This one here,' he said, pointing to the nearest contraption, 'is Tigger.'

Work was progressing fast: even a week before, the wall of graphite brick could have been hurdled by Nessheim; now it was above his head. A small elevator had been brought in, at Groves's insistence, since on his recent visit (one he had not told Nessheim about), he'd been furious to discover the leading physicists of their generation risking life and limb on wobbly scaffolding used to help build up the graphite Pile.

'How are you, Mr Nessheim?' said Fermi, shaking hands. '*Va bene?*'

'*Si.*'

Fermi smiled. 'We will make an Italian of you yet. Tell me, how is your friend Miss Madison?'

'Very well. I believe she is having lunch soon with your wife.' Talking with Fermi, Nessheim found his speech becoming a kind of formal hybrid, like the hero

260

talking to his Spanish girlfriend in *For Whom the Bell Tolls*.

Fermi stared down at the men working below. Despite his friendly welcome, there was something impenetrably moody about his gaze, though outwardly he exuded calm. On the floor next to him sat a suitcase, and Fermi was dressed in a smart double-breasted suit with wide lapels and a tie the colour of old blood. Below, several men, dressed in blackening grey overalls, were hard at work heaving the heavy graphite blocks into place. The Pile now was taller than a man, and shaped like a vast honeycomb, made of latticed layers of graphite, braced by a wooden frame of pine boards; Knuth's handiwork. Nessheim asked, 'Are you going somewhere, Professor?'

Fermi nodded. 'To Washington on the train this afternoon. Meetings tomorrow and Friday, and then back. I do not wish to be away longer than is necessary.'

'But tomorrow is Thanksgiving.'

Fermi shrugged. 'Unfortunate, I know. But General Groves does not believe in vacations in wartime.'

Lucky Mrs Groves, thought Nessheim. 'It must be important.'

Fermi said, 'Everything is important to the General. I am there to report on progress here.'

'Are you happy with things?'

Fermi nodded. 'Do not hold me to the promise, but I believe we may arrive soon at the conclusion. Perhaps as soon as next week. Originally, I had predicted we would succeed by New Year, so this is very pleasing. Even General Groves may be satisfied.' He grimaced at the improbability of this, and Nessheim laughed.

Fermi said, 'Professor Lawrence in Berkeley bet Compton that it could not be done this year. He will lose his bet, I am sure.'

'What good news. But I need to ask you something,

Professor.' Fermi looked at him, curious. 'We understand you interviewed a scientist and offered him a place on your team. Back when you were at Columbia. But he didn't come, and we were wondering why.'

'Who was that?' His tone was matter-of-fact, but he had picked up his slide rule and was fiddling with it, so his eyes didn't meet Nessheim's.

'His name is Grant. He's at Princeton.'

Fermi's expression changed to a philosophical one, though his eyes remained firmly focused on the slide rule. 'Professor Perkins and I were both impressed by him. He grasped the potential of graphite as a moderator right away.'

'So you offered him a job?'

'I did. This was after Professor Perkins died. Grant would have been perfect to help set up our prototypes.'

'But he didn't join.'

Fermi sighed. 'I was ordered to withdraw the offer.'

'By whom?'

Now Fermi was looking unhappily at Nessheim. 'The military. This was before General Groves was involved. He can be difficult, we all know that, but there is always a reason for his decisions. In this case I could see no such reason. An officer came to see me in New York. He explained that Grant had some . . . how shall I say it? Unfortunate associates, opposed to America.'

'The enemy?' It seemed incredible.

'No,' Fermi said knowingly. 'Not the enemy, if you mean the Nazis or the Japanese.'

'The Russians?'

'Closer. It was the native variety of Communists, apparently.' He said this in almost sing-song fashion, like an advertising jingle. 'Grant had friends who were members of the Party many years ago. I am sure it was a juvenile mistake. We all do dumb things when we are young, you know.'

'Sure,' said Nessheim reflexively. 'So what happened?'

Fermi shrugged. 'I had the privilege of writing to this man to say his participation would not be required after all. It was absurd, of course. I did not feel he had strong views about politics at all. And anyway, the Russian Communists are our allies now. Is that not true?'

'In theory,' said Nessheim, deadpan. From their conversation at the Quadrangle Club, he knew Fermi was no fan of the Russians, but equally he didn't seem to consider them capable of spying on their allies. Szilard had remarked on Fermi's political naivety and Nessheim saw why.

Fermi smiled at Nessheim's remark. ' "In theory" – I like that.'

'Was Grant upset?'

'He must have been. If I felt bad writing the news, he would have felt much worse receiving it. I was not happy about it at all. It did not seem just. But this was soon after Professor Perkins was killed in an accident. Horrible.' He shook his head at the memory.

'But you still needed someone, didn't you? If Grant didn't join your team, who did?'

'Professor Kalvin. He had only just arrived from Portugal. Szilard likes to say he was the last Jew to get out. Certainly he must have been the last scientist.'

'Is he around?' asked Nessheim.

'No, he's in New Mexico.'

'New Mexico? What's he doing there?'

'He and Oppenheimer are –' Fermi suddenly stopped, looking guilty for his indiscretion.

Nessheim knew not to press. He said instead, 'How did you recruit Kalvin?

Fermi seemed to relax. Then his chest began to shake

like jelly, and Nessheim realised he was trying to keep from laughing.

'What's so funny, Professor?' he asked, bewildered.

Fermi tried to recover his composure. He said, 'I should not be telling you this, but I think you will appreciate it.'

'What's that?'

'Because Kalvin had only just arrived in America, we did not know the man himself – only his work from the journals. It is very good – no question. We asked him if there was someone in this country who could speak on his behalf, someone who could supply a . . .' He hesitated and looked to Nessheim for help.

'A reference. To recommend him.'

'Exactly. And it happened there was such a man, a physicist of high reputation. The letter he wrote came and the reference was outstanding. It praised Kalvin up to the clouds.' He lifted a hand above his head with a dramatic flourish. 'I told the military idiot about it and he was pleased. Kalvin was let through.'

'And?'

'I felt much better about the earlier injustice. You see, the letter came from Princeton University. It was written by Professor Grant.'

Nessheim hurried back to the Kimbark apartment to phone Guttman but when he reached the office in D.C. Marie answered. She explained that Guttman had left early.

'Can I get him at home, Marie?'

'You could try. Tomorrow's Thanksgiving, you know.'

'They have it out here too, Marie,' he said, and she laughed. 'Where's he spending it, anyway?'

'Beats me, Jim. Maybe with some neighbours in Arlington.' Annie, thought Nessheim, and realised that the thought of her no longer stirred him. Marie added, 'I don't think he's going to his mother's in New York. I'm not sure she even recognises him any more.'

Guttman had a mother? Nessheim was taken aback. Someone had once said Guttman's wife had been an orphan, and without thinking much about it Nessheim had always assumed Guttman had been one too. He'd figured that he and Isabel had found each other in some unspecified institution, a connection that had proved to be Guttman's lifeline to the human race. To Nessheim, Guttman was a self-creation, one refined by the ministrations of his wife over the years, but always an independent agent uninfluenced by his past. Nessheim decided Marie must have got it wrong about the mother.

24

'YOU KNOW WHAT tomorrow is?' Nessheim asked, coming into the kitchen where water boiled for spaghetti and Stacey was stirring a small pot of tomato sauce.

'They call it Thanksgiving,' she said, enough acid in her voice to make him look at her.

'You going to your mom's?' he asked, trying to sound uninterested.

'No. You going to yours?' The asperity was unmistakable now.

'Of course not. She'll be with her cousins in Bremen. And their kids and grandkids and God knows who else.' He waited but Stacey kept stirring the sauce. 'So what do you think?'

'About Thanksgiving?' She put the spoon down. 'I guess I'll spend the day at my apartment.'

He realised she was angry. 'You can't do that. There are mouths to feed. Mainly mine.'

'Oh, yeah?' There was the first hint of humour in her voice.

'I'll do the dishes if you cook. That's a promise.'

She was wavering; he could tell. He went up behind her and put his arms around her shoulders, and she turned slowly, feeling soft as soap in his winter-chapped hands. He said, 'I think we should spend tomorrow together. Just to make sure I count my blessings.'

She leaned up to meet his lips with hers as he tucked his head down to kiss her. She didn't let go, and he realised she wasn't going to let him get away with just a kiss. Eventually she stood back and dropped the wooden spoon into the pot of sauce, then grabbed him again. He only just managed to turn the stove-top burner off before she had him, half-pulling, half-pushing, into the bedroom, his tie off and his shirt unbuttoned.

Later they lay in bed, side by side, exhausted.

'And you say I'm the hungry one,' he said lightly.

'That's different.'

'Why?'

'Do I have to explain?' Inexplicably she looked close to tears.

'Sure you do.' He was hoping to kid her out of the moodiness he sensed descending.

She took a deep breath. 'When I was a girl my father would get a craving for clams once a year or so. He'd drive all the way down here and buy a great sack of them from Jesselson's Steamers. He'd come home and give the cook the night off, then boil them up in a kettle the size of a ship's cauldron. I liked them well enough but my mother only ate a few – she didn't like the briny taste. My father ate them by the dozen. He'd tie a napkin around his neck and sit down with half a loaf of bread he'd use like a sponge to soak up the broth.'

'And the point is?' he asked like a benevolent Professor Fielding.

'Nothing else would do. Not a T-bone steak or oysters wrapped in bacon or veal kidneys – the other things he loved to eat. That night it had to be clams.'

'So?' asked Nessheim, wondering where this was going. 'Am I your clam?'

She didn't laugh. 'You're the type who'd take the oysters or the steak or the kidneys – or the clams. You're just hungry period.' She added, 'But I only want the clams. Even if they've got a gritty kind of shell.'

He didn't say anything. After a while she got out of bed and put on her robe, then lit a cigarette. She stood by the window, looking out at the courtyard. He said, 'I'm sorry I forgot about Thanksgiving. Something's come up'.

'You want to tell me about it?'

'I can't – I'm not even supposed to know about it.'

'Okay, though you can trust me, you know.'

'I know that.'

'I hope so.' She took a deep breath. 'Nessheim, are you going to take me up to Bremen some time?'

He felt caught flat-footed; this had not even occurred to him in passing. 'Why do you want to go there?'

'So I could meet your mom and see where you grew up. Anything wrong with that?'

'You've never done the same for me. And your mother lives ten miles away, not two hundred.'

She turned and stared at him. 'Do you like your mother?'

'I love my mother.'

'Do you like where you grew up?'

'Sure.'

'Then there's your answer.' She was fumbling in her purse. 'When can we go?'

He hesitated, visualising Stacey's first encounter with his mother. Stacey read his thoughts. 'Don't worry, I'll behave. I'll even dress the part.'

'What part's that?'

'I'll let you know – I've got the feeling auditions aren't quite over. But the costume's easy – I was thinking a dirndl, with no make-up. So how about it?'

'Let me give it some thought,' he said with even less conviction than he felt. He didn't want to rush into this. For him, Stacey meant his present, not his past.

'Are you paying me back?'

'For what?'

'For leaving you when we were first together.'

He thought about this for a moment, then said slowly, 'Maybe. Why did you do it, anyhow?'

'I felt I didn't deserve you.'

He laughed. This sounded just like the 'it's not you, it's me' that girls liked to tell guys to let them down easy. 'I didn't realise I wore a halo back then,' he said. 'Don't worry – I don't wear one now.'

'I've noticed.' But then she grew serious again. 'I didn't want to be with you because it made me feel bad about myself and bad about what I was doing to you.'

'Couldn't you have said so? You weren't doing anything wrong as far as I was concerned. I was crazy about you.'

'So have you been in love since?'

'Since when?'

'Since you were in love with me?'

Nessheim looked at her sceptically. 'What's all this love talk anyway, Stacey? You told me once you didn't believe in love.'

'We all say stupid things, especially at that age. And even later on if we're scared.'

'Scared?' He looked at her and laughed. 'What are you scared of?'

'Not you,' she said, as if stung. She looked as though she was through explaining, and stubbed out her cigarette on the little porcelain ashtray she had once lifted from the Palmer House. 'So let's have Thanksgiving together. But I really do need to go to my apartment for a while. I love Drusilla but she never could clean worth a damn, and now she's turned seventy she doesn't even pretend.'

25

THEY HAD THANKSGIVING dinner the following day at supper time. While the rest of the nation, full to the gills from their mid-afternoon meal, sat around listening to Radio City Music Hall, Stacey cooked their meal and Nessheim kept her company in the kitchen, fortifying them both with a couple of bourbon highballs. She'd found two turkey legs at the butcher's on 53rd Street, and after cutting pockets along their meaty ends she stuffed them with mushrooms and breadcrumbs, then roasted them slowly in the oven while she made succotash and a box of wild rice she'd saved for a special occasion.

When they sat down to eat, she brought out a bottle of Chianti from the drawer she used in the bedroom. Nessheim filled two sherry glasses from the straw-encased bottle and toasted Stacey. As they started to eat he said, 'How did you find the Chianti?'

'Top secret.'

'Was it Mrs Fermi?'

'That's classified information. You won't get a word out of me.'

He laughed. 'You like her, don't you?'

'Very much. We're having lunch next week.'

'You told me. She seems great. Enrico – I don't know about him. I like him well enough – he's friendly, and a pretty regular guy for someone who's won a Nobel Prize.'

'But?'

'I just sense there's something going on with him. I don't mean his work – he's not allowed to talk about it in any case. But I think something else is bothering him, and I wish I knew what it was.'

'It has to be tough for him living here. He's not your average immigrant, now, is he? There's a lot riding on his work.'

'How do you know that?'

'I wasn't born yesterday. I can tell from the way the others defer to him. Not just because he's their boss – he's also their *leader*. I don't have the faintest idea about it, but I know it's important. And I don't think you have to worry about him. It's the other guys I'd be watching.'

'Which ones?' He was amused and intrigued by the thought of Stacey sizing them up.

'That moose man.'

'Nadelhoffer?'

'That's the one. And the creepy guy – Kalvin. Though there's nothing Calvinist about him. He looks at women like they're turkey legs – what bit's chewable, what bit's bone?'

Nessheim laughed. 'So what are you doing tomorrow?'

'There're no classes because of the holiday. I thought maybe I'd knit you a muffler.'

'I bet.'

'What about you?

'I was going to drive up to Fort Sheridan and try to find a soldier for Guttman.'

'Is that the guy who called?'

'Yes.'

'So he's your boss? Now I get it.'

Nessheim didn't react.

'Can I come?' she asked.

'No way. I can do it Monday instead – then we could spend tomorrow together.'

'Did Guttman say it was important?'

'Guttman says everything's important.' Like Groves, he thought, recalling Fermi's description.

'Then you'd better do it tomorrow.'

'I'm a law student, remember. Fielding thinks I'm a good one, too.'

'Law school's faute de mieux for you, Nessheim. You wanted to do your bit. Well, Guttman's giving you a chance to.'

'I'd rather spend the day with you.'

'There's a war on, remember. Until it's finished, "rathers" don't count. You can have them in your head – who doesn't? – but you have to leave them there until the war is over. Anyway, you can give me a lift downtown on your way.'

'Why? What are you doing in the Loop?'

'Christmas is in a few weeks, you ninny. If I'm not knitting you a muffler, I'd better buy you the equivalent. Hyde Park may have a great university and a superior intellectual life, but the shopping's lousy.'

The Drive had been well ploughed and there was for the moment no more snow. He drove his own car, an old but reliable Dodge, and dropped Stacey outside Marshall Field's, arranging to meet her at one o'clock outside Carson Pirie Scott. It took him forty minutes to reach Fort Sheridan, and once there he had trouble locating anyone who would help. The original 'fort' had been swamped by the emergence of a small city – Nessheim had read that over 100,000 soldiers had already been processed through the place, and the empty lots and parkland surrounding the original fort now held row after row of barracks. A military policeman with a white helmet and olive green uniform directed him through the complicated grid of new streets to the commander's headquarters, underneath an enormous water tower that had been built in the previous century. Inside, he found the offices full of clerks scurrying in semi-panic, like the newsroom in *The Front Page*.

He also found that his credentials didn't cut much ice in this military environment. FBI badge or no, a domestic cop didn't hold much sway among people getting ready to go to war – or preparing others to do so. After a runaround from the Commander's office and a blank refusal from the Quartermaster's secretary, he tried the payroll department in desperation. A young woman with wavy hair and a corporal's stripes proved more receptive than her colleagues. Taking the slip of paper from Nessheim, she went to check it against a table full of shoeboxes, each holding several hundred index cards. She came back with three of them. 'More than one Bergen, I'm afraid. Do you have a first name?'

Nessheim shook his head. 'No. But I think he'd probably hail from New York. Does that help?

The woman looked at the cards. 'A bit. I've got one from Iowa, one from Jersey, and one from New York.'

'New York City?'

'Beats me. It says Liberty, New York.'

'You're kidding.' Nessheim knew it well; it was the town nearest a resort where he had once been unofficially trained on a mission for Guttman. It was also a hundred miles from New York City, and since Guttman had said the man Bergen worked as an elevator serviceman in Manhattan, he could not have commuted. Nor have moved there to work – Liberty was a nice spot, but a little one, and Nessheim doubted there would be a single elevator to service in the town.

'How about the third guy?' he asked.

The woman picked the card out as though it was a winning raffle ticket. She was enjoying herself. 'Elizabeth, New Jersey,' she said like a bingo caller.

273

'That's the one. Now can you tell me where I can find him? Or has he been shipped out?'

She was studying the card and her face suddenly darkened. 'Was he a friend of yours?'

'Never met him in my whole life. Why'd you say "was"?'

'He died.'

'In combat?' That was quick, he thought. Americans had only just arrived in North Africa; and how quickly could Bergen have made it to the Pacific?

'No, he died here.'

'Natural causes?'

'It doesn't say. What it does say is it involved the MPs.'

'How do I find them?' he asked, dreading the thought of finding his way again through the morass of buildings.

She saw his face and laughed. 'Don't look so gloomy. The MPs are right next door.'

He had to wait a good half-hour while the captain in charge, a man named Percival with a Kentucky twang, decided he needed to finish his early lunch, brought in on a tray by one of the ranks, all by himself. When at last Nessheim was ushered in, Captain Percival said curtly, 'State your business.'

Nessheim explained who he was. Percival made a point of not examining his credentials. Nessheim said, 'A soldier died here in the last few weeks. I wanted to know about the circumstances of his death.'

The Captain exhaled to show his indifference. 'His name?'

'Bergen – Edward Donald Bergen, native of Elizabeth, New Jersey. I don't know the regiment or what he was doing here – Basic Training, I assume.'

'Do you know how many new recruits come through

here each week? Pick a number, add a zero, and you'll still be short.'

'Sure, but how many of them die while they're here? I can't believe it would be hard to check this.'

The Captain shook his head. 'But it takes time, valuable time. Maybe I haven't got that kind of time, mister, even if you do.'

'I'm just asking for a little cooperation,' Nessheim said levelly.

'And if I say no?'

Nessheim sighed and sat down, without invitation. 'If you say no then I'll leave. Empty-handed and unhappy. You don't want that.'

'Aw, don't I now?' said the Captain sarcastically. 'You Feds really get to me, you know. You come in with your dark suits and white shirts and shiny ties and tell us what to do. If we baulk then you go all tough guy, just like you're doing to me. Yet you have no jurisdiction here – none at all. So don't try and scare me, bud. J. Edgar Hoover could walk in here himself and I wouldn't be obliged to dance. Got it?'

Nessheim sighed and took a deep breath. Then he looked at the wall behind Percival as he spoke quickly but quietly. 'I got it, all right. And that's why, when I leave here empty-handed, I'm not going to call the Bureau in Washington. I am going to pick up the phone and call General Leslie Groves. He's a big bullish sonofabitch nobody likes, but he gets the job done. In case you haven't heard of him, he built the Pentagon. Right now he's got thirty thousand men building things all over the country. I will tell him how at his direct request I came here, looking for information about the death of his wife's beloved nephew, but that unfortunately a certain Captain Percival felt he could not help me out in this slightly embarrassing task – embarrassing because

275

I know there are more important things to do, for both you and me. Anyway, after this General Groves will go up against your commanding officer, and unless your guy's a general too, I'd put my money on Groves – though you know better than me how the army works. So it's your call what I do next, Captain.'

He had said this without looking at Percival, wanting to make the man have another think without threatening him so directly that he would find it unmanly to back down. For a moment, it looked to be in the balance, as Percival considered his options and Nessheim looked out the window and saw two MPs lighting cigarettes. When he glanced over, Percival had picked up the phone on his desk. 'Send Swanson in here right away.'

They waited in silence, not looking at each other, until there was a knock on the door and a small man in uniform came in – a first lieutenant, Nessheim saw from the bars on his epaulettes. Captain Percival explained that he wanted information on Bergen's death.

The little man named Swanson nodded. 'Yes, sir. I remember it well. It was a hit-and-run – still no progress in locating the driver. We liaised with the local police.' He looked over at Nessheim.

Percival said, 'Mr Nessheim's not a local dick, Swanson. He's a Fed, so you needn't get all nervous.'

Swanson hesitated and finally said, 'Bergen got run down on Waukegan Avenue. He had told one of his buddies that he was meeting a friend from New York who was in town. I figure he was walking to catch the bus to go see this friend when it happened. He was on the road because of all the snow.'

'Did anybody see it happen?' Nessheim asked.

'Sort of. They were behind him.'

'But too far back to get a plate number,' Percival

276

interjected. It was clear he had heard about this before, and even clearer that he didn't want to hear it all again.

'Oh, it wasn't that, sir. The car didn't have a licence plate. The witness was sure about it – he'd noticed that even before the car hit Bergen.'

Nessheim said, 'Any dope on the make of car?'

Swanson shook his head regretfully. 'No. A sedan is all they could remember. A dark green sedan.'

He could see Stacey through the brass-framed glass doors of Carson Pirie Scott & Co.'s famous entranceway: Sullivan the architect had done himself proud with this building. The two-storey rotunda, with its elaborate brasswork, had already been decorated with Christmas lights.

Stacey was talking with a sales assistant, a dumpy mousy-haired woman in the store uniform of blouse and skirt. She seemed very animated and suddenly hugged Stacey and kissed her on the cheek. In Nessheim's experience, not many sales assistants did this with customers.

He tapped the horn and Stacey came out through the doors. He noticed she wasn't carrying any shopping bags.

'Brrr,' she said as she closed the passenger door. 'Home, James, as quick as you can.'

He turned on Madison heading for Lake Shore Drive. 'I thought you were going shopping.'

'I was. I just didn't buy anything. Makes a change, huh?'

'Who was that you were talking to?'

'Where?'

'In Carson's. Just now by the doors.'

'Oh, just a friend.'

'Does just a friend have a name?'

'Diane.'

'Diane who?'

'Diane Keefer. What's with all the questions?'

'Did you just happen to run into her?'

'She works at Carson's. Behind the counter since you seem so curious about her. I had coffee with her during her break. I think it was chicory and it was pretty disgusting, but they give you a cookie to hide the bad taste.'

He said, 'You've never mentioned any friend in Chicago.'

'I grew up here, remember? Diane and I went to grade school together.'

'I'm impressed you've kept up. You haven't lived here for a long time.'

She gave a small irritated sigh, then cracked her window and lit a cigarette. She blew out some smoke and said, 'If you have to know, she was in the Party with me.'

'*Was*?'

'Yes. She left at about the same time I did. She'd tell you it was doctrinal disagreements, but I think she just couldn't stand the meetings. Too much ideology, not enough men.'

'From what I saw of her, she's more likely to be embraced by the ideology.'

'Very funny,' she said crossly. 'Maybe she's not all-American in the looks department, but not everybody can be a pretty boy. She's got a good heart, and she's smart, real smart.'

'Unusual for a Communist.'

'Ex-Communist.'

'Pardon me. So what did you two ex-Communists discuss then?'

'Well,' said Stacey, in a *you are being very stupid about this* tone of voice he found unnerving because he knew it was justified, 'today she told me about her bunions, and I told her about you. It's called exchanging confidences, and it's one of the common features of something called friendship, which I would encourage you to learn more about. We can't all be misanthropes, you know.'

'I've got friends,' he said defensively.

'Of course you do. Winograd's a great guy.'

When they got back to the Kimbark apartment, Nessheim went into the kitchen. Shutting the door, he phoned Guttman's house, but there was no answer. On the off chance that Guttman was working, he tried the office as well, where to his surprise, Marie answered. When he heard a man's voice in the background he thought he'd found Guttman at last.

But Marie said, 'He's not here, Jim. He did come in at lunchtime but he left a little while ago. I told him you'd called, so he knows you're trying to reach him –'

'Do you know where he's gone? I need to speak to him urgently.'

There was something hesitant in Marie's voice. She always knew everything about what Guttman was up to; she probably knew his shoe size by now. So he pushed her: 'I need to know where he is, Marie. Like I say, it's urgent.'

'He said something about catching a train later on.'

'A train? Where's he going?'

'Didn't he tell you?'

'Tell me what? Come on, Marie.'

'Maybe he couldn't reach you, or maybe he didn't have time.' He sensed that Marie was justifying to herself an imminent disclosure, so he waited, controlling his impatience. At last she said, 'He's catching the train for Chicago.'

26

HE TOOK STACEY out to dinner on 57th Street that night. He wanted to take his mind off Guttman's impending arrival, for he was mystified by it. Why hadn't Guttman told him? Presumably he would arrive the following day, but when would he come to see Nessheim? *Would* he come to see Nessheim?

The restaurant was a low brick building with a hipped roof of pale green tiles. In front stood an enormous block of painted green wood, roughly the size and shape of an upright canoe, with '*Tropical Hut*' spelled out in wonky bamboo lettering. Inside you went down from the entrance lobby past the coat check into a big room with exotic decor: fishing nets dangled from the ceiling, threaded with brightly coloured glass lights; pictures of palm trees and grass thatched houses decorated the walls, along with masks and conch shells. All intended to conjure up some imagined Polynesian paradise.

They sat in a corner booth, partitioned off with slatted screens of split bamboo. Stacey had changed clothes, and wore a deep red roll-neck sweater and grey Oxford slacks. She'd also put on a necklace of worked gold which looked Spanish or Aztec. Nessheim didn't want to ask who'd bought it for her; even if she'd bought it for herself, he felt bad that he could never match that kind of largesse.

'What is Polynesian food anyway?' she asked. He looked at the menu, a big book full of pages offering exotic cocktails and a range of 'Polynesian specialties' – though since the waitress informed them that pineapple was impossible to obtain, most of these dishes were unavailable.

'I don't know,' he said.

'Tell you what,' said Stacey, closing her menu book with a thump. 'Let's just have the ribs.'

These proved excellent: long slabs of charcoal-barbecued ribs that had their origins in Mississippi rather than Samoa. They ate ravenously, and stuck to beer rather than the Aloha specials. As he finished and wiped his fingers with about his twelfth paper napkin, Nessheim said, 'I thought tomorrow we could walk out to The Point. It should be beautiful with all the snow, and I bet you the Lake's frozen by the shore.'

'I can't, Jim. I promised to help out with something.'

He resisted the urge to ask what. He'd grilled her enough for one day, he figured. If she wanted to tell him she would.

Eventually she said, 'Did you know Negroes can't buy houses in most of Hyde Park?'

'They can't buy houses most places. Why are you bringing that up?'

'I think it's a disgrace. This is supposed to be a liberal community – that's what President Hutchins is always claiming. Yet the university goes along with housing segregation as if it's not their concern.'

'What's that got to do with walking to The Point tomorrow – or *not* walking?'

'There's a meeting about it in Mandel Hall. I said I'd go – maybe something will come out of that.'

'I doubt it.' Stacey shot him a look, and he said, 'Don't get me wrong, I don't believe in segregation.'

'I know, some of your best friends are Negroes.'

'I don't have any friends, remember? But a Negro saved my life one time.'

'Sure,' she said, caustic. 'How?' Curious now.

'Rescued me from drowning.'

'I don't believe it. You swim like a fish.'

'God's truth.' He held his hand up as if taking the oath.

'Where was this? The pool in Ida Noyes?'

'Long Island Sound.'

'Tell me the story.'

He shook his head. He knew he kept hinting at his past, but he couldn't do more than that. Not yet, anyway.

The waitress now appeared. They were too full for dessert but ordered coffee. Nessheim said, 'I thought you'd given up politics.'

'I have. But I haven't given up right and wrong.'

'And I have?'

'I don't know. I hope not. You seem to think the war's right.'

'Of course I do. Even back home in Wisconsin, where pretty much everybody's got German roots, they recognise that Hitler has to be stopped as well as the Japanese. They're not so wild about our Russian allies, but I can't say I am either. Not since the Nazi-Russian pact – I thought that was indefensible.'

'You'll get no argument from me,' Stacey said. 'But there are some people who think the Russians need to win the war even more than we do.'

'Why's that?' It sounded kooky to him.

'Because only then can "true revolution" proceed everywhere else. That's what the Fourth International declared.' She raised both eyebrows.

'You don't believe that, do you?' he asked, trying not to sound worried. 'That we're fighting for the sake of revolution.'

'I used to.'

'So did Trotsky, and look what happened to him.'

'That's not funny.' She seemed taken aback.

'I didn't say it was. But you know, I don't think Trotsky would have been any better than Stalin if he had come out on top. Do you?'

She thought for a moment, then said reluctantly, 'No, I don't. I think he would have tried at first to be humane, but then either power would have gone to his head like it did Stalin or he would have been deposed for being too nice.'

'Too weak, don't you mean?'

She shrugged. 'Sometimes too nice and too weak are the same thing.'

There was a bitterness in her voice which hinted of experiences she was keeping to herself. Nessheim said, a little exasperated, 'I wish you'd tell me where you've been the last few years.'

'I will, when you extend me the same courtesy.'

Nessheim smiled, but added, 'At least tell me what changed your mind – you know, about Russia and revolution.'

'I don't know. Sanity returned.' She paused. 'And then I met someone.'

27

THAT NIGHT HE came out of sleep and a football-playing dream to hear an alarm clock ringing. No, it wasn't that; an early riser even in winter, Nessheim had never needed an aural prompt and didn't own one. What was it then? As he dimly re-entered the world – Stacey emitting a light snore beside him, the features of the bedroom gradually emerging – he realised that the phone was ringing down the hall in the kitchen.

He threw back the bedclothes and staggered out of the room, cursing the apartment's former occupant, the Communist philosopher upstairs, for installing the phone in the kitchen at the very rear of the apartment. He hit the light switch in the hall and weaved past the dining-room table, then grabbed the phone.

'Hello.' He forced a crispness into his voice. At this hour – the kitchen clock said midnight – it had to be news of a death or disaster, unless some lush had dialled the wrong number.

'Meester Nessheim, thank God you are there.'

Heavily accented English, a pantomime foreigner. 'Who is that?' he demanded, wondering if it was some kind of joke.

'It's Laura Fermi. I am so sorry to call, but Enrico is in Washington and I do not know what to do. I think there is someone upstairs at the very top of the house. They have been there for some time.'

'Have you called the police?'

'Police,' she said, as if it were an odd suggestion. 'No. Enrico would not allow it.'

What did that mean? 'Are the kids all right?'

'Yes. They are downstairs. You see, the door to the top floor is kept locked. But I am sure the person is there.'

'Stay put. I'll be right over.'

He put the phone down, wondering if he should call the cops – Enrico's proscription be damned. But they might be slower than he was to respond, especially once they heard Laura's accent. He went back quickly to the bedroom, where Stacey was sitting up with the bedside lamp on. 'Who was that?' She sounded scared.

He explained as he threw on his clothes. 'Why she's calling me and not the cops, I couldn't tell you,' he said crossly as he buttoned his shirt. 'I gave Fermi the number here, but I didn't expect to act as his wife's bodyguard.'

He left his suit jacket but took his gun and holster from the closet, strapping it carefully around his shoulder. When he looked over, Stacey had got up and was getting dressed. 'What are you doing?' he asked.

'I'm coming with you.'

He was putting on his shoes now. 'Don't be ridiculous. If there's a burglar in their house, I don't want you getting in the way.'

'I'll keep her calm while you flush out the bad guy. The kids know me now – I bet they're scared to death.'

He didn't have time to argue. He went out into the hall and took his heavy duffel coat from the closet. As he opened the front door he found Stacey just a step behind him, miraculously dressed, wearing the padded coat he bet she'd bought to make her look like a student.

Downstairs in the courtyard, he stopped for a moment, inhaling the dry cold air. 'I'm not going to drive – it's only a block away. I'll see you there – I'm going to run now.'

He took off then in his street shoes, and almost came

a cropper before he even reached the street, since he slid like a hockey puck on the packed icy snow. But soon he got the hang of it: he didn't try to grip the ground with his feet, but floated, skated and flew along the sidewalk.

The night was quiet, windless, the only noise an occasional car slithering along 57th Street and the harsh yap of a little dog. Against the snow-white background of the Ray School playground, the stark branches of the elms looked like finely etched figures in a pen-and-ink drawing. As he ran he wondered what he would find when he got there. What kind of burglar stuck around when the occupants stirred in a house?

The Fermi house on Woodlawn Avenue was ablaze with light. A good sign. He ran up the front steps and as he stopped on the porch the door opened and Laura stood with her hand on her heart in relief. She had brushed her hair, but wore an old quilted housecoat that had lived on two continents, and a pair of oversized slippers.

He went through into the big front room where he had watched Stacey dance while the world's leading physicists applauded. Now, standing at the back in the doorway to the kitchen were the two Fermi children, cute as bugs in their pyjamas and bathrobes. They both stared wide-eyed at Nessheim.

'He is still there,' Laura Fermi declared. 'I heard noise from the room above our bedroom, at the front of the house on the high floor.'

'Right.' He unbuttoned his duffel coat but kept it on, not wanting to scare the kids with his gun. 'I want you to stay down here with the children while I go upstairs. Is the door to the top floor still locked?'

'Yes, here is the key.' She handed it to him with a slight shiver. She looked very frightened.

'Stacey is on her way.'

'She is?' She sounded as though Christmas had come early.

'Yes, any minute now. Stay down here for now, okay?'

He went up the first flight of stairs and moved along the central corridor on the higher floor. Coming to the closed door that sealed off the staircase to the top floor, he stopped to listen for a moment. Nothing. He used the key to open the door, and in the darkness of the stairwell listened again. He heard only noises from downstairs and realised Stacey had arrived. He reached for a light switch and found it at the bottom of the dark stairwell. Kicking his shoes off, he drew the Smith & Wesson from its holster, then walked on tiptoe up to the top-floor landing.

There were two rooms towards the back of the house, their doors open. The front room, where according to Laura Fermi the noise had come from, was on his right. Its door was closed.

He stopped to think. If there were an intruder, would he be armed? Only if he had come to kill Fermi. But a hired killer would have forced his way downstairs by now. And if instead he was a burglar, he wouldn't bring a gun, not unless he wanted triple the sentence if he got caught.

The more he considered it, the odder it seemed. Finally, out of sheer impatience, he walked to the door and flung it open, while he stood to one side, out of the line of fire.

Feeling a sudden blast of cold, he reached around the door frame and touched the Bakelite light switch. He pushed it on, simultaneously moving through the doorway, his gun held level in both hands. Quantico training.

There was no one there. The room was barely

furnished: an iron bed against the far wall, a naked mattress on the springs; a single light bulb, in a papier-mâché lampshade that hung by a wire cord from the ceiling. There was also an old divan with a missing leg, a couple of side tables covered in dust, and a broken plate on the floor, which must have been knocked off one of the tables. The floor consisted of bare wooden boards, except for the centre of the room underneath the light, where two worn oriental rugs had been laid. One of them had a corner doubled up, exposing the boards beneath.

On the front side of the house a tall sash window was open a good ten inches at the bottom. He realised that was why the room was so cold. He walked to the window, pulled the upper half down and stuck his head outside. Looking up, he saw that the roof overhung the house, but no one could come down that way without falling off. Looking down, he saw it was a ten-foot drop from the window to the porch's gable below; a tricky jump at the best of times, impossible with the snow packed on the porch's roof. And that was just the way down; to climb up to the window would have required an acrobat of Olympic calibre, and a trampoline.

He pulled back into the room and closed the window. There was a sudden scratching noise not far from his feet, and he started in surprise, then looked down and found himself staring into two yellow eyes, big as marbles. They belonged to a massive tabby cat, as fat as a county-fair cabbage. It looked tetchily at Nessheim, who was satisfied now that he had identified the mysterious intruder: the cat must have nipped through the open window and roamed around the room, with a thump here (the plate), and a scratch there (the turned-up rug). Making enough racket on the resonant wooden floor to alert a nervy Laura Fermi to its presence.

Nessheim went and checked the other rooms, but found nothing there, other than a few empty suitcases and a packing crate. He went back to the room with the cat, who followed him as he opened the window again and then stood clear. After a moment's hesitation, the cat suddenly leaped on to the sill, then jumped. Seconds later, as Nessheim closed the window for good, he saw it, lit by a street lamp, scamper across Woodlawn Avenue.

He headed towards the door, stopping to flip the ruffled rug back with his foot. As he stepped on to one of the exposed boards, its far end suddenly sprang up like a see-saw. In the cavity exposed beneath, between the underlying joists, he saw something red and green. Kneeling, he reached down and brought it out. It was a chamois pouch, the size of a baseball mitt, tied shut by a leather string. Untying the string, he turned the pouch upside down and shook out its contents.

Four wads of paper landed in succession on the floorboards. Each was bound by a gutta-percha band. He riffled all four; they were fifty-dollar bills, divided into equal stacks. He counted two hundred notes in one stack. That was ten grand. Times four and you had forty thousand dollars. Jesus Christ, he thought as he holstered his gun, that was a lot of dough for a working physicist.

Downstairs the two children were sitting at the kitchen table, drinking mugs of hot milk, while Laura Fermi and Stacey stood tensely by the stove.

As Nessheim came into the room he said, 'I didn't find anyone up there. Just a cat that must have come through the window. It had made a bit of a mess.'

'*Un gatto?*'

When he nodded Laura clapped her hands in relief.

'The kids can go back to bed now,' he said. 'It's safe.'

'I'll help you,' Stacey said to Laura, and the two women herded the children upstairs. When they came back down a few minutes later, Nessheim was waiting in the kitchen. Laura said, laughing, 'I cannot believe all this was caused by one large cat.'

'I did find something else.'

Nessheim put the pouch down on the kitchen table. Laura stared at it, as if a feared enemy had returned unexpectedly. Then she burst into tears.

Stacey looked mystified. 'What have you found?'

He shook his head and waited for Laura to stop crying. 'What is it?' Stacey kept asking, until finally Laura wiped her eyes and looked at Nessheim.

He said, 'I need to know where this came from.'

Stacey looked at him as if he were crazy, so he gestured at the pouch. 'Go ahead – open it.' She untied the leather string and reached in, then gasped as she extracted the first stack of bills.

'I need to know where this came from,' repeated Nessheim. 'I'm just trying to do my job.'

Laura wiped her eyes with her fist. She said angrily, 'That is what the man in Rome said when they confiscated my family's properties because of the Jewish laws. I had known this man since I was tiny, but he said to me, "I am only doing my job. It is the law." And we then left Italy with nothing. So now you say the same thing, and the government will say that too and take the money if they put us away.'

'What do you mean, put you away?'

'They put the Japanese in camps, and now some Germans and Italians too. Why not us?'

'Because your husband is helping the United States.'

She gave this short shrift. 'And if he cannot help? If he is sick and cannot work? So they put him on some small island with other Italians. What happens to this money then?'

'If it's your money then it would still be yours. But keeping it under the floorboards doesn't seem the smartest thing to do. What if there had been a burglar and he'd found it?'

'Enrico said it was safer than a bank.'

'All right,' he said, unwilling to argue, 'but where did you get it from? You said you left Italy with nothing. This is a lot of money.'

Stacey had been listening quietly but now she said sharply to Laura, 'You don't have to answer that. It's none of his business.' She turned to him. 'You're not the IRS.'

He said firmly, 'Why don't you go check on the children, Stacey, and let me do my job?'

'Why don't you check on them instead?' she said fiercely. 'Look how upset she is. Stop bullying her.'

'I'm not,' he protested.

'Is this part of your training? Softening up the suspects.'

He ignored her, saying to Laura, 'I need to know where this comes from.'

'Why –' Stacey started to say, but Laura held her hand up. 'It's okay, I will tell you. The money is from the prize.'

'What prize?'

Stacey interjected, 'The Nobel Prize, you horse's ass.'

Laura continued, 'We collected the money in Stockholm, but did not return to Italy. The cheque was in kronor. When we got to New York, Enrico had it changed into dollars – and then into cash. He said it was our safe money. If something bad happened or we had to flee

291

again, there was this money to use. He did not want anyone to know about it – he was scared it would be taken away from us.'

'Why didn't you say so right away?'

'Because she was scared, Nessheim,' said Stacey, as if Laura wasn't standing there.

'Scared of me?'

'Scared of everything. They got out, but most people didn't. You need to remember that.'

28

ON THE WAY home they walked in silence until they reached Kimbark Avenue. Finally Nessheim sighed and said, 'I didn't know the Nobel Prize was worth that kind of money. Or that Fermi was so worried about his status here. He shouldn't be – Zinn told me that General Groves thinks Fermi's almost God.' When Stacey didn't reply, he said, 'Are you mad at me, Madison?'

'No, Nessheim. Are you mad at me?'

'Not at all. I just feel bad about that scene with Mrs Fermi. I wasn't trying to upset her, but I needed to know.'

'I wasn't trying to interfere.'

'Sure you were,' he said.

She laughed. 'Just trying to keep you on your toes, Jim. I'd like everybody in the FBI to have these reminders. I think anyone with power should be aware of when they're using it. I'm on the side of the Laura Fermis of this world. They feel powerless, you know. And they're scared.'

'You're not.'

'How do you know?' she said seriously. 'I just put up a good front. But tell me,' she said quickly, 'does anyone keep J. Edgar Hoover on his toes?'

Nessheim thought for a minute. 'Not really. In principle, the President could, but I happen to know he doesn't. Hoover's got more on him than the other way round. Believe it or not, Guttman's gone the distance with Hoover a couple of times, and somehow managed a draw.'

'How do you draw with J. Edgar Hoover?'

'That's simple – you keep your job even though he wants to get rid of you. Guttman's done it twice.'

They were on Kimbark now, getting close to home. Stacey looped her arm through his. 'Why didn't you tell me at the beginning you were still working for the FBI?'

'Partly because I wasn't sure I was. You'd have to meet Guttman to understand – a short, wide sloppy guy, nothing to look at, but sharp. He's unorthodox, and what I'm doing for him isn't official. It never is. But don't think it's a bigger job than it is. I'm just helping to make sure that nothing disrupts the work Fermi and his people are doing.'

They were inside now, and climbing the flight of stairs to his apartment. As he unlocked the door, she said, 'What's the other reason? You said "partly".'

Never any flies on her, not ever. He would have to play his best just to stay in the game with her. He said, 'I worried you wouldn't like my working for the Bureau, officially or not.'

'Nothing to do with me,' she said, following him in. She seemed suddenly distant. 'I knew anyway,' she said shortly. When he seemed surprised she added, 'Otherwise why the gun? And why the vigilance all the time? You probably aren't even aware of it, but when we go out you grow another set of eyes in the back of your head. I figured you were looking for a spy.'

'Why did you think that?' He hoped his voice sounded mildly interested and no more.

'You're playing with me again.'

'What do you mean?' he said, trying to sound aggrieved.

'"*Why did you think that?*"' she said, mimicking him with extravagant innocence. 'I *know* you've been looking for a spy. Enrico told Laura and she told me.

She assumed you would have told me already. Italian couples have no secrets from each other, unlike salt-of-the-earth Midwesterners.'

They got ready for bed, but even when Nessheim was lying under the covers Stacey stayed up, standing by the window, smoking a cigarette. He said casually, 'What are you doing at Christmas?'

She shrugged. 'Not sure.'

'Your mother's?'

'Not a chance. She's at the gin before we open the Christmas stockings.'

It sounded sad rather than astringent. 'So where will you go? Your friend at Carson Pirie Scott?'

She shook her head. 'Christmas is the one time Diane *does* see her parents.'

He waited a moment, then said lightly, 'I had an idea.'

'Yeah?' She kept herself sideways to him so he couldn't see her expression.

'Come to Wisconsin with me.'

'You mean it?'

'You'll have to sleep in my sister's room.'

'Fine. As long as you sleep there, too.'

'I'm serious,' he said, trying not laugh. 'And you have to act like I'm God's gift to mankind. Otherwise my mother won't like you.'

'And you want her to like me?'

This surprised him. 'Sure. It will make life easier while we're there. But I'm not through yet. You'll have to bring your own booze – my mother doesn't drink.'

'I'll manage – I got through Prohibition.' He could see her sly smile now.

'You were underage during Prohibition.'

'Only part of it, pal, and since when did that stop me? Anyway, that can't be what's worrying you.'

'You may not like it up there – that's what's worrying me.'

'I'll like it fine. Except for booze, it's got everything a girl could want. I've thought a lot about it.'

'How's that?' he asked, interested that she had thought about it at all.

'I can see my life there.'

'You'd go nuts after three months.'

Stacey shook her head. 'Nope. I'd have a big farmhouse with forty acres of hay-bearing fields and an orchard and a horse. Plus four kids to raise, two of them with freckles.'

'You make it sound like some Aryan paradigm.'

'You wouldn't have used that word before you went to law school. But you're wrong. It just happens their father's blood falls that way.' She looked at him appraisingly. 'You can't blame people for what they inherit. So don't "Aryan" me.'

'You'd still get bored.'

'I've been thinking about that. I'd be busy enough – those kids, and the house, the chickens, and three or four milk cows. Though let's be realistic – I'd let a local lady make the cheese.'

'What if *I* got bored?'

'You wouldn't have time. You're going to be a pillar of the community. Run for District Attorney. I've got your campaign slogan ready – *"This Time, Vote for Nessheim".*'

He groaned but was disconcerted by how inviting she made it sound. A lot better than his hazy plan of hanging up his shingle, with an office doubling as his bachelor rooms. Above the local drugstore, say, accessible by an outside staircase of pine slats rubbed grey by the elements rather than by the minimal footfall of clients.

She said, 'But this is only when the war is over.'

'That could be a long wait. What am I supposed to do in the meantime, other than finish law school?'

'I've been thinking about that a lot. You're not doing justice to yourself, Nessheim. You've been hiding.' She said this without criticism in her voice, but clinically nonetheless.

'I told you I tried to enlist. Twice.'

'You don't have to be on a landing beach in the Pacific to do your bit.'

'What else should I do?'

'You should keep working for Guttman. He sounds okay.'

'I didn't plan on joining the FBI, you know. It wasn't some boyhood dream of mine or anything. I fell into it when I had to leave college. After my injury. It's all happened by accident.'

'So what? Whose life isn't an accident? Since when did life go according to plan?'

'The Bureau's not clean as the driven snow. It may not be the bogeyman your Trotskyist friends say it is, but it's done some pretty dubious things.'

'I know that – they helped put the head of the SWP away for no good reason, and they persecuted those poor bastards who fought in Spain. But with the war on, there's nothing wrong with working for the Bureau – what you're doing is important. The problems will come later when the Bureau gets too big for its boots.'

'Hoover's already too big for his,' said Nessheim. 'But whether it's the Bureau or being a small town DA, you'd better understand one thing – I'm never going to be rich.'

'That's all right. I already am.'

'You know what I mean.'

'No.' She shook her head. 'I truly don't. All it means is that you'd never have to keep me. And I'll be more than willing to let you keep yourself. It's just that there'd be a grown-up version of a kid's cookie-jar money, which we could use every now and then to get away. Maybe to Chicago, just to see a show or two and have somebody else change the sheets. Once in a blue moon, when winter came and there wasn't much doing on the farm, we'd go get warm in Florida or California.'

'Or Mexico?' he asked, remembering Fielding's mention of her trip there. She was startled; he could tell. He added, 'Speaking of which –'

'Let's not and say we did,' she said tersely.

'How come?'

'You're spoiling this,' she warned him, and it was hard to tell if this bothered him or her the most.

'I wasn't trying to.'

'Maybe not. You're such a mix of innocent and realist.' Momentarily she looked morose, then seemed to perk up. She said, 'Mind you, until the war's over, this is just a dream.'

'Damn.'

'But that's okay. You've got to dream a bit, Nessheim. There's nothing wrong with that. Believe me – no dream, no life.'

29

SOMETHING ABOUT THE protest meeting made Nessheim nervous. He couldn't tell why, since it wasn't as if Stacey and her cadre were marching against the war – when those demonstrations took place, pacifist protestors were often beaten up; and there were literally thousands of soldiers and sailors around, as well as a populace which, though relegated to an observer's role, were itching to enact their vicarious fantasies.

When Stacey hadn't come back after an hour and a half, Nessheim went out to find her. Halfway down the block he realised he hadn't taken his gun and holster, but it was Stacey's safety he was worried about, not his own. He didn't think anyone was going to try to bump him off in the middle of a protest about segregated housing.

Mandel Hall seemed a strange venue for a protest meeting, since its owner, the university, was the main target. When he got there, he found only a janitor mopping the floor and two female students talking, their arms laden with books. 'I thought there was a meeting going on here,' he said.

'There was,' said one of the women. 'It's moved to the President's house. Pastor Simms is presenting a petition to Hutchins.'

He came out on to Woodlawn Avenue and started to walk the two blocks to the President's house near the corner of 59th Street. He had almost reached the tennis courts at 58th, by the entrance to the main Quadrangle of the university, when he noticed Stacey's car parked on the street, and looking up saw Stacey herself coming his way. She was walking with an older Negro man, a tall, dignified figure in a herringbone overcoat. He was nursing a large plum-coloured bruise on his forehead, and was letting Stacey steer him by the arm towards her car. When she saw Nessheim she called out, 'This is Reverend Simms. I want to get him in the car so he can sit down.'

Nessheim came and held the minister by the arm while Stacey rummaged for her keys. When she'd opened the passenger's door, she took the Reverend's other arm and with Nessheim's help got him on to the front seat. He looked exhausted.

Stacey closed the door carefully and Nessheim said, 'What happened?'

'Some thugs followed us to the President's house. They tried picking fights with the men in our group. There was a university cop at the front door but he didn't do a thing – probably because the hooligans were all in uniform. I was inside with Reverend Simms delivering a petition to President Hutchins, but when we came out these thugs were still there.'

'Are you okay?'

'I'm fine. I'm going to drive the Reverend home, then go to my place for a bit. Why don't you come over tonight? It would give me time to do some laundry. Drusilla's been sick all week.'

'All right, but are you sure you're okay?'

'Yes. If I'd known it'd get violent, I would have stayed away.'

He didn't believe this for a minute. 'How did the Reverend get that big welt?'

She said, 'Everybody else had left, and I was bringing the Reverend along, when the sailors started throwing snowballs at us. I asked them to stop, but they just laughed. No big deal, except one of the snowballs had a rock inside.' She gestured at Simms. 'I've never been called a nigger lover before.'

He said, 'I wish I'd been there.' He was certain Pug Face had been one of the assailants.

'I'm glad you weren't or there would have been a real fight.'

'Nah.'

'Why? What would you have done?'

'I'd have shot them.'

'Jim! Don't say that.' But she was smiling.

'I'm not going to let anyone touch the woman of my dreams.'

'I bet you say that to all the girls.'

'Nope. No veal kidneys for me. Just clams.' He made a face and she laughed. She kissed him goodbye, and he was glad he hadn't told her that he'd left his gun at home.

He watched her drive off with the wounded Reverend, then walked to Kimbark Avenue. As he reached the courtyard of his building, he saw a bulky man ahead of him, heading for his entryway. In street shoes, the man was having a hard time of it, slipping with almost every step.

Nessheim called out, 'If you'd told me you were coming, I could have warned you about the snow.'

Guttman turned around. 'I thought I'd packed my galoshes. I was wrong.'

30

THEY SAT UPSTAIRS in the apartment's living room. Nessheim had closed the bedroom door when they came in, since Stacey's nightgown lay spread across the bed like an invitation. Guttman declined a beer and sat down, then looked around. 'You've spruced this place up since I was out here.'

Had he? Nessheim looked around as well. There was a Cubist reproduction that Stacey had put up on one wall, a new standing lamp with a deco shade, and a pair of small but swanky armchairs with leather seats and steel tube frames which Stacey had brought over from her apartment. Nessheim realised how much the place had been improved, and how none of it was down to him.

But Nessheim didn't want to talk about the decor. 'I've been trying to reach you. I've found something out.' He explained what he had learned from Fermi about Grant's role in the appointment of Kalvin. 'We need to confront Kalvin and get him off the project. He's away in New Mexico with Oppenheimer, but he should be back any day now. Only Groves can get rid of Kalvin and he won't listen to me. But he will listen to you.'

To Nessheim's astonishment Guttman seemed only mildly interested.

'Harry,' Nessheim said sharply, 'we have to act. Fermi says the work at Stagg Field is reaching a critical point.'

'Sure, kid,' said Guttman, but he still seemed abstracted. Nessheim had seen this vague look before: when Isabel was going through a bad patch, a distant expression would settle on Guttman's face like an anodyne mask.

But then he seemed to come to, and he sat up on the couch. He rubbed his hands like a surgeon prepping for an operation, and looked intently at Nessheim, as if some internal decision had been made. He said, 'I've been thinking how to break this to you since I got on the train in Washington. I'm no actor and I haven't found an easy way.

'You know, since Isabel died I've come to realise that we all need somebody, one special somebody. When you're young – in college, say, and for a few years after that – that's the time for playing the field. Though even then, you may find your partner for life. I did, and I was fortunate. Because even if you've had a lot of luck with the ladies, sooner or later you realise that unless you have a special partner, life is just so goddamned *lonely.*'

He's talking about himself, Nessheim thought; he's talking about life after Isabel. Nessheim wondered where Guttman was heading with this, and for reasons he couldn't explain, he felt uneasy.

'They say love makes you blind,' Guttman continued. He took a deep breath, his eyes trained on Nessheim like headlights. 'I think that's what happened here. Because in my experience, the best infiltrations require a fall guy or a patsy.'

'What are you talking about?' Nessheim asked, disconcerted. Guttman could be wrong about things and Guttman could be pig-headed, but Guttman always made sense.

'I'm not blaming you at all but facts are facts.'

Nessheim suddenly had an intimation where this was heading. 'So far I haven't heard any,' he snapped.

'Heard any what?' asked Guttman, taken aback.

'Facts.'

'Oh,' said Guttman mildly, taking the reprimand in his stride. But then his jaw set and his expression hardened, and Nessheim saw that any hesitancy was gone.

'Somebody figured you early on, Jim. It's still a mystery to me who it was, except I don't think it was anybody here, and I know it wasn't the *Bund*. Thanks to Stephenson, I've got a lead on that, but however it happened, once they knew you were on the case, they used that information to play you like a fish.'

'Thanks a lot,' said Nessheim. 'I thought I was doing a pretty good job. And who's this "they" anyway?'

'The Soviets,' Guttman said simply. 'Our allies. They've been very clever. Originally they planted the idea in the White House that the Nazis had someone undercover here in Stagg Field. That was their high-level diversion, and it worked – the White House were alarmed by what they'd learned because they were convinced Germany was trying to build a bomb, too. So they had Frankfurter ask me to look into it unofficially. They didn't go through channels because Hoover knows nothing about the work going on here and they wanted to keep it that way.

'After seeing Frankfurter, I was sceptical, to be honest, and it turned out I was right to be – Stephenson's people have confirmed that the Germans aren't building anything remotely along the lines of what we're trying to build. But initially I couldn't be sure of this, so that's why I recruited you to have a look-see. The Russians must have been alarmed when they found out you were here. They knew you from LA and knew you were good at your job – they would have been worried you'd find their infiltrator in Fermi's Met Lab group. And sure enough you did.'

'Kalvin.'

'Yes.'

Nessheim said, 'Why didn't the Russians kill me? That would have taken care of the problem.'

'I'm sure they considered it, but you'd already proved hard to kill – they'd tried once before out in California. And they were also smart enough to realise that killing you would just confirm my suspicions – as far as they knew, I'd send somebody else in your wake.' He added ruefully, 'How would they know I didn't have anybody else to send?

'But then they did the next best thing – reinforce the idea that it was the Germans who were spying. That was the purpose of the "Rossbach" note. And that coincided with the arrival of someone ordered to get close to you.'

'Coincided?' asked Nessheim. He knew now where Guttman was headed, but wanted to delay his progress and gather his wits. It was otherwise too awful to think about.

Then Guttman said abruptly, 'It wasn't a coincidence. She set you up.'

'Watch it, Harry,' Nessheim said, and he meant it.

Guttman opened both hands, but it was not conciliatory.

'Time for the facts then,' Nessheim declared. 'There still haven't been any.'

If Guttman was piqued by this, he didn't show it, but merely pursed his lips. He said, 'Your friend was a member of the Communist Party, joining in 1931 while attending the U of C as an undergraduate. She was an active member, and attended regional and national meetings.'

Nessheim said, 'Harry, I know that Stacey was a Red.' Was that really the basis for all this? Nessheim started to relax a little. 'I also know she left the Party years ago. People change. Don't let your prejudices get in the way of seeing that.'

Guttman said patiently, 'I do know people can change. Isabel was a Trotskyite when I met her.'

Nessheim said, 'Stacey was a Trot too. She couldn't have stayed in the CP even if she'd wanted to. The Stalinists hate Trotsky more than they hate Hitler.'

'Then how is it she rejoined the CP last year?'

'I don't believe you.'

'I can show you the file. It's not hearsay – it's the Party's own list of the Hollywood branch members.'

Nessheim was stunned. He tried to think of ways to disprove this – even if it were only to himself. 'It might have been a mistake,' he said tentatively.

Guttman nodded. 'Sure. That seems to me to stretch the bounds of probability. But it is possible.'

This was said too disarmingly. Nessheim stared at Guttman. 'But there's more, isn't there?'

'There is. While she was in LA, Stacey married a man named George Tweedy, who dabbles as a movie producer. He's loaded.'

'I know about Tweedy. He's not going to be her husband for long. She's divorcing him.'

'Really?' Guttman asked, but it didn't sound genuine.

'Yes, really. He's in Reno right now. The divorce will be coming through any day.'

'That's funny. Our source reports that Tweedy was at a dinner in LA the other night, a fundraiser for Soviet citizens.'

'Bullshit.'

'Since a photograph of him at the dinner was in the *Los Angeles Times*, you may want to revise your view.'

Nessheim was starting to struggle. A counteroffensive was out of the question; all he could hope for was a truce while he digested this information. Why would

Stacey lie to him about divorcing Tweedy? He asked, 'If she's still with Tweedy, then why come here? It doesn't suggest a match made in heaven.'

'It suggests another mission for her. She'd already been to Mexico for six months without Tweedy, and that was after they were married. There's nothing romantic about the Russian intelligence people. You know that.'

'What was she doing in Mexico?' Maybe at least he'd solve that mystery.

'Who knows? But it was for the Soviets.'

Nessheim thought about this for a moment. 'Something doesn't ring true. Stacey showed up here for the very first time right after you and Groves left. I hadn't even agreed to do anything for you yet – don't you remember? If *I* didn't know I was going to be working for you again, how the hell could Stacey know that?'

'That's easy enough. Russian intelligence people in the NKVD – that's their FBI – would have kept tabs on you when you left California. You'd killed one of their men, so they weren't about to forget you. I bet they followed you all the way to Chicago. And they'd assume you were still working for the Bureau, and probably still working for me. The law school stuff was just a cover, they'd have thought. It wouldn't have even occurred to them that you'd left the Bureau. People don't resign from the NKVD.'

'But what would they hope to gain by having Stacey re-enter my life?'

'You tell me. Does she know anything about what you've been doing?'

'A bit,' he admitted. He wasn't going to lie to Guttman; to his consternation, his own doubts were growing.

'Has she met any of Fermi's group?'

'She and Mrs Fermi have become friends.'

'I bet they have,' said Guttman.

Nessheim didn't know what to say. His initial puzzlement had turned to anger, but now when Guttman got up to use the bathroom, he sat still, feeling overwhelmed by what he had been told. Stacey wasn't an ex-Communist; she had actually *rejoined* the Party. If the evidence for this was the Party's own membership roster, that seemed incontrovertible. As for George Tweedy, it seemed indisputable he wasn't fulfilling the Nevada sixty-day residency requirements, a violation which you would never chance for the sake of a dinner – if discovered you'd have to start your residency all over again.

Doubts of his own came to mind, which he could not suppress. What had made Stacey suddenly decide to go to law school, and at Chicago – two thousand miles from LA? Even Fielding had seemed puzzled by this last-minute application; he'd noted Stacey's apparent lack of interest in the law.

Then there was the break-in of his apartment. The intruder hadn't forced his way in; he had used a key. There was only one spare key, which Stacey said she'd replaced in its hiding place beneath the back stairs. It simply wasn't credible to think the intruder would have 'found' it there – it was too well hidden. Instead he must have been told where it was, and used it to get in, knowing that Nessheim and Stacey were out that night. Only Stacey could have told him that.

He was starting to feel sick – nausea and a sudden wave of flu-like ache swept over him. These were facts, all right, and they weren't even supplied by Guttman. But there was something even more terrible than facts which he had to confront.

Why had Stacey taken such a run at him? Why had she taken him up if it was not in order to take him in? *Forty acres of hay-bearing fields and an orchard* – my ass. He was in love with her, which meant he had been naively willing to believe that she loved him too. This woman, beautiful, wealthy and smart as a whip, could have any man in the world she wanted. Was it really credible that Stacey Madison would fall in love with him, football has-been, former Special Agent and neophyte law student? He had swallowed it whole – forty acres and all.

He had his head in his hands when Guttman returned and handed him a glass of whisky and water. Nessheim mutely nodded his thanks and drained it. He said, fearing his voice would break, 'Get me another one, will you?'

'Have it after I'm gone.' Guttman paused a beat, his voice now gentle. 'I'm sorry, Nessheim, but I had no choice.'

'What set you on to her?'

'It doesn't matter.' And of course to Guttman all that mattered was whether it was true.

'So where do we go from here?' Nessheim asked. There was comfort in pretending that his life had not just been ripped apart.

'I'm off to Stagg Field to see Fermi. I called him before I came here. Groves has given me authority to do whatever I need to do. I agree with you that Kalvin's got to go, and that will happen as soon as he's back from New Mexico.'

'Do you want help from me?' He didn't know what he wanted the answer to be.

'I will do. You know the set-up here, and I don't. Then at some point, we need to think how all this came about.'

'Do you want her arrested?' Nessheim was grateful that he could say this steadily.

'There's nothing to charge her with, is there? She told you a pack of lies, but as far as we know she hasn't done any damage herself – she's just got us to take our eye off the ball.'

'*My* eye, I think you mean.' He knew Guttman was being kind, but he didn't want sympathy right now.

'You can find me at Stagg Field. Or where I'm staying. It's the faculty place.'

'The Quadrangle Club?'

Guttman seemed embarrassed. 'Groves got Compton to arrange it.'

Then Guttman grabbed his coat from the chair. He stood there for a moment, looking as though he wanted to apologise. But they both knew he had nothing to apologise for.

Nessheim didn't have another whisky while he sat and thought of what to do. He was supposed to go over to Stacey's swanky apartment for a change, and if he didn't go she would no doubt come over – he'd given her back the key from under the stairs. He didn't want that; he didn't want to see her that evening, or any other time.

He had to tell her this. He found the box of stationery he used for writing to his mother, or the bank, and sat down with it at the dining-room table, pushing his law books off in one angry sweep.

In the letter he wrote, his feelings poured out in a cascade of anger and bewilderment. His bitterness grew with the recital of her lies. An hour later he would have been hard-pressed to recall the exact language he used, but the tone was poisonous and adamant. He didn't want to see her ever again.

Before he would let time temper his emotions, he found an envelope and sealed the letter inside. He went out and drove to her apartment building, gave three bucks to the doorman to deliver it by hand, then headed home, where this time after half a bottle of whisky he found reprieve, if no solace, in sleep.

31

HE WOKE TO the phone ringing. He looked at his watch, which had belonged to his father. It was two-thirty. It wouldn't be Guttman calling at this hour; it could only be Stacey. He wondered how often she'd called since receiving his letter.

Eventually it stopped. He knew he wouldn't get back to sleep, so he got up and put his clothes on. He was just dressed when the phone started ringing again, and he had left the apartment before it stopped.

He walked up to 57th Street, where the street lights made the shut storefronts and empty sidewalk look like a movie set before the actors had arrived. He walked all the way to Ellis Avenue before he even heard the sound of a car. At Stagg Field the guard was sitting behind his desk, awake, but making no effort to show he was alert. Nessheim couldn't blame him; he himself was still feeling more whisky than hangover, but knew it was going to be downhill for the next few hours. Hours? His heart sank at the prospect of the days and weeks and months ahead, as he struggled with the knowledge of Stacey's betrayal.

Zinn and his crew of young men from the stockyards were busy in the court that had become a workshop. Saws sang out in a screechy chorus, joined by the basser notes of the power drills used to bore holes for the insertion of uranium in the graphite blocks. The blocks were being carried by hand to the court next door, where Anderson was directing junior scientists on their placement. He held a big sheet of paper, on which each level of blocks had been drawn and numbered, and the alternation of plain graphite with uranium-loaded ones marked as well. A massive airtight rubber cover, commissioned by Anderson from Goodyear, enveloped the back half of the Pile on three sides like a vast balloon. It was intended, once sealed, to exclude neutron-absorbing air, though Nessheim had overheard Szilard say that there was no point to it, and that it only got in the way.

He went up on to Fermi's command post and found a director's chair with a canvas back by the instrument console. He pushed it against the wall and sat down. No one below took any notice of him. He knew now the basic outlines of the project, and recalled enough from his one physics course in college to understand that it involved a chain reaction, one which had to be controlled. Somehow the energy released was going to be harnessed to a weapon; he assumed it would have to be a bomb. It must be a very big bomb, he thought, as he leaned back in the chair, doing his best not to think about Stacey. He hoped Guttman had alerted Fermi to Kalvin by now.

He woke with no sense of the hour and, funnily enough, the whisky had not left him hungover. He put it down to the agitation he felt. He had been so gullible – he saw that now. The realisation made him feel terrible, and tense.

A man was standing a few feet away by the edge of the balcony, with his back to him. It was Fermi. He was dressed this time in the ubiquitous racquets court uniform of grey overalls and was studying the measurements record in his right hand and directing the men down below. When he stirred in his chair, Fermi turned around and smiled. 'Good morning. You have begun early today, Jim.'

He realised it was the only time Fermi had ever called him by his first name. 'Did you have a good trip?' he asked, trying not to yawn.

'As predicted, even General Groves was satisfied.' He gave a mock salute and Nessheim tried to laugh, wondering how long it would take really to laugh again. Fermi said, 'My wife tells me you have been busy while I was away. I want to thank you for your help.' He looked embarrassed.

'I was just happy the cat burglar turned out to be a cat.'

It took Fermi a moment to understand, but then he nodded. 'That is not all you found, I understand,' he said, looking slightly nervous.

Nessheim said softly, 'Your wife explained. There is no problem. Except you need to find a better hiding place.'

'I saw Assistant Director Guttman yesterday. I thought when he called to arrange an appointment, it might be about the money.'

'He knows nothing about it,' Nessheim said emphatically. 'There's no need to tell anyone.'

'Thank you. Mr Guttman explained there was a problem with one of the physicists. I believe you know about it.'

'I do.'

'I will take care of it. The man is not back yet, but I am scheduled to see him as soon as he is.'

Nessheim pointed to the Pile, which now loomed high above the balcony. 'Are you just about there?'

'Yes.'

'Will something happen?'

'Like a big bang? No, you can feel comfortable. It will merely show on this machine here when the event has occurred.' He pointed to one of the counters on the table next to Nessheim. 'It will not be a drama like Shakespeare.' He smiled, almost sadly. 'But it is,' and he paused, as if trying to put in words just how momentous it all was, 'a most important event. Szilard is sure it will change the world for ever. And not for the better.' Fermi was sombre for a moment. Then to lighten things, he said, 'Tell me, how is your Miss Madison?'

Nessheim found himself suddenly so pained that he could not pretend. 'She is not my Miss Madison any more, Professor.'

'No! What has happened?' He looked concerned. Nessheim couldn't bring himself to speak, and Fermi said gently, 'My wife says that woman adores you.' Nessheim found that his heart was pounding, and his pulse made a mockery of his stillness, sitting in the chair. Watching him closely, Fermi said, 'Of course, if you do not feel the same, then all I can say is . . .' He stopped for a moment, seeming to search for the phrase.

'Yes?' asked Nessheim, expecting an Italian exposition on the merits of true love. Charming and utterly irrelevant.

Instead Fermi said bluntly, 'I would advise you to change your mind.' And he turned on his heel and went down the stairs.

32

WHEN NESSHEIM GOT back home late that morning, the phone was ringing again. This time he went to the kitchen, took the earpiece off the wall hook and waited, not even saying hello.

'Don't worry, I'm not coming over,' Stacey said. When he didn't say anything, she said, 'Nessheim, you can't end it this way.'

'I thought I had.'

'Your letter – it's not right.'

'Sure.'

'It's *horrible*. I know you don't care about that, but it's all wrong. If you want to end it, you can't do it believing these things.'

'Watch me.'

'You have to give me a hearing. That's only fair. That's only honest.'

'Honest? Where do I start? A husband supposedly in Reno? Your Party membership? Or your new friendship with Laura Fermi?'

'I'm not in the Party.'

'So who is then? Or is it a case of mistaken identity?'

'Someone is telling you lies.'

'Yes, and we know who that is.'

She was silent for a moment. Then she said quietly, 'You're the one who wouldn't give.' She paused. 'I don't know what to say.'

Was this a confession? He didn't really care, though there was something so bare about her voice that he could not help but be touched a little.

'Just see me once,' she said. 'That's all I ask. Whatever

315

you think after that, at least you'll know the truth – whether you believe it or not.'

As if, he thought bitterly.

'Okay, I'll come over,' he said. 'I'll be there at two.'

He showered and dressed, then sat at the dining-room table, steeling himself for his encounter, trying to decide if there could be any reason Guttman was wrong. But all he could see was that Stacey had lied to him, again and again.

He heard steps coming up the back stairs. They stopped at his landing, and he wondered if Stacey was pre-empting things by coming over. Somebody pounded heavily on the back door; it couldn't be her.

He went through to the kitchen where the wall clock read five past twelve. He jerked open the door and found Winograd standing there in an oversized, red-and-black plaid Mackinaw jacket, carrying a brown grocery bag.

'Hey, fella,' Winograd said. 'I brought you a few beers to make up for drinking all of yours last time.' He shook the bag until the bottles inside clinked.

'Sorry, you've caught me at a bad time. I'm working.' He did not ask him in.

'For Fielding?'

'Constitutional Law. I'm two weeks behind.' It was safe to say this since Winograd wasn't in his class.

'What if I come back in a while? Say two o'clock?'

Nessheim shook his head. 'Sorry. I'm going out then. Seeing Stacey.'

Winograd's eyes widened. 'You still dating her, huh? You must have some secret charisma you keep hidden from the rest of us.'

Nessheim wished he hadn't mentioned her. It wasn't any of Winograd's business, and Nessheim wasn't going to theorise about what Stacey saw in him. He shook his head impatiently. 'Sorry, got to get back to work.'

'Okay,' his classmate said reluctantly.

'Another time,' said Nessheim, as Winograd started down the stairs. Nessheim closed the door and went back to the dining room. He could hear Winograd starting to whistle, a series of high notes against the background of his leaden *thump thumpa, thump thumpa*.

He had wanted to collect his thoughts, but the unexpected visit left him on edge. He felt jittery, bombarded by odd, stray notions, mostly unpleasant ones. He found himself wondering if Stacey had been seeing other guys while seeing him. He pictured her sleeping with one of her Soviet masters, then wondered if maybe right now one of them was at her apartment. He knew this was all nutty, but the thoughts were like a terrible itch that no amount of scratching could get rid of. He decided that only seeing Stacey was going to make them go away.

The sooner the better then, he concluded, impulsively deciding to go to her place early. He had to see her right away.

A slight thaw had set in, and the Dodge started easily enough, helped by a battery Nessheim had had installed in Bremen which the local garage owner had assured him could start a tank in Arctic weather. Most of the Hyde Park streets had now been ploughed, and the odd exception was slushy rather than icy, though he knew the drop in night-time temperatures would ice things up again.

The sun was quivering against the horizon through a thin white haze as he drove east, and when he turned on to South Shore Drive he could see families out at The Point, building snowmen and chucking chunks of ice against the frozen surface of Lake Michigan. He parked down the street from the entrance to Stacey's building and locked his car.

There was no sign of the doorman, and the door to the building was locked. On one side of the entrance there was a list of occupants. Nessheim pushed the button for 6B, but before anyone answered it, an elderly man opened the door on his way out, so Nessheim went in. It was Sunday, the lull day in a building like this. The ground-floor lobby was empty, though a copy of the *Tribune* lay in a mess of pages on an armchair. When he got to the elevator for Stacey's wing, he cursed, since a small sign hung from its push button saying '*Out of Order*'. He could have found the freight elevator but wasn't sure which way to go, so in his impatience he opted for the stairs. It was six storeys to Stacey's apartment, but he took them quickly, his Florsheims going rat-a-tat-tat on the hard concrete floor.

On a floor above him he heard a door open, then close with a whine, and when he got to the landing of the third floor he found a white-haired old lady, dressed to go out in a woollen overcoat with a fur collar and fur hat, looking perturbed.

'Are you the elevator man?' she asked.

'No. Can I help you, though?'

'The elevator doesn't seem to be working.'

'It's out of order. You can take the freight elevator instead.'

'Not alone. I can't open the doors.'

Nessheim nodded, since the freight elevator would have a latticed metal door that took a man's strength to open. 'I can do that for you.'

'Maybe you could just assist me down all these stairs.'

He tried not to sigh, but knew he'd have to walk her

down to the lobby. If the doorman ever showed up, he could take it from there.

Then they heard the scream.

It was a high-pitched howl that seemed to come from outside the building, through the solid masonry wall of the staircase. It lasted a long second, then stopped.

'What was that?' the old lady asked, sounding shaken.

Nessheim was already mounting the stairs, two at a time. He reached the sixth floor, where he yanked open the door and came into the lemon-coloured corridor. Ten feet along was the entrance to Stacey's apartment, and as he ran to it he heard from further down the hall a hydraulic whir of belts and cables, and he registered that the elevator was on the move again.

He was about to pound on Stacey's door when he saw that it was cracked open. Pushing it, he went into the apartment, calling her name. There was no reply. The air in the place was stuffy and hot, but when he moved along the corridor he suddenly felt a line of cold air coming from the living room. Looking in, he saw that one of the row of sliding windows facing the Lake was wide open.

There was no sign of Stacey, and no answer when he called her name again. He couldn't have said why, but he drew his gun.

He backed up into the little entrance hall, and went down the short corridor that led to the other rooms. The kitchen on one side looked spotlessly clean, and was empty. Next there was a small bedroom which Stacey used as a study – it had bookcases floor to ceiling on two of its walls. It looked as if it hadn't been used in weeks – Stacey had been doing her studying at his place on Kimbark.

He went into the bedroom, where he thought he would find her at last. Probably napping under the sheets, possibly hoping he would join her there. The bed was a mess, a tangle of sheets and a single woollen blanket. But unoccupied. On a chair by her dressing table she'd draped a black dress and a pair of nylons. He checked the bathroom, and found some strands of Stacey's hair in the sink, but no Stacey.

Puzzled and increasingly alarmed, he headed back to the hallway. From outside, through the open window in the living room, he felt the blast of cold air again. As he went to close it he heard a commotion from below. Holstering his gun so it was out of sight, he leaned out and looked down at the sidewalk.

He saw the doorman in his long black overcoat standing almost directly underneath. Nearby to him the old lady Nessheim had met on the stairs was approaching from the entrance to the building, waving a beckoning hand, doubtless wanting the doorman to get her a cab. She must have made her own way down after all.

The doorman was ignoring her and now took a step to one side. No longer blocked from Nessheim's view, a female figure lay sprawled on her front, lying half on the sidewalk, half on the adjoining strip of winter-deadened grass. She wore only a white slip, and Nessheim could see its contrast with the vestigial California tan on her bare arms and legs. Her position on the ground suggested that she was in a deep sleep, one leg bent at the knee, her arms stretched out on either side of her head, which lay turned to one side. With a beautiful untidiness, her hair flowed across one shoulder.

At first there was nothing to indicate that Stacey would not wake up, collect herself and continue with her life. Then Nessheim saw the pool of blood on the sidewalk next to her head, and he wondered if his life had ended too.

Part Six

33

THE NEWSPAPERS LEFT no doubt about their view. *'Heiress Beauty in Death Plunge'* ran the headline in the *Chicago American*; *'Fatal Fall on Shore Drive'* in the *Sun Times*, with a picture of an ambulance and two Chicago Police Department squad cars in front of Stacey's building. The other papers followed, in varying degrees of sensationalism. Even the stuffy *Tribune* splashed with the death, noting that the victim's father had been one of the city's leading businessmen.

Guttman had brought the papers when he came over from the Quadrangle Club. He'd put away the whisky bottle and washed the glasses, then fried eggs and made toast while Nessheim showered and shaved and put on a suit. Nessheim kept the door to the bedroom shut, where he'd finally fallen into whisky-induced sleep, with Stacey's nightgown clutched in his hands.

He sat at the dining-room table now, ignoring his plate while he scanned the news stories. Guttman said, 'I didn't know if you'd want to see these.'

'They're all saying suicide.'

'I know,' said Guttman unhappily.

'It wasn't.' It was about all he could hang on to since Stacey's death. 'Somebody pushed her out that window, Harry.'

Guttman said nothing.

Nessheim said, 'I heard a scream on my way up. The elevator was out of order, so I took the stairs. Suicides don't scream, Harry.'

Guttman still didn't say anything.

Nessheim pressed on: 'When I got up there the

elevator was working again. That couldn't have been a coincidence – I think whoever killed her was on their way down, having put it out of order so it would be waiting for them on the sixth floor.'

This time Guttman nodded, but it was half-hearted. Frustrated, Nessheim said, 'She wasn't the type to do herself in, Harry. You didn't know her, but you can trust me about that.'

'Okay.'

'Anyway, why would Stacey bump herself off if she thought I was coming an hour later? If she was so upset that she wanted to do herself in, then why arrange to see me at all? She *wanted* to see me, but she wasn't expecting me to come early.' He tried to control his frustration.

Guttman said, 'The police want to talk to you some more.'

'All right,' said Nessheim wearily. After finding Stacey dead on the sidewalk, he'd spent five hours being grilled, having to give his account over and over again. It had been bearable only because he been forced to react to the constant questioning, which kept him from thinking about what he had seen – and what he had lost.

A homicide detective named Palborg had arrived and honed in on his relationship with Stacey. Had there been an argument? Was she feeling down? It was obvious the police hadn't found his note to her, and he had said nothing about it. What good would it do if, like Guttman, the cops thought Stacey was working for the Reds?

Guttman said, 'I haven't told them about our conversation the other day. As far as I'm concerned, they don't need to know anything about her political associations.'

'Thanks,' said Nessheim dully.

Then Guttman surprised him. 'Actually, the cops

324

aren't sure it was a suicide either. That's why they want to talk to you again.'

'I *know* she was murdered – so do you. I want to find out why.'

Guttman shifted uncomfortably. 'There's a problem. If the police don't like your answers, they may want to arrest you. You'd never get bail in such a public case.' He nodded towards the pile of newspapers.

'Do they think *I* killed her?'

Guttman's expression gave nothing away. 'Like you, they're thinking she didn't go out the window on her own. They plan to tell the papers that tomorrow – it will make them look like they're on top of things. Making an arrest would be the icing on the cake.'

'Why me? She was dead before I entered the apartment. I heard her scream on the way down.'

'Sure, but how can you prove that? Especially when they found your prints in the apartment.'

'Of course they did. I was there – I'm not denying that.'

'Most of the prints they found are in the bedroom.' Guttman looked down at the floor, and Nessheim remembered there was a prudish streak in him. 'But they also found some on the window in the living room . . .'

'They would have done. I was at the window – that's where I saw her on the ground.'

Guttman nodded awkwardly. There was something going on here that Nessheim didn't understand, something Guttman didn't want to say but clearly felt he had to. Guttman said at last, 'The thing is, the window was open, right? I mean,' and he hesitated, 'it had to be, didn't it?'

'Yes, it was wide open.'

'Exactly. And it was open when the police first got

there. So how did your prints get on the glass? The window slides sideways to tuck behind the window next to it. Your prints would have been on it only if it were *shut*.'

Nessheim now saw what Guttman was getting at: the police were thinking he had opened the window, then somehow bundled Stacey out of it. He also realised how his prints had got there. 'The only time I stayed over there, I got up in the middle of the night and went out to the living room. I opened the window then because I wanted to hear the Lake. I'd have left prints all over it.'

It sounded lame, he knew that, and he felt the need to stare at Guttman until Guttman finally nodded. Nessheim said, 'I need some time, Harry. There are people I need to talk to.'

'What are you hoping to discover?'

'I want to find out why Stacey came to Chicago and I want to know why she lied to me. If it turns out you're right about the reasons, I'll be the first to say so. Either way, that will tell me why she was murdered.'

Guttman thought about this, then finally said, 'I have to make a couple of calls.'

'There's a phone in the kitchen,' said Nessheim, pointing next door. His voice was hoarse and flat.

'Why don't you go wait in the living room while I'm on the phone?'

It wasn't a request.

It took a while before Guttman reappeared. Nessheim paced around while he waited, at one point going into the bedroom where he picked up Stacey's nightgown, which still carried the faint aroma of her lilac scent. Back in the living room he stared out through the window towards Kimbark Avenue, where an eerily low sun had now melted most of the remaining snow. He felt numb and sick at the same time. Why had he written to Stacey? He should have talked to her face-to-face, and listened to her side of the story. Now he desperately wanted to get out of there, scared that at any moment the cops would arrive and take him out in handcuffs. Then he would never unravel the mystery of Stacey Madison. He was on the verge of grabbing his coat and running for it when Guttman came down the hall.

'I've bought you forty-eight hours. But you've got to keep your head down. I don't want the cops to spot you.'

'Why not?'

'Because they think you're in Wisconsin. I've told them you'll turn yourself in when you come back.'

'Thanks, Harry.' He knew how big a gamble Guttman was taking on him. 'There's something I didn't mention. On my way up the stairs to Stacey's apartment I ran into an old lady who was on her way down because the elevator wasn't working. I was going to help her, but then I heard the scream. The cops claim they couldn't find her – they acted like I'd invented her. But when I looked out the window of Stacey's apartment, I saw her again. She was trying to get the doorman to help her find a cab. But he –' and he stopped, not wanting his voice to break.

'Okay. Let me try and find her. Anything else?' When Nessheim shook his head dumbly, Guttman said, 'Then give me your keys, will you?'

'Why do you want my keys?'

'If you're meant to be in Wisconsin, you can't sleep here, now can you? The cops will check, believe me. So I'll stay here – they'll think I'm waiting for you to come back. And you can stay in my room at the faculty place. But keep your head down, okay?'

'All right. Let me just take my car key.' Nessheim started to work it off the key ring.

'Give me that, too – I don't want you driving your car. They'll be looking for it.'

'But I need my car.'

'You can use these,' Guttman said, handing over two keys on a thin wire hoop. 'It's not ideal, I know, but I don't see that we've got much choice. These are for Stacey's car – I parked it round the corner.'

34

THE MADISON PLACE was in mansion country, miniature estates carved out of the land adjacent to the shoreline of Lake Michigan. Easily commutable to the Loop for the wealthy businessmen who made their fortunes there, but a world away from the city, with a mix of lawns, patches of woods, and sandy beach. And gargantuan houses.

He parked outside the property, worried that arriving in Stacey's car might give her mother a Lazarus-like moment. He walked through the entrance gates, an elaborate iron pair as high as those at Stagg Field, then moved along an asphalt track, which first wound through a thin stand of birch, then suddenly opened up to reveal the house.

It was a mock-Georgian pile of orange brick, with white Doric columns the height of the roof on either side of the front door. Ivy covered the front facade, creeping over the large sash windows of the two upper floors.

He was about to push the doorbell when he saw that the front door was just ajar. He knocked and pushed simultaneously, then stepped into a big hall, with a curved staircase to one side that had more banister than stairs. A small Negro woman in a maid's uniform was dusting a side table in the hall as he came in. She didn't seem surprised by his arrival.

'Excuse me,' said Nessheim. 'I'm looking for Mrs Madison.'

'Are you the funeral man?'

In his suit and tie, Nessheim understood the confusion. 'No, ma'am.'

'You selling something? She won't see no salesman. Her daughter's passed two days ago.'

'That's what I'm here about. I knew Stacey.'

The woman gave out a noise that went *hmmpphh*. 'You'll find her mother in the conservatory. Go down the hall and turn right. It's on the far side of the living room and the first person you'll find will be Mrs M – there ain't nobody else here to see. If she offers you coffee, please say no – I ain't got time to make it. She wants the wake here and I got too much to do readying the house.'

He walked along a hall and turned into a vast living room full of chintz chairs and padded sofas with views of the shoreline several hundred yards away. He could see a big freighter a few miles out, chugging towards Gary. A pair of open French doors led into the conservatory, where he stepped into a bath-like fug of heat and potted plants. At the far end enough space had been carved out for a recliner seat, and standing next to it, staring out through the glass windows towards Lake Michigan, was Mrs Madison.

She was taller than her daughter had been, blonder with her hair swept back in a big leonine wave, and slightly heavier. There was a housecoat on the recliner which Nessheim sensed was her usual costume here, but now she wore a black wool dress. It was a little tight on her.

'Yes?' she said as he walked towards her. She had a large high-cheekboned face, with a strong jaw and set-apart hazel eyes. Like Stacey she wore little make-up. This was a woman confident of her appeal – though in a beauty contest, her daughter would have won, and Nessheim somehow sensed this would have rankled the older woman. 'Are you here about the flowers or the coffin?' From her voice and the glass in her hand he could tell she had already started on the sauce.

'Neither, Mrs Madison. I was at law school with your daughter.'

'What's your name?'

He hesitated because he was supposed to be in Wisconsin, but he couldn't see any reason why the police would hear about his visit. 'James Nessheim,' he said.

She shook her head; clearly it didn't mean anything to her. He said, 'I just wanted to pay my respects.'

'Were you friends with my daughter?'

'Yes. Good friends.'

'Did you know Tweedy?' Her voice hardened.

'Her husband? No, I didn't.'

The woman gave a derisory laugh. 'I'm not surprised. I called Tweedy last night to tell him Stacey had died. His houseboy said he was in a meeting. He hasn't called back.'

'Is there anything I can do to help?'

'The funeral's a week from Thursday – you might tell her friends. Eleven o'clock at Saint Barnabas church, here in Highland Park.'

'Do you need any help with the arrangements?'

'That's very kind, but no, thank you.' She said this as if by rote, and Nessheim could see she was already stinko. She added abruptly, 'Who did you say you were again?'

'Nessheim. Stacey called me Jim. I used to know her years ago when she was in college at the U of C. It was a big surprise for me to have her turn up in Chicago again.'

'You weren't the only one who was surprised.'

'Why did she come back to Chicago? I mean, California's full of law schools.'

'Well, it wasn't to see me, that's for sure. She was happy for my help getting in, but was she grateful enough to visit? Not on your life.'

'Well, law students are pretty busy.'

'If you say so. Anyway, she probably did it out of love.'

'For Tweedy?' he asked, confused.

'You kidding me? She never loved that schmo.'

'But she married him.'

She took a slug of her gin, tilting the upheld glass so the liquid got past the ice cubes faster. She held the glass by her side, her lipstick glistening. 'You're old enough to know not many people marry for love.'

'I'm not married.'

'Maybe that's why.' She lifted her head and viewed him appraisingly. 'Anyway, she changed.'

'How so?'

'Because of LA,' she said flatly. 'And the schmo. He was rich ... and dumb ... and liked to hang out with the Hollywood bunch. From the sound of it, half the people in pictures are Reds. So Stacey went to Mexico – I think she hoped he'd grow up a bit while she was gone. But of course he didn't, so she came out here.'

'She used to be interested in politics.'

'That went sour. Or south,' she added with a titter that ended in a slur of consonants. Sobering, she said, 'If you ask me, I think she had another guy going. In her head, anyway.'

'Who would that be?'

'Stacey stopped confiding in me when she was about twelve.' She shook her head; her great lion's mane of hair didn't move an inch. 'You see that pitcher over there? Top me up, will you? And help yourself.'

He went to the drinks trolley and picked up the pitcher. It had a lily painted on one side, and smelled of straight gin. As he refilled her glass she said, 'You sure you won't join me?'

'No, thanks.'

He stepped back and set the pitcher down on the tray, while she took a long pull on her drink. Then she said, 'You've got very fine hands for such a good-looking guy.'

'Thank you,' he said.

'You know what they say?'

'No, ma'am,' he replied, hoping to be spared the disclosure.

'Never mind,' she said.

'I think I'd better be going,' he said quietly. Stacey's mother gripped her glass so hard that the veins on her hand stood out.

'Forget about the funeral,' she hissed as he turned to go. 'It's family only.'

As he crossed into the living room he heard her start to cry, and then he heard the words she was saying in between her sobs. *My baby, my baby.*

35

As HE DROVE south along the Lake, it began to snow. Flakes the size of night moths spooled across his windshield, then stuck like pasty glue. The wipers in Stacey's car moved a beat behind, and he drove with his eyes staring until they felt strained as the road ahead alternately receded then emerged from the swirl of snow. He wanted to concentrate on his driving, but the mystery of Stacey's return was haunting him.

Was he the other guy her mother had mentioned? If so, how could Stacey in LA decide that she loved a man she hadn't seen in years? It seemed incredible. There must have been some other reason why she sought him out, something which had precipitated her flight from LA. He didn't want to believe it was because Stacey was following NKVD orders. But then what else could it have been?

He found Diane on the ground floor, working behind one of the perfume counters. Nessheim hung back, inspecting the potions and lotions arranged on an adjacent glass-topped counter until Diane came across to him. She wore the store uniform of white blouse and brown skirt that did her figure no favours. She was about his own age, with a doughy face and dull almond-coloured eyes.

'Can I help you?' she asked without enthusiasm.

'Are you Diane?'

Her eyes showed her surprise. 'Who are you?'

'I was a friend of Stacey's. I wonder if we could talk for a minute.'

'Why do you want to talk to me?' She sounded upset.

'She said you were an old friend.'

Nessheim took his ID folder out from his jacket pocket. He flipped the badge holder open, with his photo beneath it and his name in bullet type – '*SPECIAL AGENT JAMES NESSHEIM*'.

She glanced at the badge. 'I don't have to talk to you.' Her tone was only semi-defiant; she was scared.

'Look at my ID, please, Diane.'

'I can read. It says you're a Fed.'

'Read the name below the badge.'

Reluctantly she looked down. Then she picked up the badge holder and stared at it with disbelief.

'You're Nessheim?' Her voice was incredulous.

'Yes,' he said mildly.

Her face relaxed. 'I thought you were supposed to be a student now.'

'I am. She knew I was a Fed as well. There were never any flies on Stacey.'

'There sure weren't.' She added wistfully, 'Not even a cobweb. My break's in ten minutes if you can wait.'

He waited in a coffee shop around the corner, where he sat in a booth in the back facing the door. She came in twenty minutes later, and he saw she'd touched up her make-up and brushed her hair.

She slid awkwardly into the booth and sat across from him. She said nervously, 'I want to go to the funeral but I don't know when it is.'

'Next Thursday at eleven in Highland Park.' He named the church.

'Did you get that from Stacey's mom?'

'Yeah. I just came from her.'

'How is she taking it?'

He shrugged. 'Hard to say. She was half-cut when I

335

arrived. She must have started when the sun couldn't even *see* the yardarm.'

Diane gave a small smile. 'I haven't seen her since high school. She and Stacey weren't exactly close.'

She paused for a moment. 'I never would have dreamed Stacey would take her own life. It's hard for me to believe. Stacey was moody, yes – mercurial you might call it. But never really down. Something must have got to her for this to happen.' She was looking at him warily again.

'Maybe she didn't go out the window of her own accord.'

Diane's expression didn't change but her eyes widened. 'Do the police think that?'

'Yes, they think she was pushed.'

'Why would anyone do that?'

'That's what I wanted to ask you. Stacey told me you'd both been Party members for a while. The Party doesn't like people to leave.'

'Not much,' she acknowledged. 'But I only joined for the social life. Some social life,' she added tartly.

Had this woman really thought she'd find a boyfriend courtesy of the Comintern? Nessheim imagined a series of sad seductions conducted by earnest young men, who actually preferred just talking about Engels's contribution to the theory of surplus value.

He said, 'Stacey didn't stay in the Party either.'

'No. But she left for a real reason. She followed Trotsky, not Stalin, and that was unacceptable. She grew to hate the Soviets almost as much as the Nazis. That's why she went to the Fourth International.'

'The fourth what?'

'International. It was a world meeting of Trotsky's followers in '38, held in Paris. Stacey told me she attended the congress sessions during the day, and went

336

to nightclubs at night.' She laughed. 'Typical Stacey. That's where she met Tweedy. He wasn't a Trotskyist, or a Communist for that matter. He was just rich and he fell for her. Like a lot of men,' she said pointedly.

'So he took her to LA?' When Diane nodded, Nessheim added, 'I thought she lost her faith in politics.'

'Not then. Why do you think she went to Mexico?'

Why indeed? He'd assumed she'd moved on to another man. That was standard procedure for the Stacey he had known years ago. He started to say as much, but Diane cut him off. 'She wasn't Trotsky's lover if that's what you're thinking. She loved him only in the way a Baptist girl loves Jesus. She thought he could save the movement Stalin had betrayed – it was as simple as that.'

'Did she see him down there?'

'Yes. Often.'

He didn't know what to say. Diane was looking at him without suspicion now. She could see that Nessheim was feeling overwhelmed by what he was learning.

He asked, 'Was she there when Trotsky was murdered?'

'No. She left months before that.'

'Why did she leave?'

Diane looked thoughtful. 'You know, most people are looking to be loved, but Stacey was always looking for someone *to* love. She told me Trotsky was a good man, but completely unrealistic. She said that given the choice between theorising about an ideal world and actually trying to make a better one, Trotsky would always go for nirvana. She said she woke up one morning in Mexico City and decided that he might be making a contribution to political theory, but none at all to history.'

Nessheim said, 'So she went back to LA, where she

was unhappy with Tweedy and didn't like his friends. That doesn't explain why she came back to Chicago, or why she enrolled in law school.' For the first time Diane looked hesitant. Nessheim said, 'Her mother thought it was on account of some guy, but that couldn't have been me. I don't think she even knew I was here.'

'She knew, all right.'

'But she hadn't seen me in years.'

Diane said emphatically, 'She came back because of you.'

'Why? She didn't know me any more. She wasn't a fantasist.'

'I didn't say she was. But she was scared.'

'Of what? The Communists?'

Diane nodded.

Nessheim said, 'Why would they want to hurt her? She wasn't any threat to them.' He paused momentarily. 'Unless she helped them.'

'What do you mean?'

'You know, helped them get to Trotsky.'

Diane was shaking her head.

Nessheim pressed her. 'I was told that Stacey rejoined the Party while she was in LA. If she were scared of the Soviets, that wouldn't have happened.'

'It wouldn't have happened because it didn't happen. Whoever told you that is lying. It's bullshit.'

'So why was she scared?'

'Because she knew something she wasn't supposed to know.' Diane hesitated, then saw Nessheim's stricken face and continued. 'The man who killed Trotsky calls himself Jacques Mornard. Most people think he was acting on Stalin's orders and that Mornard is an alias. But nobody knows who Mornard really is.'

'Except the Russians,' said Nessheim.

Diane said quietly, 'And Stacey.'

338

It took a second to sink in. '*What?*'

He was the agitated one now, as Diane began to talk calmly, like a patient teacher talking to an ignorant class.

It seemed that when Stacey was in Paris she'd made friends with a fellow Trotskyist named Sylvia Ageloff. Both cut glamorous figures and both knew this; they leavened their socialist principles with a taste for the high life. Stacey was seeing George Tweedy, the wealthy heir to a vast canning-company fortune. Sylvia Ageloff, by contrast, fancied fiery types for her lovers, though she had an equal weakness for the well-heeled ones. Among the latter was a Belgian named Jacques Mornard, a good-looking upper-class man who in a less politicised time would have been a playboy.

Stacey hadn't liked Mornard. She didn't know why, she later explained to Diane, but something about him didn't ring true. She'd found him smarmy, in-authentic and untrustworthy. She avoided him as much as possible, which was difficult given her friendship with Sylvia; to make matters even trickier, Mornard befriended Tweedy, who was flattered to be taken up by this dashing Continental type.

Stacey's suspicions of Mornard would never have been confirmed if it hadn't been for a chance occurrence. Among the Fourth International's attendees were Republican veterans of the Spanish Civil War, some of them American, including a former U of C student named Harry Glazer whom Stacey had known when they were both undergraduates. Running into each other at the Congress, which was held in a suburb of Paris, they agreed to meet for lunch the next day at a café near the city's Luxembourg Gardens.

When Glazer arrived at the café he seemed strangely

shaken. Stacey asked what was wrong, and he explained that he felt as if he'd seen a ghost. Passing through the gardens he had found himself walking towards a Spanish man he'd last seen when they'd been fighting on the Aragon front. During the fiercest battle, they found themselves side by side in a dugout, holding a forward position for the Republican side. The Spaniard, whose name was Ramón Mercader, had been shot in the arm by a sniper just as the Francoist forces were starting to retreat, and he had been put on a stretcher and eventually shipped back to a hospital in Barcelona. That was the last time Glazer had seen the man – until ten minutes ago.

When he'd gone up to greet his old comrade in arms, however, to Glazer's astonishment the man had denied being Mercader, and insisted he was a Belgian named Jacques Mornard. Glazer initially thought it was a joke, but when he pressed him, the man grew angry and threatened to call a policeman if Glazer didn't leave him alone. When Stacey asked Glazer whether he could have been mistaken about the man's identity, he said that would normally have been perfectly possible. But this 'Belgian' had a small shaving scar on his chin – in the exact place where Mercader had had a scar as well.

The congress ended shortly thereafter, and Stacey moved to LA with George Tweedy. She lost touch with Sylvia Ageloff, and would probably have forgotten all about Jacques Mornard, if she hadn't gone to Mexico.

Growing disaffected there, Stacey had decided to leave when one day who should show up but Sylvia Ageloff, with Jacques Mornard in tow. Stacey only talked to them briefly – they were rushing off to meet the Great Man and she was getting ready to leave the country – but they seemed happy enough to see her.

Then four months later Stacey looked at the *Los*

Angeles Times at the breakfast table and saw that Trotsky had been murdered. The assassin had been arrested at once: it was Jacques Mornard. Now sitting in a Mexican prison, the killer continued to insist he was Mornard, and claimed to have killed Trotsky in a fit of rage when Trotsky didn't approve of his plans to marry Sylvia Ageloff. Everyone was sure that Mornard had been acting on Stalin's orders, but nothing could be proved when no one knew who Mornard really was.

Nessheim interjected then, pointing out again that Stacey had left Mexico months before Trotsky's murder. Why would the Russians think she knew anything about it?

Because, Diane said, Stacey had done something very stupid: she had confided in her husband, since she thought that, with all his money, he could protect her. But Tweedy thrived on gossip; he liked to show he was in the know. So Stacey's secret didn't stay secret for long.

Nessheim asked, 'Did Stacey know that Tweedy blabbed about it?'

'Not at first. But then someone tried to run her car off the road on the Cajon Pass. She said it was a miracle she wasn't killed.'

'The coupé?'

'That's right. Fire-engine red. She drove it here from California.'

Nessheim sat back, trying to make sense of her story. 'Okay, but we're back to square one. Why did Stacey come here? Her mother wasn't going to protect her.'

'No, you were.'

'Me?'

'Yes. Stacey had always carried a torch for you – you were the only man she regretted giving the heave-ho. But she wasn't being sentimental. She wasn't coming here because she was in love, but because she was scared. She said you wouldn't be scared of the Russians. It sounded like bravado to me – I didn't realise you were a G-Man.'

'So I was her cover then, her muscle.' It wasn't really a question, and he could not hide his dismay.

'At first. But that all changed. That's why she came to see me. She was so excited she didn't know what to do. She told me it was completely unexpected.'

'What was?'

'Her feelings. She said she'd suddenly found herself falling in love with you. I'm not sure she'd ever felt that way before. She told me you two were going to live in Wisconsin after the lousy war ends.' She gave a little snort. 'Stacey in an apron with four kids. I never thought I'd live to see it, but then I never thought Stacey wouldn't either . . .' She faltered, trying to check her emotions.

Nessheim was warmed by the thought that Stacey's dream of life with him had been sincere, but he also felt jealous of Diane's superior knowledge of Stacey's life.

She seemed to sense his ambivalence. 'I wasn't her best pal, you know. Our worlds were too different for that. But I was her oldest friend. In third grade I pulled her hair and made her cry.'

Diane's own eyes were openly teary now. She said, 'I wasn't telling you the truth before, when I said I joined the Party to meet guys.'

'Oh?'

'No. I joined because Stacey did. To make sure I would get to see her.' Her eyes dipped briefly, then rose to meet his.

'And that's why when she left Chicago, you . . .'

'I left the Party. Yes.' She sighed. 'You're the one person who will know how I feel right now. I hope you don't think less of me for that.'

342

He was unwilling to share Stacey with anyone just yet; he forced himself to remember Stacey's fondness for her friend. As warmly as he could, he said, 'I loved Stacey, Diane. How could I think less of anyone who loved her too?'

36

It was dusk when he reached Hyde Park, and dark by the time he parked Stacey's car discreetly under the elms by the Oriental Institute on 58th Street. He walked the block to the Quadrangle Club and stopped at reception for his room key. A young woman with a short blonde bob stood behind the counter in a smart black suit and white blouse. When he gave the number of his room she said, 'Excuse me, sir, are you Mr Nessheim?'

'I am.'

'There's a message for you from Mr Guttman.' She handed him a pink phone slip on which Guttman had scribbled, *'Stay put. See you at 6 in the bar. H.'*

The woman said, 'Will you be seeing Mr Guttman any time soon?'

He looked at his watch. 'Is an hour soon enough?'

She didn't smile, but looked relieved. 'Could you give him this then, please? It just arrived – special delivery.' And she handed him a large Manila envelope. It was carefully taped, and as he went up the stairs he saw the return address was *'The British Passport Office, 30 Rockefeller Plaza, New York City'.*

Upstairs he changed out of his suit and had a luke-warm shower since apparently the club didn't like to spoil its guests with too much hot water. He wanted to lie down and sleep until daybreak, but told himself he had to keep going. Stacey had been clear that dreams of forty acres and an apple orchard would have to wait.

He was trying not to think too much. His grief had briefly abated from learning that Stacey had not been working for the Russians, but it was quickly replaced by guilt. Why had he doubted her so readily? Guttman, sour and cynical, had persuaded him almost right away that he should not trust his feelings for Stacey, but needed to face facts. Is that why he had so easily accepted Guttman's contention that she was setting him up? The *fact* was, she hadn't been spying on him at all; the *fact* was, she had loved him. There had been no failure of love on his part – he knew he had loved Stacey – but instead an inability to accept that she had loved him too. He felt a terrible sadness now, and a growing anger – with Guttman for getting it so wrong; with himself for accepting Guttman's 'evidence' so easily.

At six he went downstairs in a blazer and grey flannel trousers and found Guttman on a stool at the dark mahogany bar. Behind them a pair of professorial types were playing billiards, in a space separated from the bar room by a waist-high wall of brick.

When the barman went to pour Nessheim a bourbon on the rocks, Guttman said, 'I've got some news. They found the old lady from Stacey's apartment building. Or rather *I* found her. Her name is Mrs Flint, and she confirmed your story about the scream.'

'Do the cops know that?'

'Not yet. There's something else. When you arrived, the doorman had gone to hail a cab on the Drive. When he was walking back he saw two guys shoot out of the building, then a minute later he saw them driving away.'

'In a dark green sedan?'

'Yep. So I phoned Palborg but he wasn't there. We're due to talk in the morning so this is no time for you to get arrested.'

Nessheim nodded.

Guttman said, 'Did you find the people you wanted to talk to?'

'I did.' He took a big swallow. The bourbon burnt his throat but warmed him, even with the ice. 'The Russians killed her. And no, Stacey wasn't working for them.'

'Then why did they –'

Nessheim cut him off. 'She knew a secret they don't want to get out.' And he told Guttman about Diane's account of Stacey's past few years. When he got to Trotsky in Mexico, Guttman's eyes widened, and when he explained what Stacey had known about Trotsky's killer, the eyes widened even more.

'So they had a reason to kill her,' said Nessheim. 'The last thing Stacey would have done was to jump out a window.'

Guttman exhaled involuntarily. He held his glass with both hands but instead of drinking he just stared moodily at it. 'I'll take your word for that.'

'That's big of you,' said Nessheim sharply.

Guttman ignored him. 'I'll talk to the police and ask them to look for the sedan and the two guys. But they'll be long gone. They would have made tracks as soon as Stacey –' Guttman stopped, mortified by what he'd been about to say.

They sat in awkward silence for a minute. Finally Nessheim said, 'You got it wrong, Harry. Completely wrong.' His voice was raised, and the barman looked over. Nessheim saw one of the billiard players raise his cue and glance at the bar. 'You said I was being taken for a ride, but it was you who was duped.'

His voice was still loud, and he got off his bar stool and stood next to Guttman. The barman hesitated, as if uncertain whether to intervene, especially when he saw the look in Nessheim's eyes. Nessheim sensed that he was close to losing control; that at any moment he might snap. But he didn't care. Right now if Guttman objected or protested, Nessheim would knock him off his bar stool.

But Guttman didn't even look at him. He sat with his shoulders hunched, both hands around his glass, and said quietly, 'I'm sorry, Jim. Truly sorry.'

And after a moment when his reaction hung in the balance, Nessheim suddenly felt himself step back from the edge. The bartender was still looking concerned, so he raised his hand to show that things were okay. He got back on his stool. 'I'm sorry, too, Harry. Sorry for believing you.'

After another long silence, Nessheim said, 'Tell me something – and I want you to level with me. Who told you Stacey had been a Communist? Who set that particular ball rolling?'

'Tatie,' said Guttman without hesitation.

'Tatie?' Nessheim stared at Guttman, who nodded vigorously.

Why would she have done that? Had she really felt so slighted by Stacey's rudeness in the Palmer House? It seemed a year ago, but was just a matter of a month or so. He tried to make sense of this, then said, 'Tatie couldn't have compiled all that info on her own.'

Guttman looked taken aback. 'You're right. But Tatie knows all the Records people in the Bureau. It's a kind of network of its own – between them, they know where all the dead bodies are buried in the files.'

'That doesn't ring true. Somebody must have instigated this.'

'Maybe.' Guttman paused. 'You know that I've been convinced that we've got a problem at the Bureau.' He looked around him carefully, but the bartender was reading at the end of the bar and the only people within earshot were the billiard players. He said, 'Tolson's got an assistant I'm worried about. A young guy named

Adams – they call him T.A. He's been hanging around Marie a lot lately, and there's something fishy about him. I got some old friends to check him out for me – just in case. It turns out he's been banging girls in a flop motel down by the Potomac. One of these broads was on my train when I left here last time; she took a big *spang* at me when I was in my compartment.' He looked at Nessheim defensively. 'No is the answer . . .

'Anyway, it's too big a coincidence. I think either T.A. is trying to set me up for a fall, probably on Tolson's orders, or it's something different – and worse. I don't know what relates to what any more, but something smells. I'm still mystified how you were found out here – and who it was who did the finding. I don't think it was the *Bund* and neither do you.'

Guttman shook the ice cubes that were all that was left of his drink, then continued. 'I got tailed when I was in New York, and when I got home Annie said there'd been somebody snooping around my house. If it was the Russians, how did they get the info on me and on you? It could only have come from inside the Bureau.'

He stopped suddenly, self-conscious that he had been talking for so long. Nessheim said, 'So we've got a complicated situation.'

'Yes, but right now, we have to leave it all aside. Our focus has to be on Kalvin and the project. Fermi says he thinks it will "go critical" tomorrow. Do you know what that means?' he asked uncertainly.

'I think so,' Nessheim said, watching the bartender filling bowls of peanuts ten feet away. He said carefully, 'If it works tomorrow, it means they can build what they want to build.'

'Got it,' said Guttman. 'I've checked and rechecked the security at Stagg. It's tighter than a drum. Kalvin won't be there for the final test – Fermi told him this afternoon that he couldn't be present. He didn't give the full reasons – he just blamed it on the military being extra-cautious, said there was concern over some of Kalvin's paperwork. He's taking him out to dinner tonight to console him, since Kalvin was supposed to be present on the big day.'

Guttman sat up straight and turned to look at Nessheim. It was always that way, thought Nessheim. Harry would snort and sneeze and shuffle around, but when the time came to lay down the law or just tell it straight, he would belly up to the bar and look you in the eye. 'I think tomorrow should go all right, but I'm still nervous. I need your help and I don't want you distracted by this other business.' Guttman shrugged. 'I know how hard it is, but right now I need you at your professional best.'

'You're telling me to be professional?'

Guttman looked uncomfortable but insisted, 'Yes.'

'I see.' Nessheim was watching the bartender; he didn't trust himself to keep his temper if he looked Guttman in the eye. 'Tell me, did you act *professionally* after Isabel died?'

'That was different.'

Nessheim scoffed. 'Why is that?' he demanded, turning now to look at Guttman. 'Because you were married? Because Isabel was sick? Because you'd been with her a long time?'

Guttman's chin jutted, but when he spoke his voice was not aggressive. 'Because she wasn't involved in my work. Because no one suggested I had anything to do with her dying. I didn't know Stacey Madison, but I can't believe she would have wanted you to go haywire at this moment. Listen, they gave me time off after Isabel died, and you want to know the truth? After four days I was climbing the goddamned walls. Sure you have to grieve, but right now there isn't time for it and second – don't kill me for saying it – you were born to *do*. Grief is *not* doing. I swear, if you stop now and surrender to how bad you feel, you'll go crazy within a week.'

He paused while the bartender put a bowl of shelled peanuts down in front of him. Guttman grabbed a handful and said, 'I'm not saying you shouldn't care about solving Stacey's murder. I'm not saying we shouldn't try to find who killed her. But we have to make sure all is safe and sound at Stagg Field first. It's bigger than the both of us – you know that, Nessheim. If you get mad now and stay mad and stay stupid, there's nothing I can do for you. And then for sure, the people who did this will get away. Do you hear me, Nessheim? Her killers will get away.'

Nessheim didn't want to look at Guttman. After a long pause he said, 'I hear you. So what do you want me to do? Stagg Field's okay, Kalvin's out of action – everything's hunky-dory.'

Guttman looked at his watch. 'I'm going to roust Kalvin's apartment. I doubt I'll find anything, but it's worth a go. My priority is getting through tomorrow unscathed, but after that I want to put this bastard away. And,' he added pointedly, 'any others we can catch. You coming with me or you staying here, sucking up more bourbon? Your choice, pal.'

Nessheim thought for a moment. He resented this tutorial of Guttman's; he was used to learning his own lessons in life. He took his wallet out and threw a bill down on the bar. 'I'm coming,' he said and got off his stool. Then he remembered. 'Hang on a minute. You had a package come – special delivery. The girl at the desk gave it to me.'

'It can wait,' said Guttman impatiently.

'It's from 30 Rockefeller Plaza.'

'Jesus, why didn't you say so?'

Upstairs Nessheim handed the envelope to Guttman, who ripped it open at one end. There was a cover letter which he took out first. 'This figures,' he said after reading for a minute. 'Kalvin came out of Portugal because he'd spent the last years in Spain. He went to Spain as a supposed scientist, and left a veteran of the Civil War.'

Nessheim remembered Kalvin commenting on Stacey's Spanish. It was clear where each of them had acquired the language – Spain and Mexico; clear too that for each of them it was a secret part of their pasts.

Guttman was still reading. He said, 'Kalvin fled to Portugal when Franco won, holed up in Lisbon, wrote letters to every physicist he knew this side of the pond, then got out on a boat for New York. There's a big gap in his résumé that's just been filled.'

'He's out of the way – that's what counts. Though I'd still like to know who he was meeting at the museum.'

'Me too,' said Guttman, struggling to extract the rest of the envelope's contents. Finally he managed to pull out two photographs the size of typing paper, printed on glossy stock.

Nessheim wondered if these were shots of Kalvin. Not much use to him, since he knew well enough what the man looked like. But Guttman continued to stare, and after a minute Nessheim ventured, 'What is it?'

'I don't believe it.' Guttman's voice had a hollowness to it; his shock was obvious. He leaned back and reclined his head against the antimacassar of his chair while his eyes looked up at the ceiling. 'Dear God,' he said.

'What is it?' But Guttman was oblivious, fighting

351

some private war of understanding on his own. Nessheim went round his chair and stood behind him. He looked down at the first photo, which was grainy, shot through a long-distance lens. It showed a woman on a walkway – from the row of doors, the place had to be a motel. A man was next to her – you couldn't see his face but his arm was thrown across her shoulder – and she was smiling. It was a smile of unabashed enjoyment. 'I think I know that face,' Nessheim said uncertainly.

Guttman brought his eyes down so they were level with the photo. 'So do I. I should do – I see it every day.'

'Christ,' said Nessheim, in sudden recognition. 'It's Marie.'

'A for All-star, Nessheim,' said Guttman wearily, lowering the photograph on to his lap.

'But what's it mean, Harry?'

'It means she's fucking T.A. in a motel room. Unless they're discussing the later works of Harriet Beecher Stowe.'

'I'm sorry,' said Nessheim. Had Harry been carrying a torch for his secretary? Marie was attractive, the right age, and always seemed devoted to Guttman. No wonder this was a blow.

Guttman shook his head. 'No, no, it's not like that. T.A. is tracking me all right – and Marie's been helping him.' He suddenly thumped his fist on the little table next to him, and the photo fell to the floor.

'Take it easy – it may not be as bad as it looks. I'm sorry about Marie, but –'

'Don't you see? Oh, shit, Nessheim, wake up. The black-haired vamp on the train – she's humping T.A. So you probably think, *big deal*. But how did she know where to find me? Only Marie knew I was on that train – and she must have told T.A. The same thing

goes for you, pal. How did they know where you lived –
Herr Rossbach and all that crap? I knew, and Marie
knew, but that's it. Oh, Jesus,' he said and slapped his
forehead with an open palm.

The other photograph was still on Guttman's lap, but
Guttman seemed too upset to look at anything now, so
Nessheim reached for it. It was also of Marie, but this
time her companion's face was visible too, as they left
the motel walkway and walked in the open past the
shabby front office. The man wore a tie you could spot
through the opening of his overcoat, which was a fine
dark Chesterfield.

Guttman had stood up and was looking over
Nessheim's shoulder. 'That's T.A. He's schtupping her
too. God, look at the smile on her face.'

But it wasn't Marie whom Nessheim was interested in.
He stared hard at the photo; there could be no doubt.
'Harry, we've got a bigger problem than you think.'

'What do you mean?'

Nessheim stabbed the photo with his finger. 'Forget
Marie – this is the guy I saw meeting Kalvin at the
museum. The same guy I followed downtown to the
FO building. He's even wearing the same coat.'

Guttman again looked stunned. Nessheim said,
'If T.A. was involved in helping Tatie, that would link
Stacey's murder to our worries about the Russians –
and T.A.'

'That's a big "if". Why do we think T.A. was helping
Tatie? Other than his being in Chicago and visiting the
Bureau here?'

'Because Tatie didn't mention him when I asked her
about the guy I followed. She just showed me the
mugshot book of current agents – in Chicago. But she
would have known T.A. was visiting. The SAC would
have introduced them, if only as a courtesy.'

'Well,' said Guttman, swallowing. He was always able to admit when he was wrong, but he didn't like it.

'And that ties the strands together. Kalvin to T.A. – Stacey, through Tatie, to T.A. It's the same group working against us. They threw out red herrings, and we took the bait. All these phoney leads – Nazis, the *Bund*, then Stacey as a femme fatale who was working for the Russians. It was all bullshit, but we believed it.'

'We caught Kalvin,' Guttman said, more in hope than defence.

'We got lucky, Harry.'

Suddenly Guttman caught sight of Nessheim's watch. 'We'd better go. Kalvin will be having supper by now.'

37

THEY LEFT THE Quadrangle Club, with Guttman leading the way. It was only once they turned the corner at 58th Street that he spoke, his breath sending little puffs of white into the air with every word. It was numbingly cold. 'You know I don't like Hoover, and Hoover doesn't like me.'

'That's pretty obvious,' said Nessheim.

'Yet Hoover leaves me alone. He's scared of what I know, and I stay clear – since I'm scared of what he's capable of. Instead he lets Tolson pick away at me. It's like having a scab that never heals. I think they both hope I'll get sick of it and resign.'

'You figure Tolson knows about T.A.'s doings?'

'No, I don't – that's the point I was coming to. Whatever Hoover is, and Tolson for that matter, neither one of them's a spy. You could show me a picture of the Director sitting on Joe Stalin's lap, and I still wouldn't believe he worked for the Russians.'

'I'm sure that's right.' There were certain conspiracies that needed to be rejected out of hand; certain lines drawn, or else you became infected with a persecution complex that was ultimately paralysing.

Guttman said, 'T.A. is a different kettle of fish. The guy's a master manipulator. Tolson seems to hold him in "great affection", shall we say, and T.A. can wrap him round his little finger. Women fall for him too, in a big way. Think of that picture – Marie looks ... what's the word?'

'Besotted?'

'That's it. I thought she might be a little bit interested

in me – I'll tell you why another time – but I realise now that Adams must have put her up to it. He's a clever, clever prick, this guy.'

'Do you think Marie's a Red?' It seemed preposterous.

'No. I think she's a dope who's fallen for a bad guy who *is* a Red. Adams spent some time in Hollywood, and Stephenson thinks he was probably recruited there, possibly by your old Russian friend Elizaveta Mukasei. So I think he *is* a foreign agent, and I think he was Kalvin's controller. Or one of them anyway – T.A. couldn't get out here very often or Tolson would start wondering why. There must be somebody based here who runs Kalvin day to day.'

They were nearing the Cloisters at the corner of Dorchester Avenue. It was a big square thirteen-storey building with four tiers of apartments. Crossing the street, Guttman suddenly turned and looked behind them. Past the adjacent playing field, seen through its iron spiked fence, were the hulking shadows of several Gothic buildings, whose blue-grey granite shone in the weak moonlight like the edifices of a ghost story. 'What is all that?' asked Guttman.

'It's the Lab School. Where the faculty kids go. John Dewey founded it.'

Guttman rubbed a finger across his lips, looking pensive. 'The Dewey Decimal System, right?'

'One and the same. Congratulations.' It seemed almost grotesque to stand here bantering with Guttman.

'Sheesh. You're supposed to be the small-town boy and I'm the city sophisticate.'

'Only according to you, Harry. I've never seen it that way myself.'

They entered the tall doorway into the apartment complex, and as they passed the doorman's little room, which had a window to watch the entrance, a Negro man inside stood up from a high stool. He was tall, with a thin narrow moustache, and wore a blue suit with a captain's peaked hat. Seeing Guttman he waved and sat down again.

'I squared him this afternoon,' said Guttman. They walked along one side of a cloistered walkway, which surrounded an open courtyard that had a shallow rectangular pool running down its centre. At one end, water burbled from the mouth of a dwarf-sized stone cherub in a passable imitation of an Italian fountain. At the back of the courtyard they crossed to the north-east tier. As they waited for the elevator, Nessheim said, 'It's a fancy building, Harry. How does Kalvin manage this?'

'He's subletting from some doctor who's gone off to stitch the wounded in the Pacific. The university owns the building, and they fixed it for him.'

They got off at the seventh floor, and Guttman took out the keys he must have got earlier from the doorman. He opened the door and they stepped into a little hall; Nessheim saw through an open doorway a magnificent view of the downtown skyline. You could even see the Palmolive Building up on North Michigan, and the sweeping beacon on its roof, used to keep aircraft from flying into it. A mile south, the dark bulk of the Loop's buildings loomed like rectangular cut-outs in a cardboard game.

Guttman switched a light on in the hallway. 'Okay, let's be careful,' he said. 'Everything you move, move it back again before you look at anything else.'

They worked together, going methodically through the rooms, switching a single light on at a time, switching it off before turning on another one. They weren't looking for Fermi-like hiding places – there simply wasn't time – but hoping that Kalvin had grown overconfident and careless.

357

In the kitchen, they checked the drawers and icebox and cleaning cupboard, which was full of dust. The dining-room sideboard contained the china and silverware which the usual tenant had left behind. The living room held a collection of curios on the built-in bookshelves and there were more bibelots on the mantelpiece, which Guttman examined and shook vigorously to no effect. They lifted the pillows of the sofa and felt under the cushions of the armchairs, but the only thing they discovered was that the room needed a good clean. They inspected the bathroom, and Guttman frowned at the lotion bottle for thinning hair, but otherwise the items they found were unremarkable. The linen closet contained a motley collection of sheets and towels and pillowcases, but nothing else.

At last they came to the bedroom, which was as gloomy as the rest of the place, but messier – the bed was unmade and there were used socks and underwear strewn on the carpet. The blinds were down, but Kalvin had left a light on here, which cast a yellow glow that made the room seem especially seedy.

Guttman gently nudged some of the underwear on the floor with his shoe. 'You have to laugh.'

'Oh, yeah?' said Nessheim, who had never felt less inclined.

'Here we are – I've lost my wife, you've lost your gal. And what do we do but sneak into some schmuck's apartment to see if there's a microdot in his boxer shorts.'

There was a suit jacket hung around the arms of a stiff-backed wooden chair, the trousers draped across the seat. Kalvin must have changed before dinner with Fermi. Nessheim carefully patted the pockets of the suit. No wallet, which Kalvin would have kept with him, but in the waist pocket of the jacket he found a small diary, with a stub of pencil shoved between its spine and pages.

'What have you got?' asked Guttman.

'His diary.' Nessheim was already paging through it.

'Anything there?'

'Nah. M.L. three o'clock. M.L. five o'clock. '

'Who's M.L.?'

Nessheim thought for a minute. 'It must be "Met Lab". That's the code name for the project. And every Wednesday has an E.F. at four o'clock. That would be Fermi.'

'Let me see,' said Guttman, and Nessheim handed him the diary.

'What's this M.S.I.?' he asked after a minute.

'When was that?'

'There are two of them. One back in August – one at the beginning of November.'

'When in November?'

'The fifth,' said Guttman.

Nessheim suddenly understood. 'The Museum of Science and Industry. That's where he met with T.A.'

Guttman handed the diary back to Nessheim and started going through Kalvin's dresser. Nessheim looked at the recent pages of the diary, which had times marked on a few of the most recent days. He realised these were probably the train times for Kalvin's trip to New Mexico and back. Groves didn't want any of the scientists taking airplanes; flying was both too risky and too intimate.

Nessheim turned more pages, looking at the days ahead, and found nothing but a few more Met Lab meetings and appointments with Fermi. Except for one item, on the very next day; it had been pencilled in and then erased. He could just make it out: '5 p.m. Tea House'. He said nothing, but felt his pulse pick up, for he had found the link he had suspected.

'Better put it back,' said Guttman. He looked at his watch. 'And we'd better get out of here. Fermi warned me that Kalvin's a fast eater.'

'Are they having supper at Fermi's house?'

'Nah. He picked some eating house on Fifty-seventh Street. Funny name – the Tropical Hut.'

They checked the place to make sure there was no sign of their intrusion, then left and took the elevator down. As they came around the far side of the decorative pool, Nessheim tapped Guttman's shoulder and gestured for him to wait. They stood there, watching as a couple moved along from the entrance towards the other east tier. Nessheim had his back against a pillar until the couple left, then breathed a sigh of relief as the elevator door closed on the figures of Professor and Mrs Fielding.

'What's the big deal?' complained Guttman as they continued towards the entrance.

'It was one of my teachers.'

'So?'

Nessheim didn't want to explain Fielding's role in Stacey's life. He said instead, 'The last man I want to see. I'm late with an assignment.'

Guttman shook his head. As they reached the entrance the doorman emerged and Guttman handed back the keys to Kalvin's apartment. 'We weren't here, Mr Smith, okay? But I thank you for your assistance.'

Smith's eyebrows arched, like a parent waiting for a child to confess. Guttman sighed, then dug into a pocket and brought out a crumpled two-dollar bill. When he shook Smith's hand, the bill disappeared.

Smith said, 'Always happy to help the war effort, sir.'

Guttman walked with Nessheim as far as 57th and Kimbark. As he hived off north he said, 'Don't worry, I'll remember to feed the cat.'

'What cat –' Nessheim started to ask, then he smiled for the first time. 'Will you be at Stagg Field tomorrow?' he asked.

'Yes. What about you?'

'No. I've got to help with the arrangements for Stacey's funeral.' Nessheim told himself it was a necessary lie. He clenched his jaw, determined to keep his feelings in check for one more day.

'I'm sorry you'll miss the climax of the project.'

'Fermi says a needle on a machine will pass a certain point and that will be it.'

Guttman said, 'That's fine by me. Success in my book means that nothing dramatic happens.'

38

IN THE MORNING Nessheim was at Stagg Field by nine, where he found four soldiers with M1 carbines guarding the main gate, and inside, three MPs rather than one behind the desk. Fermi was in the court, with a lab coat over his suit, pacing around with a pad of paper and pencil in his hand. Szilard was talking to him, and behind them Anderson and two colleagues had started pulling out the long cadmium rods from the Pile, which was now over twenty feet high, nearly reaching the ceiling of the court. It was enormous, almost as wide as it was high. Zinn had told him it held over 40,000 graphite blocks. From the counters on the balcony Nessheim could hear a steady pattern of *clickety-clicks*, indicating that the neutrons were escaping. He sensed the tension building in the room.

When Fermi saw Nessheim he came over right away and shook his hand. 'I give you deepest condolences,' he said gravely.

'Thank you. Good luck today. I am sorry I won't be here to witness it.'

Szilard had joined them and overheard the last remark. 'Be careful what you wish for. I fear that in the years ahead, you may have cause to be grateful for your absence. It is a momentous day, but not necessarily one we will all be proud of.'

'We have no choice,' Fermi said simply, and Szilard shrugged in weary acknowledgement that this was true. Nessheim said goodbye and was heading towards the main gate when Guttman came in, tie slightly askew and one of his shoes scuffed. 'I didn't expect to see you here,' Guttman said, looking worried.

'I'm leaving now. I'm not due on the North Side for an hour.'

'I'll call Palborg in a little while so you can sleep in your own bed tonight. I forgot to mention – some woman showed up yesterday to clean the place.'

Drusilla. He hoped she hadn't learned about Stacey from the doorman. He said, 'I'll try and get back as soon as I can.'

'Do what you got to do. Stacey had a mother, right?'

'You could say that.' He didn't want to explain. 'Where is Kalvin now?'

'Under house arrest. I called Groves last night after I got back to your apartment. He's been travelling so this was the first opportunity I had to tell him. He went through the roof. It doesn't make his intelligence people look very good.'

'They're not very good.'

'There's now a soldier with an M1 on the seventh floor of the Cloisters, standing guard over Kalvin's front door. Another one's on the fire escape in case Kalvin gets any ideas. The phone has been cut off, and he won't be getting any mail today. There's also half a platoon of MPs on the ground floor, to keep Kalvin from escaping in case he manages to slip a Mickey Finn to the soldier by his door.'

'Holy smokes,' said Nessheim, but he was relieved by this news. His task today would be much easier now – if he was right about the entry in Kalvin's diary.

'You'd better get going,' Guttman said, adding a little awkwardly, 'I hope it's okay.'

'Thanks, Harry,' said Nessheim gravely. Don't overdo

it, he told himself, feeling duplicitous when he saw that Guttman was moved. Nessheim had scores to settle, and he was intent on burying his emotions for now. He would have the rest of his life to grieve.

39

THE MUSEUM WAS almost empty that early in the morning; the extreme cold seemed to have deterred the usual school visits. Nessheim walked down from the entrance into the main hall, then moved right towards the Whispering Gallery. He was not surprised to find two sawhorses blocking his way, and a sign saying '*CLOSED FOR REPAIR (reopening in January)*'. Part one of his deductions had been proved right. He could only pray that he was also right about the Tea House.

He took his time going back to the club, walking along the Midway in order to avoid the Stineway drugstore on 57th, where some of the scientists liked to sit in the window booths and have coffee. He was meant to be on the North Side by now, helping with the funeral arrangements. He turned on Woodlawn, cut down an alley, then came through the club by its back entrance, passing the private tennis courts covered in snow.

Back in his room, he changed out of his suit, then lay down and tried to take a nap. When he realised he was never going to sleep, he picked up the copy of the *Tribune* he'd bought at reception, reading very slowly to kill time, and to take his mind off Stacey Madison and what he was about to do.

In North Africa, a column of American Army tanks was travelling over a hundred miles a day through Tunisia in order to join up with the British Eighth Army; their navy counterparts in the Pacific had sunk five Japanese vessels. The United Press reported that Mussolini had taken to his bed and was suffering from heart disease. On the home front, the President refused to comment on the suggestion by a British Minister of Production, Oliver Lyttelton, that the war might be over by June 1943. And to Nessheim's cynical amusement, the Secretary of the Navy promised to reveal the 'full story' of what happened at Pearl Harbor on its anniversary in five days' time.

When he finally got up he dressed in the thick woollen trousers he had first worn when he used to clear snow so his father could drive his ancient Model A into town. He also put on a T-shirt, a flannel shirt and a sweater two sizes too big that let his arms move freely. Taking his gun from the drawer where he'd put it under his dirty clothes so as not to frighten the maid, he carefully tightened the shoulder holster, though he kept the gun loose in the holster cup so it wouldn't stick if he needed it. He was hoping he would.

He put on his boots, since where he was going wouldn't have been cleared, ploughed or salted, and tied the laces carefully. Finally he put on his long woollen Chesterfield and left the room, locking it out of habit more than need.

He went out the back way of the club again after returning the room key. Outside, the sun was just setting, a pink glow diffused in stripes through the low-lying clouds. He moved east on 59th, and passed the university's cathedral-sized Rockefeller Chapel, which looked cold and forlorn, unsurprising in this most secular of institutions, then walked past the Lab School, dark now that its pupils had gone home. To his right, he noticed someone running on the Midway, a small flash of white punctuated at regular intervals by the dark background of the elms. A sailor, probably in blues but wearing his white cap, keeping in condition for the war he expected to fight in the Pacific.

He reached Harper Avenue, its wooden houses tucked

away against the steep bank of the Illinois Central line, and went through the long underpass beneath the tracks. He crossed Stony Island Avenue, then cut and juked through the traffic of the Inner Drive, drawing a horn blast from a Checker cab.

Reaching the southern edge of the Museum of Science and Industry, he slowed to a walk, looking around. No one was following him. Ahead, the museum was shutting and a large group of schoolchildren had come round from the main entrance to their waiting bus. Their teachers were the only adults in sight as Nessheim moved around the west side of the Basin, then crossed the thin steel bridge that took him on to the Wooded Island.

It was a tree-shrouded oval spit of land, sandwiched between two fish-filled lagoons. A leftover from the 1893 World's Fair, which Olmsted, the landscape architect of Central Park in New York, had designed as a wooded retreat for visitors to the great exhibition. Under pressure, he had agreed to let the Japanese build a Ho-o-den, or Phoenix Pavilion, on its north side: three redwood lacquered buildings connected by a covered walkway represented the head, body and wings of the mythical bird. Over time the structures had decayed, but were rebuilt in time for the Century of Progress Fair in 1933, joined this time by a traditional Japanese tea house that had been imported from Japan, built by hand at the cost of $20,000. The Tea Garden had been forced to close after the Japanese proprietor had been arrested by the FBI the day after Pearl Harbor and branded an enemy alien. The only visitors to the tranquil island now would be the most intrepid fishermen, willing to risk the ice on the shallow waters of the lagoon in order to fish for perch and catfish. There were a few footprints visible in the snow, and one set looked as if someone had been dragging something.

Nessheim moved along the uncleared central path. With each step his boots crunched through the crust that had hardened on the top layer of snow, like hard icing on a soft cake. He stopped to go through the decorative torii gate to the Japanese garden and followed the curving paths of snow-topped gravel, passing the double pond, which in summer was filled with a mass of flowering water lilies, and a miniature waterfall with its artfully placed rocks. The carved Japanese stone lanterns at the edge of the water were dusted with snow. He saw the Tea House itself now in the last remaining daylight. It was a small bamboo building, slightly elevated above the ground, with low upturned gables that reminded Nessheim of Frank Lloyd Wright's Robie House less than half a mile away. Except that the Japanese had got there first – centuries before.

There were more tracks in the snow here, and he stopped to take off his gloves, then put his hands into the pockets of his overcoat to keep them warm. He was about fifteen feet from the wooden building when a voice called out.

'Professor Kalvin?' The voice was Midwestern, and familiar.

'Nope,' Nessheim called back. Now he understood the funny prints in the snow.

There was silence for a minute. Then the voice said, 'Who is that?'

He climbed the three steps to the doorway. A candle in a Japanese stone lantern at the back of the room gave enough light for him to survey the place. It was the size of a large living room, almost square, completely bare but for simple wooden benches along the back wall. On one of the benches, Winograd sat with his bad leg extended straight out. Next to him sat a thick stick, maybe four feet long, propped up against the wall.

'Nessheim,' he said in astonishment. 'What are you doing out here?'

'I like to walk by the lagoon,' said Nessheim, masking his own surprise. He had never liked Winograd but he saw at once that the man had played the part brilliantly. The bumptious, slightly obnoxious classmate, interested in jazz and girls – anything but politics. No one could conceivably have taken him for a Communist. Nessheim said, 'What's your excuse?'

'I like walking here too, pardner.'

'Sounded to me like you were expecting somebody.'

'Did it?'

'Kalvin's not coming.'

Winograd said nothing for a moment, but he was incapable of sustained silence. He said, 'Professor Kalvin and I don't know each other very well. We both like walking out here, and I think we ran into each other in the museum once. He's an interesting man – he's been through a lot. He's a refugee, you know.'

He stood, picking up the stick which he held loosely in his right hand.

Nessheim said, 'Why don't you sit down again?'

'Why's that?'

'We have things to talk about.'

'Couldn't we do it some place warmer?'

'No. You stay right where you are.'

'Is that an order?'

'It's an order.'

Winograd made a show of indignation but sat down. 'Since when did you become a cop, Nessheim?'

'I think you know the answer to that.'

'If you had something on me, you'd be putting me in

cuffs and taking me downtown.' He shook his head. 'So I'm going.'

He stood up again lazily, still holding his stick. Suddenly he had it in both his hands, and had taken a quick hopping step towards Nessheim, who was already reaching for his gun. Nessheim ducked to one side as Winograd swung the hickory cudgel with incredible speed; he heard the *whoosh* as it cut through the air where his head had just been.

Failing to connect, Winograd stumbled and dropped the stick. When he regained his balance and straightened up, Nessheim had the .38 pointed right between his eyes.

'Sit down,' Nessheim said, barely controlling a sudden surge of rage. He kicked the heavy stick into the corner of the room.

Winograd fell back on the bench. 'You going to shoot me?'

'I will if I have to. Ask your comrades – I've got a track record in that department.'

Winograd swallowed, then said, 'I'm not going to squeal on anybody.' Nessheim could see that Winograd was scared but determined not to show it.

'Sure you are,' he said coldly. When he moved the gun, Winograd flinched. Nessheim said, 'Let's start with Kalvin. We've got enough to get him out of the way, so he can't do any damage now.'

'Damage?' Winograd said, nonplussed. 'That's the last thing he wants. He wants success at Stagg Field – the sooner the better. Anything to beat the Nazis.'

'Why infiltrate him into the project, then?'

Winograd looked at him with disbelief. 'Why do you think? Because Russia needs the weapon too.' He was leaning back, both shoulders pressed against the wall. 'It's knowledge the Russians want – knowledge how to do it. Any sane person would want that to happen.'

The Russians must have realised that American progress towards a bomb was unstoppable. So the Russians had decided to piggyback on the work America did.

'If it's all so benign, then why have your people been watching me?' Nessheim said.

'They liked knowing where you were.'

'They did more than that. Did you leave the "We know where you are" note for me?'

'What do you think?'

Nessheim took this for a yes. 'I guess you wanted me to think the *Bund* was on my tail. But how did you know about Rossbach?'

Winograd shrugged but said nothing.

Nessheim said, 'And it must have been your men who broke into my apartment one night. What I don't understand is how they got in. I had a key hidden, but it hadn't been touched.'

Winograd said, 'Go figure,' but he looked uneasy.

Nessheim stared at him, trying not to lose his temper. Then he saw it. 'It was the Communist philosopher in my building. He had my apartment before he moved upstairs. I never changed the locks, and he must have kept a key. Is that right?'

Winograd's eyes were locked on Nessheim's hand. Nessheim was still pointing the gun right at his head and he extended his arm slightly. Winograd promptly nodded.

'What secrets was I supposed to have?' Nessheim asked.

'They weren't looking for secrets.'

'Of course – that was Kalvin's job. But if they were looking for me, why didn't you tell them I would be out that night? You knew that – you'd asked us to your party, but Stacey told you that we had another invitation.'

Then he realised what the plan must have been. Just as Winograd said, the Russians weren't looking for secrets; they were looking for him – or rather, *waiting* for him to come home from the party. He and Stacey would have got back, tipsy and careless after an evening spent drinking punch; they'd have been easy meat for the Russians, who would have killed them both with silencers on their guns. But Nessheim had spoiled things by coming back early to get records, when there was a sole Russian in the apartment – he'd fired at Nessheim and missed, then panicked and run to the car in the alley.

Winograd stayed silent.

Nessheim asked, 'Why were they going to kill me?'

Winograd spoke at last. 'The Russians don't let enemies of the State go unpunished. You killed an agent in Los Angeles – that's not something they'd forget. And you were proving a worry here. We didn't know you had cottoned on to Kalvin, but you were trying hard enough to find out. Along with your boss, the guy in Washington – we had good information about both your activities.'

'From Adams?'

Winograd looked at him quizzically.

Nessheim said impatiently, 'Your source in the FBI. He met with Kalvin next door in the museum about a month ago.'

Winograd exhaled. 'I never even knew his name. You've figured out a lot.'

'That's how you knew about Rossbach, yes? T.A. would have checked the files.'

'You win,' said Winograd, though Nessheim sensed he might say anything to keep Nessheim from shooting him.

'Okay,' said Nessheim. He took a deep breath, trying not to show his urgency, then he said, 'Tell me what happened to Stacey.'

Winograd sighed, then winced as he moved his knee. 'There was a real chance that what she knew would get out.'

'About Trotsky?'

Winograd slowly nodded. 'It could have been very damaging to the Russian war effort. Half the capitalist governments are looking for any excuse to distance themselves from the Soviet Union. Even though it's the Russians who are keeping the Germans at bay.'

'Who rigged things to say Stacey had rejoined the CP?'

'That was my idea.'

'Yes, but who did it?'

'I told you, I won't squeal.'

'You have five seconds to do precisely that.'

It took Winograd only two seconds to reply, once Nessheim put his index finger through the trigger guard. 'We had comrades on the Coast add her name to the Party roster, then your colleague – T.A., is it? – slipped it into the Bureau files.'

How ingenious, thought Nessheim bitterly. The Bureau was used to people trying to conceal their Party memberships; it would never dream that anyone would want to *invent* a membership. The play had worked; it had been the piece of evidence presented by Guttman that had first persuaded Nessheim that Stacey was working for the Communists.

'What exactly happened in Stacey's apartment?' He was struggling to sound matter-of-fact. He knew if he didn't stay calm he would kill Winograd before learning what he wanted to know.

Winograd seemed to sense this, for he shrank back against the wall. When he spoke, his voice was thin with fear. 'When I came to see you that afternoon, the plan was to have the Russians take care of your girlfriend. Then after you and I'd had a few beers, they'd come over and deal with you. It was going to look like a homicide/suicide – you killed your girlfriend when you discovered she was a Communist agent, then went home and in a fit of remorse killed yourself. The Russians would take the gun they used on Stacey, use it on you, wipe their own prints and stick it in your hand.'

'What went wrong?'

'You did – you kept showing up early. I had gone over there to warn them you were coming in an hour or two. That was okay – it just meant they would have to kill you there as well. But then you rang the buzzer.'

'And?'

'Stacey suddenly went bananas. Somehow she got the window open and started to call out to warn you. We were desperate to shut her up and the Russians tried to pull her back in. She was like a wildcat. Finally they managed to get hold of her and then ...' Winograd paused and took a deep breath. 'They lifted her up and threw her right out the window.' He slowly lifted his eyes and looked at Nessheim. 'I didn't want that to happen. That's the God's truth.'

'I thought Communists didn't believe in God,' said Nessheim.

Winograd was silent.

'So what happened then?'

Winograd swallowed nervously. 'We couldn't wait for you – we had to get out of there fast before the cops showed up. Even so it was a close-run thing. We heard you coming out of the stairwell just as we got into the elevator.'

Winograd was starting to look exhausted. There was

a thin line of sweat coming down one side of his face. Nessheim felt sick, wondering whether if he had got to Stacey's building even earlier things might have been different. But then he would have been killed, too. There was nothing he could have done to save Stacey that day; instead, by screaming she had saved his life.

He knew Winograd would probably get off scot-free. There would be nothing to link him to Stacey's death, even if the police got lucky and caught the Russians.

'You're not planning to stick around in Chicago, are you?' he asked Winograd.

'What, and not finish Torts? What would Professor Fielding think?' He laughed weakly, but stopped when he saw Nessheim's face. 'Don't worry, I'll be gone tomorrow.'

Good, thought Nessheim. He had had enough: if he listened to much more he would kill Winograd; he was sure of that. He said, 'I'm going to leave now. For your sake, I hope we don't meet again.' He was about to holster the .38 when he thought of something. 'There's one thing I don't understand. Why didn't the Russians kill Stacey before I got there?'

'They should have. But –' Winograd stopped. There was an appalled expression on his face, like that of a man who finds he's stopped two feet from the edge of a cliff.

'Go on,' Nessheim commanded. Winograd shook his head until Nessheim pointed the gun at him again.

Winograd wouldn't look at him now. He said, 'When I got over there, I expected to find Stacey dead. But instead they had her in . . . the bedroom. They were very pissed off when I showed up – they had just started to play around with her.' He glanced anxiously at Nessheim.

Nessheim wanted to close his eyes, hoping that would

get rid of the images in his head. He looked hazily at Winograd, who said, 'I'd told them not to fool around with her, Jim. But they're Russians, after all. And you have to admit she was a tasty-looking piece.'

'What did you say?' Nessheim asked sharply.

Winograd gave a small involuntary laugh. 'I said, you have to admit she was a –'

The sound of the .38 fired in the confined space was deafening. The bullet hit Winograd in the foot of his good leg – or what had been his good leg. He doubled up and fell off the bench, rolling on to his side and clutching his bleeding foot with both hands. He opened his mouth to scream, but the pain was so agonising that he could only whimper.

Nessheim looked down at the shuddering man on the floor. 'You'll live, Winograd, and people will be out here in the morning. I'll make sure they find you. That's more than you did for Stacey.'

40

HE WALKED ALONG the Midway, on the north side of its middle strip of snow-covered grass, which had been excavated originally for a planned canal running between Jackson Park by the Lake to Washington Park a mile to the west. But it had never been filled, though in winter one section was flooded to let people ice skate. Now a solitary skater was moving in circles around the ice, backlit by the snow.

At the Quadrangle Club, he retrieved his key and went into the phone booth next to reception. He didn't bother to disguise his voice when the desk sergeant answered. 'I was walking near the Jackson Park Lagoon, at the north end. I heard shots. That's right – gunshots. Somebody was screaming blue murder. You'd better send a car to have a look. No, my name is not important, but I'd get out there if I were you.'

Upstairs, as he entered his room, he suddenly felt wobbly for the first time; he had been operating like an automaton since Stacey's death, working non-stop to find out why she had been killed, and who had killed her. There was nothing left to pursue now; he wouldn't find the Russians, and didn't think the police would either. Now he felt grief settle on him, like a great weight that he would never be able to lift. Life suddenly seemed unbearable.

He forced himself to collect his razor and toothbrush, and put them and his suit into the canvas bag he'd brought. He went downstairs to reception, where he left the room key, explaining to the woman with the bob that Mr Guttman would be repossessing the room, then left the club.

Outside, the night seemed milder now, and the moon had brushed away the clouds and sat bulb-like and low in the sky. He wondered idly how the day had gone with Fermi, and thought of the bizarre contrast between the importance of Fermi's work and the ignorance of the world at large about it.

He walked slowly along 57th Street and saw that the stores in the next block were closed; even Stineway at the end of the block had its flashing sign *'For All Your Drug Needs'* switched off. It would be nice to walk this way without worrying about scientists or spies, though the thought of becoming a full-time law student again seemed imbued by failure. Stacey had seen that he was in retreat, and for a few weeks at least had brought him to life again. His instinct now was to withdraw again, try to bury himself in the complexities of Torts and Constitutional Law, though he could hear her mocking tone if he did this. Whatever he did, a future without Stacey seemed impossible to contemplate.

Kimbark Avenue was dark, with only a few street lights on, an experiment ordered by the government to accustom the inhabitants to blackouts. Absurd, of course, since no enemy aircraft were going to penetrate this far, but he supposed it was only fair for everyone to share the burden of war. When he got to his building he saw that the lights were out in his apartment, and kicked himself for not calling Guttman first, since Guttman had his key. He must have gone out, perhaps to celebrate with Fermi and the other scientists if all had gone well. Unless he was sitting in the kitchen, out of sight from the front of the building.

Nessheim went around the corner to check the rear of the apartment. The street was deserted, and when he turned into the alley, he found it almost eerily quiet as well. He opened the back gate and crossed the small yard, and went along the thin walkway to the external flight of wooden stairs at the rear of the building. At the foot of the staircase, he paused since something caught his eye, protruding from the void under the steps. It looked like a shoe. Peering closely he saw that it *was* a shoe, and when he knelt down the shoe held a foot, which was attached to a leg, and the rest was a man. A policeman, in blue uniform.

No one would be napping there, not in 10 degrees Fahrenheit, unless they wanted to sleep for ever. Which, he realised as he looked closer, this guy was going to do. Even in the dark Nessheim could see the bullet wound in one temple, a black pencil-sized hole. A trickle of blood was seeping out; the man hadn't been dead more than a few minutes. The rescinding of Detective Palborg's orders to arrest Nessheim must not have reached the poor bastard; he must have still been watching the apartment in case Nessheim showed up.

But if the Russians had murdered the cop, then they were inside the apartment.

Nessheim put a hand out for the rough railing of the staircase and took his first step. Nothing creaked. Encouraged, he made his way up the one flight. He stayed on the wall side as he stepped on to the landing by the kitchen door, hoping they were expecting him to come in through the front.

He peeled off his overcoat and dropped it behind him, then tried the handle of the kitchen door. It moved freely, so he knew the Russians were inside. He pushed the door open very slowly, an inch at a time, then took a step up and stood on the kitchen's soft linoleum floor, waiting for his eyes to adjust to the dark, listening for any noise.

Then he heard voices, low ones from the front room. Was Guttman there? Nessheim carefully drew the Smith & Wesson out of its holster.

He took a risk and gradually eased himself through the kitchen doorway into the dining room, knowing that if anyone were there, he was a sitting duck. The room was empty; from down the hall he could hear the voices in the living room. He listened hard, but the words were an inscrutable jumble, spoken now in a high-pitched voice – no, two high-pitched voices. He realised they were speaking in Russian, and his heart sank.

Then a third, slightly lower voice said, 'You've made a hell of a mistake. I've never heard of this guy and you're in my apartment. So get the hell out.'

Nessheim wanted to cheer. It was Guttman, at his robust best.

One of the Russians said, 'We are not fools. We know whose apartment this is.'

Then the other spoke, again in Russian; his voice was more urgent now. Nessheim sensed tension building between the two men. Not good.

He squatted down and carefully unlaced his boots all the way to the last eye, taking care not to move on his heels. Standing up, he wiggled his feet, lifting them one at a time out of the boots.

He realised that there was a slight increase in light halfway down the corridor, coming from the windows at the front. He crouched down, then started to crawl his way along.

It took him a full two minutes to go ten feet. He stopped and propped himself on his elbows, his gun ready in his right hand. There was a light switch for the hall about four feet up, which he could just make out in the dark. The Russians were arguing now; when

Guttman started to interject, he was told again to shut up, this time forcibly.

Something moved in the living room ahead of him, and Nessheim could just see that it was one of the Russians, sitting in a chair in the middle of the living room, positioned to face the front door. The other Russian's voice came from further away. Nessheim figured he must be near the window, covering Guttman.

'If you're going to kill me, then get a move on,' Guttman suddenly boomed. 'I don't want to die with you pricks babbling away.'

Then Nessheim heard a movement, and he was up on his feet before he had even made a conscious decision. When he spoke he didn't shout, hoping it would confuse the gunmen for a crucial second, and said in a clear but quiet voice, 'Harry, move now.'

He pushed the light switch button and as the hallway lit up he fired at the Russian he saw by the window. There was a howl of pain. The other Russian swung his gun, and Nessheim was about to fire again when out of nowhere a burly figure was on to the man, encircling his chest with both arms.

Nessheim hesitated as the pair of men wrestled, the Russian trying to raise his gun as Guttman struggled to keep the man's arm down. Suddenly, Guttman managed to lift the Russian off his feet, and slammed his head against the wall. The Russian fell to the floor, but though stunned still brought his arm around to shoot at Nessheim. When Nessheim fired again, the Russian's arm dropped, and blood spread across his gut.

Nessheim stood still, his gun ready, finding it hard to believe the gunfight was over. The smell of cordite filled the air, and he heard Guttman trying to catch his breath. Nessheim went to the first Russian and collected his gun, then did the same for the second man.

His adrenalin surging, he made himself sit down. Guttman was kneeling on the floor, still breathing hard.

Nessheim said, 'You saved my life, Harry.'

Guttman's eyes widened. 'I was just about to say that you saved *my* life. Tell you what, let's leave the thanks stuff and call it quits.'

41

THE POLICE HAD taken their statements, the two dead Russians had been removed on gurneys, and the finger-print men wanted them out of the way. 'I could use some air,' said Guttman, and Nessheim nodded. They went out the front entrance, since the back alleyway was still filled with squad cars and policemen, stunned by the murder of their colleague whom Nessheim had found under the back stairs.

The sky was crystal clear, and you could see the stars and a crescent moon. As they moved along 56th Street Nessheim said, 'What happened at the Met Lab?'

'It worked, just as Fermi said it would. I got there a few minutes late, but you were right – Anderson told me nothing obvious occurred, just a lot of *click click clicks*. At first I thought the experiment must have failed – everybody seemed so subdued.'

'They must be exhausted. They've been working round the clock.'

'Sure, but it was more than that. I got the feeling they suddenly realised what they've done. They're scared, I think, and worried.'

'I thought the whole point was that if they didn't do it the Germans would get there first.'

'Sure, but that doesn't make the enterprise any more attractive. Funny, they brought out a bottle of wine to celebrate, and everybody signed the bottle. But there weren't any toasts, and they drank in silence. It was kind of creepy, to tell you the truth. Anyway, how about you – are the funeral arrangements all set?'

'I don't know. I didn't go to the North Side.'

Guttman stopped walking. 'How come? Did you think it would be too much for you?' He sounded sympathetic.

'No, it wasn't that. I had something I needed to follow up.' He could see that this worried Guttman. 'I found out who was running Kalvin here.'

'You did? Who?'

'A law student named Winograd. He tried to befriend me – and Stacey – and he liked to pretend he wasn't interested in politics. But he's a hundred per cent Comintern man.'

'How did you figure this out?'

'There was an entry in Kalvin's diary that he'd crossed out. For a meeting on an island over in Jackson Park. I think they used to meet in the Whispering Gallery at the museum next door, but the exhibit's closed. I put two and two together, and for a change the answer wasn't five.'

'Why didn't you tell me this last night?' Guttman sounded aggrieved.

'You had Stagg Field to worry about – you said yourself it took priority.' It sounded good, but was not the true reason. Nessheim decided to come clean: 'Plus, I didn't want you to try and stop me.'

Guttman shook his head. 'You drive me nuts sometimes, Nessheim.'

'I bet Tolson says the same about you.'

Guttman looked at him sourly. 'Have we got anything we can stick on this Winograd fellow?'

'Not really. It's pretty depressing, Harry – it turns out we got just about everything wrong. Kalvin wasn't sent to sabotage the experiment – the Russians *want* us to build this super-weapon. They just want to know how to build one too.'

'Kalvin's not going to be able to help them with that now, is he? We found him.'

'Yes, we did. But he's just the tip of the iceberg. I bet there are going to be a lot of Kalvins on this project.'

Guttman scratched his head. 'Well, I hope you're wrong. If you're right we'll just have to do the best we can to find the rest of them. I don't see an alternative, do you?' When Nessheim didn't reply, Guttman asked, 'Where is Winograd now?'

'I would think Billings Hospital.' He paused for a second. 'I'd better level with you, Harry. There may be repercussions.' He explained what had happened on the Wooded Island, recounting the conversation there, and ending with the fact that he had shot Winograd in the foot. Guttman seemed astonished, then asked why he had done it. Nessheim told the truth about that as well, explaining that he had lost all self-control when Winograd baited him about Stacey. He added, 'I had a personal agenda. He told me he was directing the two Russians we just killed. Winograd was with them in Stacey's apartment when –' He stopped, then made himself continue. 'When she died.'

Guttman sighed. 'To be honest, if I'd been in your shoes I would have shot him too – only I'd have killed him.'

He started walking again and Nessheim went with him. Guttman said, 'I doubt there will be any comeback from Winograd. How's he going to explain himself if he tries to press charges? Kalvin may not crack, but we could throw enough mud in Winograd's direction to make it widely known he worked for the Soviets. He wouldn't want that.'

'I didn't plan to shoot him, Harry. I didn't know it was going to be him. We were both equally surprised to find each other there on the island.'

Guttman said, 'I'm leaving tomorrow first thing. I want to get back and see what I can do about this T.A.

385

fellow. I have a feeling he may be away, and won't be coming back.'

'Why?'

'Kalvin may have got word to him that he's been pinched. That would scare T.A. off. He'll be on the sidelines somewhere, waiting to see how the land lies. If he thinks it's safe he'll return to the Bureau and then I'll grab the bastard. If he doesn't, we'll never see him again.'

'Wouldn't Tolson protect him?'

'Never. Oh, he'll huff and puff at first and say I've misread the whole thing. But the evidence I have is hard to dispute, and it's enough to excuse my diversions from established procedure. I don't know what will scare Tolson the most – the suggestion that he protected T.A. because he was his nancy boy, or that he unwittingly let a Soviet agent have access to the confidential files of the Bureau.'

They crossed Woodlawn and kept walking. Nessheim couldn't see anyone ahead or, glancing back, behind; then he realised no one would be following him tonight.

Guttman said, 'What about you? You got any plans?'

'I want to finish the academic quarter, Harry. That way, if I leave I have the right to come back. It's meant for people getting drafted or signing up, but I sneak in under that provision.'

' "Sneak" is not the right word. You're doing your bit and then some. Your war's been going on for a while.'

'I thought it was all over when I went to law school.'

Guttman shook his head. 'When did we first meet?'

'I think it was '37.'

'Golly, it's been a while then.'

They had reached University Avenue by now, and as if by mutual agreement turned south, so as not to proceed another block to Stagg Field. There were few street lights here, and only half of the sidewalk had been cleared entirely of snow. A man was coming towards them, walking slowly as though deep in thought, his hands stuffed in the pockets of his overcoat. They waited on the edge of a driveway to let him pass.

It was Fermi, and he stopped when he saw them both. He looked tired.

'Congratulations, Professor,' Nessheim said.

Fermi nodded absent-mindedly. 'I guess so,' he said.

'I understand the experiment went like a dream. You must be very pleased.'

'Pleased? I don't know about that. We have all worked so hard that we almost forgot what we were working to do. The result happens, and now we are made to think. I have to say, I don't like some of these thoughts.'

'It was necessary, Professor,' Guttman said.

'Necessary – like a necessary evil?' Fermi shook his head. 'I am not so sure of that. I hope it will win the war, if nothing else can. But my fear is that after that it will only cause new wars. Szilard says he is not surprised I feel this way – he has felt like that for a long time.' Fermi looked at Guttman; he seemed slightly bewildered. 'He said I have been an innocent for too long.'

Nessheim didn't hesitate. 'Nobody's innocent after today.'

They said goodnight to Fermi and continued towards the Quadrangle Club. A jazzy convertible drove past, red like Stacey's, which gave Nessheim a jolt. Eventually he said, 'Harry, can I ask you something?'

His tone made Guttman look at Nessheim, then look away. 'Sure, Jim.'

'Does it ever get better?'

Guttman sighed, thinking about this. 'Hard to say. I don't want to die any more, if that's "better". Other than that, I take it one day at a time.'

They had reached the club, and Guttman stopped in front of the awning over its front walkway. 'You said a minute ago "if I leave". What would you do if you did?'

Nessheim tried to gather his thoughts. He been wrong to think his war was over, whatever the army doctors said. He might not get the chance to fight in the Pacific or North Africa or one day in Europe, but he would still have battles to fight, even if they took place here at home. If not all the enemies of America were in plain view, they were out there just the same. There was no getting around this any more, no hopes for a peaceful life while the world was at war. In this, as in so many things about him, Stacey had been unerring – most of all, in her insistence that this was no time for 'rathers'.

He said to Guttman, 'I'd like to stay with the Bureau. If you can use my services.'

Guttman was silent for a moment. He extended his hand and the two men shook. He said, 'Let me give it some thought. Something will come up. It always has before.'

Acknowledgements

I would like to thank Joanna Taylor, Susan Sandon, Jocasta Hamilton and Selina Walker at Random House UK for their encouragement and advice as I wrote this book; my agents Clare Alexander and Gillon Aitken were also supportive – as always. Mary Chamberlain once again proved an invaluable copy-editor, and I am grateful as well to Dan Crissman, Tracy Carns and Peter Mayer at The Overlook Press.

The Hyde Park Historical Society in Chicago is a remarkable organisation and an excellent source of information about that neighbourhood's past. My thanks go also to Pranav Jain at the University of Chicago. Sam Radin was encouraging throughout.

Willard Keeney, my uncle, helped with details of transportation from an earlier era, and made many wider and useful editorial suggestions – as did my brothers, Dan and James Rosenheim. I'd also like to thank Laura and Sabrina Rosenheim for their patience. Finally, Clare Howell kept me at it, and helped in so many respects, which the dedication of this book can only begin to convey.